RETURN TO HARDEMAN COUNTY

C.J. PETIT

Printed in the United States of America

First Printing, 2019

ASIN: 9781093374940

TABLE OF CONTENTS

C.J. PETIT

PROLOGUE

Hardeman County, Texas
May 11, 1860

"Why are you planning on moving so many, Ellis?" asked Pete Orris as his brother-in-law, John Keeler, looked on.

"I don't like all that talk that's comin' from back east. I figure once the election's done, all hell's gonna break loose. There's war comin', and I aim to get ready for it."

"Ellis, you're not thinking right. Even if those boys back east start a war, it won't have anything to do with us out here. We'll probably be better off when the demand for beef goes up."

Ellis shook his head and said, "I don't trust 'em, Pete. It's gonna be like dominoes and sooner or later, we'll be in it, too. It's just the way of things. I'm just lettin' you know in case you want to tag along."

Pete glanced at John then replied, "I appreciate your asking, Ellis, but I can't see clearing out all of your cattle just because you believe there's going be a big war."

"I ain't clearin' out all of 'em, Pete, just most of 'em."

"Well, either way, if it's okay with you, I'll just add about thirty head to your herd for the drive to Abilene."

Ellis nodded then said, "Fair 'nuff. I'm roundin' 'em up now and plannin' on headin' north in four days, so if you can bring yours over by then, I'll add 'em to the herd. I'll charge you two dollars a head for movin' em."

"Thanks, Ellis," Pete said before Ellis gave him a short salute, turned and stepped off the Orris ranch house porch.

As he rode off, John Keeler asked, "You don't figure he's right about a war comin', do ya?"

Pete rubbed the back of his neck and replied, "He might be, but even if he's right about that, I can't see Texas going along with it. Let's go inside."

John laughed and said, "That Ellis sure is a worryin' kinda feller," as he followed Pete into the house.

Pete's wife, Mary Jo and her sister, Sara Mae, had been listening to the discussion and had mixed reactions.

When their husbands returned to the main room, Sara Mae asked, "Do you think Ellis is right?"

"Hell, no," replied John, "even if they raised a ruckus, it wouldn't make a bit of difference to us."

Mary Jo asked, "He's taking a big risk then, isn't he?"

Pete answered, "I think so. If there isn't a war, then he'll almost have to start from scratch again, but at least he'll have a good chunk of money this time."

Sonny, John and Sara Mae's six-year old, asked, "Papa, if there's a war, you ain't goin', are ya?"

John looked at his son and his four-year-old daughter, Mandy, but didn't reply as he turned and left the room.

———

As he rode the three miles back to his ranch house, Ellis was wishing that Pete was right and he was wrong but felt in his bones that there was going to be a war and even Texas would be involved. He may have wished for the best, but he was planning for the worst.

At least Pete and that bastard brother-in-law of his would be staying on Pete's ranch and not following him when the flags and bullets started flying.

CHAPTER 1

Abilene, Kansas
July 16, 1860

Ellis walked out of the cattle buyer's office with his draft for payment for the 426 head that he'd delivered to the pens. He'd started with almost five hundred of the critters, and between deaths and leaving some with the Indians in the Nations as payment for crossing their lands, he was pleased to have finished the drive with as many as he had. It had been a long, hot journey and in addition to the almost seventy animals, he'd lost six horses, two drovers and almost lost the chow wagon, too. Neither of the men who had died were married, so he didn't need to give their pay to their widows.

With the rumors of war that seemed to be growing louder, the price on beef was already being speculated to a new high at $24.87 a head, so the enormous draft of over ten thousand dollars should serve his purpose. He'd have to pay six hundred dollars to Pete Orris for the twenty-six critters wearing the Big O brand that survived the drive, and after paying off the boys, he'd still have over eight thousand dollars.

Ellis was always a man who thought ahead, from the day he'd arrived in Hardeman County from East Texas in 1850, and negotiated with the Comanche for his ranch, trading a small herd of horses and four beef cattle for the land nestled between the two opposing lines of the High Hills. The aptly named Fresh Water Creek ran parallel with the northern border of the High Hills before emptying into the Red River.

The Comanche really didn't want the land as the band that had been there was moving west anyway, and the new state of Texas readily accepted the deed to the ranch as it hoped to increase the population of Texans living on the west side of the state. At the time, there were only forty-six white people living in the large county.

It was only four years ago that Pete Orris and his wife, Mary Jo, had founded the Big O ranch just to the west of his property, although Ellis never was able to find out how he'd bought it or from whom. It was a smaller ranch, only four sections, and its western border was at the edge of Hardeman County. A year later, his brother-in-law, John Keeler, brought his family to help run the place, but they only hired part time help during busy times of the year. Ellis had never asked where he got the money to buy the cattle that he'd bought from the Slash W either, but that wasn't his business. It was probably for the same reason he'd come so far into West Texas; the land was dirt cheap and his cash was limited back then.

He liked Pete Orris and thought he was a good man. His wife was a real head-turner and his own hands talked about her constantly, but he'd warned them to treat both of the women with respect when they saw them. John's wife, Sara Mae was older, smaller and not nearly as pretty as her younger sister. She had two children with her husband, John, and Ellis thought she was very underappreciated by her husband. Whenever he'd had the chance to talk to her, she'd impressed him with her manner and her quick wit. While not possessing her younger sister's physical gifts, she was still a handsome young woman, and Ellis' deep secret was that he was smitten with her.

Her husband, John, had rubbed him wrong from the first day he'd met him almost three years earlier. It wasn't anything

6

specific, but it was just his attitude and the way he treated his wife and children that irritated him so much. Ellis tried to avoid even talking to the man whenever he had to go to the Big O. Those two kids sure were cute, too.

But whatever was happening at the Big O and in the Keeler family, wasn't his business. His business right now was getting everything ready for the war that he was sure to start soon.

Ellis' herd, before he drove most of them to Abilene, had numbered almost five hundred and he had a foreman and four full-time hands to keep it running. Now it had all changed just because of his premonition.

Ellis walked into the First National Bank in Abilene strode to the desk of a clerk then took a seat.

"What can I do for you, mister?" the clerk asked, perhaps not as politely as he should have.

Ellis withdrew the draft and said, "I need to open an account, deposit this and then make some withdrawals."

The clerk glanced at the draft and his demeanor shifted immediately.

"Very good, sir," he said as he began pulling out some forms.

Ellis signed the draft and said, "I need thirty-five hundred dollars in bills, a thousand in gold, and the rest can stay in your bank."

The clerk's pen stopped momentarily as he was filling out the first form then continued. These Texas cattlemen always liked to have their gold, but the bank was equipped to handle it.

7

After their business was concluded, Ellis had the forty gold double eagles and twenty gold eagles in a heavy leather sack in his left jacket pocket and had the currency in his right pocket along with some blank bank drafts and the account book. He shook hands with the bank clerk then walked outside to find his boys.

In their previous drives, he'd just paid them off and then joined them in a big celebration but this time would be different. This was going to be a more serious discussion when he paid them off.

He still found them in Bristow's Saloon and joined them and the two remaining drovers and the cook that they'd hired for the drive.

"Okay, boys," Ellis said after he'd taken a seat, "it's time to settle up."

There were eight smiling faces around the two tables as he paid off each man his wages in bank notes.

After counting out the last of the cash, he said, "Now, boys, you all know that I figure a war's comin', and I'm not alone in thinkin' that way. I'm only going to need three of you to come back to Texas with me, but you can keep your horses and rigs and take one extra mount from the remuda."

He turned to his foreman, Jim Abigail, and asked, "Jim, are you comin' back?"

"You bet, boss."

He then asked, "Rufus, could I talk to you in back for a minute?"

Rufus nodded and replied, "Sure, boss," before standing and walking with Ellis to the quiet back end of the saloon.

When they were alone, Ellis said, "Rufus, I know you're the best hand I got, but I think it would be a good idea for you to stay here in Kansas."

"Boss, it don't matter. I'm just a cowhand."

"I wish that were so, Rufus, but we both know better. Just 'cause your owner set you free don't mean nothin' if those boys get all riled up."

"I ain't worried, boss. There ain't many folks around down there anyway."

"Not now, but I just ain't all that sure that it's gonna stay that way."

"Don't you want me to come back with ya?"

"You know better than that, Rufus. I just don't want to see you hangin' from some damned tree."

Rufus laughed and said, "Anybody who tries that will find out how good I am with this Colt."

Ellis nodded, then put his hand on Rufus' shoulder before saying, "Okay, Rufus, let's go back and talk to the boys. Who else do we bring back with us?"

"I'd say Lou. He's a good man."

"That would be my guess, too," Ellis said before they began to walk back to the tables of cowhands.

After telling Lou Gordon that he'd be returning to the ranch to work, Ellis let the boys celebrate in the saloon while he left through the batwing doors and turned right on the busy boardwalk.

He walked briskly two blocks then carefully crossed the crowded main street to M. Liston's Gunsmithing and Firearms. He needed to get more ammunition for his Colt Dragoon and his Remington Model 1841 rifled musket. He was almost out of the .54 ball shot for the musket and wasn't much better with the .44s for the Dragoon.

When he entered the well-appointed business, he almost bumped into an inattentive customer just exiting.

"Pardon, mister," the man said as he looked at Ellis, "but I kinda got distracted."

Ellis noticed the reason for his distraction as he held a repeating rifle in his hands and suspected that it was one of the new Henry repeating rifles that had replaced their Volcanic models.

"No problem, mister. Nice gun."

The man grinned and replied, "You bet. I can't wait to try it either," then hurried out of the shop.

Forty minutes later, Ellis was leaving the shop with his heavy load of replacement ammunition for his Colt and Remington, a brand-new Henry repeater and six boxes of the .44 rimfire cartridges that he knew he'd never find down in Texas, at least for a few years. When war came, he wasn't about to take the new gun with him either. He'd use his Remington, knowing that the Henry would be waiting for him when he returned, if he returned.

The ride back to Texas didn't take nearly as long, and Ellis, Jim Abigail, Rufus Green and Lou Gordon each had a spare mount in addition to the much smaller remuda that they herded along with them. Ellis had specifically chosen the horses that he was bringing back with him and anticipated that they would soon form the new herd that would be waiting for him when he returned. All of them were younger mares and their stallion was still waiting for them at his ranch with another eight mares. The cattle that were still grazing back in Texas were selected for the same reason.

It was a relatively pleasant return, with only a little fuss from a small band of Comanche who had wanted to relieve them of some of the mares, but really hadn't made a whole-hearted effort.

It was the past the middle of August when the four riders and spare horses finally crossed onto the ranch, but none of them were that sure of the actual date.

After they left the horses in the corral, the three ranch hands carried their saddlebags and bedrolls to the bunkhouse while Ellis brought his things into the house. He had to make two trips because of the addition of the new Henry and ammunition, but once inside, he was glad to be home.

He set his two sets of saddlebags on the floor of his bedroom and leaned the Remington and Henry against the far wall. He smiled as he noticed how clean the house was and expected it was thanks to either Mary Jo Orris or Sara Mae Keeler, but probably both. He hadn't asked them to take care of the house but appreciated the work. He'd slip them each a ten-dollar note when their husbands weren't looking.

That reminded him that he'd have to ride over to the Big O soon to pay John for his cattle. He should be pleased with the amount as it was more than either had anticipated.

But right now, he needed to clean up and put on some coffee. Without a cook, he'd have to handle the cooking for a while. Today and tomorrow, they'd live off the tins of food still in the pantry and what they had left from their long ride back, then he would have to make a wagon trip into Fort Madrid, ten miles southeast of the ranch. It used to be an old army fort but was now a trading post that had added a few buildings but not enough to call itself a town yet. Naturally, the first added building was a saloon and a poor excuse for a whore house that only worked three older women. The owner of the establishment, Tyler Mutter, was always telling the boys that he'd add some younger girls, but never had.

Ellis returned to the kitchen and started a fire in the cookstove using the old, dried-out wood stacked in the wood box, and didn't even have to use kindling because it was so dry. Soon after he'd closed the door, the cookstove began popping as the iron settled back after months of disuse.

He primed the pump then filled the coffeepot, figuring he really should have washed it first, but just shrugged and put it on the hot plate.

While the coffee water was heating, he returned to the bedroom, removed the set of saddlebags containing the gold and pulled the heavy sack from inside and just slipped it into his canvas jacket's pocket. But he found it was just too danged heavy and quickly pulled it back out and returned it to the saddlebags.

The remaining cash was in his left jacket pocket, so he took out the wad and counted out the six hundred dollars for Jim Orris and shoved it into his left pants pocket. He then slipped another hundred into his right pants pocket before returning the remaining bills into the left-hand jacket pocket. He put the two ten-dollar bills for the wives into his vest pocket then on a whim, he put two silver dollars with them for Sara Mae's two kids. He imagined that neither of them had even had a nickel to call their own and they could do some serious damage to the Ernie Smith's store in Fort Madrid with that much money.

He smiled as he imagined the joy on the faces of the two Keeler children. He surely liked those two young'uns. He really wanted to sneak in some small talk with Sara Mae Keeler too, and would prefer that her husband wasn't around, not that he seemed to care.

He returned to the kitchen, took off his jacket, vest and shirt and then washed in the sink before turning and pouring a large scoop of coffee into the hot water.

After pouring himself a cup of coffee, he was dressing when Jim Abigail walked into the house followed by Rufus and Lou.

"We saw the smoke and figured you'd have some coffee goin'," Jim said as he took a cup from the shelf.

Rufus and Lou then took cups and Rufus filled all three while Ellis finished dressing.

"You headin' over to the Big O, boss?" asked Jim before taking a sip.

"Yup. I'll pay off Pete and then come back to whip up some chow."

"I'll take care of the cookin', boss," offered Rufus, "you don't do so good."

Ellis laughed and said, "I'll admit to that, Rufus, and you got yourself a new job, just don't be askin' for no raise."

"Mind if I come along when you go to the Big O?" asked Jim.

13

"Nope. If you wanna come along, it's a free country, at least for a while."

"Boss, what are your plans now? There's only about forty head out there. That ain't enough to keep all of us busy."

"No, it ain't. But now that we're back, I'll fill you in on what I'm thinkin'."

They all took seats at the kitchen table before Ellis began to talk.

"I figure this war that's comin' ain't gonna stick to the east like everybody thinks. We got all those cotton growers down south and Galveston has its finger in the illegal slave trade, too. Once those states back east get all riled up, Austin won't be far behind."

"If that happens, are you gonna go off to war?" asked Lou.

"I'm a Texan, Lou. If Texas declares war, then I gotta go. What you boys do is up to you. Now, Rufus, I already told you that you shoulda stayed in Kansas, but now that you're here, you have to be ready to make another long ride if it gets bad. You head west to Colorado or north to Kansas or even Nebraska. I don't figure anything bad will happen in them places. But until then, we're going to set the ranch up to kinda run on its own."

"How are you gonna do that?" asked Jim.

"I already started by selling most of the herd. The ones that are left are all prime animals and mostly cows and some calves. You know that. Now, up on the northwest corner of the ranch is that gap between the hills that we ain't ever used. That's where we'll drive the cattle when things start happenin' back east. We'll leave the horses there, too."

"How long do you figure it's gonna take for us to whip them Yankees?" asked Lou with a snicker.

Ellis sighed as he replied, "We're gonna get our butts whipped, boys. That's why I'm doin' all this. Now, I ain't about to say that them Yankees are better fighters than us. Hell, most of 'em probably don't even know what end of a gun the bullet comes out, but there are a lot more of 'em and in case you boys haven't noticed, all of the factories are up north, too. We can't even make guns down here. They have a big navy too, and can just sit them ships off of our ports and keep things from goin' in and out."

"*You think we're gonna lose?*" asked a startled Jim Abigail.

"It'll take a while, but I figure that's what's gonna happen unless the new president is a real gutless feller and can't put up with seein' dead soldiers. If he's got the sand to stick it out, we ain't got a chance and then, we'll have real problems."

Lou asked, "You tellin' me that a long war with the Yankees won't even be the biggest problem?"

"Oh, it'll be bad, but think about it, boys. We lose all of those young fellers in the war, then some of those Yankees will want to punish the South for startin' the war. I'll bet it'll be like an invasion of Yankees tryin' to milk every drop they can out of us troublemakers. That's when we might have our own problem."

"I hope you're wrong, boss," said Rufus as he shook his head slowly.

"So, do I, Rufus. So, do I."

They quietly finished their coffee, then Ellis and Jim left the house to saddle some fresh horses for the ride to the Big O.

———

Twenty-five minutes later, they left Slash W land and entered the neighboring Big O, the ranch house and barn just eight hundred yards ahead.

Ellis spotted the two Keeler children near the back door and wondered what they were doing. They were both huddled over and seemed intent on whatever it was, and it was only when the horses were within two hundred yards that both turned his way, saw Ellis and Jim then quickly stood.

The boy said something to his sister before she ran inside to tell the adults and as the boy began walking toward them, Ellis spotted the horned frog they had cornered making his escape.

By the time they reached the back porch, the two sisters, now with different last names, exited the house with the little girl.

"Afternoon, Ellis," Mary Jo said as Ellis and Jim pulled their mounts to a stop.

"Afternoon, Mary Jo. Is that lucky husband of yours home?"

"No. He and John are at Fort Madrid getting some supplies."

"Well, ma'am, I came by with the money from his cattle sale. I need to show him the bill of sale from the cattle buyer in Abilene, so he knows that I'm not cheatin' him out of any of the money I owe him."

Mary Jo smiled and said, "Now, we know better than that, Ellis. I'm sure it's the right amount."

Ellis pulled the bill of sale from his right saddlebag and handed it to her as he said, "If you want to take a look, Mary Jo, you can see where the buyer wrote twenty-six of your critters were sold at $24.87 each and I was charging him two dollars a head to drive 'em to Kansas, so the amount is just under six hundred dollars."

Mary Jo handed it to her sister and said, "Why don't you and your foreman step down, Ellis. It's difficult to do business while you're sitting up there."

Ellis smiled, tipped his hat then said, "Yes, ma'am," before he and Jim both dismounted.

Ellis reached into his pants pocket and pulled out the thirty twenty-dollar bills for the sale and handed the currency to Mary Jo while Sara Mae examined the bill of sale.

Ellis glanced at Sara Mae, smiled and watched her as she examined the document. He knew that Sara Mae wasn't really looking for any evidence of cheating. Ellis believed she was almost showing off. She may not be able to compete with her younger sister in looks, but she sure was as smart as a whip.

Sara Mae returned the bill of sale, smiled and said, "You're shortchanging yourself five dollars and thirty-eight cents, Ellis."

"That's okay, Sara Mae, I'd just as soon not have to do the cypherin'," he replied, "By the way, I want to thank you and Mary Jo for takin' care of my place while we were up in Kansas."

"That's quite alright. It was just some dusting once a week."

"Well, I appreciate it, and I figure you both could use some money of your own, so I set aside ten dollars for you and Mary Jo," Ellis said as he pulled the two ten-dollar notes from his vest pocket and held them out to Sara Mae, who shook her head.

"No, that's quite alright," she replied even as Mary Jo took the two bills and handed one to her protesting older sister.

Mary Jo then smiled at Ellis and said, "Thank you, Ellis. Sara Mae was just trying to impress you."

Sara Mae blushed but still smiled, which to Ellis made her almost as pretty as Mary Jo, then she said, "Thank you, Ellis."

"Now, don't you go be givin' that to your husband, Sara Mae. That's your money to buy yourself somethin' nice."

Her smile widened with laugh lines appearing at the corners of her eyes as she looked at Ellis' brown eyes which matched her own and replied, "We'll see."

Jim Abigail smiled at Mary Jo as he said, "We figured you ladies worked a lot harder than us menfolk."

Mary Jo turned her smile to the foreman while Ellis dropped to his heels to face Sara Mae's two silent children.

He pushed his hat to the back of his head and smiled at the two youngsters.

"Now, my comin' in here makin' all that noise and scarin' away that horned frog you had cornered wasn't a very neighborly thing to do. So, if it's okay with your mama, I'd like to make it right."

Sonny smiled back and asked, "How?"

Ellis reached back into his vest pocket, pulled out the two silver dollars and handed one to each child as their four brown eyes kept growing in astonishment.

"*A whole dollar? For me?*" exclaimed Sonny.

Four-year-old Mandy had no idea what the difference between a penny and a silver dollar was but if Sonny was excited to have one, then she had to be, too.

Sara Mae was about to tell Ellis that it was too much to give to the children but seeing the expression on their faces made it impossible. She had no idea when they'd be able to spend it, but it was a gift after all, so she reverted back to her mother's handbook.

"What do you say?" she asked.

Sonny blurted, "Thank you, Mister White!"

The previously silent Mandy smiled and replied softly, "Thank you."

Ellis rose and replied, "You're welcome," then a sudden notion popped into his head and he said, "Now, I've got to go down to Fort Madrid tomorrow to get some supplies, and seein' as how your papa is already done your family shoppin', if you both want to come along for the ride, you're both more'n welcome."

Sonny looked plaintively at his mother and pleaded, "Can we go, Mama?"

She knew it was a day-long trip, but she trusted Ellis and knew he would treat her children better than her husband and always had.

"Alright. If your father agrees to let you go tomorrow, then when Mister White stops by with his wagon, you can go along."

Sonny was all grins, but Mandy was more subdued, having never been off the ranch before.

Ellis then shook Sonny's hand and said, "I'll see you young-uns tomorrow mornin'."

"Thank you, Mister White," Sonny replied.

Sara Mae was still smiling at Ellis when he turned and said, "I'll take good care of 'em, Sara Mae."

"I know you will, Ellis," she answered softly.

After a long, ten-second pause, Ellis tipped his hat to Sara Mae, turned and mounted his gelding then had to wait for Jim to stop chatting with Mary Jo about something that he couldn't hear.

Finally, Jim realized that his boss was already on his horse grinned once at Mary Jo then tipped his hat to the sisters before he turned and mounted.

After they'd ridden off, Mary Jo asked, "What are you going to buy with your money?"

Sara Mae replied, "I'm going to hide it away in case I need it."

"That's a silly thing to do. John will find it sooner or later," Mary Jo said as they turned to go back to the house to finish their laundry.

Sara Mae stood for a few more seconds watching Ellis ride away then sighed and followed Mary Jo.

————

As the sun began to set, Pete Orris and John Keeler returned to the ranch with the wagonload of supplies.

Before they unloaded the wagon, they entered the house to tell their wives that they'd returned and to have some coffee.

When they walked into the kitchen, Mary Jo said, "Mister White stopped by and dropped off the cash from the cattle sale."

Pete grinned as he accepted the six hundred dollars from his wife and asked, "How many head did he sell?"

Mary Jo looked at her older sister, and Sara Mae replied, "He sold twenty-six head at $24.87 each and deducted the two dollars per head that you agreed to pay him to move them to Abilene. So, the total was $594.68, and he rounded it off to six hundred."

"I'm kind of surprised he got that many to Abilene, as hot as its been," Pete said as he counted the bills.

"How do we know he didn't get all thirty of 'em there?" asked John.

Pete looked at his brother-in-law then replied, "John, don't be so damned untrusting. Ellis is as honest a man as I've ever met. If anything, he probably added a critter or two to the total."

John just shrugged.

Pete then handed John a hundred dollars before he walked to the cold room, pulled a cracked pot from the darkest corner, then extracted a leather pouch and slid the wad of bills inside. There wasn't a real bank anywhere nearby not that Pete would have trusted it anyway, but for those who didn't want to keep their money in their homes, Ernie Smith's store in Fort Madrid had a safe that they could use, for a fee of course. He had no idea where his brother-in-law kept his money, assuming he had saved any of the money he'd been given the past three years.

While Pete was banking his cash in the pot, Sara Mae said to John, "Mister White said he'd going to Fort Madrid in the morning and asked if Sonny and Mandy could ride along with him."

"Why would he want to do that?"

"He gave them each a coin to spend and I know that Sonny would really want to go."

"I don't care. If Ellis wants to put up with 'em all day, that's okay with me."

Sonny looked at his mother and smiled and she smiled back at him while Mandy still just sat silently nearby, unsure of whether it was going to be as much fun tomorrow as Sonny seemed to believe.

Once the money matters were settled, Mary Jo and Sara Mae began to cook dinner as the two husbands went back outside to start unloading the wagon.

————

About an hour after daybreak the next morning, Ellis drove his wagon up to the back of the Big O ranch house. He had

Rufus with him but mounted on his tall mahogany gelding because of the space needed for the two children on the driver's seat.

The empty wagon had barely trundled to a stop when the back door flew open and a jubilant Sonny Keeler bounced onto the porch with his young sister walking slowly behind him.

"Good mornin', Master Keeler," Ellis said as he stepped down.

"Good morning, Mister White," Sonny said as he hopped down from the short porch.

Pete Orris and John Keeler stepped out behind them.

"Thanks for moving the cattle, Ellis," Pete said as he followed Sonny off the porch.

"No problem, Pete. Lost a couple of drovers though."

"Anybody I know?"

"Greenie Lamonte and Hank Dundee."

Pete just nodded, recognizing that death was just a hazard of the job.

Ellis helped Sonny onto the driver's seat then lifted Mandy next to him before turning back to their father.

"I'll have 'em back before you know it."

John was halfway through his turn back to the house when he replied, "Yeah. Take your time."

Ellis glanced at Pete then smiled turned and climbed onto the driver's seat. He took the reins and started the wagon moving to the access road as Ellis returned to the house.

Rufus pulled up to the side of the wagon and said, "That was kinda different."

"You mean what John said?"

"Yup."

Ellis nodded in agreement as he turned the wagon onto the trail toward Fort Madrid, but knew it wasn't much different at all for that poor excuse for a man.

Once underway, Ellis asked Sonny what he was planning on buying with his fortune expecting to hear him reply candy or maybe a slingshot.

"I want to buy my mama a present."

Mandy then quickly said, "Me, too."

Ellis smiled at the children and said, "Well, I reckon that we'll see what we can do."

"Do you really think that there's gonna be a war like you said before, Mister White?" asked Sonny.

"Well, son, I hope I'm wrong, but it sure looks that way."

"Why would there be a war with just Americans?"

Ellis pointed his thumb at Rufus and replied, "Because of folks like Rufus over there. Rufus used to be owned by a man in Louisiana named Will Thornhill. Just before he died, Mister Thornhill gave Rufus a piece of paper that said he wasn't a slave no more and he came to Texas where he worked for me.

Rufus is one of the best men I've ever met, but a lot of folks think it's okay to buy and sell colored folks, and most of 'em live in the South. There's a lot of talk up North about freein' all of the slaves and the folks down South who own these big farms that have them slaves don't like it. This election for president that's comin' up might push some of the states to leave the Union and the Union ain't gonna put up with it. That's what will start the war."

Sonny glanced over at Rufus, who was pretending not to be listening and asked, "You'd go and fight so they could keep ownin' slaves?"

Ellis paused then replied, "Not for that, son. I think slavery is just plain stupid besides bein' wrong. If there's a war, I'll fight for Texas because I'm a Texan. But just like I told your pa, I don't think we can win and then after the dust clears, slavery will go away with it."

"Then why have a war at all?"

"That, Mister Keeler, is the biggest question of 'em all. Why have a war at all?"

Ellis then slipped into a few minutes of silence as the thoughts raised by Sonny's questions festered in his mind. *What if the South won?* If the North was serious about the war, then there was no chance at all, but there was always the unexpected. *What if one of the European powers suddenly decided to back the South because of the cotton that would no longer be available for their mills?* He was specifically thinking about merry old England. If any of those folks in the Old World decided to throw in with the southerners, it would be them.

But after those few minutes, Ellis concluded that what he thought didn't matter a lick. He'd just pick up his Remington rifle and ride off to fight for Texas and whatever happened was beyond his control. At least his ranch was ready, and he had all that cash sitting in a bank in Kansas to boot.

He then asked, "So, what were you and your sister plannin' on doin' with that horned frog if you caught him?"

Sonny grinned and he and his young sister began happily chattering.

————

It was just before noon when they reached Fort Madrid and Ellis noticed two new buildings had been added to the trading post. One was a feed and grain store and the other was a bakery.

Ellis treated for lunch at the small café before he gave his list of supplies to the proprietor, Ernie Smith.

"I'll pick up what you got on your shelves while you get the big stuff out of your storeroom, Ernie," Ellis said.

"Fair 'nuff," Ernie replied as he accepted the sheet.

"You losin' business with that new feed and grain store and bakery?"

"Nope. I own 'em both," Ernie replied with a grin before leaving the counter to go to his storeroom.

Ellis shook his head and grinned. Ernie pretty much owned the settlement except for the saloon and whorehouse, but he was mostly an honest man and Ellis liked him.

He and Rufus then began walking the aisles making their selections while Sonny and Mandy hunted for a present for their mother.

Twenty minutes later, the counter was full of tins of food and assorted other supplies, but Ellis noticed that Sonny and Mandy were still searching.

He turned, spotted them in an aisle then walked that way where he found the children examining a well-sewn woman's yellow print dress and when Ellis approached, they looked up at him.

"Mister White, how much is this dress?" Sonny asked.

Ellis had to hunt for the price tag and said, "Two dollars and fifteen cents."

"Oh. That's too much, isn't it?"

"Well, Mister Keeler, I'll tell you what. Mister Smith, the store owner, always gives me a discount because I always pay in cash, so why don't you take that pretty dress for your pretty mama and I'm sure it will be fine."

Sonny and Mandy both smiled as Sonny lifted the dress from the rack and handed it to Ellis.

Ellis walked to the counter, set the dress on the stack of things he'd ordered then turned back to Sonny and said, "Now, I'll need to take those silver dollars from you, so you can pay for the dress."

Both children quickly pulled their money from their pocket and handed them to Ellis without hesitation or even the tiniest drop in their smiles.

Ellis dropped the coins into his pocket then said, "With my discount, I figure you each have a dime left over to buy something else for yourselves. So, you can get yourselves some penny candy and maybe, if we go next door to the new bakery, you'll be able to buy some cookies, too."

"Thank you, Mister White," they said as they rushed to the glass-faced part of the counter that protected the four boxes of penny candy.

Ellis glanced at the smiling face of Ernie Smith and just tipped his head in the direction of the children before leaving the counter.

He knew where he was going and when he reached the display, he selected a small pocketknife then headed back to where the children had found the yellow print dress and bought some hair ribbons and a small hair brush.

While the children were eagerly pointing out their candy choices, Ellis caught Ernie's eye, showed him the pocket knife, hair brush and ribbons then slipped them into his jacket pockets after Ernie nodded.

They loaded the wagon then after a brief stop at the bakery where Ellis bought two large bags full of molasses cookies for everyone including Jim and Lou back at the ranch, they were soon rolling out of Fort Madrid.

Once the trading post was out of sight, Sonny and Mandy were sucking on some of their candy when Ellis reached into his pocket and pulled out the pocketknife.

"Now how in tarnation did that get there?" he asked in astonishment as he held the knife in front of him.

Sonny's eyes were welded to the knife as Ellis said, "Well, I sure don't have no need for this 'cause I got a bigger one in my pocket."

Sonny was itching to ask but knew it was impolite, so he just sat on the bouncing wagon seat mesmerized by the knife as Rufus trotted alongside smiling at the ongoing play.

Ellis kept his eyes ahead of him as he slid his hand and the knife to his right and asked, "You wouldn't want to take this off my hands, would ya?"

Sonny breathlessly asked, "Do you mean it, Mister White? I can have the pocketknife?"

"Well, I sure don't need it."

He watched Sonny's small fingers wrap around the precious knife and was glad he'd made the decision to bring them along and even happier with his plan to buy the knife.

He drove for another ten minutes without saying another word before he turned to Mandy and said, "That was pretty funny, wasn't it? I mean, finding that knife in my pocket without knowin' it was even there."

Mandy just nodded.

"You know what? I haven't even checked my other pocket. I wonder if there's another knife in there."

Mandy watched Ellis' hand slip into his jacket pocket then was stunned as he withdrew a hairbrush and it wasn't even big, so she could use it.

"Now, how about that? Here I was all surprised about the pocketknife, but this really makes me think I'm goin' rattlesnake crazy. How would this hairbrush wind up in there? If I didn't need a pocketknife, I sure don't need no girly hairbrush. Why the other fellers would be makin' fun of me till horses grew horns. Miss Keeler, would you save me from bein' called all those bad names and take this hairbrush?"

Mandy smiled took the hairbrush from his fingers and said, "Thank you, Mister White," then immediately began pulling it through her long brown hair.

Ellis then reached into one of the bags of molasses cookies, removed one and tossed it to Rufus who caught it in midair and took a big bite to keep from laughing. He then put one into his mouth before giving one to each of the children.

Once they cookies were distributed, Ellis launched into an off-key 'Git Along, Little Dogies' and was quickly joined by the much more on-key, deep bass of Rufus before the children both added their voices to the song.

As soon as that tune was finished, Rufus began singing 'The Old Chisholm Trail' and Ellis didn't bother singing but just listened to his ranch hand's strong voice as it echoed across the Texas landscape.

When he ended his solo, he looked at the three faces that were watching him then embarrassingly said, "Sorry, boss. You pick the next one."

"It's gonna be ugly, Rufus, but here goes," Ellis said before starting 'The Yellow Rose of Texas' sure that even the children would know the lyrics.

———

An hour later, their voices had been worn down even after using the canteens and Ellis figured they were another hour out of the Big O, so he put the second bag of cookies into the bag with the dress that they'd bought for their mother. He then reached into the magic jacket pocket again and as he pulled the three shining hair ribbons from his pocket, Mandy squealed.

"Will wonders never cease," he said as he held the ribbons out to Mandy.

"You'd better take these, ma'am. I'd sure look funny wearin' 'em around my ranch."

Mandy giggled as she took the ribbons and asked, "Are they for me or my mama?"

"I think your mama would be happy to see you wearin' one of those ribbons in your hair when we got back. Which color do you want?"

"Can I wear the red one?" she asked as she pulled it free from the blue and yellow ones.

"Of course, you can. I'll even tie it on for you if Rufus over there promises not to tell anybody."

Mandy glanced at Rufus who laughed and said, "I ain't promisin' nothin', but I guess if I look away, I won't see what's goin' on."

Mandy looked quickly back to Ellis handed him the scarlet ribbon, and he tied a loose knot with a big bow behind her hair.

"There you go, Miss Keeler, and may I tell you you're just about the prettiest lady these old bachelor eyes ever set upon."

"Thank you, Mister White," Mandy replied as she reached behind her head and ran her small hand down the length of her hair stopping to feel the ribbon.

Little Mandy Keeler was very happy she'd come along on the trip after all and couldn't wait to see the look on her mama's face when she saw the ribbon.

———

When Ellis turned the wagon down the Big O's access road, he spotted two riders up with the ranch's herd about a couple of miles north of the house. Technically they were on his property, but he didn't mind especially with his reduced herd. Right now, Pete Orris had more critters than he did.

Ellis pulled the wagon to a stop set the brake and hopped down as Sonny scrambled down from the wagon on his side. He lifted a smiling Mandy from the driver's seat then took the bag with the dress the second bag of cookies and their penny candy from the bed behind the seat and gave it to Sonny.

Normally, Ellis would have taken a little extra time to talk to Sara Mae but this time it was about her children, not him.

"Well, folks, I'm real happy that you joined us today. You made a long boring ride into a real good time. Now you make sure that your mama gets some of those cookies."

"Thank you, Mister White," both children replied in chorus as they smiled at him.

"You're welcome. Now me and Rufus gotta get those supplies to my ranch."

"Okay," Sonny said as he and Mandy stepped away from the wagon.

Sara Mae and Mary Jo had heard the wagon's approach and stepped out just as the Ellis was preparing to climb back into the driver's seat.

Sara Mae saw the ribbon around Mandy's brushed hair and the hairbrush in her hand then smiled at Ellis and walked closer to the wagon. His decision not to talk to her was at most half-hearted anyway.

"Thank you for making my children so happy, Ellis."

"I wish I could do more for both of 'em, Sara Mae. They're fine children and they think mighty highly of their mama."

"I'm quite fond of them as well."

"Well, you take care, ma'am. We've gotta get this load back to my house."

"Thank you again, Ellis," Sara Mae said as the warm smile stayed on her face.

Ellis climbed aboard released the hand brake then snapped the reins and as the wagon began to roll, he waved at everyone but his eyes lingered on Sara Mae before he turned and headed the wagon almost due east. If he used the trail to return to his ranch house, it would take an hour, but he followed a more direct route that he'd marked out when Pete first started building the ranch. He'd had his men help with the construction of the house and barn when they could, so it was a well-worn path.

As the wagon rolled away, Mary Jo entered the house followed by Sara Mae and her excited children.

Once inside, they took seats around the kitchen table and Sara Mae smiled at them as she asked, "So, Mandy, I see that you bought yourself a hair ribbon and a hairbrush. What else did you buy? That was a lot of money."

"It's in this bag with a bag of cookies that Mister White bought for everyone. He said you should have some," said Sonny.

Sara Mae blushed slightly as Sonny pulled out the bag of cookies and set it on the table then with Mandy standing beside him wearing a big smile, he pulled the yellow print dress from the bag and held it out to her.

"We bought this for you, Mama."

Sara Mae's eyes were filling with tears as she accepted the dress set it on her lap then reached over and hugged her children

She sniffed and said, "That was your money. You should have bought something for yourselves."

"I got a pocket knife and Mandy got a hairbrush and some hair ribbons, too."

Mary Jo walked beside the chair and said, "Maybe we should have gone along."

Sara Mae didn't reply but opened the bag of cookies from the bag and offered one to her sister before taking one herself.

"We have some penny candy, too," Mandy said as she produced a small bag of hard candy then added, "Mister White said the hair ribbons were for you too, and said that you were pretty when we showed him the dress."

Sara Mae blushed again as she glanced at her sister who was obviously suppressing a smile before looking back at her children.

"Well, you two did very well for yourselves," Sara Mae said before kissing each of them on the cheeks.

Before she rose, she glanced at the price tag on the dress and knew that Ellis had allowed them to overspend what he'd given them and then bought them the pocketknife and hairbrush. It was just one more example that slammed home her heartfelt knowledge that she had married the wrong man.

————

It took Ellis, Rufus, Jim and Lou almost an hour to unload the supplies and put them in place. Neither Ellis nor Rufus told Jim and Lou about the children coming along on the day long trip for supplies.

That night, Ellis wondered if he'd ever have children of his own. He'd already done what he had dreamt of doing when he built the Slash W and hadn't spent a lot of time on the other part of his dream because there simply wasn't time. Now with the almost inevitability of a long conflict between the states, he doubted if that would ever be possible.

But then there was Sara Mae. He knew all of his ranch hands talked about Mary Jo, but Ellis had a felt a strong connection to her almost from the first time they'd talked. If she hadn't been married to such a poor excuse for a man, he'd just be happy for her. But John Keeler wasn't even at that level and Ellis wished he'd been able to make life better for Sara Mae and the children.

————

Over the next few months as the critical November election neared, Ellis, working with his three men, prepared the ranch as best they could following Ellis' long-term plan.

He'd tried the Henry twice to get the feel for the innovative repeater and before he'd finished a single box of the cartridges, he felt comfortable enough with the rifle to just clean it and oil it before putting it aside. He did spend more time in target practice with his Remington and his Dragoon to prepare himself and that required additional purchases of ammunition when they made their supply runs to Fort Madrid, which had added a butcher's shop also owned by Ernie Smith.

Ellis kept the cash in his own private bank in the house for supplies and to pay the three men. Even before the election, the country was already splitting apart as new political parties were created based on how much support they gave to either slavery or its abolition. It was that fracturing of the proponents of slavery that almost guaranteed that Mr. Abraham Lincoln from Illinois, while not an abolitionist himself, would become the sixteenth president of the United States and maybe its last as a complete union.

Several states had already seceded even before he was elected, and even though Texas wasn't among them, Ellis knew it was just a matter of time. It was just a question of who would light the fuse before the shooting began.

Ellis was preparing to begin the final steps of setting up the ranch for his extended absence and already had long talks with the three men about what would happen.

As soon as Texas made its decision about joining the other Southern states, he'd leave the ranch and ride east to join the army. He hadn't been surprised that Jim and Lou both said that they'd stay and keep an eye on the ranch while he was gone, so he told them he'd set aside enough cash to last them for a while. He tried to convince Rufus to take his advice and head west, but Rufus said he would stay on the Slash W to keep the other two in line which made Jim and Lou laugh, but Ellis wasn't sure it was a joke.

As 1861 arrived, Ellis was almost ready. He'd taken the leather pouch of gold coins from the cattle sale and at night, when the men were in the bunkhouse, he rode to the northwest corner of the ranch and dug a small hole at the base of a boulder, buried the bag then after covering it with dirt, slid a smaller rock over the top.

He returned to the barn, unsaddled his horse then entered his house to finish his preparations. He took the remaining cash, set aside enough for three years' salaries for the three men then added another four hundred for supplies. There shouldn't be much need beyond food because the horses and cattle that he'd leave behind in the northwest corner of the ranch would take care of themselves.

He took the remaining hundred and fifty-two dollars in cash and put it into a small box on his dresser. He then took the Henry rifle and its five and a half boxes of cartridges and carried them out to the barn. He climbed into the loft, walked to a corner and slid the oiled tarp he'd stored there earlier. He laid the repeater onto the canvas, folded it over carefully, then set the boxes of ammunition nearby before covering the lot with a smaller, dry canvas. He then shoveled some loose hay onto the tarp and figured it would suffice then climbed down from the hay loft and left the barn.

It wasn't until the second week in February that word finally reached Fort Madrid of Texas' vote of secession. Not one shot had been fired yet, but the war was here.

After returning from that supply run with the news, Ellis had to make his final preparations and called in the three men to join him.

"Well, boss, it looks like you were right all along," Lou said as they sat around the kitchen table.

"I wish I'd been wrong. This is gonna be real bad."

"You takin' two horses with ya?" asked Jim.

"Nope. I'm just takin' the red gelding. He's older and I probably won't be able to hang onto him anyway if they put me in the infantry. They'll probably take him and give him to some officer."

"What happens now?" asked Lou.

"I'll pack some clothes, food, my guns and ammunition and ride to Henrietta. I'll find out when I get there where I need to go and sign up."

"Boss," Rufus asked, "what happens if you...you know, don't make it."

"Well, if the war's over, and I'm not back six months after that then that's your problem. I left enough cash in the box on my dresser that should last for three years."

The room lapsed into a morbid silence for a few minutes before Ellis said, "Don't worry about me, boys. I don't figure on doin' anything stupid."

They all laughed before Ellis stood then shook each man's hand and as he held Rufus' hand, he said in a low voice, "Any sign of trouble, Rufus, you get your black behind out west to Colorado."

Rufus smiled and said, "If it gets that bad, you can count on it."

Ellis smiled before the boys all left the kitchen to give their boss time to pack.

———

Early the next morning, Ellis mounted the red gelding, waved to the boys and headed out of the ranch but headed southwest toward the Big O. He wanted to tell Pete that he was leaving and if he needed any help to just ask the boys. He'd told Rufus to give him anything he needed, but the real reason for the side trip was that he really wanted to see Sara Mae one more time to imprint that image in his mind. He wasn't convinced that he'd survive what lay ahead and was resigned to whatever fate awaited him, but he wanted to give himself this one last gift.

When he arrived there was smoke coming out of the cookstove pipe, so he stopped in the back and was stepping down when Pete opened the door then he and John stepped onto the porch and he said, "You're stopping by early, Ellis. We were just coming by to see you. Are you already going to Henrietta to sign up?"

"Yup. I just figured I'd stop by and let you know that I told the boys to give you any help you'd need while I was gone."

"Well, that's kind of you, Ellis, but John and I are coming with you. He was a bit ornery about it, but I talked him into it."

Ellis looked at his neighbor shook his head and said, "Pete, I don't figure that's a good idea. You got your families to think about."

John turned to Pete and said, "I told you that, Pete. We should stay. At least let me stay here and keep Mary Jo safe."

Pete shook his head and snapped, "We've been all over this, John. You're coming!"

Ellis noticed that John had said he wanted to stay to keep Mary Jo safe not Sara Mae and his children. The reason that John probably wanted to stay probably had nothing to do with keeping anyone safe. Ellis thought he was a coward in addition to all of his other less-than-admirable traits.

The two women both walked onto the porch as Ellis continued to shake his head, then he looked at the wives and said, "Couldn't you two ladies talk Pete into stayin'? He should stay here with you, Mary Jo and not goin' off with me 'cause he figures he's gotta prove himself or somethin'."

Before Mary Jo could reply, Pete said, "I'm not trying to prove anything, Ellis. I'm a Texan just like you and I'm going either with you or without you."

Ellis sighed then figured he'd have a few days to be able to talk him out of his decision, so he just nodded and said, "I'll wait while you both get ready to go."

Pete kissed Mary Jo and whispered something to her that brought tears to her eyes before she turned and almost ran back into the house.

Pete and John then stepped from the porch and walked to the barn. Ellis noting the lack of tears on Sara Mae's face as well as the non-existent goodbye kiss from her husband and not even a wave.

Sara Mae walked to the edge of the porch and said softly, "Be careful, Ellis. Keep an eye on Pete. He's a good man, but I think he should have stayed, too. I think you're right about how long this is going to be, too."

"I hope I'm wrong, Sara Mae," he said, "but I'll do all I can to keep both of 'em safe."

"Just you make sure you stay safe, Ellis. Don't worry about my husband. I know that you understand what he is and what he isn't, and I know him even better than that."

Ellis replied, "I know, Sara Mae, and I'm really sorry."

Sara Mae smiled and said, "Now that he's gone, I'll be able to wear that yellow dress that you bought for me and let my children believe that they had. You're a good man, Ellis Mitchell White."

Ellis took a deep breath and said, "I swear, Sara Mae, you're the most woman I've ever met, and I promise I won't do anythin' stupid out there."

Sara Mae said softly, "You never do, Ellis," then turned and walked back into the house.

Ellis watched Sara Mae leave before he turned back to the gelding, rubbed his neck then climbed into the saddle and walked the gelding toward the barn. It was a hell of a way to go off to war.

CHAPTER 2

May 19, 1864
Northeast Texas

Ellis was slowing his breathing as he centered the crosshairs of the Amadon telescopic sight of his J.F. Brown sniper rifle. He had the Yankee colonel with an almost perfect shooting solution but held his shot.

He hadn't asked to be the regimental sniper, but no one else had offered to take the job after the last man who served in the position had been hanged by the Yankees. He'd been 'volunteered' by Colonel Bushnell and was close to mutiny before taking the rifle. Now he was doing something he considered cowardly and reprehensible and cursed the colonel for even asking for volunteers much less making him take the job.

The one advantage was that he operated alone and was no longer subject to the confusing and often conflicting orders that came down from on high. Now he was very alone more than two miles from his regiment as they were engaged in what had been categorized as a reorganizing movement. It the Yankees hadn't had similar problems the whole damned campaign would have been an abject disaster.

He'd probably shot twenty Yankee soldiers since he'd signed up more than three years ago and had only been wounded twice. He'd been sick three times lost a lot of weight and now probably weighed as much as he did when he was sixteen.

Ellis took one more look at the colonel and tried to mentally will him to leave the chart table, but he still stood there pointing at some line on a map and shouting to a captain to his right. *Move, damn you!* But the commanding officer still stood in place as he gestured and argued. Ellis knew he'd waited long enough.

He then held his breath and slowly squeezed the trigger. The long rifle bucked as the .45 caliber bullet spun out of the long barrel followed by smoke, flame and sound. He waited for almost a full second to watch the impact and when it smashed into the chart table between the two officers he grinned then quickly jumped to his feet and began a quick but quiet exit from the location knowing it would soon be populated by bluecoats.

Twenty minutes later when he knew that it was unlikely that the Yankees would be pursuing him, he slowed and began to think up an excuse for the miss if it came to that.

The officers in his and other regiments were still trying to paint a rosy picture of the battles against the Yankees, but every single one of the boys in gray or butternut knew better. Besides the news provided by the occasional Yankee newspaper that filtered through the lines just seeing the larger, better-equipped armies in blue spoke volumes. Those first few years, the fights had been much different as he and the other boys in his brigade seemed to almost terrify their opponents. Now not only were the Federals better equipped, better fed and in his opinion, better led their morale and fighting prowess was much improved.

But despite the obvious, Ellis still didn't believe he'd get back to his ranch before 1867. There were many times that the desire to return to his ranch almost drove him to just walk away as many men did, but he convinced himself that despite the lost cause it would be dishonorable to just give up.

He often wondered about his ranch. He hadn't heard a word about it since he rode away which wasn't surprising. Pete Orris had been assigned to a different brigade, but John Keeler was with him since they stepped off and even had been in his company before he'd been given the sniper job. Yet John barely talked to him for many reasons, so when Ellis had asked about his ranch, John would just shrug and tell him that he hadn't heard about it from Sara Mae.

Whenever he mentioned her name, it conjured up the memory of that last smile from her before she turned and walked into the house. That was more than three years ago, and he wondered if she was still even capable of smiling.

He stopped to take a drink from his canteen and get his bearing when he heard some whooping from his right past the thick trees. It was closer to Confederate lines than the Union's, so he loaded his rifle then began to walk in the direction of the excitement, expecting to find a group of soldiers who had created their own version of mash. It wouldn't be the first time and John Keeler was one of those who always seemed to be involved.

The shouts were getting louder as Ellis stepped through the trees and he finally was able to pick out words. Once he understood what was happening, he broke into a trot and soon popped into a clearing.

"*What the hell do you think you're doin', Private Keeler?*" he shouted as he approached the group.

John turned to him and yelled back, "What does it look like we're doin,' Sarrr-gent? We found this Yankee spy and we're gonna hang him."

"The hell you are! Take that noose from around his neck right now!"

44

One of the other men snapped, "C'mon, Sergeant White, this here Yankee captain was where he didn't belong, and we caught him."

Ellis reached the group then without asking, he pulled the noose from around the officer's neck then led him away a few feet leaving his wrists still bound.

"He's nothin' more than a regular prisoner. You oughta know that. If you hanged him then you could be hanged yourself."

"They hanged Sergeant Immelmann," John argued.

"He was a sniper just like me. We hang theirs, too. Now I'm making this an order. You all head back to camp and I'll take the prisoner. Tell Captain Forsythe what happened, too."

The men began to walk away but not before John Keeler mumbled, "Yankee lover."

Ellis watched them all disappear into the woods before he turned to the captain and said, "I ain't no Yankee lover, but what they was doin' was just plumb wrong."

The captain didn't reply but waited as Ellis cut his wrists' bonds.

Ellis then said, "I'll escort you closer to your lines, so this don't happen again. I don't know what got into those boys."

Captain Mike Dunston replied, "It wasn't all of them. Just that one who called you a Yankee-lover seemed intent on putting that noose around my neck."

"Well, John was never one of my favorite people anyway," he said as they began walking away from the Confederate lines.

They had barely walked two hundred yards when the tables were suddenly turned and Ellis found himself under four Yankee rifles as one of the pickets shouted, "Halt! Who goes there?"

Captain Dunston returned the challenge, yelling back, "I'm Captain Dunston of the 54th Ohio in Smith's Corps."

"Come through with your prisoner, Captain," the picket replied.

Ellis knew he was in serious trouble as the sniper rifle seemed to triple its weight in his hand but not for long as one of the Federal picket men ripped it from his grip.

Two of the pickets walked with him and the captain to the Union camp he had just visited for a different reason when he'd just blown apart their colonel's chart table. He suspected that the near miss probably wouldn't endear him to them either.

As they approached the large collection of tents with none of the fungus that seemed to be on every one of the Confederate tents, Ellis began looking around for nearby trees that would be used for his execution. Maybe they'd shoot him instead. Even now, he was almost amused by the irony of the situation. He hadn't shot the colonel who was about to condemn him and by rescuing the officer who was about to hang, he'd traded places. But in this case, his amusement didn't reach the level of generating any laughter.

He was made to stand with two rifles pointed at him as the captain walked into the command tent. He could hear voices talking loudly from inside before the colonel threw back the tent flap and strode toward him, followed by the captain.

"Are you the bastard who almost killed me an hour ago?" he shouted.

Ellis looked at his angry, dark blue eyes and replied, "No, sir. If I wanted to hit you, or the captain standin' next to you, I woulda."

The colonel blustered, "Are you telling me that you missed on purpose?"

"Yes, sir. I'm new at this whole sniper business and didn't like it much. I don't mind shootin' you Yankees out there in the battlefield but wasn't happy about shootin' men who weren't shootin' back."

The colonel's eyes narrowed as he scanned Ellis then finally said to the soldier behind him, "Give me that sniper rifle he had with him."

"Yes, sir," the private said as he held out the rifle to his commanding officer.

After taking the J.F. Brown, he asked, "Is it loaded?"

"Yes, sir."

"Alright, I'll tell you what, Sergeant, if you can prove to me that you really tried to miss then maybe, just maybe, you won't hang."

He handed the rifle to Ellis who tried to keep himself calm for the upcoming shot as he scanned the environment.

"I was about four hundred yards east of here when I took that shot, so I figure that's about where you have that campfire set up over yonder. Is that about right?"

Everyone's head turned to see the distant campfire and the captain said, "I'd say closer to four hundred and fifty yards."

The colonel then nodded and said, "Alright, Sergeant, I want you to hit the blackened rock at the top of the fire pit."

Ellis sighed then tried to focus on the target. He'd hoped that he'd only have to hit the campfire itself not a particular rock, but he didn't have a say in the matter.

He cocked the hammer then said, "Yes, sir," before bringing the heavy rifle to bear. Normally, he'd use a prone position, but he wanted a backup plan. If he missed, just a heartbeat later, he'd be running as fast as that bullet and that would be hard to do if he was still on his stomach.

He had the lens caps off as he sighted the rock through the long-tubed offset scope and let out his breath before squeezing the trigger. He didn't keep his eye near the scope after the rifle fired but quickly dropped his hands as the rock exploded into thousands of shards and splinters of rock.

Ellis exhaled at his reprieve then turned to the colonel for his judgement.

The officer slowly turned to meet Ellis' eyes and said, "That was good shooting. I wish my men were that accurate with their weapons."

"We can't afford to waste ammunition, Colonel," Ellis replied.

The colonel turned to Captain Dunston and said, "I want you both to come into my tent."

One of the pickets asked, "What about his pistol, Sir? Do you want me to take it?"

"No. Let him keep his rifle, too. It's empty."

Ellis then followed the two officers into the command tent and after the colonel sat down, he said, "Take a seat, Sergeant. You too, Mike."

Ellis was surprised to hear such familiarity between a commanding officer and a subordinate and didn't comment, but soon discovered the reason for the lack of military decorum.

"Sergeant, I'm Colonel Ralph Dunston and I appreciate your actions in saving my son. I apologize for that display out front, but I couldn't do anything less and maintain the respect of my men. Now, what can I do with you?"

"Colonel, if it's alright with you, I'd just as soon go home to my ranch in west Texas. I haven't seen it in more than three years now, and I'm gettin' kinda tired of this war."

"Aren't we all. If I offer you parole, then you'd accept it and promise never to take up arms against the Union again?"

"Yes, sir."

He turned to his son and said, "Mike draw up a letter of parole for the sergeant and I'll let you handle the particulars."

"Yes, Sir. I'll do that."

Captain Dunston waved Ellis to follow and both soldiers, one wearing a reasonably clean and intact blue uniform and the other a mismatched gray blouse and faded blue britches, left the command tent.

Ellis drew glances from the Yankee soldiers as he walked with the captain through the encampment carrying his J.F. Brown rifle, but none seemed overly hostile when they did. Ellis couldn't help but notice the level of supplies and equipment that they had available.

When he'd been setting up to shoot Colonel Dunston, he'd only had a limited view of the camp but seeing the readily available supplies even this far from their warehouses and train lines reinforced his belief that the war was in its death throes and that his parole was just an early gift.

The captain turned into a tent that was almost as large as the command tent and Ellis followed into the dark interior.

"Have a seat, Sergeant," Captain Dunston said as he removed his awkward sabre.

"Thank you, Sir," Ellis replied as he sat on a collapsible chair near a well-made cot.

After hanging his hat, Captain Dunston said, "I never did get your name."

"Ellis White."

"Do you mind if I call you Ellis? Technically, you're a civilian now."

"No, sir. Ellis is fine."

"Call me Mike. I owe you that it more ways than you can imagine. You not only saved my ass from getting hanged, although they were really going to put that rope around my neck and not my behind, but you didn't shoot my father and that, to me, was even more important. I wouldn't want to be the one to break the news to my mother. I'm their only son. I have four sisters back in Ohio, but I know that he's been worried that I'd be killed before the end of this war more than getting shot himself."

"I imagine that woulda been kinda bad."

Mike took a seat on the cot and asked, "Where are you from, if you don't mind my asking?"

"I have a ranch out in Hardeman County between the High Hills."

"Where's that? The only part of Texas I've seen is right here. We were supposed to head for New Orleans, but things never seem to work out the way they should."

"It's just about two hundred miles due west from here."

"How long have you been in the war?"

"From the start. Me and two other fellers from next door left in February of '61 right after Texas left the Union. One of 'em was the bastard who had that noose around your neck and called me a Yankee lover."

"He sure seemed like a son-of-a-bitch to me, too. Do you mind if I ask why you joined up to fight against the Union? Quite a few of you Texas boys are wearing blue."

"It ain't no secret. I'm a Texan and Texas needed me to fight, so I did."

"Did you think you were going to win?"

"Not a chance, unless one of them European countries threw in with us because they needed our cotton, but that wasn't very likely."

"But you still joined up."

"Like I said, Texas needed me. How long have you been fightin'?"

"Since June of '63. I had just graduated from Oberlin College and my father was offered a commission as a lieutenant colonel with the 58th Ohio Infantry as a replacement. I joined him as his adjutant."

"What did he do before the war?"

"He owns a pipe making plant in Columbus. He didn't even know what a lieutenant colonel was before they asked him to be one."

"Did you study soldierin' at college?"

Mike smiled and replied, "No. I have a degree in divinity."

Ellis smiled and just shook his head.

"How about you, Ellis? How did you wind up in such an empty space in west Texas? I know it's empty because we never even thought about sending any troops that far west. There's nothing of value out there."

"That's the truth of it. All it's good for is grazing cattle which is why I went there."

"So, how did you wind up where there weren't a lot of white folks?"

Ellis ran his hand through his dark brown hair and replied, "Well, it was a bit different, I'll give you that. I never knew my pa 'cause he lit out before I was born leavin' my ma alone with her folks. My ma died when I was three, but I never knew why. I was raised by my grandparents on their ranch about fifty miles southwest of here, near Cooper.

"It wasn't a big spread, and I was ridin' horses and workin' the cattle when I was ten. My grandma died when I was twelve and my grandpa died when I was nineteen, so I inherited the place. I didn't want to stay there, though. I figured it wasn't really mine, so I sold it and with a couple of friends just drove the small herd west. We stopped at Fort Madrid, a trading post in Hardeman County and the owner told us that I might be able to work a deal with the Comanche, so I did."

"You drove a herd of cattle into Comanche territory?"

"It weren't so bad. After we worked out a deal, I started buildin' my ranch. It took a while, but I finally figured I was where I wanted to be and then the war kinda made a mess out of it."

"You might be lucky that your ranch was so far west. Between the two armies, they've just about stripped every ranch and farm wherever they've visited."

"I kinda figured that would happen, so I pretty much emptied my ranch of critters in May of '60."

"That was pretty smart."

Ellis shrugged then replied, "Maybe."

Then he asked, "So, what happens now?"

"Well, I'll write up your parole paper and give it to you so none of our troops will shoot you, then you just leave in the morning. You can sleep here. I'll have another cot brought in."

"I appreciate that, but what about my guns? I wouldn't feel all that comfortable walking two hundred miles across Texas unarmed."

"I don't blame you. There are a lot of deserters out there with nothing but a nasty temper. You can take your guns with you and all of your ammunition. You'll need some food, too. I'll get you a full knapsack before you go."

"Well, I do appreciate it."

Mike then looked down at Ellis' feet and said, "Those boots are ready to fall apart, Ellis. What size to you wear?"

"Eleven."

"Stay here. I'll be right back."

Ellis nodded as Mike stood then left the tent leaving a somewhat perplexed ex-Confederate sergeant alone with his thoughts.

He knew that he'd have no problem with the navigation back home because he'd made the trip before and his unit had also marched this way on its way east. As the captain had mentioned, the problems were the number of deserters that now populated East Texas and the probable lack of horses and supplies.

Unlike his fellow soldiers, Ellis still had Union currency. He'd been paid, albeit infrequently, in Confederate notes, but they were already worth much less than their face value. He still had five of the twenty-dollar Yankee notes folded into a small pouch that he kept in his right boot. He'd had to dry them out four times over the last three years which had posed its own problem, but they were still in good condition. But even with that much Yankee cash, it was unlikely that he'd be able to buy a horse to make the journey faster. Horseflesh was being consumed by both armies at a terrifying, almost irreplaceable rate. He would have been glad to sell one of his horses for fifty dollars before the war but now even a nag was bringing three hundred. Mules weren't much better.

So, he'd start walking west in the morning and he estimated that if he managed a good pace, he could be back on his ranch in two weeks. The thought of standing in his own house again after three years of living in disgusting conditions felt like a warm blanket for his soul.

He was still running through a map in his head when the flap opened and Mike Dunston returned carrying a pair of boots, a canteen and a knapsack.

He sat down and handed the boots to Ellis as he said, "These should fit. I put some socks and other stuff in the knapsack," then set the knapsack down at Ellis' feet as Ellis examined the boots.

"These are some nice boots, Mike."

"They're officer's boots. The enlisted boots aren't nearly as good but at least they're better now. We received two cases of boots a few months ago and found that the soles were just cardboard. The telegraph lines were burning up after that one."

Ellis grinned and said, "I guess there's always greedy bastards who try to make money the easy way."

"That's the truth."

C.J. PETIT

Ellis pulled off his boots which wouldn't have lasted twenty miles much less two hundred then fished out a pair of nice, wool socks from the knapsack, slipped them on and then pulled on the new boots. He stood and took a few steps, expecting more discomfort than he felt. They'd still need breaking in, but they were a considerable improvement.

He sat down on the collapsible chair and said, "These feel real good. I reckon they'll be even better after I put a few miles behind me."

"Good. Now let's go and get something to eat. I missed lunch because I was in the company of your boys."

Ellis laughed then rose to follow Captain Dunston out of the tent leaving his rifle behind.

Without the long rifle, Ellis wasn't quite the attraction he'd been before, and he shouldn't have been surprised when he found that his supper was going to be in the officer's mess, but he was. He just hadn't given it much thought.

Once inside, he expected to be treated with disdain if not open hostility but once he'd been introduced by Captain Dunston and Colonel Dunston shook his hand, he received nothing but deferential treatment and was soon inundated with questions during the meal.

By the time Ellis returned to the captain's tent where he found a second cot, a pillow and blankets waiting for him, he was beginning to feel downright comfortable which struck him as very bizarre. He'd been at war with these men just hours before and now, he'd just shared a congenial meal with them and would be sleeping unguarded with his weapons nearby. Maybe they were all just as tired as he was with the war and just wanted to go home to Ohio.

56

During the night before they slept, he and Mike shared stories and Mike was surprised to find that Ellis not only didn't like slavery but one of his best friends was colored. Oberlin College was a hotbed of abolitionists and while Mike never slipped into the extremes, he was a firm believer that slavery was evil and had to be eliminated.

Mike spoke of his fiancée back in Ohio and showed him her picture then asked Ellis if he was married. Ellis figured that he'd never see Mike again, so he told him about Sara Mae and her children and Mike had been surprised to learn that the woman that Ellis had described as 'more woman than any other woman he'd ever met' was married to the despicable excuse for a man who had convinced the others to hang him. He then suggested that when Ellis got back to his ranch, he should just ignore John altogether because he really wasn't a husband and father anyway.

After the woman discussion, they talked about the war for a while then finally had to end the long conversation when they both knew that tomorrow had already arrived and they both would be busy.

By the time they finally drifted to sleep, each man considered the other a friend.

————

The bugle's sharp notes awakened both men early in the morning when it sounded reveille. After heading to the latrine and washing quickly in the officer's bath, they went to the officer's mess again for breakfast.

As it had been the previous evening, the questions continued but this time they were mostly about his plans and what it was like out in the emptiness of West Texas.

After breakfast, Mike and Ellis walked to the supply tent and Mike filled up another knapsack with food and in a real surprise, he added some additional ammunition for his guns.

Without saying anything, Captain Dunston took the knapsack left the supply tent and headed back to his personal tent then went inside as Ellis followed.

"I'd look mighty stupid with two Yankee knapsacks, Mike," Ellis said as he sat down.

"I know," he said before he walked to the back of the tent, then pulled out a set of large saddlebags without the distinctive U.S. markings.

"These were mine when I joined up and kept them with me for no reason at all. I have a horse but use army saddlebags. Now I'm glad I kept them."

He sat down on his cot then moved all of the food and ammunition from the knapsack filling one side of the voluminous saddlebags then slid them to Ellis.

"I really appreciate this, Mike," Ellis said as he transferred the contents of the first knapsack to the other side even adding his old boots.

"Ellis, do you need some cash? I know that Confederate money isn't worth much. I can give you twenty dollars."

Ellis grinned and said, "Remember I told you that I sold almost all of my critters in May of '60? Well, I left most of the money in a bank in Abilene then after I left most of the remaining cash from the sale with my foreman, I buried a thousand dollars in gold coins. I still have a hundred dollars in Yankee money in my boot."

"You're in better shape than I am," Mike replied with a laugh.

"I still appreciate all you did for me, Mike."

Mike said, "When you leave, I'll walk with you to the end of our lines and tell the pickets that you've been paroled. I'll send word across to the Confederate lines to your colonel if you want."

"No, that's okay. I don't want you to risk anybody just to send a message that I ain't comin' back. They'll probably figure that you all hanged me anyway. Sooner or later, they'll get the word."

Mike didn't reply but waited as Ellis stood hung the heavy saddlebags over his left shoulder and the canteen over the other then picked up his rifle. The captain then reached down, pulled up his blanket folded it twice and gave it to Ellis who hung it over his right shoulder.

The two men stood for a few seconds before they shook hands then turned and left the tent.

They walked quietly through the camp and finally after reaching the western picket line, Captain Michael Dunston told the pickets that Sergeant Ellis White had given his parole and was not to be fired upon not that it was really necessary.

They shook hands one more time before Mike said, "Have a good life, Ellis."

"You too, Mike," Ellis said before snapping to attention and saluting the officer.

Mike returned the salute then Ellis did a sharp about face and marched west, soon disappearing into the trees.

Mike watched him leave and wasn't sure what kind of life awaited him when he reached his ranch but knew that few of them really knew what to expect when they finally went home. He hoped that Ellis would take his advice about that woman that was waiting in Hardeman County but probably not for her bastard husband.

He turned back to the camp to join his father in the hope that they would be going home soon, too.

CHAPTER 3

Ellis marched for another thirty minutes before he slowed down to a more comfortable amble knowing he had a long journey ahead. He knew that there were no more Yankee army units in front of him, so he wasn't concerned about running afoul of any bluebellies, but he still stopped and reloaded his rifle.

He knew that Clarksville was just a few miles south, but he didn't want to divert his route and add more distance, so he decided to keep heading west for Paris. He should be able to reach the town by nightfall if he kept up a good pace.

After an hour and a half of walking, he reached the east-west roadway and found the going easier, but he had to stay alert for possible highwaymen and deserters. He'd toyed with just heading for the Red River and following along its southern bank but that would add a few days to the journey, and he'd be more likely to run afoul of folks he didn't want to meet.

It was well past noon when he finally stopped for his first break, left the road and entered some nearby trees where he found a moss-covered rock and sat down.

He lowered his saddlebags to the ground took out the bag of beef jerky and took out three pieces before returning it to the saddlebags. As he chewed on the jerky, he tried to calculate the time it would take to reach his ranch and thought that optimistically, he might be able to reach it in one week and not two. It would take long days of almost non-stop walking, but he had been marching for three years now ever since the army had confiscated his horse. He didn't doubt that he could manage the forced march, but he was concerned about what he might encounter along the way.

He'd read about the devastation in the southern states to the east but hadn't seen a lot of it in Texas although he hadn't seen much of Texas since he joined up. He'd get an idea when he reached Paris and maybe he could buy himself a good meal. He'd use all eighty-two dollars of Confederate bills until they were gone which might just be after that first good meal before he began using his Federal notes.

After taking a deep drink from his canteen, he screwed the top back on then stood and headed back for the road and then onto Paris.

The afternoon walk was uneventful and as the sun was setting, Ellis spotted Paris on the horizon. He hadn't seen any traffic at all on the road which had surprised him as he had expected to be passed by the stagecoach run between Boston and Paris or the return run if it had already passed by before he reached the road. He hadn't seen a rider or another walking traveler either.

When he reached Paris an hour later, he didn't see any of the ravages of war at all and headed for a small café that seemed to be open but had an empty hitching post out front.

He entered the eatery and found an empty table which wasn't difficult as he was the only diner.

It still took almost a minute for a waitress to arrive who seemed enormously pleased to see him despite his dusty, unkempt appearance.

"What can I get for you, sir?" she asked as she smiled.

"Well, ma'am, I'm mighty hungry, so whatever you got ready sounds good, and lots of coffee."

"I'm sorry, we don't have any coffee, but we do have some chicory that's pretty good. Is that alright?"

"Yes, ma'am. That's fine."

"I'll be right back," she replied with another smile before scooting back to the kitchen.

Ellis scanned the diner and wondered why it was so empty at what should be dinnertime. He was still wondering when the door opened and an older gentleman entered with a white-haired woman who was probably his wife and two younger women then after glancing at Ellis, he walked to a nearby table and held out a chair for his wife while the two women took their seats. Once seated, all of the women glanced at him and one of the younger ones smiled.

Ellis smiled back out of courtesy but before he could give it another thought, the waitress returned with a pot of chicory coffee and a cup. She set the cup on the table, poured his coffee substitute then smiled again and quickly left.

The door opened again and in almost a mirror image of the first group of new diners entered consisting of a gray-haired man two younger women and a boy and girl of about ten but no white-haired wife.

Again, they all glanced his way, even the children before Ellis took a sip of his dark coffee-like brew and looked at the kitchen door hoping that the waitress would return.

She arrived two minutes later with a plate of what looked like chicken in gravy, some mashed potatoes and a piece of cornbread.

She set it down and said, "Here you go, sir."

"Thank you, ma'am," Ellis said but not asking what was buried under the gravy.

He began eating as the waitress left to help the new arrivals then looked around for any indication of the cost for the dinner and found nothing displayed anywhere to help.

He finished his food and stretched out his chicory coffee that wasn't as bad as he'd been drinking for more than a year. He had been hoping to see how others paid for their meals, but finally decided he'd ask the waitress.

"Ma'am, how much do I owe you?"

"It's a dollar and a half in Confederate money and twenty cents in real money."

Ellis smiled at the reference but pulled out a five-dollar Confederate note and handed it to her while saying, "Keep the change, ma'am."

She accepted the bill then turned to help the other customers leaving Ellis to polish off the coffee. After draining the cup he stood hung his blanket and saddlebags over his shoulders then picked up his rifle before leaving the café.

Once in the street, Ellis decided against spending any more of either color money on a hotel and figured that his best bet would be to wait until morning and buy some more supplies at the dry goods store with one of his greenbacks so he could get change. The only problem would be that the change would probably be in Confederate money which led him to change his mind again.

The weather was warm, and he had a full stomach, so once his decision was reached, he began walking out of Paris on the road to Bonham. He had no intention of walking even halfway tonight but if he could put another ten miles behind him, he'd be that much closer to his ranch. The moon was almost full giving him a clear view of the empty roadway.

Ellis walked for another two hours before fatigue began to set in and he finally decided to get some sleep. He turned north off the road, found some trees then set down his saddlebags, rifle and his blanket. Using the spare clothing side of the saddlebag as his pillow, he stretched out on his blanket and relaxed with his rifle by his left side. He was still wearing his pistol and unless it became annoying overnight, he'd leave it on.

As he laid on the cooling earth waiting for slumber to overtake him, he wondered what was so different about Paris from what he had expected. The money problem he had anticipated as was the lack of horse traffic, but there was something else. He had almost slipped into sleep when it dawned on him and should have been more obvious than the other changes; there were no young men. He'd only seen older men in the short time he'd spent in Paris, and although there were probably some around most were still off in the army or would never return.

He let morbid curiosity ask how it was in West Texas where he knew of many men who hadn't gone off to fight at all. As Mike had mentioned, some had actually gone North to join the Union army but there were a few that stayed, maybe to take advantage of the situation.

Luckily, he told himself, he didn't have anything to worry about. Jim Abigail, Lou Gordon and Rufus Green would all still be there, and he should be able to have the Slash W back to full operation within a year. He just hoped that Rufus was okay. If he wasn't there, then hopefully he'd made his way to safety up north.

But once he'd had the nagging mystery of the missing men solved, he shifted his thoughts back to Sara Mae. That image he'd burned into his memory had done its job, and he wondered what she looked like now. It had been three years, so she'd be twenty-seven now. Sonny would be nine and Mandy would be seven.

He knew there would be enormous physical changes in the children but believed that Sara Mae wouldn't look much different. He smiled as he pictured her wearing that yellow dress and maybe a ribbon in her hair. But just as he'd told Mike Dunston, it didn't matter what he felt because her husband was still alive and well in East Texas and keeping himself alive and well was the only thing that he seemed to be good at doing.

———

The next four days were almost repetitions of the first with little road traffic although he did finally see a stagecoach pass by from Montague heading west after he'd passed through Greenville.

He'd kept a steady and hard, driving pace every day and managed to walk more than forty miles in one day. His new boots while a bit tight at the start, had broken in nicely and would be able to see him through to the ranch and probably last a couple of years after that. He smiled when he thought of cardboard boots and how angry those Yankee soldiers must have been when they made that discovery.

He'd stopped at both Sherman and Gainesville to buy supplies and have some cooked food using up the last of his Confederate currency in Gainesville.

Yesterday he'd been soaked by a driving rain that only lasted for two hours, but he appreciated the chance to bathe when he stripped and washed himself with a bar of soap that he'd bought in Sherman but just air-dried himself after the rain stopped. He really needed a shave as he'd left his shaving kit at the camp with his other things. Luckily, there wasn't much else that he left behind, but he knew he was looking pretty bad with his curly black beard and long hair.

All things considered, everything was going very well until he was just two hours out of Montague. The area south of the roadway was heavily forested, and Ellis had become complacent after six days of walking. That complacency almost cost him dearly.

He never knew what suddenly alerted him to the unexpected danger, whether it was the sudden rush of an owl awakened from his daytime slumber or the loud snap of a twig, but the reason never mattered as he suddenly halted and dropped to the ground with his rifle slamming butt first into the roadway.

A rifle shot rang out in just the same instant as his own rifle dropped onto the dust and he reached for his big Colt as his saddlebags, blanket and canteen were all shaken loose when he'd fallen.

Two men quickly raced out of the woods, one carrying a smoking rifle and the second aiming his pistol. The pistol shooter fired as they ran toward him now less than sixty yards away.

Ellis rolled into his side with his heavy Dragoon in his hand and took aim at the pistol shooter on his right. He fired without really aiming and the pistol bounced back in recoil as it spat its .44 caliber round at the man. He missed, but the shooter jerked to his left to avoid the shot then bounced off of his partner before regaining his balance and taking a second quick shot without slowing down.

Ellis felt the ground above his head explode as he took aim for his second shot and at less than forty yards, he fired again. This time, the racing piece of lead slammed almost dead center into the pistol shooter's gut exploding his abdominal aorta before drilling into his lumbar spine and stopping.

The shooter's blood pressure dropped to nothing, but his momentum kept him going for another six feet before he plowed face first into the dirt.

The second man, who had his knife drawn quickly realized his precarious position then dropped his rifle and knife to the ground and began to crawl to retrieve his partner's smoking revolver just eight feet away.

Ellis watched him drop then his mad creeping dash to get the weapon but still had his sights where he needed them to be and as the highwayman reached his right hand out to grab the pistol, Ellis fired.

His third bullet smashed into the man's chest just below his outstretched arm on his right side, destroyed two ribs then plunged across his right lung before mangling the upper lobe of his left lung and lodging against a rib on the opposite side.

Ellis quickly scrambled to his feet leaving his rifle where it was then carefully jogged to the second man who had the better chance of being alive, although it wasn't much.

He kept the Dragoon pointed at the man but by the time he was close, he realized it wasn't necessary then slowly holstered his revolver.

He rolled over each man then went through their pockets, finding thirty-eight dollars in Confederate bills and six dollars and fifteen cents in 'real' money. He picked up the pistol and was surprised to find a Remington Model 1861 New Army. It was a lot newer than his Colt Dragoon and fired the same .44 caliber ball round. It probably weighed a pound less, too.

He slipped the pistol into the back of his waist then pulled the man's gunbelt off and checked the ammunition pouch finding enough powder and shot for just three more rounds, and no more percussion caps.

He then turned took three steps and picked up the rifle that had they had used to try and drygulch him and wasn't that surprised after finding the Remington that it was a Sharps 1852 carbine. He then glanced back at the two men and was sure that they were deserters but wasn't sure if they were Union or Confederates. They were both wearing good boots and light blue britches but had gray blouses.

It didn't matter to him, but he didn't want anybody to find the bodies so easily, so he set the Sharps down and then began to drag the rifle shooter's body back to the trees. It served two purposes for going that way. The first was to hide the bodies, and the second was to find their source of supplies. Neither man had much on him and that meant there were more spoils of battle in the trees.

He dropped the first body just a few feet behind the trees before returning for the pistol shooter's corpse. After leaving them both together for the scavengers, he walked deeper into the trees and after a minute, he popped into a small clearing and blinked. *They had horses!*

Ellis walked slowly to the two animals who were just grazing in the clearing. They both raised their heads and watched him as he drew closer and began to sing *The Yellow Rose of Texas* in an off-key, but soothing tone.

He reached the closer animal, a dark brown gelding with two white stockings and a star on his forehead and began to rub his neck as he continued to sing.

He smiled at the horse then, keeping his hand on the first horse's neck, he approached the second animal, a black mare with four white stockings and no other markings at all. She was a very handsome lady.

He then touched the mare's neck with his fingertips and said, "Lady, you just made my day," before reaching down and taking her reins. After taking the gelding's reins in his left hand, he began to lead them to the trees. Once among the trunks, he tied them off to inspect their saddlebags.

There were some tins of beans and some jerky in one side of the first set, some clothing and a towel in the second but little else. The saddlebags on the mare however, produced some real finds beyond the same kind of food and clothes. There was ammunition for the Sharps, a box of percussion caps, and a shaving kit.

But it was the saddled horses that were the real treasure. He quickly checked their haunches for brands and found only one, the expected CSA and that was on the gelding. The Confederate States of America owed him a horse anyway, so he didn't care if he kept the gelding and as far as he was concerned, the black mare was an unbranded mustang.

He untied their reins mounted the mare and telling himself to adjust the stirrups later for his additional four inches of height over the rifle shooter. Both horses had scabbards, so he'd be able to carry both rifles.

For a man who was almost dead less than a half an hour earlier, it was a happy Ellis White who trotted the two horses out of the trees stopped to pick up his rifle, saddlebags, canteen and blanket then the Sharps. He put the Remington pistol in the saddlebags with the shooter's gunbelt, squeezing it in with the Sharps ammunition.

He didn't have any rope, so he just attached the gelding's reins to the back of the mare's saddle and finally continued his ride to Montague, knowing that the rest of his trip would now be much shorter.

As he approached the town, he had second thoughts about entering the place in case the two bodies he'd left behind were locals, although he doubted it, so he shifted to the south and circled around Montague before picking up the road again and heading west. The next town of any size was Henrietta which was the closest one to his ranch, and Ellis planned to stay there for a whole day.

It was there where he'd get a better read on what to expect when he returned home and spend some of that Yankee money he'd been holding onto for all those years. Maybe he'd even stay in a hotel, but he was sure he'd get a shave, haircut and a bath.

———

Ellis reached Henrietta the next afternoon and as he walked the horses into town, he began his examination of the town for the changes he knew had to be there. As he'd traveled west, he'd noticed that although there were still not nearly as many men as there should have been, it wasn't as pronounced the further west he'd traveled. He saw several young couples strolling on the boardwalk, and the wheeled and horse traffic was heavier although still not what he'd hoped to find.

As he pulled up in front of Wharton's Dry Goods, he glanced to his left and was somewhat puzzled by the sign on the neighboring business: WAR WIDOW'S LAUNDRY.

He stepped down from the mare and entered the store.

"Howdy, mister," the man behind the counter said with a smile.

"Howdy."

"Lookin' for anything in particular?"

"I'll know it when I see it," Ellis replied, generating a chuckle in the proprietor.

He walked the aisles and noticed the lack of some products and the preponderance of others which were mostly homemade. He began to pick up basic supplies, but nothing big yet. He'd need to go to the livery and see about exchanging the riding saddle on the gelding for a pack saddle.

He paid for the order with his first twenty-dollar greenback, which he could tell pleased the store owner immensely. Ellis then told him that he'd be back in the morning for a bigger order and told him to keep the change on account which pleased him even more.

After Ellis loaded the supplies into his overfilled saddlebags, he decided he may as well help the war widows and get his laundry done, including the two extra shirts he'd picked up. The only britches he'd found in the store were just too small.

He plucked out the clothes that needed cleaning, some desperately then carried them through the already open door of the laundry where he spotted a young, handsome woman behind the counter. She was probably about twenty-one or so with light brown hair and blue eyes that were smiling at him as much as the rest of her face was.

When he set his clothes on the counter, he asked, "How long will this take?"

She looked at him curiously and asked, "For the cleaning, a day. For anything else, well, that's up to you."

Ellis was confused and replied, "Just the cleaning is fine."

She scooped up the clothes dropped them into a numbered basket then said, "That'll be twenty cents if you have Federal money or two dollars for Confederate and your number is seventeen."

Ellis reached into his pocket pulled out one of the outlaw's Yankee dollar bills and handed it to her and told her to keep the change.

Then he asked, "Ma'am, what did you mean by 'anything else'?"

She looked at the Federal note then smiled and asked, "Are you married?"

Ellis was never a bashful or modest man, but her surprising question did set him back.

"No, ma'am. Never been."

"All of the women that work here are widows, courtesy of men's foolishness. At least you didn't leave your wife behind to satisfy some urge to go and legally shoot someone. Some of the women are anxious to find husbands and there aren't many healthy young men anymore. So, they offer services to some men to entice them into marriage. I don't do that which is why I asked about anything else. If you were here for another reason, I'd call one of the other women."

Ellis understood and was surprised that his mind shifted into sympathy rather than lust. Their husbands may have died but now, they'd have to do anything to keep themselves alive and in the conditions that would be in the South for years, it would be a hard life at best.

"Ma'am, as much as I'd like to help, I have to get back to my ranch in Hardeman County and see if it's still there."

"Well, that's not too far away. If everything works out, maybe you can come back and help one of the widows. My name is Linda Harrison, by the way."

Ellis shook her hand and said, "Nice to meet you, Linda. I'm Ellis White."

She smiled as she held onto his hand then reluctantly let go and said, "You can pick up your clothes tomorrow at ten, Mister White."

"Ellis, Linda. My name is Ellis," he said before smiling and leaving the laundry.

Once on the boardwalk, he blew out his breath knowing that Linda was probably watching him then turned back to the dry goods store where he untied his horses, mounted the mare and turned her and the gelding toward the closest livery.

As he walked his horse, he couldn't help but think about Linda's plight and that of all of the other women that worked there and around the entire country. He estimated that there would be almost a half a million widows by the time the war was over and more millions of men returning with lost limbs and other serious wounds. His two wounds weren't that impressive when compared to what happened to others, just a slice across his behind and a hole in his left bicep that didn't even touch the bone. Neither had become infected, either.

He reached the livery and despite the gelding's brand, he didn't have any problems with the liveryman who promised to shoe both animals for a good price while they were being stabled. He then worked out a deal for trading the riding saddle for a pack saddle and two panniers. He paid him all of the Confederate cash he had from the two highwaymen then walked down the street with his saddlebags over his shoulder.

He stopped at the bank and asked if he could exchange his twenty-dollar notes for smaller denominations of Federal money and despite being charged a five percent 'handling' fee, he was glad to finally have nothing but five and one-dollar bills and lots of silver. It made for an impressive wad of cash even though its value was less than the four pieces of paper he'd handed over.

Now that he didn't have to worry about getting any more change, he stopped at the barber and had the works which set him back twenty cents. Then with his raw face and naked neck, he walked to the diner had a real dinner with clearly identified steak then checked into the hotel.

All in all, it had been a profitable day by the time he pulled the blankets up to his clean chin and closed his eyes. In two more days, he'd be home. If he pushed it, he could make it in a day but didn't want to arrive late in the day with tired horses.

He was finding it hard to sleep as he knew he was almost finished with his journey and the war. Then without intentionally trying to recall it, the image of Sara Mae smiling at him while she stood on the back porch of the Big O flashed into his mind. When it did, he briefly considered heading to that ranch rather than his own but knew that would probably just make his conundrum deeper. He simply couldn't do what Mike Dunston had suggested that he do. She may be more woman than any other woman he'd ever met, but she was John Keeler's woman, not his.

————

After getting his newly shod horses the next morning then filling the panniers with his big order from the dry goods store, Ellis finally walked to the laundry to get his clean clothes.

As he entered, he wasn't surprised to find Linda Harrison behind the counter, and she'd obviously spent some extra time making herself even prettier than the first time he'd entered which was impressive indeed. Linda Harrison must have placed a bullseye on his back.

"Good morning, Ellis. You look very nice this morning," she said with a smile as he passed the threshold.

"Good morning, Linda. I'm number seventeen."

Linda laughed as she said, "You don't have to tell me that, Ellis. I'd remember you without a number."

Ellis didn't know what to say as he waited for her to get his clothes.

She didn't have to walk far before she returned with the basket of neatly folded clothing and set it on the counter.

"Ellis, could I ask you a question? You don't have to answer if you don't wish to."

"No, go ahead," he replied, expecting something with a marital ring to it.

"Did you desert from the army?"

A startled Ellis replied quickly, "No, no, I didn't. I was captured by a Union picket line near the Red River north of Boston and they gave me my parole. Did you want to see the paper?"

"No, I'm sorry. I didn't mean to offend you, and I know this sounds silly, but I didn't want you to go to your ranch and leave me with that potential stain on your image. You impress me as a very good man, Ellis, and I wanted to remember you that way. I wasn't that fortunate in my choice of husbands and I know that good men can be hard to find."

"Linda, I never ran from any gunfire and never will. I'll admit that I was gettin' mighty tired of all the fightin' and dyin', but we all were, even the Union boys who caught me. I wish I coulda been there and saved your husband, but we can't change nothin' that's already been."

"I know but, trust me, Walt wasn't worth saving. Did you get wounded at all?"

"I was only shot twice, but not too bad."

Linda wanted to stretch out the conversation and asked, "What's the name of your ranch?"

"The Slash W. It's right between the two rows of the High Hills and has Fresh Water Creek runnin' right through the top of it. Before I left in '61, I sold almost all of my critters and now I gotta build it back up. I left some there to start makin' their own herd, but I don't know what to expect. I'll find out tomorrow."

"I hope everything works out for you, Ellis."

Ellis was enjoying talking to Linda Harrison but knew that he had to get out of the laundry and out of Henrietta before she made an offer he couldn't refuse after years of celibacy, so he said, "Well, I've gotta get going, Linda. It was nice meetin' ya."

"I enjoyed talking to you too, Ellis."

He smiled as he picked up his clothes then quickly turned and left the laundry and didn't waste any time before putting the newly cleaned laundry into one of the panniers, mounting and turning the mare westward. The brown gelding was now attached with a proper trail rope and the rest of the coil was hung from the mare's saddle.

As he left Henrietta, he kept thinking about Linda Harrison and how much she seemed to want to go with him. He had to admit that she was an impressive young woman and was almost as pretty as Mary Jo, but neither Linda nor Mary Jo measured up to Sara Mae as a woman. He thought there was a good chance that John Keeler would just go somewhere else and abandon his family after the war or maybe he'd desert again. He was that kind of a man.

As poor of an opinion he had of John Keeler before they left Hardeman County, it only grew worse once he spent a lot of time with him. After they enlisted and John was in the same company, Ellis would see constant reminders of John's failings as a man. He was always a discipline problem which wasn't his concern until he was promoted to sergeant and then it became a serious problem when John expected special treatment and favors.

Ellis had not only denied him what he expected but had turned him in to the captain twice for drunkenness.

John had skirted close to courts-martial offenses three times over the past year and a half. Twice, he'd deserted but was caught by the pickets, so he was just charged with leaving his post. The third time, he'd struck a commissioned officer, a pompous lieutenant that no one liked, and the commanding officer had ruled it an accidental event.

But the worst offense, at least to Ellis and not the army, was the way he talked about Sara Mae and the children. It was as if they weren't people at all. He spoke lasciviously about Mary Jo and how he'd been able to spy on her when no one was looking, but he called his own wife a cow and even worse.

Sara Mae was hardly a cow, or even a cute heifer, but a handsome young woman. Yet as poorly as he spoke of his wife, in those rare instances when he mentioned his children, he sounded almost ashamed for having sired them at all and that totally baffled Ellis beyond making him angry.

There were times when he'd heard John talk of Sara Mae or the children with disgust and contempt dripping from his words that he was close to shooting the bastard, but what was worse was that he knew he was only hearing a small part of the vitriol that John was spewing about his wife and children.

The memories of that one day he'd spent with the children when they went to Fort Madrid was one of the only truly bright recollections that was capable of pushing away the disconsolation of endless conflict, disease and boredom. He remembered Sonny's open-mouthed stare as he beheld the pocketknife and Mandy's excited face when she saw the ribbons and even now those recollections made him smile.

His memories of Sara Mae were beyond just making him smile. They made him think and realize what he didn't have. She was such a sweet, caring woman who deserved so much better than what she had. He knew that her children were the center of her world but no woman with her reservoir of love should be denied love herself.

After he returned to his ranch, he'd ride over to the Big O and see how they were doing. He had to give them news anyway or at least that was his excuse. Despite the dilemma that blocked him from anything beyond just friendly conversation, he really wanted to see Sara Mae and the children.

———

After leaving Henrietta, the road became more like a long pair of wagon ruts. He had to stop for breaks more often and had to make sure that water was nearby as well. At least it wasn't summer yet or finding water would be much more difficult. With the recent spring rains even some of the gullies had running water now.

After his shootout with the two deserters, he was more aware of his surroundings, but the trees had thinned out noticeably and most of the heavier growth was up north following the Red River which now was about two hours' ride away should he need to go into the Indian Territories which he didn't think likely.

But that line of distant trees was like a roadmap to his ranch, which he now estimated was only about ten hours' ride away. He guessed he was in Wichita County now and the number of large streams confirmed it. He'd stop after he reached Wilbarger County and camp. Hardeman County bordered Wilbarger County and unless he was way off, when he entered Hardeman County, as long as he kept the Red River in sight off his right shoulder, he should pop right onto the eastern boundary of his ranch.

He tried not to break his established pace as he grew ever closer to his home, but it was difficult. He'd stop and water the horses, let them graze for a minute or two, then mount again.

He finally pulled over to set up camp as the sun went down, unsure if he was still in Wichita County or Wilbarger, but it didn't matter. He estimated that he'd reach his ranch around mid-day tomorrow.

Ellis found it difficult to sleep as he lay staring at the half moon overhead. He listened to the familiar sounds of the night and was grateful that he was far enough from the river to keep the mosquito squads to manageable level.

Tomorrow he'd see his ranch again and renew his friendship with Rufus. For more than one reason, he often regretted his decision to make Jim Abigail the foreman, but what had stuck with him over the past three years was the almost cheerful way that Jim had made his farewells as if he was glad that Ellis was going off to war. Maybe he was hoping that Ellis wouldn't survive, and he'd take over the ranch for good. *Wouldn't he be surprised tomorrow?*

But either tomorrow or the next day, he'd see Sara Mae again and would have to restrain himself and just talk to her no differently than he spoke to Mary Jo, but it would be hard.

It wasn't until almost midnight that Ellis finally slipped into a deep sleep.

———

Just an hour after dawn the next morning, a freshly shaved, ex-CSA Sergeant Ellis White was leading the CSA-branded brown gelding as he rode the black mare out of his camp and headed west at a medium trot.

Ellis knew he was being too optimistic in expecting to find his house, barn and bunkhouse all in good shape, but it was hard to imagine them as run-down as much as some of the other ranches and farms he'd seen along his journey. His boys should still be there, even though he'd only left enough money to last three years and it was past that now, but only by a few months. But even more important than the amount was that it was all in Yankee dollars, so for the past couple of years, they were worth more than their face value.

Just three hours later, he reached one of the last creeks in Wilbarger County then stayed in the saddle as the mare and gelding drank and he just took off his gray Confederate hat wiped the sweat from his forehead then pulled it back on. He let the animals drink for a little longer then pulled the mare's head up and they splashed out of the creek, climbed the shallow bank then set off at the same medium trot.

An hour later, Ellis grinned when he spotted the first of the southern line of the High Hills that marked the border of his ranch then shifted the mare's direction slightly to the north to enter his ranch from the east. He'd toyed with the idea of riding into Fort Madrid and getting the news of what had happened in his absence, but he was far too anxious now.

More than three years of war and all the misery that accompanied it were now behind him as he watched the hills grow larger and his ranch grow nearer. He'd be entering from the southeast corner, so his house would still be three miles away and if any of the cattle and horses were still there, they'd be almost nine miles away on the opposite corner, so he wouldn't get his first glimpse of what made the Slash W his for another forty minutes, but Ellis was already giddy as he kept scanning land that was so familiar yet so new at the same time.

The giddiness hadn't left him as he made the turn west around the southeasternmost hill and knew he'd see his house and barn soon but still kept the horses at a medium trot as they didn't seem to have been infected by his enthusiasm. Maybe if the mare knew that there was a stallion waiting for her, she'd move faster, he thought as he snickered.

Then at long last, he saw the top of his barn and then the house. With an incredible sense of relief, he picked up smoke coming from the house's cookstove pipe and unless it was squatters which he had to admit was possible that meant that the boys were still there, and somebody was cooking lunch. It was late morning if not early afternoon, so he was hungry and almost believed that they were expecting him but knew it was a silly thing to even pop into his mind.

He noticed that the windmill was still turning, pumping groundwater into the large trough at its base, but it was missing a blade and he'd have to fix that. He wondered why Jim had let it get that way.

When he was less than a mile out, he began to look for animals but didn't see any which surprised him for a moment until he figured that they'd put their horses into the barn for the night. He didn't expect to see any cattle or horses in the northwest corner as it was still too far to see with the undulating land that made up the Slash W.

His heart was pounding and a grin threatened to split his face in two as he pulled the mare to a stop behind the back door, dismounted in a flash then tied off the reins and without hesitation, hopped onto the porch threw open the door and shouted, "I'm back!"

Then his smile evaporated and was replaced by a stunned look as he found himself staring down two barrels of twelve-gauge shotgun.

If that wasn't enough of a shock, it was made much worse when he realized that it was Sara Mae Keeler who was staring at him with both triggers back.

"Sara Mae?" he finally asked in a hushed voice.

"Ellis?" she asked softly.

"Yes, ma'am. I'm sorry to scare you," he replied as he looked at her not seeing any difference in her face from the last time that he'd seen her.

His heart was pounding against his chest as he gazed at her, but his mind was exploding with questions about her presence and the absence of his three ranch hands.

"Is the war over?" she asked as she lowered the shotgun.

"No, ma'am. I was caught and paroled."

Sara Mae stared at him for a few seconds then released the shotgun's hammers before setting it on the kitchen table.

"I'm sorry, Ellis, but I thought you might be someone else."

"Well, I'm not. Now can you please tell me what you're doin' here? And where are your young'uns?"

"Mandy is in the bedroom hiding," she answered then turned and said loudly, "Mandy, it's okay. It's Mister White."

Ellis noticed the absence of her son, Sonny, but put off that question before he asked, "Sara Mae, you never told me why you're here."

"It'll take some time, I'm afraid. How much do you know about what happened after you left?"

84

"Not a damned thing."

"Nothing at all? Didn't John tell you?"

"No, ma'am. He didn't say nary a word, and I asked lotsa times."

Sara Mae just shook her head as Mandy slowly entered the kitchen and said, "I only wrote to him so he could tell you what had happened. I should have sent those letters to you instead."

Ellis then looked at Mandy smiled and said, "Well, howdy there, young lady. You sure grew a whole bunch since the time we went shoppin' in Fort Madrid."

Mandy smiled back then replied, "I didn't know it was you, Mister White. I saw a rider coming and warned my mama. She grabbed the shotgun and told me to go into the bedroom."

"Well, mamas are always a lot smarter than men folk, so she did the right thing. I mighta been some bandit or king of the outlaws."

"Ellis, would you like some coffee?" Sara Mae asked.

"Real coffee?"

"Well, mostly chicory with a little real coffee," she said.

"I'd appreciate it, ma'am, and then you can tell me what I been missin'."

She nodded then took down two cups set them on the cookstove and poured the coffee.

As she did, Ellis scanned the kitchen and didn't find anything missing yet which was a relief although the pantry was almost empty. But it was even cleaner and neater than it had been when he left and attributed that to Sara Mae. He wondered why she was there with just her daughter and how long she'd been there.

Sara Mae set the two cups on the table then sat down to join Mandy.

She held her cup in both hands as she began to explain the circumstances that put her into his ranch house.

"After you left with John and Pete, things were pretty normal for quite some time. Your foreman, Jim Abigail, and Lou Gordon would take care of our cattle and horses and make trips into Fort Madrid for supplies. Then the following summer, in '62, things changed. Jim began paying more attention to Mary Jo, and she told me that it worried her after a while. I think there was a bit of a competition between Jim and Lou to get her attention and that caused more problems but nothing really bad happened because of all the work in keeping up the two ranches.

"We were almost out of money by the end of '62 because Pete hadn't expected the war to last that long, but Jim and Lou would take a head or two into Fort Madrid and trade them for supplies which kept us going for a month at a time. We still had about forty head left by September of last year when everything went bad."

"How bad?" Ellis asked quietly with his full cup of coffee still untouched.

Sara Mae exhaled sharply and said, "Mary Jo got word that Pete had been killed in Louisiana, and that was the trigger."

"Who told her that? He wasn't in my brigade, but I didn't hear nothin' of the sort, and I would have."

"Some man returned from his unit and told Ernie Smith in Fort Madrid, then he told Jim and Lou when they were making a supply run."

More questions were already popping into Ellis' head, but he'd save them for later as Sara Mae continued.

"Anyway, once they found out that she was a widow, both of them proposed to her the same day and that led to violence and Jim killed Lou in a knife fight. There's no law anywhere closer than Henrietta, so they just buried him and then Jim married Mary Jo."

Ellis just looked into her brown eyes and waited for the rest of the story that would explain why she was in his house with Mandy and not back at the Big O with Sonny.

"The day after they returned from getting married in Henrietta, Jim told me that I needed to move out so he could be alone with his wife, so I came here. I've been here with Mandy since last September."

"And your sister allowed that?"

"I don't think she had any choice, Ellis. I think she was afraid, but never said anything."

"How do you get by with supplies?"

"Mary Jo drops some off when she can, but basically I make do. I used the shotgun to do some hunting but now I'm out of shells. I raise some potatoes and onions, too."

Ellis then asked, "Sara Mae, what happened to Rufus?"

"I don't know. He used to stop by and talk to Sonny, but Jim seemed really mad when he did, so he stopped coming. I know he wasn't here when we moved in because I hoped we'd have some protection from Comanches."

"You don't have to worry about the Comanches. They know I bought this land from them years ago and they keep their word unlike those damned politicians in Washington. Did Jim or Lou say anything about him leaving? I told him to go west as soon as I left, but he said he'd stick around."

"But I do have to worry about Comanches!" she exclaimed as tears suddenly erupted from her eyes, "They took my Sonny!"

That news surprised Ellis more than the previous revelations, and it showed as his face registered his disbelief.

Sara Mae then shocked him when her face darkened and she spat, "You don't believe me, do you? You think those savages are just like us, but they took my Sonny away and now all I have is Mandy."

Ellis bypassed her accusations and vitriol and addressed her worries alone when he replied, "Now, Sara Mae, before you start accusin' a whole people of doin' somethin' like that, why don't you tell me what happened and why you figure it was the Comanches that did it."

"Right after the knife fight, Sonny ran away, and I thought he had gone to your ranch because he was so scared. Jim went looking for him the next morning and told me that he found unshod hoofprints everywhere and that the Comanches had taken him to be one of them because they needed warriors."

"Well, ma'am, part of what he said is true. They do need warriors, but the Comanches, for all their fierce reputation are basically horse traders and thieves. You don't want to rile 'em up any but then again, it still wouldn't be as bad as when we riled up those Yankees. Besides, they only drop by on occasion to do some tradin'. Tomorrow, I'll ride over to the Big O and talk to Jim and find out more. Either way, I'll go and get your son back."

Sara Mae blinked then wiped her cheeks and asked, "You can do that? It's been almost eight months."

"Yes, ma'am. I know where their village was before I left and with the Yankee army all tied up back east, I doubt if they moved. Now before we go any further, I need to ask you a couple of questions. Did you see that knife fight?"

"No. They had it out in the barn."

"Where was Sonny when it happened?"

"I don't know. Why?"

"Sara Mae, you may be a real fine mother, but you gotta understand boys. If they know there's a fight comin', they're wanna go and watch. I wouldn't be a bit surprised if Sonny snuck out, watched the fight and if Lou didn't have his knife in his hand when Jim stabbed him, then it would be murder. If he saw a murder, then he'd run to tell someone he could trust. Now you told me that Rufus used to talk to him, and I'd be kinda surprised if your boy didn't trust him right off. Rufus was that kinda man. If he ran over to my ranch and told Rufus what he saw, then he'd hide Sonny and maybe tell Jim that story about the Comanches to keep him safe."

"But he's gone, too. How will you know where they are?"

"Like I said, ma'am. I'll talk to Jim Abigail in the mornin', get the read of the man then come back here and let you know. After I do that, I'll head over to the Comanche village and have a chat with 'em. If everything works out, I'll be back by the next day with your boy."

"Thank you, Ellis. I'm sorry for being so upset and saying such stupid things."

"That's perfectly understandable, Sara Mae. I know what Sonny means to you."

"Ellis," she asked as she stared into her full cup of lukewarm chicory coffee, "now that you're back, where can Mandy and I live?"

"You can stay here as long as you need to, Sara Mae, and before you ask, I have no intention of not sleeping in my own room and my own bed after all those years. I know you're a married woman with two young'uns, so you don't have to worry about anything. I'll treat you with respect."

"I wasn't going to suggest that you not sleep in your own home, Ellis," she replied quietly.

"Good, then that's settled. Now I've got to unload my horses, then I want to take a ride up to the northwest corner to check and see how many animals I still have up there. Will you and Mandy be all right?"

"Do you have any more shotgun shells?"

"Nope, but I can give you a loaded pistol if you'd like. Have you ever shot a revolver before?"

"Is it hard?"

"No, ma'am. I'll give you the basics when I bring my things inside," he answered before rising and walking to the door.

As he approached the open doorway, Sara Mae said, "Thank you, Ellis."

He tipped his hat and said, "You're welcome, Sara Mae," then left the house.

While he was unloading the pack horse, Ellis was thinking hard about what she'd told him. Boys may be adventurous and sometimes do stupid things, but he wouldn't have run if he'd just seen a plain old knife fight. He might have lost his dinner, but there'd be no reason to run. He'd head back into the house, blurt out to his mother what he'd witnessed and that would be that.

The next part of the puzzle was Rufus. If he was on the ranch by himself when Sonny came running for safety, why wouldn't he just stay and protect him? He had his own Dragoon revolver and was better with the pistol than either Jim or Lou.

In a way, he was to blame for all of this. Not for going to war but for leaving Jim Abigail in charge. There had been times over the years where Jim had overstepped his bounds as foreman, acting almost as the owner of the Slash W and that had really shown itself on the day he'd ridden off with Pete and John Keeler.

He cursed himself again for not making Rufus the foreman, despite Rufus' own advice. If the other hands couldn't handle it, he could have hired more colored ranch hands. But that was all water under the bridge now. Jim Abigail was now Mary Jo's husband and the owner of the Big O.

———

After bringing the two panniers into the kitchen and setting them on the floor, he then brought in his three sets of saddlebags and his two rifles.

Sara Mae and Mandy watched when he set the Sharps and J.F. Brown against the wall removed the Remington pistol and gunbelt from the saddlebag then set it on the table and slid the pistol from the holster.

"Sara Mae, this pistol is loaded, and I don't want to unload it to show you how to use it. I'll take you through the steps before firing and that should be good enough. Okay?"

"Okay."

Ellis demonstrated how he expected her to use the pistol, not how he would. Her hands were too small to handle the Remington and was glad he wasn't having to give her his Dragoon. He showed her how to hold it with two hands, cock the hammer then aim and fire. It was as basic a shooting lesson as possible, but it was all about making her feel safer and he doubted if she'd ever use the gun.

"Think you can handle it, ma'am?" he asked as he slid the revolver into its leather home.

"Yes. I think so."

"Good. Now I've got to go outside and take care of the horses. Can you empty the food from the packs there while I'm doin' that?"

"We can do that. I was getting ready to cook when you arrived, so I'll just add another portion. I'll have it ready in about an hour."

Ellis smiled then said, "I appreciate that, ma'am," before trotting out of the kitchen and after two long strides, he stepped onto the dirt untied the mare and led the two horses to the trough where he let them drink before taking them to the barn.

His mind was still a torrent of questions as he walked across the hard-packed dirt. *When did Rufus leave and where did he go? What really happened to Sonny Keeler? Was that a fair fight on the Big O?* Then there was something else that he'd noticed. Sara Mae hadn't asked about her husband. All she'd asked was if he had given Ellis any news and seemed surprised that he hadn't and then made the comment about sending letters to him. But the thought of receiving precious letters from Sara Mae over the years actually gave him goosebumps as he imagined how they would have progressed.

He knew that she'd been writing periodically to John, although he never wrote back. After listening to the way that he spoke of her and his children, he hadn't been surprised by his lack of replies. That lack of interest wasn't any surprise, given that he'd had a more emotional farewell with Sara Mae than John had.

"What an idiot you are, John Keeler," he said aloud as he approached the barn.

He opened the barn doors and before he led the horses inside, he did a quick visual inspection. Just as the house had been, it was well-kept but empty except for the wagon and his tools and a large tarp-covered lump in the corner, which hadn't been there when he'd left.

He led the horses inside then began stripping the pack horse. He'd be using the mare in a few minutes to check the northwest corner for critters before coming back and having lunch.

After stripping off the pack saddle, he set it on a stall board, then left both horses to get his Henry, hoping it was still there. He climbed the back ladder, scrambled into the loft and strode to the dark corner where he'd left it more than three years earlier.

Ellis found the hay still there which was a good sign and quickly began pawing the hay out of the way, scattering it across the loft floor. He found his oiled tarp unfolded it and smiled when he saw the still shining brass sides of the Henry rifle. He picked it up but didn't do anything with it yet before he began stacking the five boxes of cartridges. He emptied the half-box into his jacket pocket walked to the ladder and set the five boxes on the floor near the cutout then climbed down. Once on the barn floor, he leaned the rifle against the wall, then made five more trips up the ladder to retrieve the cartridges. He very briefly considered just dropping the boxes to the barn floor, but even he realized that it wasn't a good idea.

He'd left the rifle unloaded, so the spring that pushed the cartridges down the magazine tube wouldn't lose its springiness. But before he loaded it, he'd clean and oil the rifle to make sure that first shot after more than three years' storage worked the way it was intended.

He then glanced at the tarp in the corner, stepped over and pulled it free then discovered his two saddles and the rest of his tack along with the wagon's harness. He ran his finger over the leather and found it to be still smooth and supple. In the dry Texas air even if they'd been covered, they should have been dryer than this. It was just another mystery he'd have to solve as he pulled the canvas tarp back over the saddles but was more than happy to have found them.

———

While Ellis was outside in the barn, Sara Mae and Mandy began unloading the panniers, placing the much-needed supplies on shelves in the pantry.

"Mama, is Mister White going to find Sonny? I miss him."

"I hope so, darling. It's been a long time, though."

Then as Mandy picked up a tin of beans, she asked, "If Mister White is home, does that means papa is coming home, too?"

Sara Mae paused before replying, "No, sweetheart, I don't think so. Not yet, anyway. Mister White was sent home by the Yankee soldiers."

Mandy set the beans on the counter and said, "Good."

Sara Mae pretended not to hear her daughter's comment as she finished emptying the first pannier and then moved to the second.

After opening the covering flap, the first items she found were his neatly folded clothes which made her smile as she lifted them from the pannier. *What kind of man folds his clothes, especially after what he must have been through?*

As she turned to put them on the table, a small sheet of paper drifted from among the folds and fluttered to the floor. She set the stack of laundry on the table, then picked up the sheet and read:

Please don't forget my name.
I'll never forget yours. Ellis White.
I'm staying at Morgan's Boarding House if I'm not at the laundry.

With Affection,
Linda Harrison

She blushed after reading the note feeling as if she'd invaded his private life then slipped the note back under the clothes and quickly continued unpacking.

———

Ellis was carrying the Henry as he hopped onto the back porch and entered the kitchen where Sara Mae was putting the last of the supplies away.

"I left your clothes on the table," she said as she set a bag of salt on the top shelf.

"Thank you, ma'am. I had 'em cleaned at a laundry in Henrietta just before I left."

"Oh."

"Sara Mae, I'm gonna ride out to the northwest corner and check on my critters, if any are there. I'll be back in time for that lunch you promised."

Sara Mae was still embarrassed about the note, so she didn't look his way when she replied, "Alright."

Ellis exchanged the Henry for the Sharps. Not only was it loaded, but it was a breech loader, so he could have it reloaded in less than half the time it took to load the muzzle loading J.F. Brown. He even had more ammunition for the Sharps.

He left the house, slid the Sharps into the scabbard then mounted and turned the mare to the northwest and set off at a medium trot. As he rode, he let his mind just inhale being back on his ranch again.

He'd been gone more than three years, but every rock and bush seemed as if it hadn't changed probably because they hadn't. And then there was the presence of Sara Mae. He'd been shocked to see her in his kitchen and doubted that the shotgun she had pointed at his face was even a factor in his reaction. To him, she was even more handsome than when he'd left and now, she was living in his house. Ellis was pleased and terrified at the prospect and continued to think about the dilemma her presence was causing him as he rode northwest.

Less than ten minutes after leaving the house, he spotted cattle in the distance and was surprised by the number of animals that the almost automatic count his brain gave him. He'd left thirty-two critters, but mostly cows. Now, after a quick guess, he was looking at well over a hundred head which was mathematically and biologically impossible. If twenty of the cows had calved that first year and half were heifers then those ten wouldn't produce their own calves for another two years or so.

He'd have expected some losses to draught, theft and accidents, too. He'd have to wait until he was closer to get a better count and the makeup of the new herd, but he did notice that there were no horses at all, which didn't surprise him one bit. The Comanches would have happily relieved him of the herd after he'd gone. It would be another reason for visiting their village tomorrow and he might be able to convince them to give him back some of the animals.

He crossed two dry gullies before reaching Fresh Water Creek and the herd then walked the mare among the critters, finding a lot of youngsters. What did surprise him was that all were wearing the Slash W brand. He'd expected to find a few Big O animals mixed in with his as well as a few mavericks.

He'd increased his own herd over the years by finding and branding mavericks, and he was sure that there were even more out on the free range now because of the war. The armies had taken the herds of the more accessible ranches but wouldn't have taken the time to do a real roundup. There were always strays off by their lonesome.

He had actually planned on starting his new herd by rounding up mavericks, but here it was and almost intact. He did an actual count of the cattle in the single herd, knowing that there were probably more in the thick brush and the trees to the north and came up with a hundred and eighteen animals.

Satisfied that at least the cattle question was mostly solved, he turned the mare back toward the house and set her to a medium trot.

His world was slowly beginning to resolve back into a manageable form. There were still a lot of things that needed to be handled but somehow, finding the cattle restored Ellis White, Sergeant, Confederate States of America to Ellis White, the rancher.

He rode straight into the barn, dismounted and began unsaddling the mare. As pretty as she was, Ellis decided that unlike his other mounts, she deserved a proper name. For just a moment, he toyed with naming her Linda because of that young lady in Henrietta was just about the prettiest lady that he'd ever met, but decided that was a bad idea because every time he talked to the mare, it would remind him of the lady in the laundry, and he had no intention of going back, especially now that Sara Mae was living in his house.

Then as he thought about a name for the mare, for some obscure reason, his goofy brain made a connection to of all things, an election slogan; 'Tippecanoe and Tyler, Too'. He didn't even care about politics much, but that stupid saying just stuck in his mind.

So, he looked at the mare and asked, "How about Tippy?"

The mare didn't seem to mind the name, so he slapped her rump softly and christened her Tippy.

He took his Sharps from its scabbard then headed for the house. The sun was about halfway down on the horizon, so at this time of the year, it had to be after four o'clock and despite his earlier almost defiant statement about wanting to sleep in his own house and his own bed, he began to rethink the whole idea of sleeping so close to Sara Mae.

Before he even reached the porch, he could smell the aroma of good food wafting from the open door making his stomach growl in protest. Sara Mae Keeler may make him uncomfortable by being there, but regular, well-prepared meals were worth the discomfort. He'd have to make a serious supply run to Fort Madrid soon, but he'd need those horses back for the wagon before he could.

He entered the kitchen, smiled at Mandy and said, "Somethin' smells mighty good."

"Mama's making stew."

"Well, that sounds good to me. What are you ladies gonna be eatin'?"

Mandy was about to say something when Ellis laughed as he set the Sharps with the other two rifles.

"You're just being funny," Mandy said.

"Yes, ma'am. It feels real good to be able to be funny again."

"Are you going to find Sonny?" she asked.

"I'm gonna try, ma'am," he answered before turning to Sara Mae and saying, "I'll get those clothes off the table and put 'em in my room."

"That's a good idea," she said without turning from the cookstove.

Ellis scooped up his clothes then walked down the hallway to the third door and after he opened it, he entered his bedroom for the first time in over three years. Not surprisingly, he found it neater than when he'd left. He had expected it after seeing how Sara Mae had tidied up the rest of the house.

He set the clothes on his dresser then pulled open his top drawer and found his old clothes that he hadn't taken with him. That did surprise him. He'd worn the uniform for so long that he'd forgotten that he even had any regular clothes. He'd left most of them behind expecting that his boys would use them when their own clothes wore out, but not only were his clothes all there, but they were clean and folded neatly just as the laundry clothes were. He'd been surprised not to find Sara Mae's clothes there, but maybe she'd moved them while he was out checking the herd.

He hadn't gained his twenty pounds back, so they'd be a bit looser than before but after a couple of months of steadily eating real food, he should be back to his normal two hundred pounds.

He closed the top drawer and had to go to the bottom drawer to find one that was empty then began placing the clothes into the drawer. If the other drawers hadn't been so neatly packed, he might not have bothered but now, he didn't want to have one all messy and the others so neat.

When he lifted his pair of clean britches, a sheet of paper floated to the floor. He picked it up and read the feminine handwriting then stood staring at the note for a full minute, full of mixed thoughts. She sure was a pretty lady and obviously interested, but it didn't matter.

Sara Mae and Mandy were in his house now and needed him to be there, and he'd rather have a married Sara Mae than a widowed Linda Harrison or any other woman anyway.

He crumpled up the note and jammed it into his right pants pocket before putting the rest of the clothes away. The feeling of contentment that had begun to emerge after finding the cattle was pushed aside because of that note. It reminded him of what he didn't have and what he couldn't have. He didn't have a wife and he couldn't have the woman who would be living with him. Meanwhile, her husband, the man who never should have left her to run off to war was off in East Texas and thought of her and her children less than he thought of the holey, unwashed socks that he wore.

Ellis left his bedroom in a more somber mood than when he'd entered and almost felt like going outside and shooting a few rounds through the Sharps when he reached the kitchen and Mandy smiled at him.

"The food's ready, Mister White."

Having a cute, seven-year-old girl smiling at you has a way of dissipating even the foulest of moods, so Ellis smiled back and said, "Why, thank you, ma'am."

Sara Mae had recovered from her embarrassment and had ladled out the stew into three bowls and set them on the table. After filling two cups with chicory-coffee, she sat down.

"I found the herd of cattle up on Fresh Water Creek, Sara Mae. I counted over a hundred and ten critters and was kinda surprised to find all of 'em wearin' the Slash W brand."

"Why?" she asked as she blew on her spoonful of hot stew, "didn't you expect to find them?"

"Not that many and not all of them branded. I didn't have any horses, though. I figure I'll ask the Comanches tomorrow when I go and talk to 'em."

Sara Mae took a bite of her stew and began chewing as Mandy devoured hers while Ellis watched and ate more slowly.

"This is mighty tasty, ma'am," he said after he'd swallowed his first bite.

"Thank you. Considering what I had to work with before, this was quite simple."

"Well, ma'am, when I get some horses back, then I'll make a supply trip into Fort Madrid. How much has changed down there since I was gone?"

"You didn't stop there on your return?"

"No, ma'am. I was kinda anxious to see my place."

"Well, it's bigger now, but I haven't seen it in almost a year. The only change I know about is that they have a telegraph now."

"Now that's good news. Do they have an operator, too?"

"I assume so."

Ellis was very happy with that news. With the telegraph, he'd be able to have some of his money wired down from the bank in Abilene. He'd stored the codes and account information with the gold, so he'd have access to the six thousand plus dollars in that account. It had just been sitting there drawing interest for three years. His only worry on that front was if the bank had failed during the war as many had. At least it had been a substantial bank, so he hoped it was still operating.

His mood bounced a little higher again as he continued to eat and even the chicory-coffee was tasting better.

"Where did you get two horses, Ellis?" Sara Mae asked as she set her spoon in her empty bowl.

"I was waylaid by a couple of deserters east of Montague. The first feller missed with that Sharps rifle over there, and then after I dropped, they charged at me. The other one was firing a pistol and I guess the one with the Sharps was just his partner and didn't wanna get left behind.

"I got lucky and shot the pistol shooter with my second shot and then had to shoot the other one when he was goin' for the pistol on the ground. I found their horses in a small clearing in the trees. I was kinda tired of walkin' by then, so I was mighty grateful for those two animals. I just named the black mare Tippy."

C.J. PETIT

Sara Mae smiled and asked, "Tippy?"

"You know, Tippecanoe and Tyler, too. She was a mare, so I called her Tippy. She didn't seem to mind."

"I imagine not."

"I found my two saddles and tack in the barn under a tarp. They were in a lot better shape than they shoulda been. Do you know why that was?"

"No, we didn't go into the barn very often."

Ellis nodded then said, "Sara Mae, a lot of what's been goin' on has my head spinnin', so it's probably gonna take some long talkin' for me to get a rope around all of it."

"I'll help all I can, but there's a lot even I don't know."

Ellis nodded as he tried not to stare at her.

"Well, I've got to clean up," Sara Mae said as she stood and picked up Mandy's bowl then her own.

As she reached for Ellis' bowl, he rose took his bowl, cup and spoon and said, "I'll help, Sara Mae. I'm kinda used to it."

"Alright, if you insist. I'm not about to argue."

After pumping the sink full of water, Ellis then took the pot that Sara had used to make the stew and waited for her to wash the three bowls before she stepped aside and let him handle the messier job.

As she watched Ellis do the menial chore, she couldn't help but compare him to her husband. It was really no contest. Even before that marvelous day when he'd returned from Abilene and given her ten dollars and each of the children a

104

dollar, she knew that Ellis White was special, even if he didn't. Why he'd never married was a genuine puzzle to her, but she harbored a deep and inexplicable desire that he never did, and it was why that note had bothered her so much.

She had married John Keeler because she was the oldest daughter of a rancher north of Fort Griffin and he had been a ranch hand and little else. She had married as it was expected of her when she reached the advanced age of seventeen and become pregnant with Sonny almost immediately after the wedding and delivered him just two days after her eighteenth birthday.

By the time Mandy arrived two years later, John had already been spending more time with the other boys than with her and her two endlessly crying, stinking babies, as he put it. Sara Mae's plight wasn't even noticed by the rest of her family. She was just doing her duty as the oldest daughter. The dowry that she'd been given was almost gone when Mary Jo finally selected Pete Orris, the son of a nearby rancher, to be her husband and that changed everything.

When Mary Jo married Pete, there was a bit of a row after Pete decided to use Mary Jo's dowry to start his own ranch but needed to spend as little as possible on the land to allow him to build a house and buy some cattle. So, just a month after their marriage, they took a wagon north and almost disappeared.

Almost a year later, John received a letter from Pete promising to make him a partner at the ranch. It seemed that Mary Jo missed her older sister and Pete needed the help anyway, so John, without asking her opinion uprooted her and the children and took them to the Big O which was hardly the big spread that John had expected, but they didn't have the means to return and there had been so much family turmoil left behind that they probably wouldn't have been welcomed back anyway.

So, they had stayed, and John behaved himself because of Pete. When Pete had announced his decision to do his duty to the state, she hadn't been surprised when John had offered to remain behind and manage the ranch.

Pete had been adamant that he should go with him and she believed it had only been John's wish to be free of her and the children that had convinced him to leave. That farewell scene on the porch where John had made his final pitch to stay to 'protect' Mary Jo had frightened her, believing that Ellis, of all people, would be the one to convince Pete to let John remain behind.

Now as she watched Ellis, she knew that her husband was still alive or Ellis would have told her, and that meant that he'd be returning soon. Even she knew the war was all but lost even if the Southern generals and politicians didn't.

She finished drying as Ellis rinsed the heavy pot and set it on the counter before her and let the water drain from the sink.

"There you go, ma'am, all nice and clean for tomorrow's cookin'," he said as he smiled at her.

"Thank you, Ellis," she replied, smiling back.

"I've got to clean and oil that Henry before I load it, so I'll take it out on the front porch and do it there 'cause the cleanin' fluid is kinda stinky."

"That's fine."

Ellis turned stepped across the kitchen then picked up the Henry and walked down the hallway to his room where he found his cleaning kit in the saddlebags. He then stepped across the front room, opened the front door and walked onto the porch leaving the door open.

He sat on the edge of the porch and began to clean the Henry. It really didn't need the cleaning as much as it did the oiling, but it would have been downright stupid to oil it then clean the new oil off right away with the fluid.

He'd finished cleaning when Sara Mae exited the house and asked, "Do you mind if I watch, Ellis?"

"Not at all, Sara Mae. Have a seat. We'll be havin' a nice sunset here shortly and we really need to talk."

Sara sat on the porch two feet to Ellis' right and asked, "Ellis, what can you tell me about John?"

He kept his attention on the Henry as he oiled the repeater and replied, "He was okay when I left."

"I mean, had he been wounded or anything?"

"No, ma'am. Nary a scratch."

"How about you?"

"I had a couple of Minie balls find my hide, but nothin' serious."

"That was a strange rifle you brought back with you."

"It's a sniper rifle. I was carryin' a regular Springfield musket when our sniper got hanged by the Yankees just a couple of weeks ago. The colonel wanted another sniper, but nobody wanted the job, so he kinda volunteered me. I never got to shoot nobody with it, though. It shoots real nice and all, but I felt kinda like I was cheatin', so I shot the chart table the Yankee colonel was usin' then ran.

"I come across some of our fellers who were gonna hang some Yankee captain who was doin' some scoutin', and after I stopped them and was escortin' him back to his lines, I got captured myself by their pickets. They usually hang snipers, so I figured I was a goner, but the captain told his colonel, the man I was gonna shoot that I saved him from hangin', and they gave me parole."

"They even let you keep your sniper rifle?"

"Yes, ma'am. The captain and me, we kinda hit it off, and he even gave me these boots," he said as he lifted his feet from the ground.

"He gave me a bunch of food and that big set of saddlebags, too. He wrote his name and address in the inside flap of the saddlebags and I intend to write to him after the war. He was from up in Ohio. The other odd thing was that the colonel I decided not to shoot was his pappy."

"No wonder they were so grateful. When do you think John will come back?"

"I can't see the war lastin' much longer. If they'd asked the smart generals, like Bobby Lee or Grant or even Sherman, it woulda been over months ago, but there are too many generals that fill the politicians with even that small bit of hope that they can pull off some kinda miracle and them politicians are only too eager to listen. I figure even they'll have to give it up before another year's out. I'd figure a few months, but things tend to slow down the winter months, even in the South."

"So, you think John will return here in a year?"

"Maybe sooner."

"Oh," she said then started to say, "but what if I don't..." but quickly stopped, not wanting to say what she really needed to say because she knew how it would make her sound.

Ellis glanced over at Sara Mae and was going to comment on what she was about to ask and could understand why she would. If he'd been married to that bastard, he would have shot him, but he wasn't a woman and was grateful for that difference as he sat beside Sara Mae. He just didn't comprehend the full context of what her question would have been.

Sara Mae then wanted to ask one thing, but instead approached the topic from a different direction and said, "I hope you don't mind my doing your laundry in your absence. I thought you might need them when you returned, and they were all just stuffed in the drawers."

"No, ma'am, I sure do appreciate it. I was never to fond of doin' the laundry anyway."

"Maybe they'll open a laundry in Fort Madrid like they have in Henrietta."

"I hope not, Sara Mae. That laundry was called the War Widow's Laundry, and it wasn't just to have clothes done either. There were a bunch of widows in the place and I was told that men would come in and, um, meet the ladies when they dropped off their laundry and the women would try to, um, well, um, see if they could convince the single ones to marry 'em."

"Really? Did one of them try to convince you?"

C.J. PETIT

"Yes, ma'am. A pretty young widow named Linda Harrison pretty much asked me that and even left a note in my clothes."

"Are you going to go back to Henrietta soon?"

"No, ma'am. I have too many things to do here, and besides you and Mandy are here now and you need protection and a place to stay until your husband comes back."

"After he comes back, will you go and see if she's still there?" she asked quietly.

Ellis honestly replied, "I have no idea what's gonna happen in the next few days, Sara Mae, and I ain't about to look that far ahead. Besides, as pretty as she is, I don't figure she'll have to wait long as soon as them young fellers start drifting back into town."

"Don't you think you made an impression on her? I mean, she sent you that note, didn't she?"

Ellis laughed and replied, "Oh, I figure she was more impressed that I paid in Yankee dollars and she probably puts those notes in all of the customers, and maybe all of the widows do."

Ellis had finished oiling the Henry, so he flipped it upside down at an angle, slid the slider up the bottom of the feeding tube slot, compressing the long spring and twisted it to open the tube for loading. He then began carefully feeding the .44 caliber rimfire Henry cartridges into the tube as Sara Mae watched.

"I've never seen a rifle do that before. Where did you get it?"

110

"I bought it in Abilene when we went on that cattle drive. I wasn't about to take it to war because I figured I'd run out of my own ammunition after a few months and carryin' around a useless rifle woulda been a waste. I bought it for when I got back and stored it in the barn. It holds fifteen cartridges and instead of having to stop and reload after each shot, I can just shift that lever down there and it pops the used brass out of the top and pulls a fresh cartridge into firing position. I'll be able to fire a dozen rounds before a single shot rifle gets to fire two."

"That's very impressive."

"I haven't fired it yet since I got back, but when I go to see the Comanches tomorrow, I'll bring it along and the Sharps, too. I don't expect any trouble from the Injuns, but they ain't the ones I'm worried about."

"Who are you worried about?"

"Jim Abigail. When Mary Jo dropped off those supplies for you, did she say if he had anyone else working the ranch?"

"No, but I never asked."

Ellis dropped the last cartridge into the tube then turned the tube cap back into position and slowly lowered the coiled spring into position.

"The only thing that kinda spooks me about the Henry is the way it loads. If I do it wrong or too fast, it could set off those cartridges and that would be bad."

"I imagine so."

Even though he still had a lot of questions, he knew that either Sara Mae didn't know the answers, or they might be too personal, and he might not want those questions answered anyway.

"Well, Sara, I got a lot to do tomorrow, so I'd just as soon turn in," he said as he rose and stood on the porch.

If Sara Mae hadn't been married, he might have offered to help her stand, but instead he just waited as she got to her feet and walked into the house and he followed.

"Good night, Ellis," she said with a smile before she entered the last bedroom.

"Good night, Sara Mae," Ellis replied before entering his room and closing the door.

After stripping down to his birthday suit, Ellis slid beneath his blankets in his own bed and rested his head on his own pillow for the first time in over three years. He was home again and tomorrow, he'd begin restoring his ranch and hopefully, he'd find Sonny, although he had a bad premonition that both Sonny and Rufus were buried somewhere on the ranch. Before he rode off to see the Comanches, he'd make a circuit of the area around the house and barn to look for evidence of any recent holes being dug. There would be settling as the bodies decomposed, a fact he had seen hundreds of time since he left his ranch what now seemed like a decade ago.

But tonight, he'd just let his mind float through images of the lady sleeping a few feet away. It was still going to be a dilemma having her there, but he would rather have her in the house than back at the Big O with Jim Abigail or even worse, with her husband.

CHAPTER 4

Ellis dressed quickly before sunrise the next morning in deference to Sara Mae and Mandy. Normally, he'd just walk buck naked out to the back porch and not even bother walking the extra fifty yards to the privy, but things were different now.

He quickly trotted down the hallway, zipped through the kitchen and almost ran to the privy, barely making it in time, realizing that he'd have to make this adjustment to the way of starting his day more quickly.

He returned and started the cookstove fire before washing his face and then lathering and beginning the sometime painful job of removing two days' worth of beard. He really needed to buy a new razor. The one he'd recovered from the highwaymen had too many nicks in the blade and was almost as dull as Sara Mae's husband. He snickered at the thought and nicked himself in the process.

He had just finished shaving when Sara Mae exited the bedroom already dressed and Ellis noticed she was wearing the yellow print dress that her children had bought her three years earlier. It was surprisingly new-looking, and it made her seem younger and almost girlish. He also couldn't help but notice that it fit her much better than the threadbare red checked dress she'd been wearing when he arrived.

She hadn't tied her hair in that tight bun she normally wore either, but instead left it long and obviously brushed. She didn't even seem nearly as tired as she did when he first met her at the Big O and seemed positively fetching even more so than he had recalled from their parting. Sara Mae had his complete attention.

"Good mornin', Sara Mae," Ellis said as he smiled at her, trying to mask the approval in his eyes.

She smiled back and said, "Good morning, Ellis."

After she hadn't raced to the privy, Ellis assumed that she had awakened before him, used the small house and returned to her room without a lot of noise.

"You look mighty handsome this mornin', Sara Mae," Ellis said, but instantly regretted it when Sara blushed a very deep red.

"I'm sorry, Sara Mae. That kinda slipped out."

"No, no. It's alright. It's just that no one has ever said that to me before."

"Well, that's kinda sad if you ask me," he replied not mentioning her husband specifically.

Her blush stayed put as she said, "Anyway, I'll take over cooking breakfast. When will you be leaving?"

"As soon as I'm finished eatin'. I'll go and saddle Tippy right now and I'll take some food for the ride. Then I'll head down to the Big O and have my little chat with Jim. When I'm finished, I'll swing by here on my way to the Comanche village and let you know what he said and what I think about it."

"I'll pack some food for you while you're at the Big O."

"Thank you, Sara Mae. Is there anythin' that you want me to tell Mary Jo?"

Sara thought about it and then shook her head before saying, "I can't think of anything, and I don't believe she'd tell you anyway."

"Okay. I'll be back in a bit," he said before walking out the open door.

He hadn't asked Sara Mae why she thought that Mary Jo wouldn't tell him anything, because she'd already mentioned that she thought her sister was afraid of Jim Abagail. If Ellis could get talk to her away from Jim Abigail, he'd tell her that she was safe now and if she wanted to return with him to the Slash W and stay with Sara Mae, she could. A lot would depend on Jim Abigail, and it bothered him that he'd read the man so badly.

He was still wearing the remnants of his Confederate uniform as he left the ranch house for a reason. He figured that there might be a chance that they'd be bloodied sometime today and didn't want to ruin any of his clean clothes. If he returned, he'd turn them into rags.

He saddled Tippy then led her out to the trough, let her drink and then led her to the back hitchrail where he tied her reins, hopped onto the porch and entered the house.

"One of these days, I'll make a proper breakfast with eggs," Sara Mae said as he walked to the table and took a seat.

"And I'll get us some real coffee too, ma'am," Ellis said before digging into the bean and bacon breakfast.

Sara Mae sat and ate with him while Mandy ate some mush that Ellis couldn't identify.

Ellis smiled at Mandy and said, "Why, Mandy, I swear you're as pretty as a bluebonnet in bloom this mornin'."

Mandy grinned, swallowed and replied, "Thank you, Uncle Ellis."

"You're welcome, Niece Mandy."

Sara Mae had suggested that Mandy call him Uncle Ellis rather than Mister White, and Ellis appreciated it as he hoped it made her more comfortable to have him around.

He quickly finished his breakfast but didn't have time to help with the cleanup in the kitchen as his cleanup at the Big O and with the Comanches would be much more difficult.

"I should be back in a couple of hours, Sara Mae. I'll let you know how that went and then I'll head northwest."

"Good luck, Ellis," she said as he smiled at her and tipped his hat.

Sara Mae and Mandy watched him leave then mount his black mare through the open door and Mandy said, "I hope he finds Sonny, Mama."

"So, do I."

————

Ellis walked Tippy around the back of the barn leaving about a hundred feet as he scanned the earth for any signs of a depression, but by the time he'd ridden a complete circle, he'd come up empty and set off to the southwest and the Big O.

He was curious about how many head of cattle he'd find on the smaller ranch and if Jim had hired any ranch hands. He could understand why he might not, after he'd wrangled Mary Jo. He was still curious about how he was able to marry her if

116

there had been no official notice of Pete's death. The war caused a great deal of miscommunication but still, it was a big step to take based on hearsay, and he hadn't heard a whisper of Pete's death.

Before he left Slash W land, he spotted the Big O herd or what was left of it. Instead of the forty to fifty animals he expected to see based on what Sara Mae had told him, he guessed there were less than thirty even allowing for strays on the smaller ranch.

He spotted a rider leaving the ranch house and it didn't take long to identify the horse that he was riding as the one he'd given to Jim Abigail three years ago. It was a dappled gray gelding with four white stockings, so it was easy to pick out. It had been one of the best animals in the remuda.

Obviously, Jim soon spotted him but failed to recognize him and pulled his rifle from the horse's scabbard when they were still eight hundred yards apart.

Ellis gambled and put both hands in the air as he let the mare continue to trot toward his old foreman. If he saw that rifle drop to a shooting position, he'd grab his Henry and let Jim find out how many bullets he could send his way in just a few seconds.

When Jim Abigail was within two hundred yards, he pulled his gelding to a halt and shouted, "You're on my land, mister! Who are you and what are you doin' here?"

Ellis shouted back, "I come to visit, Jim. I know I lost some weight, but I still own the Slash W."

Jim Abigail slowly slid the rifle into his scabbard as he nudged his gelding forward.

Ellis continued to stare at him to get a read of the man after having noted that Jim had referred to the ranch as 'his land' and not even the Big O.

When they were just a hundred feet apart, both slowed their horses to a walk and then stopped just six feet away from each other.

"Well, I'll be damned! What in tarnation are you doin' back? Is the war over?"

"Nope. I got myself cornered by a Union picket line, got taken into their camp and had to sign a parole rather than get hanged. I was carryin' a sniper rifle at the time."

"So, what brings you here?"

"Information, Jim. What happened while I was gone? I got Mrs. Keeler and her daughter livin' in my place and she told me her boy got taken by Comanches. That doesn't seem right to me. What happened?"

"Well, I figure she told you what happened twixt me and Lou. He got all kinda lit up when Mary Jo agreed to marry me and said he was gonna kill me. We had it out in the barn so none of the women or young'uns would see it, and I got him with my sticker first, and I buried him. I got back to the house and had to have Mary Jo fix me up 'cause Lou sliced me on my arm.

"Then Sara Mae come in a while later and tells me her boy's missin'. I had to wait for a while, but I went over there the next mornin' and the place was empty. I did some lookin' around, but there just wasn't nobody anywhere. I told Sara Mae that the Comanches probably took him to be a warrior 'cause I figured he was probably dead somewhere and I wanted to give her some hope he was still alive. Hell, you woulda done the same."

Ellis just grunted then asked, "Why did you send Mrs. Keeler and her daughter to my place? She woulda been a lot safer with you and Mary Jo."

"Hell, Ellis, we was, you know, busy. I didn't want those kids watchin' and listenin'. It just wasn't right and your place bein' empty and all, well, it was the smart thing to do. I sent Mary Jo over there with supplies, too."

"How is Mary Jo? Mrs. Keeler hasn't seen her in a couple of months and is kinda worried."

Jim paused for a few seconds then answered, "That's 'cause she's kinda big. She's gonna have a baby in a few months."

"Mind if I talk to her?" he asked.

"She's kinda embarrassed about bein' so big and doesn't want to see anybody. That's why she ain't gone over to see her sister for a couple of months. I guess the pretty ones don't like bein' so fat."

Ellis grunted again then asked, "How'd you all get married without anything official about Pete's death?"

"Aw, they don't care none. I guess there are so many widows these days that don't have no papers, it's just the way it is."

"What happened to your herd? Mrs. Keeler said that there were forty head when she left, but it looks like you're down to about twenty-four."

"I trade 'em for supplies down at Fort Madrid. They don't take Confederate money anymore and the money you left us ran out in August last year."

Ellis knew there was something wrong in his calculations, but let it ride for now.

Finally, he asked, "What happened to Rufus, Jim?"

"Beats me, Ellis. He used to come around and see Sara Mae's boy, but stopped last summer and I ain't seen him since. I reckon he finally took your advice and skedaddled."

Ellis nodded then said, "Well, I just wanted to stop by and see how you was doin'. You haven't been able to hire any hands have you?"

"Nope, but you might get some old fellers down at Fort Madrid that are lookin' for work."

"Maybe I'll do that. I'll catch you later, Jim," Ellis said before wheeling Tippy around and heading back to his ranch to talk to Sara Mae.

Jim watched him ride away then turned his horse back to the Big O's ranch house and tell Mary Jo that Ellis was back and refresh his warning about saying anything to anybody. But his unexpected arrival meant he'd have to think about changing his original plans. He didn't expect Ellis to remain ignorant very long and knew he'd never have a chance in a gunfight. He was sure that Ellis had been practicing a lot over the last few years, if one called it target practice.

Ellis had Tippy at a medium trot and soon reached his land. He had done the math in his head about the money and had come up almost a thousand dollars shy of the amount he'd left for them to spend, and that was assuming that Jim had continued to pay Rufus, which he was beginning to suspect wasn't true.

He was a bit surprised that Mary Jo hadn't told Sara Mae about her pregnancy even before she stopped visiting, and then thought maybe she had, but Sara Mae hadn't mentioned it because she thought it was a woman thing.

When he reached the ranch house thirty minutes later, he pulled up to the trough, and let Tippy drink while he went inside.

He barely crossed the threshold when Sara Mae hopped up from the kitchen table and asked, "What did he say? Did you talk to Mary Jo?"

Ellis pulled off his hat ran his fingers through his hair and replied, "Well, Sara Mae, I never did see Mary Jo. I ran into Jim out in the fields. First of all, you didn't tell me that Mary Jo was gonna have a baby."

Sara's mouth dropped open before she exclaimed, "*She's pregnant?*"

Ellis smiled and replied, "I thought you had figured out how that worked by now, ma'am."

"I know very well how it works, but how far along is she?"

"Jim said she was gonna have the baby in a few months."

"Then why hasn't she asked for my help? She'll need me there when she goes into labor."

"The story that Jim was sayin' was that she was embarrassed to be so big."

Sara Mae shook her head and said, "That's not right, Ellis. She wanted to have a baby in the worst way, and I know if she'd found out she was pregnant, she would have told me and would have been proud to have that big belly. Besides, the timing is all wrong. I don't see how she could be that big when she was perfectly slim when I saw her a couple of months ago."

"I ain't too sure he was tellin' the truth anyway, Sara Mae. I think that was a lie like just about everything else he told me. He said he run out of money to run the Slash W last year, but I gave him enough to run it for three years. Even if he had to pay Rufus right up till yesterday, he still was about a thousand dollars short. The story he told me about the knife fight and what happened afterwards was different from what you told me, too. Did he get sliced by Lou Gordon in the fight?"

"Not that I noticed. Did he say that he did?"

"He did and said that Mary Jo had to fix him up. Now, he might've thrown that out there 'cause he was worried about somethin' and wanted to make sure I knew that Lou had his knife. Anyway, he said that when he came to the Slash W, he didn't find anything or anyone at all and told you that the Comanche took Sonny to be a warrior so you wouldn't be upset. He figured that Sonny was already dead somewhere."

"Do you believe that?" she asked quietly.

"Sara Mae," he replied softly, "you gotta understand that there's a chance that's true, but don't get too upset yet. I got a feelin' that Sonny is out there, and I aim to find him. Give me a chance to go out to the Comanche village and see what I can find. I'll be back tomorrow."

Sara Mae nodded slowly, but Ellis could see how much the realization hurt. As much as he disagreed with Jim Abigail's lie, he knew that he had just almost extinguished that small flame of hope by repeating the story and then confirming at least its possibility.

Then he said, "Sara Mae, do you have any scissors?"

"I have some in my sewing box. Why?"

"I'd like to bring them with me. Sonny is probably going to need a haircut."

Sara Mae laughed lightly as she wiped her wet eyes and replied, "I'll get them for you."

Ellis smiled as she left then exhaled and picked up the food she'd packed for his trip. By the time she returned with the scissors, he was ready to go.

He accepted the scissors, smiled at Sara Mae and said, "I'll see you and Mandy tomorrow, Sara Mae, and God willin', I'll be bringin' home your boy."

She nodded and watched as he turned and left the kitchen then waited for the hoofbeats to fade before smiling at Mandy, who'd listened to everything but had remained silent.

"He'll find Sonny, Mandy, and give him a haircut before he comes home."

Mandy nodded but then stood, walked to her mother and put her arms around her before she began to cry.

Sara Mae held her sobbing daughter in her arms and began to silently weep.

———

Ellis set Tippy off at a medium trot to the northwest, following the tracks he'd made late yesterday. He hoped his request for scissors wasn't just a weak attempt to restore Sara Mae's spirits.

As he rode, he began to suspect that although the Comanches probably hadn't taken Sonny, he'd find the boy with the Indians and began to believe that somehow, Rufus was involved with his disappearance. It was the only thing that really made any sense. Sonny disappeared shortly after Rufus disappeared, and the well-conditioned leather back in the barn was a measure of care and respect that Jim Abigail never had, but Rufus had in abundance. It was all just speculation now, but he hoped that in a few hours, those suspicions would be confirmed and if they were, he'd have a lot more of his many remaining questions answered.

He crossed the gullies then Fresh Water Creek before riding through his herd and swinging to the west of the northern string of High Hills that marked the boundary of the Slash W.

———

"Ellis is back? Is the war over?" asked Mary Jo with wide eyes.

"Nope. He said he was paroled, but I figure he deserted. He was still wearin' that gray suit."

"You know him better than that. He would never desert and then lie about it. What did he say?"

"Not much. He asked about Sonny, the cattle, and why your sister was there, but nothin' else."

"Is he coming to the house?" she asked hopefully.

"Nope. I did tell him you were havin' our kid in a few months, though."

"Why did you tell him that? I'm not even pregnant!"

"Because, missy, I aim to get you that way and I figure we can start right now."

He took her hand and almost hauled her to the bedroom as Mary Jo closed her eyes. *Why had this all happened to her?* Once she'd heard that Ellis was back, a bright flame of hope had erupted within her heart but now, it was fading quickly as Jim reasserted his dominance over her life.

———

Ellis made two rest breaks since passing Fresh Water Creek to let Tippy graze and drink. He'd had a rolled flour tortilla with some spiced beef that Sara Mae had made for him and enjoyed each succulent bite but saved the rest for later. He sure could get used to having a woman in the house, especially that woman, the most woman he'd ever met.

It was early afternoon when he spotted the Comanche village and knew he was already under the eyes of the scouts as he trotted the mare closer to the collection of hide-covered dwelling that wasn't nearly as large as he'd recalled.

He was still a good six hundred yards out when he squinted into the afternoon sun then dropped the bill of his hat slightly as he tried to focus on one of the Comanches crossing from the right to the left in the camp with his woman by his side.

The reason he had picked up the warrior initially was because of his height. He was a half a head taller than the other warriors, but it was that head itself that gave him pause and the reason to stare. His hair was the total opposite of the straight, glossy hair of the Comanche and almost all of the Indian tribes. It was tightly curled, and he smiled when he realized he was looking at the head of Rufus Green.

Why he was there and what he could tell him about Sonny if anything, would provide for an interesting conversation. But the very presence of Rufus reinforced his belief that Sonny was somewhere in the village as well.

He kept the same pace to avoid raising any alarm and slowed as he approached the outer edge of the village, and Rufus finally glanced his way. Ellis could see his eyes narrow as he tried to identify the tall, thin rider entering the village on a black mare. Then the light came on, and he could see the marvelous smile as he heard Rufus' deep, booming voice shout, "Ellis!"

He said something quickly to the woman next to him then began jogging toward him as the woman walked behind him at a slower, more dignified pace.

When he was close, Ellis dismounted wearing a huge grin of his own and the two men were soon meshed as they pounded on each other's backs.

"Is the war over, boss?" Rufus asked as they separated.

"Nope. I figure them fools are gonna go at it for another year or so, but I got paroled when I got captured, so I'm back. There are a lotta things I need to figure out before I can get the ranch restarted, but I can't tell you how happy I am to see you again. So, what happened? Why are you here?"

Rufus turned to the Comanche woman and said, "Boss, I'd like you to meet my wife, Silver Dove. She's gonna have our baby soon."

Ellis tipped his hat and said in Comanche, "I wish you every happiness, Silver Dove."

Silver Dove returned his smile and replied, "Thank you. Rufus speaks of you often and told me you would return to make everything right."

"I'll do what I can."

Then he turned back to Rufus and said, "Rufus, what drove me wasn't so much to find you, but…"

Rufus interrupted him and said, "I know," then turned and bellowed, "Sonny! Mister White is here!"

Ellis turned to where Rufus was looking and soon a much taller Sonny Keeler popped out of a tipi on the other side of the camp and began jogging toward Rufus and Ellis. He was wearing his regular clothes, which surprised Ellis after almost eight months, but the britches had obviously been cut to allow for his greater height. He still looked healthy, which didn't surprise him, nor did his need for a haircut.

Sonny, now nine years old, stopped before the two men and asked, "Do I have to go back, Uncle Rufus?"

Rufus nodded and replied, "It's your home, Sonny. Your mother and sister both miss you and I'm sure that Mister White will protect you, too."

Sonny looked up at Ellis and asked, "How are my mama and Mandy?"

"They're fine. They're living on my ranch now and so will you. You don't have to go back to the Big O ever."

"What about my father? Is he back, too?"

"No. He's still back in East Texas. The Union army caught me and made me promise not to fight anymore and sent me home."

Ellis didn't have to ask if Sonny wanted his father to return because the tone of his question already provided the answer.

"What happened, Rufus?" Ellis asked.

"Let's go into my tipi and Silver Dove can make us something to eat. Sonny's been living with us for a while now."

"I figured that. The last time I saw him, he didn't even reach belt high," Ellis said as he took Tippy's reins and they all began walking to the tipi.

One of the warriors approached and told Ellis that he'd make sure the mare was cared for, so Ellis handed him the reins without question which reminded him to ask about his missing herd of horses.

Once inside, Silver Dawn began preparing their food while Rufus, Ellis and Sonny sat on old buffalo robes.

"Before I tell you the story, boss, can you tell me about the war. How bad was it?"

"Probably not any different than most of 'em. Chaos, boredom, sickness and dyin'. All that talk about glory and honor are hogwash."

"Did you get shot?"

"A couple of times, but not bad."

"Did my father get shot?" asked Sonny.

"No, sir. When I left, he was as fit as a fiddle."

"You lost weight, though, boss."

"I'll get it back if Sonny's mama keeps cookin'. So, tell me what happened. I got a good idea about the knife fight, but after that it gets kinda murky."

"Well, I'll start from when you left, 'cause I don't figure you heard anythin' about that yet."

"You're right. I only got from when Jim married Pete's widow, which still kinda smells bad."

"It should. Anyway, after you left, things ran pretty good for a few months. We took care of the cattle and the Big O herd, too. Then Jim and Lou began spendin' more time at the Big O, and I figure it was 'cause of Mrs. Orris. That left more work for me, but that was okay. Me and Jim never got along all that good anyway."

"I know, and it was my fault, Rufus. I'm plumb sorry."

"That's plain old horse manure, boss. Anyway, the herds were both doin' pretty good, even the horses. It was like the war wasn't even goin' on out here. Things began changin' when Jim figured that you might not be comin' back and tried to convince me and Lou that we should just act like the ranch was ours.

"We told him to not even think about it and he dropped it. He stopped payin' me after that, and one day, I found my pistol gone and knew I was in trouble. That was last summer. So, I lit out but instead of goin' west like you said, I rode to the Comanche village. See, I'd made kind of deal with Chief Long Elk about the herd. Them horses were gettin' too busy for even three of us to manage, so the deal was that they'd take the herd and could use them and keep half of the foals until you returned. If you didn't come back, then they could keep the herd. I think they were kinda hopin' the Yankees would get ya."

Ellis laughed and said, "I bet they were, too."

"Anyway, I'd made that deal in the fall of '62 then they picked up the herd and I had a good count of the horses, too. Not that they'd cheat you or anything. So, when I took off last summer, I came here and stayed. I was already kinda been sweet on Silver Dove before I showed up permanent, so we got married."

"What happened at the Big O?"

Rufus said, "Sonny, you tell Mister White what you told me."

Sonny nodded then looked at Ellis and said, "Well, sir, like Uncle Rufus told you, those two men from the Slash W kinda took to thinkin' that Aunt Mary Jo wasn't married even before they found out that my Uncle Pete was killed. So, when they did find out, they started yellin' at each other and Mister Abigail told Mister Gordon to go out to the barn. They went out there and I kinda waited until they were inside then snuck out and walked behind the barn to watch through a crack between the boards.

"At first, they were just yellin' and pushin' each other and then Mister Abigail pulled his knife real sudden and just pushed it into Mister Gordon's belly. It was horrible. When Mister Gordon fell down, Mister Abigail kicked him a few times, then he looked right at me before leavin' the barn. I knew he saw me, so I raced away as fast as I could and kept goin'. It was already gettin' dark, so he must not have seen where I went. I slowed down and walked all the way to your ranch figurin' Uncle Rufus would be there, but he wasn't. It was empty, so I went into the house and instead of sleeping on a bed, I slid underneath a bed in case he came lookin' for me 'cause I know I left a trail."

"He came the next mornin', didn't he?" asked Ellis.

"Yes, sir. I was still asleep when I heard the door open and he walked through the house. I was really afraid, and I had to pee really bad too, but I waited until he left and finally ran outside. He was already gone, but I was too afraid to go back."

Rufus then picked up the story, saying, "I'd been stopping by the ranch house to check on it and keep your leather oiled and got there in the afternoon. I found Sonny, he told me what happened, and he said he was too afraid to go back, so I brought him here."

Ellis looked at Sonny and said, "I don't think he saw you, Sonny, but I'm gonna have to come up with some story about where you been these past eight months. I'll tell everyone but your mama that you were lost and some Comanches found you wanderin' around and brought you here for protection."

"Okay. When can we go home?" he asked.

"Whenever you feel ready. I know your mama and sister miss you and want you back in the worst way. I'll bet you can even talk her into makin' some cookies."

"Cookies sound good," Sonny said with a smile.

Rufus asked, "Can you stay the night, boss? We have a lot of catchin' up to do."

"You bet. What are your plans now that I'm back, Rufus?"

"If it's all the same with you, boss. I'm gonna stay in the village. They like me."

"They know a good man when they seem him, Rufus," he said before asking, "What happened to Jim, Rufus? I know he always fancied himself as the boss, but why did he go so wrong?"

Rufus shrugged and replied, "He was always careful to be just regular when you was around, but the rest of us saw it."

"Why didn't you tell me?"

"It wasn't my place, boss. The other boys felt the same way."

"What happened to the money, Rufus? Mrs. Keeler told me it ran out last year and they had to start tradin' cattle for supplies. It shoulda lasted 'til spring of this year."

"Like I said, he stopped payin' me early last year, and Lou figured he was hidin' the money for somethin'. We just couldn't figure out what it was."

"Okay. I'll worry about that later. Now tomorrow, I'm gonna need a horse for Sonny and the two draft horses for the wagon. The rest can stay here."

"Sonny can ride bareback now, but I have an extra saddle."

As Silver Dove brought the food and set it on the blanket, Ellis said, "So, tell me how your life is now, Rufus."

Rufus smiled at Silver Dove then replied, "Well, boss, it's kinda hard, but I like it here. When I arrived to talk about the horses…"

As they ate, Ellis listened as Rufus spoke of his new life and how different it was from his two previous lives, the first as a slave and the second as a cowhand. Here, he was not only liked, but respected. As his hands moved as he spoke, Ellis glanced at Silver Dove and saw the love she had for her husband and understood a lot more than what Rufus was saying. He was a bit jealous of what Rufus had found, too.

He and Rufus were about the same age and soon, Rufus would be a father and have a family around him. Then he looked at Sonny as he watched Rufus and saw the respect and admiration in his eyes.

Sonny was three years older now, but there was a huge difference between a six-year-old child and a nine-year-old boy. Sonny was learning how to be a good man from Rufus and was sure that his own father did nothing to encourage or help him.

Sonny would be returning to his ranch tomorrow and would be his responsibility until his father returned, and Ellis vowed to make sure that he'd do all he could to earn the same respect and admiration that he gave to Rufus. He'd do his damndest to help Sonny become a good man, even if it meant having to do it after his useless father made it back, if he ever did.

When Rufus finished, he asked, "Now, boss, tell us about what happened after you rode off."

Ellis wiped his mouth thanked Silver Dove then began to tell the long narrative about his time in the army from the day he enlisted in Henrietta, the march east with no training at all then their first engagement.

Ellis remembered each fight as vividly as if it had happened yesterday, and unlike many others who refused to talk about their wartime experiences, he wanted to share those memories. He didn't gloss over the cruelty, the horror or the despair. He talked of those he'd shot and the two times he'd been wounded and the many near misses. He talked about the incredibly disgusting lack of sanitation and rampant disease in the large camps, the swarms of bugs and snakes that lived with them adding to their misery and the constant boredom between the terrors of battle.

When he finally finished with his last day, when he'd been sent off on a sniper mission, failed and stopped the hanging of a Union captain, his voice began to lose its intensity as he spoke of his capture, his parole and the friendship he'd forged with a man who'd been his enemy the day before.

But the excitement returned when he began narrating about his almost religious pilgrimage to his ranch, including the gunfight near Montague.

Because Sonny wasn't there when he reached the ranch, he included finding his mother and sister in his house and then his meeting with Jim Abigail.

By the time he completed his tale, it was after sunset and the inside of the tipi was illuminated only by the embers of the cooking fire.

"So, that, Rufus, is how I got to be here."

"That's one helluva story, boss," Rufus replied.

Ellis glanced over at Sonny, who'd been mesmerized the entire time, smiled then looked back at Rufus and said, "I feel like a walk to stretch my legs. Wanna come along, Rufus?"

Rufus nodded then both men rose, and Rufus said, "We'll be back soon, Silver Dove."

Silver Dove smiled and replied, "Sonny and I will probably be sleeping by then."

"Then have good dreams, my wife," Rufus said before kissing her softly.

Rufus and Ellis then exited the tipi and began to walk across the village, drawing the occasional glance from warriors but nothing more.

"I figure you wanna talk about somethin'," Rufus said.

"I got a couple of problems, Rufus. First off is Jim Abigail. He married Mary Jo Orris and said that Pete was dead, but I never heard that. Now, he was in a different unit, so I didn't see him much, but usually when one of the fellers that we knew was killed, we'd hear about it. I don't know Mary Jo all that good to figure out what went on between 'em, but I always figured she and Pete got along right good."

"I thought that way, too. But like I said, I was kept off of that ranch while all that was goin' on."

"Then there's Jim himself. I don't trust the man and figure that he might make a play for the Slash W now that he knows I'm back. My guess is that he was holdin' that money to buy the ranch after the war knowin' that nobody would have any real cash. Now that I'm back, that would throw that plan into the dust bin."

"You need help?"

"Not yet, Rufus. Besides, you got a baby on the way. I think I'll go into Fort Madrid and get some supplies and see about hiring a couple of old boys that Jim said were there lookin' for work."

"What's the other problem?"

"Mrs. Keeler and her young'uns. You've been doin' real good with Sonny, and I aim to keep him headin' that way while he's in my house, but I don't like her husband at all. John Keeler is a worthless excuse for a man. He talked about his wife like she was a critter and those nice kids like they were just a pair of unwanted vermin. I'm kinda worried about gettin' too attached to 'em and then have that bastard come waltzin' back and takin' em away and makin' their lives bad again."

"Sonny said that his father didn't like him or his sister. He didn't beat 'em or anything, but I figure that was only because Pete Orris was in the same house. I think the boy is hopin' his father don't come back."

"That's what I figured myself. I think Mrs. Keeler and Mandy feel that way, too. I guess all I can do is to make 'em all feel good as long as I can," he replied then paused and said, "I didn't say anything in front of Sonny, but that group that tried to lynch the Yankee captain was led by John Keeler. He was always in trouble for somethin' and when the bullets started flyin', he always had an excuse for not bein' where he was supposed to be. He had a group of three other slackers in the company that did the same thing and were with him when they tried to string up Captain Dunston."

"I don't figure Sonny would be all that surprised if you told him, boss."

"Well, I'm still gonna keep it to myself, at least for a while. I'm not even gonna face off Jim Abigail until I figure it's necessary. Right now, I want to get the ranch back to runnin' good and keep Sara Mae and hers safe."

"You still sweet on Mrs. Keeler, boss?" Rufus asked with a grin.

Ellis was going to deny it but paused before he replied.

The pause generated a snicker from Rufus before Ellis finally replied, "She's married, Rufus."

Rufus' grin stayed put as he said, "Uh-uh."

The two men then turned and walked back to the tipi as Ellis thought about John Keeler. *Why would he even want to return to a wife and children he didn't even like?*

———

Two hundred and eleven miles east of the Comanche village, the Confederate campfires were scattered around their camp as the men lined up to fill their plates with whatever the cooks managed to scrape together.

John Keeler, Hick Smith, Eustice Smothers, and Al Hartman had all filled their plates and were sitting in their own circle fifteen feet from the fire.

"I'm tellin ya, boys, he was hanged by them Yankees. He was caught with that sniper rifle and they captured him and hanged him. He ain't been back for over a week now and even the colonel thinks he was hanged," John said.

Eustace snorted then said, "So? What do we care? He was a bastard when he was here, so I say good riddance."

John set his plate down so he could use his hands and said, "Don't you get it? I told you boys how he cleared his ranch of his cattle and then drove 'em to Abilene before the war. He musta made over ten thousand Yankee dollars for a herd that size. He paid off the drovers and came back, then we all enlisted a few months later. He musta still had over eight thousand dollars on him by then, but he didn't have it with him when we enlisted, did he?"

Hick snickered before saying, "So, he's a rich dead body rotting from some tree."

"Yeah, but that money is still somewhere on that ranch of his. It's gotta be somewhere on the ranch 'cause the closest bank is in Henrietta, and he never went past Fort Madrid before we all rode to Henrietta to enlist. If we all head that way before anybody else gets their hands on the ranch and looks around, we could find the cash and be rich!"

Al Hartman asked, "You figure on desertin'?"

The subject had come up before and none of them had objected, but it had always been a matter of timing and incentive. Now there was definitely an incentive.

"When we get the chance. I figure we can start storin' food and then, when the brigade starts marchin' east again, we kinda hang back and then disappear into them woods."

"I'm in," Eustace said eagerly.

"Me, too," added Hick.

Al added, "Alright, John, but the brigade ain't gonna go anywhere for at least a week."

"That'll give us time to get what we need," he replied then smiled, picked up his plate and began to eat with gusto.

———

At the Slash W, Sara Mae tucked Mandy into bed, kissed her on the forehead then stepped out of the bedroom. She walked into her bedroom then took off her yellow dress, put on her one nightdress and blew out the lamp before she slid beneath the blankets. The Remington pistol was on the nightstand near the head of the bed.

Sara Mae closed her eyes and just let her mind wander in preparation for sleep. She didn't want to believe that Sonny was dead but knew that it was a very real possibility. She hoped that Ellis would ride in tomorrow with her son, but thought it was unlikely. But even if he did return with Sonny, *what would happen to them after that?* She knew that Ellis would let her stay in his house, but when John returned, *what would happen then?* They couldn't move back to the Big O because Jim Abigail wouldn't allow it.

Sara Mae was growing more despondent with each new thought and was almost on the verge of tears when she had to roll over and when she did, she opened her eyes and saw the gleaming barrel of the revolver just two feet away.

She stared at the steel glinting in the moonlight coming through the window then closed her eyes again and began to see the face of the man who had given it to her. The same man who had taken her children into Fort Madrid let them overspend the money he'd given them then bought them gifts and sang with them on the drive back. Sonny and Mandy had talked about it for weeks, even though they didn't see Ellis for a long time afterward.

Her husband, after being annoyed that Ellis had spent time with the children and bought them things, had ignored it and them. He had noticed the yellow dress and had asked where she had gotten it. When she told him that it was a gift from the children, she thought he was going to hit her, but Pete was in the next room with Mary Jo, so all he had done was glare at her. She hadn't worn the dress even after she had moved into the Slash W ranch house. She had already decided that the only man who would see her wearing the dress was Ellis White.

Now she lived here and soon Ellis would be returning, hopefully with Sonny. But even if he didn't find her son, he'd return to help her and Mandy, and Sara Mae decided then that she would do all she could to stay and made one other important decision that dissolved her own worries about John Keeler. She would convince Ellis to be her real husband, and if John returned at all, and she doubted if he would then she'd tell him that she divorced him, even if it was only in her own mind, heart and soul. The difficulty, she was sure, was convincing Ellis to believe it and accept her as his wife.

Once she'd made that decision, Sara Mae sighed, then rolled back onto her back and let her mind wander into a more pleasant dream realm before she fell asleep.

———

Mary Jo lay in bed with Jim Abigail wondering how this had all happened. She had stopped short of begging Pete not to go, yet he went anyway, but at least he took John with him. She despised the man and pitied her older sister. He hadn't beaten her or the children, but Mary Jo didn't doubt that he had it in him.

Now she had this one lying next to her treating her like his wife even though she wasn't. At first, he and Lou had been very polite and helpful to her and Sara Mae handling the cattle and bringing supplies. She'd been her usual, friendly self despite Sara Mae's warnings then even after she could tell that both men were interested in her, she knew that the presence of her married sister and her children would keep them at bay.

She should have talked to Sara Mae more, but it had happened so gradually over the years that the bigger change went almost unnoticed. They were always busy with all of the housework and maintaining the ranch and now trying to grow vegetables that she simply hadn't had the time to worry.

It had still been getting worse over the following year despite the inhibitions, then things turned even more downhill when the new year of 1863 arrived. The money that Pete had given to her before he left ran out, then they started exchanging cattle for supplies and Mary Jo estimated that by the time Pete returned, there wouldn't be any cattle left.

Then came the word that Pete had been killed, and she was devastated, but within a day of that news, she received two proposals of marriage and turned them both down, not wanting to believe that Pete was dead and not really caring for either man. She never had a chance to talk to Sara Mae about it before the challenge and the fight that created chaos in the Big O ranch house.

After Lou had been killed, Jim Abigail had told her privately that she was now his wife, the ranch was his and if she had a problem with it, then he'd let her join her husband and he'd move onto her older sister. With the threat came a warning that if she told anyone, he'd follow through on his promise.

She'd submitted and was now Jim Abigail's property, because that's how he saw her. She was allowed to take supplies to Sara Mae, but even if she'd told her sister what was happening to her, Mary Jo knew that she was just as isolated as she was and could do nothing to help and just knowing would endanger her older sister and her children.

The only exciting news she'd heard was today's revelation of Ellis White's return and he was at now at his ranch house. She was happy that her sister was safe but knew that Jim would keep a closer watch over her now, so she couldn't make a mad dash to the Slash W ranch house the three miles away.

She hoped that Ellis would come to the house but knew it would probably get him killed. Mostly, though, as she drifted off to sleep, she wished that Pete was still alive.

———

Eight miles east of John Keeler's regiment, Sergeant Pete Orris was slipping into his small tent. There were two large holes in the left side, but it kept out the dew.

The last few days in the camp had been boring, but he knew they'd be moving out in a few days to cross the Mississippi River into Louisiana to attack the Federals. It was more of a harassing campaign than a full-scale battle as they were outmatched in every possible military arena as they had been for almost the entire war. But this time, it was almost to the point of absurdity.

They were dependent on finding guns, ammunition, boots and even Union uniforms that would be bleached instead of getting any new supplies. Their units were just over half strength and they were losing men to desertion every day. When the army started east again, he didn't doubt that they'd lose a lot more. The Texas boys weren't keen on dying in Louisiana or any other state anymore. They lost men in every state where there'd been a fight, and even Pete hoped that someone would see the light and put a stop to the killing.

As he stretched out in his tent, the only thing that kept his morale from plummeting was the hope of returning to the Big O and Mary Jo. He hadn't gotten a letter from her in months, but that wasn't unusual. They hadn't been paid in over a year, either.

CHAPTER 5

A freshly trimmed Sonny mounted the small horse that had been given to him from Ellis' herd, as Ellis sat in the saddle. The two draft horses were attached with a trail rope to Tippy.

Rufus and Silver Dove were standing beside Ellis' horse looking up at him.

"Keep in touch, Rufus. Give me a few days and stop by with Silver Dove before she gets too heavy with that baby."

"We might do that, boss. I kinda want to see what happens."

"I'm hopin' things stay quiet for a week or so, anyway."

He glanced over at Sonny, who was in the saddle and had the reins in his hands then smiled down at Rufus and said, "Well, we'll be off. Thanks for takin' care of Sonny and everything else, Rufus."

Rufus didn't reply but waved as Ellis and Sonny started their mounts at a walk out of the village.

As they left, Rufus wasn't sure if he'd ever be able to visit the ranch as the chief had said that they were moving the village in another month to get closer to the herds of deer.

He and Silver Dove waved once more as Ellis and Sonny both waved before they returned to their village.

———

Once underway, Ellis said, "You know, Sonny, I kinda thought you'd be wearin' buckskins when I found ya."

"Uncle Rufus said that you'd be comin' to get me and he wanted me to remember where I came from."

"Why did he figure I'd be comin' to get ya?"

"He said you would, but I never asked why."

Ellis figured that it was because Rufus didn't want to spook Sonny by telling him that his father would be coming after him or that he thought that Sonny's father wouldn't bother.

Ellis then asked, "Did you ever catch that horned frog?"

"No, sir, but we kinda stopped lookin'."

Ellis laughed and said, "You know it's not a frog, don't ya? It ain't no toad, neither. I had an officer straighten me out on that one. He told me it was really a lizard."

Sonny grinned and asked, "A lizard? Really? Like a snake?"

"Nope. A snake is a reptile, and I didn't need no officer to tell me that. A lizard has legs."

Sonny nodded, then asked, "Are we gonna stay in your house?"

"Yup, that's the idea. I'm gonna put you to work, though. You gotta earn your keep."

"That's okay. I like to work."

"So, do I, but a lotta folks think it's a waste of time."

"Like my father," Sonny said.

"Sonny, what do you think of your father?"

The horses walked another hundred feet before he answered, "I ain't sure. He's my father, so I guess I gotta like him, but he sure don't like me, Mandy or our mama. Do you like him?"

For just a few horse steps, Ellis thought about deflecting the question but then replied, "No, sir. I'll admit that I don't. I was with him in the war and he was nothin' but trouble. There were a couple of times they almost hanged him, but they needed the bodies. I was his sergeant before they made me a sniper and he was a real troublemaker. I wasn't gonna tell you about it, but after what you just told me, I figured I had to be honest with ya."

"Did he try to hang that Yankee captain you talked about?"

"He was the one who started the lynchin'."

"I figured that might be the way of it. What happens when my father comes back?"

"Well, son, let's not worry about that now, okay. Let's get back and make your mama and sister two happy ladies. Then you and me will start puttin' the ranch back together. I need a good man to help me with that."

Sonny grinned and replied, "Okay."

"Now, just after we reach the northwest border of my ranch, we gotta stop, so I can dig up a buried treasure."

"*A treasure?* Do you have a map and everything?"

Ellis laughed and answered, "No, sir. I don't need a map,
'cause I'm the one who put it there. Remember the day I gave
you and Mandy that silver dollar?"

"Yes, sir. That was the best day ever!"

"Well, I had a bunch of other Yankee dollars that I left in a
bank up in Kansas, but I kept some with me, figurin' that if
there was a war, I'd need it. But I didn't want all of it in paper
money, so I got a thousand dollars in gold and buried it under
a rock. Nobody else in the whole world knows about it except
us. Well, the horses know about it too, but they ain't gonna tell
anybody."

Sonny laughed but was still excited about seeing a
treasure. This was turning out to be an exciting ride and it just
started!

————

Sara Mae had just finished washing the dishes and had set
them to dry before she picked up her mug of pseudo-coffee
and walked to the kitchen window. She'd moved the pistol to
the kitchen and put it on the counter near the sink.

She had borrowed Mandy's hairbrush and spent ten
minutes running it through her long brown hair and wished she
had one of the ribbons that Ellis had bought for Mandy. She
was wearing the yellow dress again because Ellis had told her
that she looked 'mighty handsome' when she wore it last and
now, wanted to keep impressing him. Her only questions were
how and when to suggest what she wanted.

She had been fantasizing about Ellis for years now and
here she was living in his home, but she wasn't sure that he'd
agree to becoming her husband-in-fact. Ellis simply was one
of those men who believed that things that were right were

right and if they weren't right, they were wrong. What she wanted to propose was definitely in the gray area, and her concern was that if she suggested that she join him in his bed, he'd see her as less honorable, and that was the last thing she wanted to happen. Then she amended that to the second worst thing she wanted to happen after she added the return of the man who'd married her ten years ago.

She knew that Ellis wouldn't be returning before noon, but she simply couldn't focus her mind on much else. She could almost visualize him riding from the northwest with Sonny beside him, but her rational mind told her that it wasn't going to happen.

"Mama, are you okay?" Mandy asked as she skipped into the kitchen.

Sara Mae turned around smiled and replied, "Yes, Mandy, I'm fine. I'm just anxious to see Sonny again."

"Can he be back so soon?"

"No, but I'm too excited to do anything else."

"Can you brush my hair, too? I like it better when you do it."

"Of course, I will. That will keep my mind busy, too," Sara Mae replied as she set her coffee cup down picked up the pistol and followed Mandy into her bedroom.

As she stroked the brush through Mandy's light brown hair, she wondered if a question about the new sleeping arrangements after Sonny was returned would be the way to make her suggestion. After all, Sonny had his own room now that he was nine, and she'd been sleeping in Ellis' room. She'd ask Ellis if he would want her to move out of his room to share a room with Mandy. Maybe, he'd be able to use the inconvenience as an excuse. It was a slim chance at best, but it was the best she could manage to conjure up.

———

Two hours ago, they'd stopped to rest the horses and let them graze and drink for ten minutes, but Ellis was going to make this return trip faster than the outbound journey. They were less than an hour from the rock where he'd hidden the gold, and he knew that it was extremely unlikely that anyone would have found his cache but was still a bit anxious to get it out of the ground.

Sonny had been talking almost non-stop about his life, but Ellis quickly noticed that they all revolved around his mother. He wasn't sure if Sonny was intentionally avoiding mentioning his father or just talking about the things he wanted to remember.

Ellis could see the High Hills and Fresh Water Creek in the distance and knew they were close.

"There's the corner of my ranch, Sonny!" Ellis shouted as he pointed at the western edge of the hills.

"We're almost at the treasure!"

"Yes, sir."

Twenty-five minutes later, Ellis pulled Tippy to a stop then dropped to the ground and waited for Sonny to dismount.

They wordlessly approached the big boulder then when they reached the rock, Ellis bent over picked up the smaller rock then tossed it aside before dropping to his heels.

He slid his big knife out its sheath on his gunbelt then slipped the tip into the earth until it stopped.

"Well, son, it's still there," he said as he withdrew the blade and slid it back into its sheath.

He used his fingers to pull away the few inches of dirt then after his fingers felt the soft leather, he grabbed the bag and pulled it free.

Sonny's eyes were like pie plates as Ellis untied the binding cord then dumped the sixty gold coins onto the Texas soil. Forty twenty-dollar double gold eagles and twenty ten-dollar gold eagles shone brightly in the sun as man and boy just gazed at them.

Ellis then held the bag open and said, "Well, Mister Keeler, time to go to work. Start droppin' them gold pieces back into the bag."

Sonny was grinning as he began to pick up the heavy coins and dramatically started dropping them into the dirty leather bag.

Ellis was surprised that the bag hadn't rotted through after more than three years underground but figured it was because it was so dry. The codes for the access to his bank account in Abilene were inside, too. They weren't very complex anyway.

Once the coins were safely stored again, Ellis put them into his saddlebags then they mounted for the final six miles to the house.

————

Sara Mae had resumed her watch through the window, but the heat finally made her drag two chairs to the back porch so

Mandy could join her in the slight, cooling breeze. At least there was the short porch overhead to keep away most of the blazing sun.

As they sat, Mandy asked, "Will Sonny be different now?"

The question startled Sara Mae. It had been almost eight months since Sonny had been taken by the Comanches and that was a long time for a boy his age. If Ellis found him, *what would he be like? Would he come back in buckskins and not be her little boy anymore?* He could have grown an inch or two by now, too.

She finally answered, "I don't know, sweetheart. He'll be bigger, I think."

"I know. I was just wondering if he was going to be, you know, different."

Sara Mae sighed and said, "We'll see when he gets here, Mandy. Mister White might not be able to find him. He could have run to Fort Madrid and is hiding there."

Mandy nodded then stood quickly pointed and shouted, "Here they come!"

Sara Mae had been looking at Mandy but whipped her head to the north then shot to her feet putting her hand above her eyes to block the bright afternoon Texas sun and saw a dust cloud coming from the northwest. It was much too large to be made by a single rider, so she kept her eyes focused on the distant cloud but thought about where she'd left the pistol. They could be Comanches.

Within a minute, she was able to make out the specks of two riders and her heart began to pound.

Mandy began to bounce as she exclaimed, "I see them! I see them!"

Sara Mae didn't want to give in to her hopes yet because she wasn't a seven-year-old girl and knew there was still a chance it wasn't Ellis bringing her son home but with each passing second that hope grew.

———

Ellis spotted the yellow dress long before they had been able to identify him and Sonny, and so had his sidekick. He had to tell Sonny to keep to the current pace as he expected that the boy wanted to race the tired gelding the last couple of miles.

"Always take care of your horse, Sonny. He's givin' you a ride, so you owe him some consideration."

"Yes, sir. I was just happy to see my mama again."

"When I tell you to go, you can run that gelding at a fast trot to get to the house. I'll stay slow a bit 'cause of the draft horses and that'll give you and your mama some time to get acquainted again."

"Is she really gonna be happy to see me?"

Ellis grinned at him and replied, "Son, you'd better be ready to be hugged and kissed like you was just a cute little girl. And don't you go makin' no fuss about it, either. You just let her know how much you missed her and Mandy, too. It ain't embarrassin' to show how you feel about 'em."

"Okay."

After another three minutes, they were close enough for Ellis to let them know who he was in case they hadn't figured it out yet, so he pulled off his hat and waved it high over his head before pulling it back on.

"They're waving back!" Sonny shouted and began to wave wildly.

Ellis couldn't help but smile at the boy and was looking forward to watching the reunion.

When they were about eight hundred yards out Ellis said loudly, "Go ahead, Sonny."

Sonny didn't reply but kicked the gelding into a fast trot and left Ellis behind as he kept Tippy and the two draft horses at a slow trot.

————

Ellis' hat wave had finally convinced Sara Mae that it was safe to let her emotions go and found herself chilled in the afternoon heat as she wrapped her arms around her and watched them approach.

Time was barely moving for her and she didn't even hear Mandy's excited chatter as Ellis and Sonny grew ever larger in their eyes.

Then Sonny's horse suddenly bolted away from Ellis and came racing toward the house. She noticed that he wasn't wearing buckskins and had short hair, so maybe he'd be her Sonny after all.

Sonny pulled the gelding to a stop and without using the stirrups, he hopped down from the saddle then tumbled to the ground before quickly popping back to his feet and racing onto the porch. He didn't wait for his mother to embrace him as he threw his arms around her waist.

"I'm home, Mama!" he exclaimed as she held his head to her chest.

Before she said a word, the expected kisses arrived, and Sonny didn't mind a bit.

After a few seconds of uncontrolled release, a teary Sara Mae said, "Thank God that you're safe, Sonny. I was so scared, and it had been so very long. Are you all right?"

"I'm fine, Mama. Uncle Rufus took me to the Comanche village and he and Silver Dove took care of me."

"Silver Dove?"

"That's his wife. She's really pretty and is gonna have his baby, too."

"Well, you can tell me all about it later. Mandy wants to welcome you home, too."

Sonny released his mother then turned to Mandy and surprised her when he hugged her too.

Sara Mae then looked across the Texas landscape to watch Ellis approach. She waved and smiled as he brought the horses closer to the house with her heart swelling with gratitude and love for the man who had already given her so much.

Ellis was already smiling and waved back as he kept the horses at a slow trot and soon reached the back of the house pulled Tippy to a stop then dismounted and stepped onto the porch.

"Thank you so very much, Ellis," she said as she gazed up at him with her big brown eyes.

"It was a real pleasure, Sara Mae. Sonny has a lot to tell ya and I have some news of my own, but I need to take care of the horses, so why don't you all head into the house and I'll be in shortly."

Sara Mae then surprised him when she stepped forward and hugged him tightly as she said, "I can never thank you enough, Ellis."

Ellis put his arms around Sara Mae, telling himself it was just because he had no other place to put them and replied, "You're very welcome, Sara Mae."

Sara Mae hadn't really planned to be so forward so soon, but for some reason, it had seemed not only appropriate but necessary. But once she had Ellis in her arms, those three years of enforced celibacy awakened long-dormant desires and caused her both distress and exultation in the experience. She felt that she was letting her intentions be known before even talking to him.

She stepped back and said, "I'm sorry for being so forward, but I was so grateful for having Sonny back that I lost all sense."

"No, that's all right, Sara Mae. I'll be honest enough to admit that I didn't mind it at all."

A relieved Sara Mae smiled and said, "We'll go inside now."

Ellis smiled back tipped his hat then replied, "Yes, ma'am," and left the porch to collect the four horses.

Sara Mae watched him step off the porch sighed then looked back at Sonny and Mandy, who were both staring at her then took their hands and walked back through the open door leaving the chairs for Ellis to bring back into the house.

Ellis led the horses to the trough chastising himself for allowing his own base urges to turn a simple expression of gratitude into something more than it was. She may not have a good man for a husband, but he was still her husband. The very idea made him gnash his teeth. He wanted that woman in the worst way and the cowardly bastard who had married her didn't even care if she lived or died.

Once he got the horses into the barn and began removing Tippy's saddle, he pushed those thoughts aside as he knew he needed to concentrate on getting the ranch back to a semblance of normal operation and how to deal with Jim Abigail.

Jim Abigail was a difficult issue because Ellis knew that he had no rights to do anything, but that wouldn't prevent him from setting things right. It would have to wait, though.

Then there was the whole question of the Big O. From what he'd been told, he'd married Mary Jo Orris and now was the owner of the Big O. The big question he really had about the Big O situation was Mary Jo herself. *Did she really agree to marry Jim Abigail? Did she really marry him at all? Did she really believe that her husband was dead?*

From what Sara Mae had told him, she didn't think Mary Jo even liked Jim Abigail, and he didn't think that Pete was dead, either. This whole episode stunk to high heaven.

With the new telegraph in Fort Madrid, he would have suspected that war news would reach the town much faster than it had before when it was dependent on the freighters and travelers from Henrietta. He still didn't think that Pete had been killed, mainly because he'd gotten word just eight months earlier about how he'd taken a serious shot to the gut.

They'd gotten the Minie ball out without any serious damage to his insides and he hadn't come down with an infection, which was almost miraculous considering the conditions in which they had become accustomed. As far as he knew, Pete had returned to the field just two weeks after being shot. He hadn't told Sara Mae yet because he really hadn't spent that much time talking to her. That would change now, and he'd want to find out more about the Big O, although any action would have to be delayed unless it was forced on him.

After unsaddling Sonny's horse, he set them into stalls, leaving only one open, but he'd put them in the corral soon anyway. He just needed to get some hay tomorrow when they made the supply run to Fort Madrid. He'd have to talk to Sara Mae about that, too.

He hefted his heavy, gold-laden saddlebags over his right shoulder and pulled his Henry and the Sharps from their scabbards before he left the barn and walked to the house. He still had his Yankee currency that he'd converted to smaller bills and change, so he wouldn't need the gold coins yet.

His original idea of being able to have money wired to him from his bank had been dashed when he realized that Ernie Smith probably didn't have any cash and what good would a wire transfer be for him, anyway. The gold would last him quite some time, but at least he could wire the bank in Abilene to ask for his balance. That would tell him that the bank was still running, and his money was still there.

Ellis hopped onto the porch, passed through the threshold and smiled at the three Keelers sitting around the table chatting. They stopped talking and turned their eyes to him as he leaned his rifles against the wall.

Sara Mae immediately stood walked to the cookstove and said, "I saved you some leftovers from last night's dinner. Sonny already finished his while he told us about what happened."

He hung his hat on a peg then replied, "That sounds good, Sara Mae. I appreciate it."

After dropping his saddlebags on the floor near the table, he took a seat then picked up the glass of water and drained it. He immediately had to stand up again, walk to the pump and fill it before returning to his chair.

Sara Mae set a bowl of chili with a piece of cornbread before him before sitting down.

Ellis took a bite of the chili, smiled and said, "This is mighty tasty chili, Sara."

"Thank you, Ellis."

He swallowed his chili then said, "Now that Sonny's back, I figure we can start makin' things better around here. Tomorrow we're gonna take the wagon into Fort Madrid and get some hay and supplies. Now everyone here, including my ornery self, could use some more clothes. We need a bunch of other things that houses need too, like kerosene, soap, and firewood. Sara Mae, when we get there, I need you to make sure that I don't forget anything."

"Are you going to barter with cattle? Mary Jo said that Ernie Smith doesn't take Confederate money at all anymore."

Ellis took another big bite of chili then reached into his pants pocket and pulled out the wad of Yankee currency and set it on the table.

He chewed for another few seconds swallowed then after swallowing a big gulp of water, he said, "Now there's about eighty dollars altogether right there. That'll take care of tomorrow and probably one more trip. But then, me and Sonny stopped and found some buried treasure on the ride back."

"*Treasure?*" Mandy shouted before her mother could react.

Ellis grinned and said, "Yes, ma'am," then pulled the saddlebags onto his lap, extracted the dirty leather sack then set the saddlebags back on the floor.

Sonny was already smiling and watching for his mother's reaction when Ellis opened the bag then dumped its contents on the table near the paper notes.

Sara Mae was stunned as she looked at the mound of gold coins that was more than all the money than she'd ever seen in her life combined.

"Where did you get it, Ellis?" she asked softly.

"Remember when I sold all my cattle before I left? Well, I had the bank in Abilene give me a thousand dollars in gold and some cash, but then I opened an account in the bank and left most of the money up there. I paid off the hands and left enough money with Jim Abigail to run this place for three years. Rufus told me that he's most likely got a good half of it with him now, probably aimin' to use it to buy the Slash W once he found out I was dead."

"Now that he knows you're alive, what will he do with it?"

"I got no idea, but I'm sure gonna keep an eye on him."

"Ellis, where can you keep that much money on the ranch?"

"If nobody knows it's here then it's not gonna be a problem, so none of us can ever talk about the gold until it comes out. As soon as I spend one of those coins, the word's gonna get out anyway, but the longer we can keep that from happenin' the better."

"I won't tell anybody," Sonny said loudly.

"Me neither," Mandy added.

Sara Mae then said, "Ellis, I haven't been to Fort Madrid in a long time and I don't know what they have there anymore. It could be gone now for all I know."

"Well, ma'am, I reckon we'll just have to find out what's there tomorrow. So, what you need to do is write out a list of what you need, and I'll handle the rest. Don't forget to remind me about them shotgun shells, either."

Sara Mae smiled and said, "Alright. But I don't have a pencil or anything else to write with."

"I have one in my room, but paper's a bit hard to come by. I have my parole paper, but I don't wanna start usin' it for anything but what it is. We don't need paper anyway. We can use an old board or a scrap of leather and buy some paper and pencils tomorrow. I'll head out to the barn shortly to see if I can find somethin' that works. I'll move the pouch of gold out there and I'll tell you where I put it. Okay?"

"Okay," Sara Mae answered with a smile that included both relief and a host of other emotions as she realized just how much Ellis was trusting her and making her feel like she was already a part of his life.

Ellis smiled back then began to eat his chili again. Sonny had already told his mother about his time with Rufus and the Comanches, but he hadn't mentioned the barn fight. He'd already told Ellis that he thought that he should be the one to tell his mother about the murder because it was so gruesome.

"Mama, can I talk to Sonny by myself now?" Mandy asked.

"Of course, dear, why don't you both go into your room."

"Okay," she replied then dropped to the floor and waited for Sonny to stand before walking with him into her room and closing the door while Sara Mae watched them leave with a smile.

"It's so wonderful having Sonny back. I had given up almost all hope of ever seeing him again, but then you returned, and I thought there was a chance even after eight months. Then I was worried he'd come back…well, different. But aside from being a bit taller, he's still my son and it's a joy that's hard to describe."

"I imagine so, Sara Mae. I can't imagine it myself, never havin' kids at all, but I can see how happy you were when you saw him again. It made me real happy, too. I told myself when I was in the Comanche village that I was gonna do all I could to help Sonny become a good man. Rufus helped a lot, and I aim to keep doin' that even if his father comes back."

Sara Mae looked at Ellis then said, "I don't want him to come back, Ellis. I know that sounds shameful and faithless, but it's how I feel. I've been married to that man for almost ten years and from the very start of the marriage, he's acted as if I was nothing but a maid or a loose woman. He ignored our children even before we came to the Big O, and once we were here, he spent more time with Pete and Mary Jo than he did with me and his children. More than that, I know what kind of man he is.

"He's a coward and a conniver. He barely talked to me, yet I know what he was hoping would happen when Pete said he was going to go with you. I think he was planning on sending me away and forcing himself on Mary Jo. He only left because Pete wasn't going to leave without him, and he wanted to get away from me and the children. I'm surprised he didn't desert to come back and try to take Mary Jo and the Big O."

Ellis said, "He did try and desert, at least twice that I know about. He was caught both times and almost got hanged the first time. It was only 'cause the colonel needed the bodies for cannon fodder that he didn't. The same thing happened the second time, but that meant he was watched a lot closer. I already told Sonny back at the Comanche village because he asked me if I liked his father, and I was honest with him.

"John always seemed to find a way not to be in the line of fire when we engaged the Yankees and never got a scratch. I swear he never got sick like most of us, either, but I can't figure out how he avoided that. It might have been 'cause he and a few of the other slackers made their own mash liquor."

"That sounds like something he'd do. When he did leave, I thought things would be better, and they were until Jim Abigail and Lou Gordon began spending so much time trying to attract Mary Jo."

"Tell me about that, Sara Mae. Did Mary Jo show any interest at all?"

"Well, you have to understand, Ellis, we were both lonely, but I had my children. Mary Jo had no one but me and it's not the same. She was friendly and maybe that encouraged them, but it wasn't her intent. She was just more outgoing than I was and didn't realize what trouble she was in until it was too late. But I don't think it would have mattered to Jim Abigail if she'd thrown a dirty diaper at him. They never looked at me, by the way."

"Why not? You're a handsome young woman."

"Thank you for saying that, but Mary Jo is younger, much prettier and has a nicer figure than I do. Plus, she didn't have any children. Anyway, I still don't think she realized how bad it had become until that day that they returned from Fort Madrid with the supplies and told her that Pete had died, then Lou quickly asked her to marry him before Jim did the same. That's what led to the knife fight."

Ellis asked, "Sara Mae, I just figured out why that story about Pete mighta come this way. Pete was shot in the gut just about that time but recovered pretty fast. I heard about it from some of the boys 'cause they knew we were from the same place. That's why I was kinda surprised to hear you say that Mary Jo was a widow and had married Jim Abigail. If Pete had been killed, I probably woulda heard about it."

"She was pretty devastated by the news, but after that, I was pretty much kept in the dark. Mary Jo didn't confide in me at all before they went off to Henrietta to get married."

"There's somethin' else there, too. I don't think they ever went to Henrietta. It's a long ride and I can't see 'em gettin' married quick and then comin' back right away."

"But they were gone for three days," Sara Mae protested.

"Yes, ma'am. They most likely trotted right over to this house and stayed here for a couple of days before goin' back.

Jim most likely enjoyed being private and all but didn't know where Rufus was or if he would come back, so he took Mary Jo back to the Big O and kicked you and your young'uns out."

"That all makes sense, but Sonny said that Rufus took care of your leather, but I never saw him."

"He never came back after he picked up Sonny, thinkin' that Jim Abigail would hurt Sonny, but wouldn't hurt you or Mandy. He was countin' on me comin' to get him when the war was over."

"Oh. I'm so very glad you're back early, Ellis."

"Me too, Sara Mae. Now let's go and hide the gold," he said as he scooped up the bills and non-gold coins, stuffed them into his pants pocket then slid the gold back into the leather bag.

He then rose waited for Sara Mae then they left the kitchen crossed the porch and headed for the barn.

"And ideas where we should hide the bag?" he asked as they strolled side-by-side.

"Well, it'll have to be someplace that's not obvious."

"Yes, ma'am, that's kind obvious."

Sara laughed then hooked her arm through his as they stepped across the hard ground.

Ellis wasn't about to object, but as they soon entered the barn, she released his arm and both began to scan the barn for hiding spots. It didn't take Ellis long to find the ideal location for their bank.

He handed the bag to Sara Mae then walked to the heavy anvil that was part of his makeshift smithy in the back corner of the right side of the barn. He bent his knees, slid his arms under the end of the anvil and with a loud grunt, he lifted the two hundred pounds of steel turned it two feet to his left and set it down gently on the floor.

"Lord, I miss those extra twenty pounds!" he exclaimed as he stood straight and stretched his back while Sara Mae watched closely.

He then lifted the loose heavy oak plank that supported the anvil and set it aside before taking a spade from the back wall and digging a small hole. Sara Mae handed him the pouch, then he set it into the barely large enough hole pulled the oak plank back into its original location then stood, took a deep breath and lifted the anvil back into position.

Once it was in place he blew out his breath rubbed his abused back then kicked the dirt around to cover the deep impression the anvil had made in the dirt.

"If they want the gold, they'll have to work for it and thieves don't like to work or they wouldn't be thieves in the first place."

Sara laughed and said, "When you have to get it out of there, I'll make sure you have those extra twenty pounds."

Ellis grinned and replied, "If you keep feedin' me so good, then I'll probably have a big belly that weighs twenty pounds on its own."

"I don't think so, Ellis. I think you'll always be a handsome man."

Ellis was close to blushing as he replied, "Now, Sara Mae, I figure you're just gettin' even for me tellin' you that you were a handsome young lady, but we both know better. That husband of yours is better lookin' than I am."

"But he's not a man," she answered before taking his arm again.

Ellis set a slow pace out of the barn leaving the doors open to get some air inside for the horses.

As they walked, Sara Mae asked, "Ellis, where will Sonny sleep now? I believe he's getting too big to sleep with Mandy."

"Can't Mandy sleep with you then?" he asked, afraid to mention the only other answer.

"I suppose that would work," answered a disappointed Sara Mae, but at least she hadn't made a more direct approach.

"I know I told you that I'd sleep in the house 'cause it was mine, but that was 'cause I was so anxious to be back in my own place again. But if you want to sleep in my room, I could move out to the bunkhouse."

"No, I'd rather you stay in the house. I'd feel safer with you close by."

Ellis smiled at Sara then nodded and replied, "Okay. I'll stay."

They entered the kitchen again and while Sara Mae prepared to make dinner, Ellis walked to his bedroom, found his stubby pencil then began looking for something to use as a replacement for paper. It didn't take long. He took off his Confederate sergeant's shirt, tossed it on the bed then opened the drawer and removed one of his clean, folded shirts and quickly put it on. As he did, he recalled the smiling face of Linda Harrison and surprised himself a bit when all he thought was that he hoped she found a husband who treated her well. As far as he was concerned, he was off the list of eligible bachelors. He'd probably have to wait until the end of the war to finalize Sara Mae's fate with John Keeler, but he believed she was worth the wait.

Once he was fully dressed again, he took Sara Mae's scissors from the saddlebags and began to snip at the shirt, removing both sleeves then cutting the broad remaining cloth into four sheets.

"Good enough," he mumbled to himself then set one down on the top of the dresser.

He started his own list to see how the pencil worked on the tired cotton and was pleased with the results. The light gray fabric made a good background and the pencil worked well as long as he didn't keep the point too sharp.

He added hay at the top of the list then shotgun shells and then of all things, chickens. He'd decided on the ride back as they passed the cattle herd, that he'd bring two cows that had recently calved back to the barn with their calves and share their milk. He could do that each spring as cows calved and be able to have fresh milk and butter for Sara Mae and the children. That had then triggered his idea about trying to add a few chickens to the ranch. He could let them run loose until he built a coop for them, but with the cow and chickens, they'd be able to have butter, milk and eggs for breakfast and the occasional chicken dinner. He decided that he'd hold off telling Sara Mae of his plans until tomorrow.

He stuffed his own list into his pocket then picked up the three remaining cloth sheets and left his room to find Sara Mae.

"I have some writing cloth and a pencil for your list, ma'am," he announced as he walked into the kitchen holding up the aforementioned items.

Sara Mae was already looking in his direction since she'd heard his footsteps and smiled at him as he entered.

"That looks like pieces of your shirt," she said.

"That's what it is, ma'am. I cut up my Confederate shirt and later tonight, my Confederate britches follow. The flat pieces work pretty good for writin' on, too."

Sara Mae then asked, "Ellis, could I have the sleeves with your sergeant's stripes?"

Ellis was surprised but replied, "Sure. They're in my room and I'll bring them out in a while."

She smiled before she said, "Thank you," then returned to cooking as Ellis set the sheets of cloth and the pencil on the counter near the sink and took a seat at the table watching Sara Mae.

"Sara Mae, Sonny told me what he saw in the barn when Jim and Lou had their fight and he said that Lou never had a knife in his hand. It was murder, pure and simple. That's why he ran. He figured that Jim had seen him and thought that he'd come after him, so he lit out. He was terrified."

Sara Mae quickly turned and asked, "Do you think that's true? Is Sonny in danger?"

"No, ma'am. I don't believe he is. When you're spyin' on somebody, you can see all of them, but they'd have to be real lucky to even see your eye. Trust me on that one. Sonny was just an eight-year-old boy and when Jim looked in his direction, to him, it was like Jim was starin' right at him. After we get back tomorrow and get everything put away, I'll head over there and let him know that Sonny's back. I'll give him some story about the Comanches takin' him away and bringin' him back 'cause they were movin' their village. I'll watch his eyes and see how he takes the news. I'll be able to tell."

"Can you talk to Mary Jo, too? I'm worried about her."

"If I can, but I got a feelin' that Jim don't want either of us talkin' to her. I'm not so sure she's with child, either, just from the way he told me and what you said. It wasn't like he was all happy about it. It was more like a way of sayin' that they were married and there was nothin' I could do about it. He didn't even smile, and I never saw any man who was tellin' one of the other boys that he was gonna be a papa and not be wearin' a big grin when he did it."

"I trust you to do it right, Ellis. You've done nothing but impress me since you've returned."

"That's 'cause I only been back a couple of days, Sara Mae. Give me a few more and you'll be wonderin' what kinda idiot you're sharin' a house with."

Sara Mae laughed and said, "I don't think that's about to happen, Mister White."

"Don't say I didn't warn ya, Mrs., I mean, Sara Mae."

Sara then smiled and said, "Thank you for not addressing me as Mrs. Keeler. As far as I'm concerned, my name is Sara Mae Lanigan. That man back near the Mississippi River isn't my husband anymore. One of these days, I'll have my children's names changed too if I can."

Ellis just nodded smiled back then stood and said, "I'm going back out to the barn and look around for some spare lumber. I know I had some before I left, but it mighta been used. I didn't bother lookin' in the loft when I was up there 'cause I was busy gettin' my Henry rifle."

"What do you need the wood for?" she asked.

"It's a surprise," he replied with a grin before leaving the kitchen, crossing the short back porch and heading for the barn.

Ellis had definitely not missed Sara Mae's statement about John not being her husband any longer, and he agreed that he didn't deserve to be. *But what difference would that be to him?*

He had stored a dozen eight-foot 1 x 12 boards in a stack in the dark northern edge of the loft, and if they were still there, and he was judicious in the use of the wood, he could build a chicken coop frame with it and maybe even a couple of nesting boxes for the hens to lay eggs. He'd just need some fencing and some nails. He had an idea about where to find the chickens, too. Ed and Mabel Anderson had a chicken farm before the war but wasn't sure they still had any of the birds, or if they even had a farm anymore.

He climbed the ladder to the loft and had to bend at the waist to get close enough to look under the eaves of the roof but spotted the boards. Now the question would be one of condition, so he slid the boards out one at a time and found that none had warped and would work well for the chicken coop after he split them into thinner strips. He could get three, eight-foot long 1 x 4s out of each of the board, but it would take a lot of cutting.

He left the boards where they were then after leaving the loft, he exited the barn and headed for the bunkhouse. He'd been back two days now and hadn't had a chance to see its condition. After being spoiled by the neatness of the house, he expected to be disappointed by what he found inside.

He swung the door open and saw the four bunks with bare mattresses and pillows, with the blankets folded neatly at the foot of each bunk. He wasn't sure if it was Sara Mae's work or Rufus had kept it so neat, but he sure was grateful. He planned on asking around sometime soon to see if he could hire a couple of old-timers who might want to be ranch hands again and having the bunkhouse ready for them would make it easier.

He walked inside, shook the hanging lamp and almost expected to find coal oil sloshing around inside, but it was dry as it should be after sitting there with the Texas heat evaporating the kerosene. He'd have to add lamp wicks to his own list when he returned to the house.

He then began taking off the blankets and then the pillows and placing them on the opposite bunk before yanking up the mattress to check underneath the wooden slats. It was more to make sure that no unwanted critters had decided to call the bunkhouse home than anything else, but he didn't find a snake or a furry animal in the first two, so he lowered the mattresses, moved all of the blankets and pillows from the other two, then lifted the two mattresses on the second set, again finding nothing moving, but did find something else.

Carved into one of the wooden slats was a short note from Rufus.

SONNY WITH ME IN COMANCHE CAMP

Ellis smiled lowered both mattresses then set the blankets and pillows back in place before leaving the bunkhouse and closing the door to keep out the snakes that weren't there yet.

No wonder Rufus hadn't been that surprised to see him. He'd never mentioned the carved message and assumed it was because Rufus thought that he'd found it. It didn't matter in the end, but it was just another instance of what a good man he was and what a mistake Ellis had made when he appointed Jim Abigail as his foreman.

When he entered the house, he found both children sitting at the table, and Mandy was talking to her mother. She stopped when Ellis passed through the doorway and Sara Mae turned to look at him.

"Did you find your boards?"

"Yes, ma'am. It reminded me of a couple of things that I need to add to my list, so I'll borrow the pencil for a few seconds."

He walked to the counter picked up the pencil then sat next to Sonny, pulled his cloth list from his pocket and added nails, wicks and grease to the list then replaced the pencil and stuffed his list back into his left pants pocket.

"Are we coming tomorrow, Uncle Ellis?" asked Mandy.

"Oh, I think we might have room for two more on that driver's seat, unless you'd rather stay here and keep all the rattlesnakes away."

Mandy shook her head rapidly and answered, "No, sir. I was just asking."

"I was just funnin' with ya, Mandy. Even if you said you wanted to stay and play with all of the horned frogs, we'd still be takin' you with us."

"Are there really rattlesnakes, Uncle Ellis?" asked Sonny, taking a cue from Mandy.

Ellis was a bit surprised and asked, "You ain't never seen one? They're all over the place. I saw three of the big ones on the way back from the Comanche village, but figured you didn't care 'cause you'd seen 'em before."

"No, sir. We never went very far past the house. That's why we were so excited to see that horned frog when you first got back."

"Well, you gotta be careful when you get further away from the house. Don't go stickin' your hand where you can't see and if you hear rattlin', look for the snake and slowly back away. He's only warnin' ya that you're too close and as long as you don't get any closer, you'll be okay."

"I hope I don't see one," Mandy said.

"That's not very likely, sweetheart. As long as you know how they act, you don't have anything to worry about."

"Okay, but I still don't want to see one," she replied.

The three-way discussion about snakes, coyotes and wolves continued while Sara prepared dinner and just listened to Ellis as he talked and listened to her children. He'd been back two days and had already spent more time talking to her and her children than John had in the last two years.

The longer she was with Ellis, the more hopeful she was that she never saw her husband's face again and that she would soon join Ellis in the first bedroom.

———

The rumors were flying through John Keeler's regiment about a pending move across the Mississippi in a few days, and he, Hick Smith, Eustice Smothers, and Al Hartman began to seriously set their plans in motion for their desertion. What made the possibility of success greater was the arrival of several long boats to transport the troops across the river.

They were all tied to the southern bank of the nearby Red River and even had their oars on the floors of the boats. They were normally crewed by eight men at the oars, but that was because they'd each be carrying heavy loads of soldiers and supplies. Four men would be able to row against the Red River current without too much problem. With the food that they'd start accumulating, John figured they'd make their escape from the war tomorrow night and row all the way to where the Fresh Water Creek emptied into the Red River. Then it would just be a five or six mile walk to the Slash W where they would find all that money that Ellis White had left behind. If Jim Abigail, Lou Gordon and that colored hand were still there, well, too bad. Each of his boys would have his rifle with him and be able to make short work of all of them. After all, they were hardened veterans and those three were just regular, stay-at-home cowboys.

———

Pete had heard the same rumors of the pending engagement and had asked his captain if they were true. After he'd received official confirmation, he then returned to his tired bunch of men and passed the word. In three days, they'd cross the Mississippi to engage the tail end of Yankee General Banks' army.

After briefing his men, Pete walked to his tent to write a letter to Mary Jo. He hadn't heard from her in months but had only posted one letter to her during that time himself. It was time to write to her and let her know of his sudden, morose belief that this next engagement would be last. He'd been fortunate since that gut wound and almost believed it was nothing more than a warning and that the next time, he wouldn't be so lucky.

He wrote:

My Darling Mary Jo,

In three days, we cross the Mississippi to engage a much more powerful Union army in what I know now is a lost cause. I should have listened to Ellis before I followed this foolhardy path and still be with you and maybe we'd have a child by now. In some ways, I don't regret my decision, but they are far outweighed by how much I miss you.

I know this sounds terribly morose, but I don't think I am going to survive this next battle. I haven't had this feeling before, and maybe it's just because I took a belly wound and survived. I don't know. But if I leave you a widow, I want you to understand how much I love you and will always treasure the days we spent together.

I hope I'm wrong, my love, and will soon be returning to you to embrace you and feel the softness of your lips again. It is what has sustained me though the long months since I left your side.

If I do fall, please don't mourn for me to the exclusion of living your life. I heard that Ellis has been hanged, but then the rumors started arriving that he'd been paroled, so if he does come back, seek him out and ask him to care for you. He's a good man and will treat you as you deserve to be treated. I know he's sweet on Sara Mae, and if he was smart, he should act like John was dead and keep her as his wife, but he can keep you safe, too.

But no matter what happens, always think of me with the same deep affection that I have always held for you. This war cannot last much longer, and I will do all I can to stay safe so that I may return to you. You are the center of my world, Mary Jo, and if I don't come back to you, I will be waiting for you in the joy of the next life where I will never leave you.

Your Loving Husband,

Pete

Pete read his completed letter then carefully folded it and addressed the outside. They had no envelopes but had glue that they could use to seal the paper before posting it. He knew that there was only about a fair chance that his letter would reach the Big O but wanted Mary Jo to hear from him at least once more.

He left his tent then posted the letter before getting his plate and cup and joining the chow line.

———

After they'd finished dinner, Ellis helped Sara Mae with the cleanup while the children went outside to see if there were any rattlesnakes nearby.

"Are you going to give me a hint about what you're going to do with the boards now, Ellis?" she asked as she smiled at him.

"I suppose I'll tell you the whole plan as you'd figure it out soon enough anyway. When we get into Fort Madrid tomorrow, I want to see if I can buy some chickens. I needed to see if those boards were still there to build a chicken coop behind the barn. That way we'd have eggs anytime we wanted, and we'd let some chicks hatch, too."

175

"That's a wonderful idea!"

"Then the second part was that the day after we get back, I was going to ride out to the herd and bring back a couple of cows with their young calves, so we'd be able to share the milk with their young'uns and have fresh milk and butter, too."

"Why, Mister White, you astound me! With my potatoes and onions, we'd be almost self-sufficient."

"That's the idea, ma'am. Each year, I'd just bring those two cows back to the herd and borrow another pair. While we're at Fort Madrid, we can see if they have other kinds of seeds for vegetables, too."

Sara Mae may have been pleased with the idea of fresh milk, eggs and vegetables, but she was much more pleased when Ellis had casually added the 'next year' into the mix.

"That all sounds so perfect."

"I'm glad you're happy, Miss Lanigan. You deserve better treatment than you and the children have been gettin'."

Sara looked into his dark brown eyes, smiled and said softly, "Thank you, Ellis, for everything."

Ellis shared the look, smiled back and just managed a nod.

The moment was interrupted when Sonny and Mandy flew into the kitchen and Sonny yelled, "I saw one! I saw a rattlesnake!"

"Me, too!" exclaimed Mandy.

"Where was he?" asked Ellis as he turned, walked to the wall and snatched his unused Henry.

176

"I'll show you," Sonny said before he turned and trotted onto the porch.

Ellis didn't care so much about the snake's presence but shooting the reptile would serve two purposes: he'd test the rifle's accuracy after its long storage, and they'd have fresh meat.

Sonny waited for Ellis to leave the porch and they began to walk as Sara Mae and Mandy stepped onto the porch but stopped to watch.

Ellis kept his eyes peeled as Sonny walked northeast and he soon spotted the snake about sixty feet away as it lay coiled behind a big rock. It wasn't making any noise, but it was watching them and flicking its forked tongue to smell their presence. The snakes also had a way of sensing the heat of their prey or any threats with pits on their faces. Ellis wasn't sure that they worked all that well in the heat that was present right now, but he had no intention of getting close enough to find out.

"Sonny, stay about six feet to my left and a bit behind me."

"Okay."

They stepped another ten feet before snake began his warning rattle. Ellis immediately stopped, glanced to his left to make sure that Sonny was where he expected him to be then raised his Henry levered in its first cartridge then set his iron sights on the big snake's head. He guessed this one was almost six feet long and that meant he was seriously dangerous.

He let out his breath and squeezed the trigger.

The Henry cracked as it spat out its .44 caliber round and the bullet crossed the forty-eight feet in an instant, exploding the big viper's head before the rest of the body collapsed on itself.

"Wow! You got him!" exclaimed Sonny.

"Yes, sir. This is a mighty fine firearm. I was kinda worried about it sittin' so long, but it sure shoots good."

"Now what?"

"Now, young man, we go and get that snake and I'll slice him up for the meat. I'll give you the rattle as a present for findin' him, too."

Sonny grinned as they began to walk to the snake.

Sara Mae and Mandy watched as Ellis reached down and pulled up the monstrous reptile, turned and held it high to them with a big smile.

Neither Sara Mae nor Mandy returned his smile and were both a bit surprised when he and Sonny headed back, and Ellis still had the snake in his hand.

When they were close, Sara Mae asked, "Why are you bringing the snake?"

"The meat is really good. I've had it before and sure woulda liked some when we were in Louisiana. Whatever they were feedin' us wasn't close to bein' this tasty. I'm gonna give Sonny the rattle, too."

"Are you sure that you're not just saying that as a joke?"

"No, ma'am. It's no joke. You'll see."

"If you say so, Ellis, but Mandy and I will be going back inside now."

Ellis nodded as both hands were full then he and Sonny headed for the bunkhouse.

"How come we're not gonna cut it in the barn?" he asked.

"The smell would spook the horses. I'll show you how it's done, but I need you to go to the kitchen and ask your mama for a tin plate and a cuttin' board."

"Okay," Sonny replied before racing to the house.

Ellis reached the bunkhouse set down the Henry then opened the door then snatched the repeater and entered the bunkhouse. He leaned the rifle against the wall and dropped the snake's carcass onto the floor. It was a big boy, about five and a half feet in length. It was the biggest he'd ever seen and was a bit surprised that he'd missed it, but he had been gone for three years.

Sonny returned with the plate and cutting board, so Ellis pulled out his big knife and showed him how to remove what was left of the head, the rattle and tail then skin the snake, remove the spine and peel off the valuable skin. He finally sliced up the meat and put them onto the tin plate.

When he was finished, he handed the long rattle to Sonny, who grinned and immediately began to shake it. Ellis left the skin on the floor, pinning the corners under the bunk footings, picked up the head, tossed it out the door as far as he could, then picked up the plate of meat and his Henry.

"Okay, son, let's bring this meat into the house."

"Yes, sir," Sonny said as he finally stopped playing with his rattle and slipped it into his pocket.

As they left the bunkhouse, Sonny closed the door and Ellis kicked the snake's head as far away from the structure as possible. He figured a coyote would snatch it soon enough.

When they entered the kitchen, Ellis set the Henry against the wall and showed the big pile of rattlesnake meat to Sara Mae.

"This'll keep for a day or two if I throw some salt on it, so I figure it'll be nice and tender when we get back tomorrow."

Sara looked at the lean meat and thought as long as she didn't spend too much time recalling its source, she'd be able to eat some.

"Okay."

Ellis then sprinkled some salt on the fresh meat, moving the pieces around to make sure they all were coated then dropped the meat into a pot before he covered it with the top and carried it into the cold room. The cold room was only about fifteen degrees cooler than the rest of the house, but it was a big difference to the food that was stored inside.

With everything settled, all that remained was for Sara Mae to finish her list and then they'd prepare for tomorrow's trip into Fort Madrid. They had all taken seats at the table to talk about the lists when the topic suddenly changed.

Mandy asked, "Mama, am I sleeping with Sonny?"

"No, sweetheart, you'll be sleeping with me now. Sonny's getting to be a big boy and needs his own bed."

"But I'm getting big, too, Mama," she complained.

Sara Mae glanced at Ellis for a heartbeat then looked back to her daughter and replied, "We're just guests here, Mandy. I'll be able to give you hugs if you have a nightmare, too."

Mandy was satisfied with her mother's reply and nodded as she replied, "It okay, then."

Ellis had caught the glance and was a bit irked by Sara Mae's comment about being 'just guests', and said, "You're not guests, Sara Mae. You belong here now. You've lived here for the past eight months while I was back east. You took care of the house and made it nicer than when I left it. This is your home."

Sara Mae smiled at Ellis then replied, "I'm sorry, Ellis. I was just trying to explain things to Mandy. I know you've made us feel like family after just two days."

"I'm sorry too, Sara Mae. I shouldn't have taken it wrong. I just was kinda worried you'd think that you, Sonny and Mandy were just visitin' and didn't matter to me at all."

She asked softly, "Do we matter to you, Ellis?"

"Now, that, ma'am, is a loaded question, don't you think?" he asked in return before saying, "I think we might need to take a walk, Sara Mae."

She nodded and said, "Sonny, we'll be right back," then stood as Ellis rose.

Ellis followed Sara Mae out of the kitchen and across the porch, still trying to find the right way of answering her question.

Once they reached the packed dirt behind the house, Ellis stuffed his hands into his pockets and Sara crossed her hands on the small of her back as they began to stroll.

"Sara Mae, this is kinda hard for me 'cause I'm not very good with words, but first off, I do want to tell you that you and Sonny and Mandy matter an awful lot to me and have for longer than I can say. I'll even be honest enough to tell you that for some time, I been breakin' the tenth commandment and covetin' my neighbor's wife. Now I ain't exactly a religious feller, but the way I look at it, feelin' that way and doin' anything about it is two different things. I never could figure out why the Bible says that just thinkin' somethin' is a sin."

Sara didn't look at Ellis as she walked alongside him but hearing him say that he coveted her was a revelation in the extreme and almost created goosebumps in the heat of a late Texas spring day.

"Anyway, I never said anything 'cause it wasn't right, but I felt real bad for the way John treated you and those two short folk. When we were in camp and I heard him talkin' about you and them like you were like rocks holdin' him down or worse, it really riled me somethin' fierce. A man like that doesn't deserve a good woman like you, and he sure doesn't deserve to be around your children. I'll even be more honest and tell you, Sara Mae, that you are the most woman I ever met."

Sara laughed lightly and said, "I hardly think so, Ellis. I'm nowhere near as pretty or as comely as Mary Jo and I'm sure that the woman you met in the laundry was prettier, too."

"That ain't what I meant, Sara. I said you were the most woman and I meant it. You're just talkin' about the outside, but you're smart, honest, real nice to talk to, and you have a deep heart that can hold more love than anybody else I ever met. It's like the difference between what makes a man a man. Now your husband is probably better lookin' than I am, and I know he's not so skinny, either. He's younger than I am, too. But I don't figure he's anywhere close to bein' the man I am, and that's not braggin', it's just the way it is."

"I agree with you about John, Ellis. And I'll confess something to you, too. From almost the first time I met you, I knew that I'd married the wrong man. Each time we talked, that gap between you and the man that shared my bed widened. Now it's a chasm and I feel somewhat ashamed to admit that I hope he never returns."

"I been hopin' the same thing, Sara Mae, but I'm pretty sure he's gonna finish this war without a scar to prove he was in it. He might even try desertin' again."

"Would he come back here?"

"I ain't so sure. There ain't any reason for him to make that long ride or walk unless he had somethin' pullin' him back."

"And it certainly isn't me or the children, is it?"

"No, Sara Mae, it ain't. But back to your question. After all I just said, if you can't figure out how much you and Sonny and Mandy matter to me, then you ain't nearly as smart as I figured you were."

"I don't have to be that smart to understand that you do, Ellis."

"Good."

Sara Mae then asked softly, "Then where am I sleeping tonight?"

Ellis looked down at the ground said, "Sara, can we keep it the way we figured for a while? I need to get a handle on things a bit better, but it don't mean that I don't want it to change. I just need a few days. Is that okay?"

Sara smiled then nodded and replied, "Yes, Ellis, it's okay, and I understand. I'm really not a brazen woman, but it's been so long."

Ellis exhaled sharply and said, "Thank you, Sara Mae, and I don't think you're a brazen woman at all. Like I said, you're the most woman I ever met, and just to let you know, it's probably been a lot longer for me."

They made a wide turn back toward the house as Sara smiled slightly and asked, "Really? Would it be too bold to ask how long?"

"The way we been talkin', I figure it's not that bold at all. Let me do some quick figurin'," he replied as they continued to stroll.

After a few more steps, Ellis said, "Six years, six months and three days."

Sara laughed and asked, "Why so exact? I was expecting something like 'about five years or so'."

"It was in Henrietta and it was New Year's Eve. I took all the boys to town to have a party and we all enjoyed the favors of some of the ladies."

"You've never been to visit them in Fort Madrid or those camp followers I heard about?"

"No, ma'am. The whores in Fort Madrid are kinda, well, not healthy. The camp followers weren't any better. I saw too many of the other boys with all sorts of bad things on their privates for visitin' those women."

"This has been a very enlightening walk, Ellis," Sara Mae said as they approached the porch.

"That, ma'am, is the honest-to-God truth, but I'm real happy we talked the way we did, too."

"So, am I. We'll have to do this often."

"I think that's a good idea, Sara Mae."

Just before they stepped onto the porch, Sara Mae looked at Ellis, smiled then said, "It's going to be a long, difficult wait, Ellis."

Ellis returned her smile then nodded and said, "Amen to that, ma'am."

They entered the kitchen, and Sara Mae crossed to the opposite side took down one of the pieces of gray cloth and the pencil then sat down and said, "Okay, let's get working on this list."

———

That night, as Ellis lay on top of is blankets in the warm Texas night, he thought about Sara Mae lying in her bed in the next room. It was driving him to distraction, and he kept trying to focus on what they would be doing tomorrow, but it didn't matter. As he told Sara Mae, she and the children are all that mattered.

But Sara Mae's obvious suggestion to join him in his bed had pushed his moral dilemma to the front of his mind. He wanted her to be here with him, but that damned piece of paper making her John's wife still gnawed at him. *Why couldn't he just get past it as most men would?* It wasn't as if he just lusted after Sara Mae. He knew he loved her completely and she owned his heart, mind and soul. It was the rest of him that was causing the problem.

But even with his tortured state of mind, he was able to finally drift off to sleep.

———

Sara Mae, as she lay in her bed with Mandy tucked in close, wasn't so lucky as she had no other mental distractions now. All she could think about was Ellis. She'd told him how lonely she'd been, but she didn't dare to say how much and how long she had really desired for him to be with her. It might make him reshape his opinion of her as a good woman.

Now he was back and sleeping right nearby, but unlike Ellis, knowing that John was still alive and still her husband made no difference to her at all. Even now, she seriously thought of fulfilling one of her fantasies and sneaking into his bedroom, undressing then curling up beside him and feeling his skin pressing against her. She closed her eyes and shivered with the thought, but still stayed in the bed with Mandy. She simply didn't know how much longer she could keep her desires in check.

Sara Mae didn't fall asleep until almost one o'clock in the morning as she continued to let her mind imagine what it would be like if she were just one room away.

CHAPTER 6

Ellis had the two draft horses in harness by eight o'clock. He'd rolled the wagon out of the barn a few feet to see if the wheels needed greasing and wasn't surprised that they seemed okay, at least for today's trip.

After pulling the wagon to a stop before the back porch, he pulled the hand brake, hopped down then trotted onto the porch and entered the kitchen.

"The wagon's waitin', folks," he said loudly to the empty room.

"We're coming!" Sara Mae shouted from her bedroom as Sonny walked into the kitchen.

"Do you wanna drive the wagon for a bit, Sonny?" he asked.

"Can I?"

"Beats me. Can you?" Ellis asked with a grin.

"I never did before. Is it hard?"

"No, sir. You just drive them two horses using the reins like you do when you're ridin', only it's a lot slower."

Sonny was all grins and nodded as Sara Mae and Mandy stepped out from the hall.

Ellis smiled at Sara Mae and said, "Okay, ladies, let's head to Fort Madrid. I hope it's still there."

He followed Sara Mae and the children outside, closed the door and helped Sara Mae onto the driver's seat and then gave an assist to Mandy but let Sonny climb up on his own.

After clambering into the seat beside Sara Mae, Ellis released the brake and flicked the reins.

Once they were underway, Mandy asked, "Are we going to sing this time, Uncle Ellis?"

"Absolutely, ma'am. What would you like to sing first?"

"Can we sing Mustang Gray?" she asked as she looked past her mother to Ellis.

"Okay, ma'am. It's your choice, so you start first."

Mandy smiled and began singing, "There was a brave old Texan, they called him Mustang Gray…"

Everyone else joined in as the wagon trundled southeast toward Fort Madrid.

———

Eleven songs and two hours later, it was a happy group that rolled the wagon into the settlement that Ellis quickly noticed had actually added a couple of buildings rather than lose any.

"It looks bigger than I thought," Sara Mae said as she scanned the structures.

"It's bigger than when I left, so that's a good thing. We'll go to the Ernie's store first."

As they rolled closer, Ellis spotted the telegraph line which ended at the original sutler's store, but now had a sign that said SMITH'S DRY GOODS AND SUNDRIES. Ernie had been making improvements. He could see foot traffic and a couple of wagons and one rider, but no one he recognized.

He had let Sonny drive the wagon the last mile or so and watched as he leaned back, pulled the reins taut and shouted, "Whoa!", bringing the team to stop. Ellis then watched as the boy pulled the handbrake to its locked position.

"You did a good job, Sonny," he said, "I figured you might forget about the handbrake."

Sonny smiled at him and replied, "Thank you, Uncle Ellis."

Ellis hopped down, helped Sara Mae and then Mandy down and when everyone was on the ground, they stepped onto the storefront boardwalk and headed inside.

No sooner had he cleared the doorway when Ernie Smith spotted Ellis and shouted, "Well, glory be! Is that you, Ellis?"

Ellis grinned, walked to the counter and shook Ernie's hand.

"Yes, sir. Got myself caught by some Yankee pickets a couple of weeks ago and they didn't want to waste any prisoner camp space on me, so they give me my parole."

"You back in your ranch now?"

"Yes, sir. I have Mrs. Keeler and her young'uns stayin' with me, too. They was there when I arrived and I ain't about to send 'em away."

Ernie smiled at Sara Mae and said, "Mornin', ma'am."

Sara returned his smile and replied, "Good morning, Mister Smith."

C.J. PETIT

Ellis turned to Sara and said, "Sara, why don't you start browsin' and see if you can find some clothes and anything else you forgot to put on your list."

"We'll do that, Ellis," she answered then guided her children down the surprisingly well-stocked aisles that had even more than what he'd seen in Henrietta.

Ellis had been almost stunned to see just how much was available way out here in West Texas, but he needed to talk to Ernie.

Ernie watched them leave then asked, "What happened to her husband, Ellis?"

"He's still out there, Ernie, and I don't mind tellin' you that I was ashamed to have that man in our brigade. I was his sergeant and he tried desertin' twice, struck an officer and was caught making his own mash. Every time the bullets started flyin', he was nowhere to be found. For a good woman like Sara Mae to be married to a man like that makes my blood boil."

"You get shot at all?"

"Twice, but not too bad," he replied then said, "Ernie, I notice that you got a telegraph now. Do you have an operator?"

"Yup. You're lookin' at him. The key sits right at the back of the counter. We don't get a lot of messages, though."

"Well, I need to send a telegram to a bank in Kansas and ask how much money I got up there. Can we do that?"

"Sure. It'll take a day or two to get a reply, though."

"That's okay. I'll do that shortly. Now my next question is how do you get paid? Confederate money ain't worth that much anymore and I was told that you don't even take it anymore. Folks have been tellin' me that everybody's barterin', but I have some Yankee money, too."

Ernie smiled and said, "I'll take Confederate money, but like you said, it ain't worth much these days. Yankee money is more'n welcome, but most folks do some tradin'."

"I'll be payin' with Yankee cash, Ernie. I have two lists for you. It's a pretty big order, so let me know how much it's gonna cost."

"I'll do that," he replied, then leaned forward and dropped his voice to a conspiratorial level as he said, "Ellis, I kinda need your help with somethin' that's been botherin' me for months now."

"What is it, Ernie?"

"Well, you probably know about how Mrs. Orris and your foreman got hitched after somebody said that her husband died."

"Yup, I heard, and I ain't all that sure it's not some kinda monkey business, either."

"That's what's got me bothered, see. About two months after they got hitched, I got a letter from Pete Orris for her. I figured at first it had been lost and then found again, but Pete had put the date on the back, and it was only two weeks old. I held it here for a couple of days and then Jim Abigail come by for supplies and picked it up, sayin' he'd give it to her. He was her husband, so I had to give it to him, but I felt kinda sick about it. I don't figure he ever did give it to her, either."

"I never did figure that Pete died. I heard when he took a gut shot about that time that the word came back here that he'd been killed, but nobody ever told me he was killed, and they woulda."

"Can you handle this for me, Ellis? I don't know what to do."

"I'll take care of it, Ernie. Don't worry about it. I already got a problem with what happened in a fight with Lou Gordon. He stabbed Lou, but Lou didn't have his knife in his hand. That's murder, Ernie, but I need to get him to admit to it before I take care of him. If you get another letter from Pete, hold it and don't let Jim Abigail know about it. Okay?"

Ernie exhaled then nodded and said, "Thanks, Ellis. That takes a load off my mind."

"Good. Now, here's those lists. I also want to pick up a few chickens. You wouldn't have any, would ya?"

"Nope, least ways not many live ones. But you know the Andersons?"

"Yup. They got that farm just south of town and a bit east, but I wasn't sure that they still had any chickens."

"Well, they lost their cattle a couple of years ago and just got the chickens now, and a lot of 'em. They bring me eggs to sell and I know they got a whole passel of the birds. Once a every two weeks, Mrs. Anderson brings some of the birds for the butcher, too."

"Thanks, Ernie."

Ernie looked at Ellis' list and didn't say that there were any problems with filling it, so Ellis walked down the aisle and found Sara Mae looking at dresses. The children were already two aisles over.

She smiled at him as he approached and then when he was close, she said, "My yellow dress cost over two dollars three years ago, but the price tags have two amounts. This dress is four dollars and fifty cents in Confederate dollars, but only forty cents in Union money."

"I guess we'll be able to fill the whole order after all. You make sure you get what you want, Sara Mae. I'm kinda surprised that Ernie's got such good stock, and I have a feelin' that he's got a black-market supplier down south. I ain't gonna complain, though."

"Neither am I."

Ellis decided not to tell her about Pete yet, but picked out two pairs of britches, three shirts and some underpants before returning to the counter, setting them down then returning to do his own browsing. He picked up three pads of paper, a dozen pencils, two chalkboards and a big box of chalk so he wouldn't have to cut up any more shirts and also added a copy of *McGuffey's Reader*.

He found things that were rare, and almost giggled when he found a box of privacy paper near the soaps. He hadn't seen it in over three years. The biggest surprise was when he spotted sacks of honest-to-God coffee. He even found some tea for Sara Mae. As Sara Mae had mentioned earlier, everything had two prices and the difference on the foodstuff was bigger than that on the dress that she'd shown him.

When they'd finished loading the wagon, the total for the enormous order was $46.89 in Yankee dollars, which Ellis gladly paid. They left enough room for some hay, which he'd already paid for as it was next door in Ernie's feed and grain

193

store, as was the bag of oats, some vegetable seeds, and a bag of chicken feed.

He then sent his telegram to the First National Bank in Abilene to verify his current balance.

After having a nice lunch at Ernie's Café, they drove to the feed and grain store where he picked up his hay, oats, seeds and chicken feed. He had to pay another three dollars for the chicken wire fencing and a dozen two by four boards that he was happy to find.

Before they left Fort Madrid, Ellis stopped at the bakery for a bag of cookies, bread, and a huckleberry pie. Sara Mae said she could do the baking, but Ellis said it she'd be busy enough over the next day just getting all the things put away, and she had thanked him for his consideration.

After a stop at Ernie's butcher for a ham, two slabs of bacon and some sausages, Ellis dropped off his old boots at the cobbler who shared space with the blacksmith.

As the almost overloaded wagon rolled out of Fort Madrid, Ellis still had twenty-three dollars left of his original stash of cash from the cattle sale four years ago. He felt much better about their situation now that he understood how well-stocked Ernie Smith's little settlement was. In a few days, he'd be back for the chickens after he built the coop then check for a reply from the bank and see about finding those ranch hands.

"Well, Sara Mae, that was quite a surprise. Real coffee is in that wagon bed and some tea, too."

"I can't believe I was able to buy so many clothes for Sonny and Mandy. They've never had so much before."

"You better have bought some for yourself, too, ma'am."

194

"Oh, I did. I bought three new dresses and two new nightdresses. I even bought a new pair of shoes."

"Good for you. Did you see that Ernie even had privacy paper?"

"I noticed."

Sonny said, "Mama bought me a nightshirt. I never had one before. Do you wear a nightshirt, Uncle Ellis?"

Ellis looked at Sonny and replied, "No, sir. Never have."

Sara Mae glanced at him and asked, "No? What do you wear to bed, may I ask?"

Ellis grinned at her and replied, "Exactly what I was wearing when I came into this world. I had to sleep in my uniform for most of the nights for the past three years and I ain't about to go back."

"Then I'll be sure not to enter your bedroom uninvited," Sara Mae said with a smile.

"No, ma'am."

"I have a nightdress too, Uncle Ellis, just like mama's, only smaller," Mandy said, needing to join the conversation.

"You'd be pretty even if you was wearin' a burlap sack, Mandy," Ellis said as he leaned forward to look past Sara Mae.

Mandy smiled then sat back in the seat.

"You know, Sara Mae, I think it might be a good idea to find a buckboard. The wagon is good for heavy haulin', like this big order, but it's kinda slow. I know where I can get one for a good price and we have the horses. It'd give us enough room for some shoppin', but we'd get to Fort Madrid a lot faster."

"That would be wonderful. I could make the trip myself, couldn't I?"

"Yes, ma'am, as long as you kept the shotgun close by."

The rest of the trip back to the ranch was spent talking about the marvelous things that were piled behind them. Ernie Smith may have been getting supplied by shady methods, but however he managed to fill his shelves was a real boon to Ellis and his newfound family.

By the time Ellis rolled the wagon to a stop behind the house, it was late in the afternoon and he knew he had a lot of work ahead of him.

"Okay, folks, let's get this wagon unloaded," he said as he hopped onto the ground then helped Sara Mae and Mandy down.

It was a group effort to remove all of the supplies. Ellis handled the heavy items, like the barrel of flour, but everyone pitched in with gusto, rediscovering items that they'd forgotten about.

When all of the household items were stacked in the kitchen, Ellis said, "I'll move the wagon over to the barn and unload the rest."

"I'll put your new clothes away, Ellis, but I won't leave any notes," Sara Mae said as she began to stack tins of food onto the pantry shelves.

Ellis raised his eyebrows but didn't say anything when he saw her laughing eyes.

"Can I help you with the rest?" Sonny asked.

"You figure I was gonna make you help the womenfolk? You come along, son. We got man's work to do."

Sonny grinned and trotted out the door behind Ellis as his mother watched with a smile on her face.

After rolling the wagon the two hundred feet to the barn, Ellis and Sonny began to remove the last of the wagon's contents. Sonny was limited to what he could carry, but Ellis let him push his strength, so he knew that he was doing real work.

"When are we gonna build the chicken coop, Uncle Ellis?"

"I figure we can start tomorrow mornin'. It won't take that long now that we got those two by fours. We only gotta build three sides 'cause the barn wall will be the back, but we need to make sure that coyotes and foxes can't get inside, too."

"What about rattlesnakes?"

"Nope, they won't be able to sneak in either. We're gonna use them boards up in the loft to make sure of that."

Sonny nodded, feeling like a grown-up already.

After unloading the last of the supplies, he finally unharnessed the team, then he and Sonny brushed them down while they grazed on some of the hay.

Ellis carried the box with the four sacks of vegetable seeds into the house, knowing that if he left them in the barn, they'd become target number one for the mice he knew were nesting somewhere in the deep corners. Maybe he'd find a dog to help with that issue. Cats weren't nearly as good as folks thought they were for getting rid of mice. If they didn't feel like chasing after the varmints, they wouldn't. Now a dog, on the other hand, if you train him to find the mice, they'd do it. Besides dogs could scare away the bigger troublemakers, both two and four-legged varieties.

By the time Sonny and Ellis reached the kitchen, the floor was clear of boxes, sacks and cans, but the pantry was chock full, and the cold room had its shelves filled.

"Now this is how it oughta be, Sara Mae," Ellis said as he set the box of seeds on the floor.

"It was actually difficult finding places for everything. I had to be inventive."

"Well, you're the smart one in the house, ma'am," he said as he smiled at her.

"Don't sell yourself short, Mister White."

"Just bein' honest, ma'am. Now how about if I fix us some rattlesnake?"

"I'll be more than happy to let you do that, but I'll watch. I need a lesson on how to cook reptile."

Ellis laughed then walked to the cold room picked up the pot with the seasoned snake meat then returned and set it on the cookstove before taking out the large skillet. He opened the firebox door and soon had a strong fire going. He closed the firebox door opened the oven door and placed four potatoes on the baking rack.

Sonny had gone off to the bedroom to talk to Mandy, so Ellis figured it was time to tell Sara Mae about Pete's letter.

With her just a few inches on his left, he dropped some fat onto the skillet and as he waited for it to melt, he removed the pot's lid and set it aside.

"Sara Mae, when I was talkin' to Ernie, he told me that he'd gotten a letter for Mary Jo from Pete a couple of months after she married Jim Abigail and Jim was the one who picked it up."

Sara exclaimed, *"He's alive?* You were right, Ellis!"

Ellis nodded then said, "I told Ernie if he got any more to hold 'em and I'd pick 'em up, but I need to tell Mary Jo and that might be a problem."

"Why? Can't you just go down there and tell her and let Jim Abigail know?"

"I don't figure it's gonna be that easy. I always figured you and Mary Jo got along pretty good. Is that right?"

"Yes. We were very close."

"So, how come she ain't been visitin' regular? You said she dropped off supplies. Why didn't she come and stay for a bit and just talk?"

Sara replied, "I thought she was afraid, but never said anything."

"What if Jim told her that he'd come here and hurt everybody if she said a word about what was goin' on at the Big O? She'd be too afraid to say a thing to you, so she'd drop off the supplies, make some small talk and leave. Don't that seem about right?"

Sara's eyes widened as she replied, "Yes, it does. She even told me that I shouldn't visit because she said that Jim wanted his private time."

"I was wonderin' ever since I heard about all of the queer things about what was goin' on at the Big O what Mary Jo was doin' 'cause none of it made much sense. The only thing that worked was when I finally figured out that Jim murdered Lou in that fight, then came back to the house and musta made it kinda plain to Mary Jo that he was the only man around now and he made the rules."

"What can you do, Ellis?"

"I wasn't sure until I was unloadin' the wagon. Then I figured that Jim still needs supplies himself and sooner or later, he's gotta go to Fort Madrid, and he'd have to leave in the mornin' so he could make it back during the day. So, between me and Sonny, we can keep an eye on the Big O every mornin', and when he leaves, I'll go down there and talk to Mary Jo and then wait for Jim to come back. Then I'll have a serious talk with him."

Sara Mae smiled and said, "And you said I was the smartest person in the house, Ellis. I think you deserve that title."

Ellis smiled back then replied, "I figure that argument's gonna be goin' on for years, ma'am."

Sara exhaled then said softly, "Years."

Ellis was going to say something else, but just took a deep breath and turned back to the cookstove and began tossing rattlesnake steaks into the grease covered skillet.

Sara handed him a spatula and as she watched him sprinkle pepper on the steaks, he asked, "Now that we have all the supplies, Sara, could you chop up a half of one of them cloves of garlic?"

"My! My! Aren't you the chef?" she asked before she turned to the counter, picked up a butcher's knife and a clove of garlic.

As Ellis cooked the meat, Sara had to admit it smelled awfully good.

She watched him cook and found it hard to believe how comfortable she was with her new life after such a short time. It was as if those ten years with John were nothing more than a bad dream that was only made livable because of Sonny and Mandy. The potential return of her husband she'd finally relegated to an unknown future that may never happen, but this was her present and she hoped it was her future.

An hour later when everyone sat down at the table with their snake and potatoes complete with butter, fresh bread, and real coffee, all eyes were on Ellis as he took his first bite of the rattlesnake.

Then Sonny cut a piece, shoved it between his lips and exclaimed with his half-full mouth, "This is really good!"

Dinner then progressed normally, and Sara had to admit that the meat was every bit as good as Ellis had said it was.

As they ate, they talked about the chicken coop and its future tenants and Sara Mae told them about the cows that would be arriving shortly to give them milk and butter.

"When I get a chance, I'll dig up the ground near your potato and onion patch for those vegetable seeds, Sara Mae," Ellis said as he sipped his coffee.

"I have it just to the west of the windmill, so I can use the water."

"That reminds me. I gotta get up there and fix that broken blade."

Sara nodded with a smile on her face. This was just normal, daily conversation between a husband and wife, even though Ellis wasn't her husband and would be sleeping in a different room. It still gave her a real sense of home and hope that he wouldn't be sleeping alone much longer.

They finished the meal with some of the huckleberry pie and everyone seemed to be more than content. They were happy and they were a family.

After Sonny and Mandy went off to Sonny's room to use their chalkboards, Ellis helped Sara with the cleanup and as he scrubbed the skillet, he felt the same contentment of home that Sara Mae was enjoying. What was more, for the first time in his life, Ellis Mitchell White felt whole.

———

That night as he lay atop his bed in the same suit that he'd been born wearing, he dwelled on that young woman next door. Having a woman wasn't as simple as bedding her. She had to be part of him, and he had to be part of her. Sara Mae was definitely already a part of him, a very large part. He didn't doubt that she felt the same way, either. Sooner or later, they'd share this bed and each other, but there was still that annoying part of her husband somewhere near the Mississippi

River, and Ellis knew that he'd only be completely one with Sara Mae when he knew John wouldn't be returning.

Sara Mae was in one of her new nightdresses with Mandy already asleep beside her wearing one of hers. Her mind was full of Ellis and partly because of how he'd described his sleeping preference. That image made her happily uncomfortable.

She wondered what would happen if John suddenly returned and claimed his husbandly rights and tried to take her back. She knew it was highly unlikely that he would, but John knew about Ellis' sale of the cattle and that he'd gone off to war just a few months later, too. *What if he returned and instead of taking her back, demanded that Ellis buy her and the children?* It would be just like him, too.

Sara Mae finally sighed and refocused on Ellis lying on his bed next door in all his glory. It was a pleasant way for her to fill her mind despite the frustration it caused.

———

The object of both of their concerns was meeting with Hick Smith, Eustice Smothers, and Al Hartman in the moonlit camp near his tent.

"I got us all assigned to picket duty tomorrow night, so there ain't gonna be anybody watchin'."

"How'd you get 'em to do that, John?" asked Eustice.

"Since they made that ass-kisser Tom Dempsey the sergeant, he don't care about nothin' as long as he gets his behind rubbed."

The three listeners all snickered before Hick Smith asked, "What time are we gonna head out?"

"It's gotta be real late, after midnight, I figure. I'll come and round you up when it's time. Make sure you got your bags of food and ammunition. We take the boat that's furthest west and then we'll be off. Nobody will even know we're gone for a couple of hours."

"Sounds good, John. Now, tell us again about how much money Ellis had from sellin' his cattle," Al Hartman said with unhidden glee.

———

Ellis had done his measuring for the chicken coop just an hour after sunrise. With Sonny's help, he'd moved the boards from the loft, then they'd carried all of the necessary tools and materials to the back of the barn and started to work.

"Sonny, I was tellin' your mama yesterday about somethin' that Ernie told me back at Fort Madrid. He said that your Uncle Pete sent a letter to your Aunt Mary Jo after they all said he was dead. Now I aim to go down to the Big O and talk to her, but I figure it'll be a might dangerous if Jim Abigail is there. So, you and me, we're gonna be like scouts and keep an eye on the Big O ranch house to wait for him to leave to go to Fort Madrid for supplies. Once he's gone, I'm headin' down there."

"Are we gonna ride down close?"

"No, sir. He'd have to drive that wagon on the trail that passes the Slash W, and that's less than a mile away. We only have to watch early in the mornin', too. I figure that as long as we're working outside, we'll see the wagon pass, so it's only when I'm doin' somethin' in the barn or I'm out north with the herd that you have to watch."

"If you ain't around, how will I let you know that he's gone?"

"Well, I'll let you think about it for a tad, then you give me the answer."

As Ellis began cutting the two by fours on the two sawhorses he'd made when he was building the house and barn more than ten years earlier, Sonny thought about it.

It only took him thirty seconds before he said, "If he's going into town, then I don't have to go fast, do I? I can just ride out and tell you."

Ellis smiled at him and replied, "That's it, son. You just hop on one of the horses and bareback your way to the herd."

Sonny was prouder that Ellis had trusted him figure it out than he had been about solving the problem. His father had never asked him about anything at all.

As Ellis had estimated, building the chicken coop didn't take long at all. It was a simple frame with a door that was little more than an opening. The door itself wouldn't be hinged, at least not yet, but simply tied in place with heavy cord.

After putting the steel chicken wire mesh fence around the frame, Ellis began cutting the wide boards and using them to cover the lowest sides of the coop, leaving gaps for the sunlight. He didn't doubt that a resourceful fox or some burrowing critter could get past the coop's walls, but the chickens would be pretty well protected when the job was done.

They each took a long drink from the canteen they'd brought with them, draining it before packing up the tools and leftover boards and chicken wire and returning them to the barn.

"You know what we need, Sonny?" Ellis asked as they walked out of the barn.

"Chickens?" he replied with a giggle.

"Chickens is one thing, but I figure a dog would be a fine addition to the critters on the ranch. He could guard the chickens and get rid of the mice in the barn, too."

"*A dog? You're gonna get a dog?*" he asked excitedly.

"Unless you want a rattlesnake," Ellis answered as he closed the barn doors.

"No, sir. But where would you find a dog?"

"The same place where I'm gonna get that buckboard I told your mama about. There's a rancher named Abe Chesterfield that has a decent ranch about two miles east of Fort Madrid. When I came back after sellin' my cattle, I ran into Abe Chesterfield at Ernie's and he asked me if I needed a buckboard. I didn't at the time, and he might not have it anymore, but I know he always had one of his dogs with him. They were coon dogs and pretty handy critters. So, I gotta head down to Fort Madrid in a day or two anyway, so I might as well swing by the place and see if I can buy the buckboard and maybe come back with a coon dog or two."

"That would be great!"

Ellis grinned and said, "I figured you'd think that way."

They walked to the trough, took off their shirts and quickly washed off the sawdust and dirt that had attached itself to their sweaty skin then dressed again before heading back into the house for lunch.

"How's the chicken coop going?" Sara Mae asked as they entered.

"It's ready for the chickens, Mama," Sonny replied.

"That was fast. Why don't you two working men have a seat and I'll give you something to eat."

"Yes, ma'am," Ellis replied before heading over to the table and joining Mandy and Sonny.

———

Three miles southwest, Mary Jo sat at the table with Jim Abigail having the food she'd prepared, and he'd complained about until she pointed to the almost empty pantry.

For almost eight months now, she'd endured an almost prison-like existence. Even the brief trips to the Slash W had seemed little more than a short parole.

The news that Ellis White had returned had given her a glimmer of hope, but after two days of continued isolation, her brief period of relative happiness had gradually worn down to an even lower condition.

Why he'd told Ellis that she was pregnant still bothered her. She'd taken precautions after each of their couplings, which had become less frequent as he seemed to be tiring of her. And it was that gradual shift from daily rutting to the less excited romps that had her more worried. He hadn't said anything that indicated she was in danger, but he'd become more distant.

Then Ellis had arrived and his moods had changed significantly. He hadn't even taken her the last two nights but had stayed awake in the bed just thinking about something.

She was sure that he was planning on trying to kill Ellis and maybe Sara Mae and her children. Maybe he was thinking of keeping both women to entertain him. She just had no real clue about his intentions as he rarely spoke to her.

She knew he'd have to make a supply run soon and then she'd have her opportunity to run to the Slash W. With Ellis there, she didn't have to worry any longer about the threats. She'd warn Ellis and he'd be ready. She knew that Jim was almost terrified of Ellis.

"I'm gonna head into Fort Madrid tomorrow, so I'm gonna go and pick out a couple of head of cattle to trade in a little while," Jim mumbled as he poked at his food.

"Okay," Mary Jo replied startled to think he might have read her mind.

Jim finished his lunch then without saying another word, stood then snatched his hat from the nearby chair and walked out of the back door to saddle his horse.

Mary Jo then took the plates and walked to the sink where she could watch him through the window. If the Big O had been as large as the Slash W, she'd seriously consider making her escape while he was off picking out the cattle, but he'd only be a mile away at the most and she wouldn't get far. She'd make her break tomorrow morning after he'd gone.

———

"You ever milk a cow, Sonny?" Ellis asked as he threw the saddle over Tippy's back.

"No, sir."

"Well, you'll be learnin' soon enough. I'll be back in about two hours with a cow and her calf. When she's all nice and settled, I'll show you how it's done. Maybe your mama will want to help."

"She sure likes you a lot, Uncle Ellis."

"She's a fine woman, Sonny. I wish your father was a better man."

"I don't want him back. I think you and mama should be together."

Ellis turned to look at Sonny and replied, "So, do I, son. But she's still married to you father and there ain't nothin' I can do about it."

Sonny mumbled, "I don't care."

Ellis was tightening the cinches as he said, "I wish I didn't."

"How will you know if he ain't comin' back?"

"That, son, is a real good question," Ellis said as he stood and took Tippy's reins.

They walked out of the barn and as Ellis mounted, he said, "I'll be back soon with our new milk factory," then waved and set Tippy off at a medium trot.

Sonny watched him ride away then walked quickly to the house.

After entering through the open doorway, he walked behind his mother who was sitting with Mandy at the table teaching her the alphabet and plopped into the next open chair.

He waited for her to stop talking then said, "Mama, I asked Uncle Ellis why you and him can't be together, and he said it was 'cause papa is still alive. I don't care and I know Mandy doesn't either. How come you can't have him be our father?"

Sara Mae was somewhat surprised by both the question and his apparent permission but replied, "Sonny, I married your father and Mister White thinks that we can't be together until that is no longer true. I wish that I could do what you want even more than you can imagine, but it can't be."

"Never?"

"No, not never. But let us worry about that. Okay? Just be patient and know that we are never going to leave this house."

"Okay, I guess. I just want you to be happy, Mama."

"I know, sweetheart, and I am very grateful that you do, but now you understand how things are."

Mandy just asked, "Is Uncle Ellis going to be our new papa soon?"

Sara Mae kissed her daughter and replied, "I hope so, Mandy. I hope so."

———

Ellis was riding northwest toward the herd and as he looked to his left, he spotted a dust cloud on the western part of his land where those Big O cattle had been grazing the day after he'd returned. He kept Tippy at the same pace and knew it had to be Jim Abigail and gave a passing thought of heading that way and confronting him, but Jim would see him coming and probably turn back to the ranch house before they had a chance to chat. He'd stick with his original plan, but the fact that Jim was heading out to the herd could only mean one thing. He was going to round up a head or two to take into Fort Madrid, and that meant tomorrow. If he'd had a ranch hand or two, then he could be going out there to do some normal care for the critters, but on his lonesome there was almost no possibility of that.

He kept Tippy going and only took the occasional glance back at the Big O herd that was little more than black specks on the horizon now.

By the time he reached his own herd, picked out a cow with a young calf, roped her and began walking her back to the barn, he didn't see any movement on the Big O. Whatever Jim Abigail was doing was already done and he just led the slow moving cow with her trotting calf southeast.

Having seen Jim Abigail picking up that steer gave him advance notice of his trip to Fort Madrid, so he'd have Tippy saddled first thing in the morning and after that wagon and steer passed by his access road, he'd give Jim another hour, then he'd make a quick ride over to the Big O to talk to Mary Jo. That would be one interesting conversation, and he expected that there was a very good chance that he'd be returning with her to the Slash W.

It took over an hour to get the cow back to the barn, and he had to settle her into a stall as her anxious calf looked on. He tossed in a bunch of hay to keep her happy, then as he began unsaddling Tippy, he heard footsteps and turned expecting to see Sonny but was very pleased to see Sara Mae enter the barn.

"Well, this is a pleasant surprise, Sara Mae," he said as he lowered the saddle to the floor.

Sara Mae walked closer glanced at the cow then said, "I had an interesting conversation with Sonny after you left and thought it would be a good idea to talk to you before you went inside."

"I can imagine what it's about, too," he said as he pulled off the saddle blanket.

"You'd be right if you thought he asked why we couldn't be together."

"That's what I figured. It's only been a few days and he already figures that I should be his papa, and not just to show him man things."

"I know. Mandy feels the same way and by now, I'm sure that you know that I do, too."

"We all do, but there's that one problem that's livin' about two hundred miles east of here."

"Yes. That's what I told them. This is very hard for me, Ellis, and I'm sure that it's not any easier for you."

"That, ma'am, ain't the half of it. I can't get you outta my mind, and thinkin' about you sleepin' just a few feet away in your nightdress is makin' it pretty hard to get to sleep."

"How do you think I feel? You sleep naked, for God's sake, and that's making me too excited to sleep for hours."

Ellis smiled and said, "Now, that's good news, Sara Mae."

"What's so good about it?" she asked but with a small smile.

"It's good that you're all excited, 'cause when we finally don't have to worry about them vows, it means that it's gonna be one helluva night we spend together."

Her slight smile widened into a broad one as she replied, "I suppose there is that."

Then Ellis changed the direction of the conversation by saying, "Oh, when I was headin' out to get the cow, I spotted Jim Abigail ridin' out to his herd probably to grab a steer or two to do some tradin' in Fort Madrid tomorrow. So, I'll saddle Tippy in the mornin' before breakfast, and after he goes past the house, I'll wait a while then head over to the Big O and talk to Mary Jo."

"Will you bring her back here, Ellis?" asked Sara Mae excitedly.

"Yes, ma'am. If she wants to leave, and I expect she does, I'll bring her back, then I'll head back to the Big O and wait for Jim Abigail to return and we'll have a nice, friendly talk."

"I'll keep the shotgun ready, just in case."

"That's why you're the smartest person on this ranch, ma'am."

Sara laughed then said, "And so the debate continues. Are you really going to just have a friendly talk?"

"Well, kinda. It'll be friendly, but I'll have my Colt pointed his way to let him know I'm serious."

"Ellis, what will you do if he admits to killing Lou Gordon?"

"He won't, but if he does then I'll worry about that when the time comes. Tomorrow is all about Mary Jo. We make sure she's safe and then I can deal with Jim Abigail."

Sara Mae smiled, then Ellis removed Tippy's bridle picked up the brush and began to stroke the black mare.

"She is a pretty lady," Sara Mae said.

"She is. Do you want her, Sara Mae? I'll be headin' back to the Comanche village to get my herd of horses soon and I'll pick one of them for me. The gelding that I brought with me is for our new buckboard and the horse that Sonny rode from the village is his. I'll let Mandy pick one out of the herd when I get it back, too."

Sara walked close to Ellis and stroked the mare's chest.

"Thank you, Ellis. I'd love to have her."

"Good. If you want to change her name, you can."

"No. I like Tippy. It's a good name."

Ellis then asked, "Can you milk a cow, Sara Mae?"

"Of course, I can. I thought that would be my job anyway."

"Good, then you can show Sonny how to do it. You'll have to take turns with her calf, though."

She laughed and replied, "That's okay. I'll manage."

Ellis nodded then as he bent over to put the brush on its shelf, he bumped into Sara Mae, and she began to stumble backwards. He dropped the brush quickly and caught her in his arms.

As he steadied her, he looked down into her deep brown eyes as she gazed into his. Instead of letting her go, he pulled her closer and Sara Mae slowly slid her hand behind Ellis' neck and pulled herself closer with her eyes still locked on his.

Ellis felt her softness pressed against him as he leaned down and kissed her.

Sara Mae felt her toes curl and an electric shock shot down her back as she kissed him back, feeling his hard body pushed against her torso. She wanted this so badly and wanted him to know just how much as she began to slide her hips against him slowly all too aware of the effect she was having on him.

Ellis was lost as he felt her move and then let his hands slide across her back until he felt her soft curves and pulled her tightly against him.

After the long, passionate kiss ended, he began to kiss her neck as she moaned in delight at the extraordinary pleasure she was already experiencing. She'd had two children with John, but nothing had prepared her for this.

Ellis was even worse and then after kissing her neck, began to kiss her hungry lips again as his back was pressed against Tippy and his hands wandered all over Sara Mae's backside.

When their second kiss ended, Ellis whispered, "Sara Mae, we have to stop. Lord knows I don't want it to, but we have to."

Sara had her eyes closed and was still out of touch with reality as she whispered back, "What did you say?"

"Sweetheart, we gotta stop. You know how much I want you, but we gotta stop."

Sara sighed then said, "I know. This was just so sudden, but I don't regret it for a moment. I love you, Ellis. I want you."

"I love you too, Sara Mae, and want you just as much. We'll be there soon. I promise."

"One more kiss? Please?" she asked softly.

Ellis smiled then kissed her again, and Sara Mae made the most of it as she took her left hand from behind his neck, pulled his right hand from her behind and placed it on her right breast.

Ellis spent the remainder of the long kiss letting her know that he appreciated the gesture.

When Sara finally stepped back, Ellis said, "Now, Sara Mae, you surprised me."

Sara was all smiles as she replied, "I should think so. Why did you tell me that?"

"I always thought that you were, um, less, um, bumpy than you are."

Sara laughed and said, "I've had two children, Ellis. I may not be a cow, but I fed them both."

"I guess it's just because of what you wear underneath that I never noticed before."

"That's the idea. As a wife and mother, I wasn't supposed to advertise. I guess that was a good thing given what's happened to Mary Jo. Lou Gordon might have settled for me if he'd known."

Ellis stepped closer again, put his hands on her shoulders and said, "No man who would ever have you for a wife would ever be settlin', Sara Mae. Like I told you before, you're the most woman I've ever met, and that was before I discovered your hidden secret. I loved you for you, Sara Mae, and always will."

Sara Mae smiled then kissed him again but for a different reason then said, "I love you for all the right reasons, Ellis."

Ellis smiled back at her then said, "We'd better be headed back to the house, ma'am. I wouldn't want our young'uns to be thinkin' we're doin' anything out here that we just told 'em we wouldn't be doin'."

Sara took his arm, laughed then replied, "They would be very happy to think that we were doing what we said we wouldn't do."

"I imagine so, ma'am," he replied as they exited the barn with their arms linked.

Both knew that falling asleep tonight would be almost impossible.

———

Jim Abigail had spotted Ellis as he was riding northwest to his herd but didn't think twice about it. He was just going to check on his animals.

He'd picked out two steers, brought them back to the corral and left them inside with some hay and let them drink at the trough. Normally, he'd get a full wagonload of supplies for the cattle that should last him and Mary Jo for two months, but not this time.

As Mary Jo had noticed, he was getting tired of her, but it wasn't because she was any less pretty or didn't excite him. It was her almost sulky attitude. It had been getting worse with each passing week, and he attributed it to the absence of her sister. More than once, he'd been close to riding over to the Slash W and taking Sara Mae back with him even with that daughter of hers, but was concerned about Rufus possibly returning, so he hadn't.

Now just as he had convinced himself that Rufus was really gone, Ellis had suddenly returned and that had thrown everything into chaos. He'd expected Ellis to come visiting over the next two days and was ready if he showed up, but he hadn't. Jim figured he was diddling Sara Mae and didn't have any free time.

He knew that Ellis had always fancied Sara Mae, and even though he never said anything directly, he often talked about how that husband of hers didn't deserve such a good woman and things like that, but Jim knew he wanted the woman and now he had her. But his return had made him change his long-term plan, too.

He still had almost eleven hundred dollars of the Yankee cash that Ellis had left him to run the ranch while he was gone and had planned on using the money to buy the Slash W once he got word that Ellis had been killed, knowing that Ellis must have hidden the rest of his money somewhere on the ranch. He'd searched in all the obvious places, but Rufus had seemed to be watching. But with Ellis' return, that plan wasn't going to happen.

His only other option now was to make a run with the money and that was the real reason for the supply run. He'd stick Mary Jo in the second bedroom tomorrow, strap her down then saddle his horse with his things, take the wagon, the cattle and team into Fort Madrid, get what he could for the cattle then trade the wagon and one of the wagon team horses for a pack saddle, fill it with the supplies and light out for Henrietta.

He figured that Mary Jo if she escaped, would run to the Slash W and tell Ellis but by then, he'd be long gone, and Ellis would probably just let him go. He didn't think Ellis knew about the money.

So, after setting the cattle in the corral and unsaddling the dappled gray gelding, he headed to the house with his saddlebags over his shoulder still finalizing his plans for tomorrow's run. If he'd been smarter, he would have just left his horse saddled with the money in his saddlebags. The he could have trailed one of the other horses and ridden into Fort Madrid, bought his supplies then disappeared. But he was so determined to keep every possible Yankee note that he took the much more complicated and longer route of trading the cattle for what he needed. He didn't take any more cattle so if Ellis saw him, he wouldn't be suspicious.

He entered the house found Mary Jo at the stove but didn't say a word as he passed through the kitchen into the bedroom and closed the door to pack his things.

Mary Jo hadn't even looked his way as he passed by. She'd seen him ride in leading the two steers and didn't see anything odd about his behavior, so she just continued to cook.

———

Throughout dinner, Ellis and Sara Mae kept glancing at each other without saying what was on their minds nor was a single syllable necessary.

Ellis told Sonny and Mandy about what was going to happen tomorrow, and both were excited with the possibility of seeing their aunt again.

"Does she know I'm back?" asked Sonny.

"No, sir. Why don't we let that be a surprise? When she walks in the house, you just say good mornin', like it's nothin' important and you can see her surprised face."

Sonny grinned and replied, "That sounds like fun."

Mandy, of course, asked, "Where will Aunt Mary Jo sleep?"

Ellis really hadn't thought about that yet, and neither had Sara Mae, so Ellis replied, "Let's see what happens when she gets here. She might wanna go back to the Big O."

"I don't think she wants to be there," said Sonny, "I think she's scared."

Ellis was surprised because he'd never said anything about it before, but said, "I think so too, Sonny. But she won't be anymore."

"Good."

After the children went to Sonny's room so he could show his sister how to write her letters, Ellis again helped Sara with the cleanup but this time, they intentionally managed to sneak in a few kisses and touches. It wasn't anything dramatic but just enough to keep the romantic fires alive as if they needed any more stoking.

The sun was setting, and everyone was on the porch, sitting on the edge. Sara Mae was close against Ellis which was noticed and appreciated by her children as they watched nature's daily show. Ellis finally gave in and slipped his hand around Sara Mae's waist and she followed suit.

"We need some rockin' chairs," Ellis said.

"How about a porch swing?" Sara Mae suggested as she looked up at the porch supports.

Ellis glanced up and said, "That would work, ma'am. That was mighty smart thinkin'."

Sara Mae laughed and squeezed him closer letting the beauty of the sunset, the presence of her happy children and Ellis' love make it a perfect evening.

When the red sky finally began to turn a deep purple, they stood and returned to the house. Ellis had Sara Mae's hand tightly in his as they entered the main room and he closed the door behind him.

Sonny walked ahead, said, "Good night," then turned into his room and closed the door.

Mandy then kissed her mother, said, "Good night, Mama," and walked into the center bedroom and closed the door.

Ellis and Sara Mae looked at each other and a second later, both burst into laughter, probably confusing both children who were getting undressed in their closed bedrooms.

When their laughter subsided, Ellis pulled Sara Mae close, kissed her softly and said just as softly, "Good night, my love."

Sara smiled and replied, "I'm going to have very pleasant dreams tonight, sweetheart."

He kissed her once more before he stepped back, blew out his breath to make his point, then entered his room and closed the door.

Sara sighed then opened the door to the center bedroom surprising Mandy and said, "I thought you'd have your nightdress on already, young lady."

"Oh."

Sara then helped Mandy finish changing into her nightdress then undressed herself, folded her new dress then set it on the dresser and removed her somewhat restrictive camisole. If Mary Jo wasn't going to be coming tomorrow, she'd dispense with the undergarment to impress Ellis. She may have had two children, but she wanted to have more, and she didn't want to have them with that man back near the Mississippi River.

———

That man was just taking his position on the picket line. The man he'd replaced didn't ask why he had his knapsack and canteen with him. It wasn't that out of place, and he was happy to be relieved, so he quickly left the spot and headed back to camp.

The insects were buzzing like crazy as John began his slow walk around his post. Why the general had insisted they make camp so close to the river junction was beyond him. Every damned mosquito God put on this earth must live within this one square mile. He was squashing them as they landed on his neck to punch into his skin and wished there was some way to kill them all. He hated them worse than he hated the Yankees, and that was considerable.

It was close to midnight now and the camp was already quiet. He'd planned on waiting for another couple of hours, but the mosquitoes had pushed him to an early departure, so he began to walk north, keeping the camp's low fires to his right.

Hick Smith was distracted by his own battle with the mosquitoes, and when he heard rustling to his left almost shouted a challenge. Then just as he opened his mouth, he slammed it shut and John Keeler stepped through the brush and waved at him to follow.

After ten minutes, they'd picked Eustice Smothers and Al Hartman then all four deserting soldiers worked their way in the forested darkness as quietly as they could heading northwest for the Red River and the long boats.

It took them another twenty minutes to find their way to the boats and selected the one on the far left. John stood at the bow and accepted each man's knapsack then his rifle, placed them in the boat and then climbed inside. He carefully stepped along the craft, sat down in the second set of seats amidships and picked up one of the oars. He'd never rowed a boat before but figured it couldn't be too hard. None of the others had either, but it was too late to learn.

After Hick Smith joined him on the seat and took the other oar, Eustice Smothers and Al Hartman shoved the boat off of the bank into the Red River and clambered inside as it drifted into the channel.

They both sat in the first seat, took up their oars and then they tried to straighten the boat into the current. By the time they managed it, they were already a few hundred yards downstream, but then they struggled to figure out how to get the boat moving in the direction that they wanted it to go and wound up almost a mile downstream from their starting point before they began to make headway.

It was two o'clock in the morning when the longboat finally reached its starting point and the four deserters were marginally functioning as a rowing crew.

They had two hundred plus miles ahead of them and even as they were gliding through the water, John Keeler was beginning to think that taking the land route might have been a better idea after all. He guessed that it would take them six days to get all the way to where the Fresh Water Creek emptied into the Red River, but if they found all of Ellis White's money, it would be worth it.

He didn't give his wife and children any thought of all.

———

The man who gave them a lot of thought had finally managed to fall asleep after tortured memories of his time in the barn with Sara Mae and she didn't drift off for an hour after that.

CHAPTER 7

Jim Abigail didn't bother even letting Mary Jo make breakfast. After she returned from the privy which he thought was very considerate of himself, he told her to go into the second bedroom without an explanation then once she was inside, he told her to lay on the bed and close her eyes.

Mary Jo was terrified believing that Jim was going to kill her now that Ellis was back.

But when she felt him wrapping a rope around her left wrist, she almost cried in relief, but still didn't ask him what he was doing. She believed that the best thing she could do now was to silently acquiesce which is pretty much what she'd been doing for the past few months.

She kept her eyes closed as he tied off her other wrist and then her ankles before he wordlessly left the room. When she heard him leave the house, she opened her eyes and looked at her bindings. As an experienced ranch hand, he was pretty good at tying knots and she doubted if she'd be able to free herself, so she simply relaxed to save her energy and closed her eyes again. There was nothing she could do at all. Even screaming wouldn't help as it wouldn't be heard by anyone.

Mary Jo just lay on the bed and tried to think of a way to free herself, but almost gave up the idea before she started. To keep her hopelessness at bay, she began to recall the happy memories of her life with Pete and wished she had given him children. Why she hadn't was a mystery because they'd certainly tried hard enough, even after Sara Mae and that useless husband of hers arrived. She remembered Pete commenting how quiet it was in their bedroom and Mary Jo had said it was because of the children, but she knew better.

How her sister managed to have two children by that bastard was the real mystery. Maybe they weren't his at all. That idea appealed to her, so as she lay strapped to the bed in the rising Texas heat, Mary Jo Orris began to giggle as she tried to imagine her almost prudish older sister having an extramarital affair. She didn't even think that Sara Mae was capable of enjoying what she and Pete had relished.

As she was giggling, Jim Abigail had saddled his horse then harnessed the team and rolled the wagon out of the barn. He attached the gray gelding's trail rope to the back of the wagon, then went to the corral, brought out the two cattle and tied their trail rope to the other side. Satisfied that he was ready, he clambered into the driver's seat, released the hand brake and snapped the reins.

He rolled the wagon down the access road and turned left to head to Fort Madrid, feeling an enormous sense of freedom and release. He'd miss Mary Jo's favors, but she could be replaced easily, especially with as many widows that would be more than anxious to warm his bed. He'd even heard about a whole laundry full of them in Henrietta.

———

"There he goes," Ellis said as he watched through the front window of the house.

"Why does he have his horse?" asked Sonny.

"That, Mister Keeler, is an excellent question, and I'm not too sure I like my answer, either."

"What's wrong, Ellis?" Sara Mae asked anxiously.

"It looks like he's clearin' out. There ain't no reason for him to be trailin' his saddled horse unless he wasn't plannin' on comin' back."

"Do you think he hurt Mary Jo?"

"I ain't sure, but I ain't gonna wait no hour now, neither. I've got Tippy saddled, and I'm gonna go over there right now. I'll come back here as soon as I find out what's goin' on."

"Hurry, please, Ellis," Sara said anxiously.

"Yes, ma'am," he replied as he grabbed his old gray CSA hat and trotted out of the front room, crossed the porch and jogged to the barn.

As he crossed the ground, he was genuinely worried about Mary Jo. He may have hated John Keeler, but if Jim Abigail had hurt Mary Jo, then he'd shoot the man without a qualm.

He reached the barn, quickly mounted Tippy, and once out of the doors, set her at a fast trot following the trail to the Big O. He had the Sharps in the scabbard leaving the Henry and the J.F Brown in the kitchen.

———

As much as Colonel Avery Bushnell was angered by the desertion of the four men, he was much more furious that they'd taken one of the precious longboats to make their escape. He wouldn't have bothered with them otherwise because desertions weren't uncommon but stealing that boat certainly mattered.

He'd dispatched four men on horseback to head along the river to find them knowing they couldn't make that much speed going against the current and they'd be tired soon enough.

———

He was right on both counts as John and his partners had pulled to the shore after rowing just eight miles. Aside from not having slept all night, their arms weren't used to the rowing motion, so they'd beached the craft and collapsed on the shore with stiff arms and backs.

They slept for almost three hours before Hick Smith was awakened when he heard the sound of horses and nudged the others. Each man grabbed his loaded musket and crawled to the top of the bank and found places to conceal themselves.

The four men that had been sent to find them were searching the river for a moving boat and hadn't spotted the beached long boat yet as they continued to ride at a decent pace.

"Hold your fire 'till they're real close," John loud whispered.

It was really unnecessary as they all knew they'd probably only get one shot before any survivors turned and raced back to the camp to get help, but his second instructions weren't expected.

"If any of 'em are left, rush 'em with bayonets."

For some reason, shooting fellow soldiers didn't bother Eustice Smothers and Al Hartman as much as the thought of sticking them with an eighteen-inch blade of steel, but Hick Smith didn't care much either way.

They held their fire until the four riders were within fifty yards and suddenly one of them shouted, "The boat's right there on the shore!"

John fired first, followed immediately by the others. Two of the riders were thrown from their mounts and the other two pulled their rifles as the four deserters all hopped up from the brush and charged at them with their bayonets at the ready, screaming the rebel yell.

The two empty horses had both bolted away and disappeared into the trees while one of the two remaining riders brought his carbine level, aimed and fired, but missed his target, Hick Smith, who dashed the last twenty yards and reached up and plunged his bayonet into the gut of the man who'd just tried to shoot him.

The rider screamed and grabbed at Hick's musket barrel, but as his life's blood poured across his front, he just glared at Hick and shouted, "You cowardly bastard!" then fell face forward as Hick pulled his bayonet out of the man.

John's victim tried to get a shot off, but never got the hammer cocked when John rammed his bayonet into the man's chest just below his ribcage then immediately yanked it free.

The last rider just stared at his killer with wide eyes before slowly leaning forward then tumbling to the ground.

The entire action lasted less than a minute and a half.

John Keeler and the other all examined the four soldiers and recognized every one of them, as they knew they would.

Nothing more was said as they turned to go back to the boat. They didn't want to waste any time trying to hunt down the horses and suspected that by the time they did, more soldiers would be coming, either Yankee or rebel, drawn by the gunfire. They weren't sure how far they were away from either camp.

Twenty minutes later, they were rowing west again.

———

Ellis didn't slow Tippy in his dash to the Big O because there was no point. Either Mary Jo was alive, or she wasn't, but if she was alive, she might need his help. He still wondered how he could have missed so much in Jim Abigail after all those years.

He pulled the black mare to a dusty halt, dismounted and dropped the reins. He didn't bother pulling his pistol as he stepped onto the small back porch and without a knock, entered the house and shouted, "Mary Jo?"

Mary Jo had actually drifted to sleep and wasn't sure the voice she heard was real, but still yelled, "In here!"

When she heard heavy footsteps, she felt like crying then when she spotted Ellis entering the room she did.

Ellis quickly pulled his knife and began to cut her bonds as he asked, "What happened, Mary Jo?"

"I don't know, but Jim tied me up and left. I don't think he's coming back."

"I don't either. How are you?"

"I'm much better now that you're here. How are Sara Mae and the children?"

"Happy," was his short reply as he walked to the head of the bed to cut her wrist ties.

"Jim said you returned, and I think that's why he decided to run."

"I'm sure it was, ma'am," he said as he cut her last binding and helped her to a sitting position and sat next to her.

"Now, I aim to go and run him down in a little while. It's no rush 'cause he's drivin' that wagon and trailin' a horse and a couple of steers. But can I guess you want to come to the Slash W and stay with your sister and her young'uns?"

"Yes. I don't want to stay here."

"Okay. We'll do that in a few minutes. I'm gonna go and get you some water and be right back."

"Thank you, Ellis."

Ellis smiled at her and said, "You ain't heard the half of it, Mary Jo," then left the bedroom and headed for the kitchen.

He pumped a glass full of water drank it quickly then refilled it and brought it back to the bedroom and gave it to Mary Jo, who drained it almost as rapidly.

"What did you mean when you said I haven't heard the half of it?" she asked.

"When I was in Fort Madrid, Ernie Smith said that two months after you and Jim got hitched…"

Mary Jo interrupted him, saying, "We were never married. He just took me to your house and had his way with me. He threatened to kill me and then Sara Mae and her children if I said anything. I'm pretty sure he killed Lou Gordon, too."

"Yes, ma'am. I kinda figured that too, and Sonny told me the story that made it the truth. Anyway, two months after Jim killed Lou, Ernie got a letter for you from Pete."

Mary Jo's hand flew to her mouth in shock as she stared at Ellis with wide eyes.

"*Pete's alive?*" she exclaimed.

"I'm pretty sure, ma'am. When I got back and folks told me that Pete had been killed in September, I was surprised 'cause even though he was in a different outfit, I woulda heard about it and I didn't. I even heard how he'd gotten shot but came out okay. I'm pretty sure he's all right."

Then her eyes closed and she whispered, "He's going to be so ashamed of me."

"No, Mary Jo, he won't be one lick ashamed of you at all. If there's one thing I'm sure about is that Pete is a good man, and he loves you like a man is supposed to love his woman. He'll just hate Jim Abigail for lyin' to you and makin' you do what you did. Of course, I aim to make sure he hates a corpse by the time he gets back."

Mary Jo opened her eyes smiled at Ellis and said quietly, "Thank you, Ellis. You're as good a man as my Pete. I wish Sara Mae had married you and not John. I think she's smitten with you; you know."

Ellis smiled back and said, "I know, ma'am, and I ain't ashamed to admit that Sara Mae owns my heart and soul, too. I wish it could be all of me but, well, there's that one problem back east."

"I don't think that should stop you, Ellis. He was never a real husband to Sara Mae."

"I know he wasn't, but a promise is a promise and one made to God is kinda the biggest one we can make. I wish it weren't so, but it is."

Mary Jo sighed then said, "I think we can go now."

Ellis stood took Mary Jo's hand and they walked from the bedroom into the kitchen and left the house. He mounted Tippy then lifted Mary Jo onto the saddle and put his arm around her waist and she pulled herself close before he turned the black mare back toward the Slash W.

Having as pretty and well-formed woman so close to him, especially after yesterday's close encounter with Sara Mae, made the ride very difficult and if Mary Jo noticed, and he was sure that she did, she was polite enough not to comment.

"What happened, Ellis?"

Ellis had Tippy at a slow trot because of the added load, so he thought he had enough time to give her a quick rundown of what had happened since he returned, which he did. There was even enough time for her to tell him briefly what had happened to her.

———

Sara Mae and the children were all sitting on the edge of the front porch watching the southwest and soon spotted the dust cloud and seconds later saw Ellis riding with Mary Jo in his lap.

"It's Aunt Mary Jo! Uncle Ellis got her!" shouted Sonny as he popped to his feet.

Sara Mae stood and smiled, happy to see her sister, yet at the same time feeling a twinge of jealousy that she was so close to Ellis and knowing how pretty she was didn't help. But she pushed the feeling aside as she watched them approach anxiously awaiting the story she had to tell.

———

"It looks like everybody's waitin' to see you, Mary Jo," Ellis said when he spotted Sara Mae and the children on the porch where he expected to see them.

"Sara Mae is probably waiting for you more than me," she said as she smiled.

Ellis didn't comment as he picked up the pace a bit. He would have waved, but his hands were full of Mary Jo.

Five minutes later, he pulled Tippy to a stop in front of the house and lowered Mary Jo to the ground where she was hugged by her sister.

Ellis then said, "Sara Mae, I'm going to saddle the gelding and head after Jim Abigail. He's makin' a run for it, and I don't want him gettin' too far ahead."

Sara Mae looked up at Ellis and replied, "Be careful, Ellis."

"Yes, ma'am," he replied then tipped his hat and set Tippy at slow trot to the trough under the windmill. He wasn't sure how far Abigail had gone, but he guessed about halfway to Fort Madrid.

He dismounted at the trough, and while Tippy drank, he trotted into the kitchen, snatched his Henry then left the house before the sisters and the children reached the hallway.

Ellis took Tippy's reins and led her quickly to the corral where the gelding watched.

Ten minutes later, he was sitting in the saddle again and as he turned to ride away, he waved at Sara Mae, Mary Jo, Sonny and Mandy before setting off at a fast trot.

———

Jim had already passed the halfway point and was already planning on his journey to Henrietta later. He wasn't going to stay very long in Fort Madrid because of Ellis. His old boss was the wild card now, and Jim had no idea what he was going to do or how much he knew. He was counting on Ellis remaining at his own ranch and trying to restore it to what it had been.

Having Sara Mae there was added insurance against him riding to the Big O and looking for Mary Jo. His only real concern on that front was that he had ridden past the Slash W on his way to Fort Madrid. He'd studiously watched the distant ranch house as he drove past and hadn't seen anyone, so he thought he was safe, but he was still nervous.

That nervousness had him checking his backtrail every few minutes, but after the first hour, he became less intent. He still looked behind him, but not so often.

———

Ellis picked up the dust from the wagon and trailers forty minutes after leaving the ranch and kept the fast trot to close the gap. Once he was within a mile or so, he'd slow down to a medium trot, so he didn't appear to be chasing after Jim. He might get close enough to be able to talk to him but doubted it even then. He'd tied up Mary Jo and Ellis figured once he'd been spotted, Jim wouldn't be in a talking mood.

———

Jim hadn't checked his backtrail in almost thirty minutes when he twisted in the driver's seat and spotted a rider about two miles behind him and moving fast. He didn't have to guess

235

who was in that saddle but took another couple of minutes to think about the best way to deal with the problem.

If he abandoned the wagon and cattle, he might be able to just get away on his horse, but he knew that Ellis probably found Mary Jo and wouldn't give up the chase. But he also knew Ellis well enough to know that he wouldn't shoot him straight out, and that was his advantage.

He decided that he'd act as if he hadn't seen Ellis, and then let him get close. He'd have the jump on him if he had his Colt already loose in his holster and took the first shot. He could probably get two shots off before Ellis even got his Dragoon out of his holster.

His plan set, he loosed the trigger loop on his Colt New Army pistol then kept driving the wagon toward Fort Madrid, waiting for Ellis to arrive.

———

Ellis had seen Jim Abigail turn in the wagon's seat, so he knew he'd been spotted. That meant that there was no reason to slow the horse, but he slowed the gelding for a different reason. He needed the extra time to think.

He kept watching the wagon to see what Jim was going to do. After he had done nothing for two minutes, Ellis figured that Jim had decided not to run and that left him only two options; he could either try and talk his way out, or he could shoot his way out. His ex-foreman's behavior since he'd gone off to war made Ellis almost certain that Jim was going to try and get the drop on him. He really had no other choice.

Ellis released his Dragoon's hammer loop and figured he'd come up on the right side. If Jim's hammer loop was already off, or he went for his pistol, Ellis would have to beat him in a short-range gunfight.

He was pretty good with the pistol, but its size was a disadvantage when it came to pulling it free of the holster quickly. He knew that Jim had a Colt New Army, which was a lighter, less cumbersome revolver, so he'd have a slight advantage.

But Ellis had been in a lot of gunfights over the past three years and had to use his Dragoon on many occasions. He doubted that Jim had to use his pistol that often, so he counted on his added experience to negate Jim's ease of use advantage.

He kept the gelding trotting and gaining on the wagon and when Jim hadn't turned again when he was within a half mile, he was certain that he was setting up for a shot.

The idea of getting into a close-range gunfight was a lot different than what he'd experienced in the army. In those situations, it was a chaotic melee of gunfire, and when he'd had to pull his pistol, it was when the lines had converged, and all hell was breaking loose. There was no time to dwell on what was happening. He just pointed the pistol and fired before he was gunned down, but always keeping track of the number of shots he had remaining.

This time, the number of filled cylinders didn't matter. The only thing that would matter would be the first shot or maybe the second, but no more.

He was within four hundred yards now and tried to concentrate on the deadly task at hand, yet his mind kept taking him back to the barn and the accidental but welcome time with Sara Mae. He wanted desperately to return to the

Slash W, and it wasn't because of the house, the cattle, or even the missing horses.

Ellis was still unfocused by the time he was a hundred yards behind the wagon when his gelding snorted loudly at the scent of the horses, snapping his mind back into the business at hand. He patted the horse's neck in gratitude then took a deep breath before he angled the horse to the right side of the road.

———

Jim had been expecting Ellis to arrive a couple of minutes earlier and had avoided the temptation to turn and see where he was, but with each passing second, he was growing more agitated. *Where was he?* Then even though he had previously shoved aside the notion of Ellis White shooting him without warning, that possibility began to creep into his mind. Maybe he'd talked to Mary Jo and she'd told him everything and Ellis had already decided to execute him.

Now it wasn't just the Texas heat that was making him sweat as the wagon continued to roll south. His nerves were as taut as a guitar string when he finally heard Ellis' horse approaching behind him.

Ellis was just twenty yards back when he shouted, "Mornin', Jim. Where you headed?"

Jim turned to look at Ellis and yelled back, "Where does it look like I'm goin'? I'm headin' to Fort Madrid for some supplies."

"Why are you trailin' your saddled horse?"

"I need to get the wagon fixed and I'm gonna ride back."

Ellis' heart was pounding as he approached the right side of the wagon and slowed the gelding to a barely faster pace.

"Don't go lyin' to me, Jim. I know what you did, and I reckon it's time to face the music."

Jim wanted to pull his pistol, but Ellis was too far back and in a terrible position, so he replied, "How you figure? You gonna shoot me, Ellis?"

"If I have to. I read you all wrong, Jim. I figured you were a better man than this. You murdered Lou, drove off Rufus, and then lied to Mary Jo about Pete and kept her like a prisoner."

Jim didn't argue any of the points because it wasn't going to help, but what he did was to suddenly pull back on the reins, bringing the wagon to a sudden stop, startling Ellis and giving Jim the advantage that he had hoped it would.

He went from pulling on the reins to pulling his Colt in one motion, twisted in the seat with his pistol drawn and cocked then searched for Ellis.

After the sudden, unexpected stop, Ellis had lost two or three seconds and was cursing himself as he pulled his Colt from his holster when he saw Jim's pistol turning toward his face. He was a dead man, but still continued drawing his Dragoon, cocking the hammer and bringing it level.

Jim fired his pistol at twelve feet, but the combination of released nerves, the rocking motion of the almost-stopped wagon, and his desire to get his shot off first, sent the bullet to Ellis' right, missing him entirely. Ellis swore he felt the heat from the passing bullet but didn't wait for Jim to fire again and squeezed the trigger of his Dragoon.

The mammoth pistol bucked in his hand, the .44 caliber round blasted out of the muzzle, and in a small fraction of a second, it slammed into Jim Abigail's right upper chest, smashed through his clavicle then eviscerated his right lung's upper lobe and ripped apart his trachea before punching into his left lung and crashing through a rib on the left side.

Jim's eyes went wide before he collapsed, folding himself over the back of the driver's seat with his life's blood pooling around him.

Ellis was cocking his hammer for a second shot by the time Jim Abigail died then held his pistol level for a few more seconds before slowly lowering it, slipping it back into his holster and pulling the hammer loop into place. There was so much blood on the wagon's seat, he knew that Jim wasn't playing possum.

He stayed sitting in the saddle for another minute as he calmed down then dismounted and tied his gelding to Jim's gray gelding. Out of curiosity, while he was there, he pulled off Jim's saddlebags and wasn't surprised to find his missing cash in the second one. He did a quick count and came up with around eleven hundred dollars. He replaced the saddlebags, then walked to the wagon, pulled Jim's body onto the bed and had to return to the gray gelding and take a canteen to wash the blood off the seat before climbing back on board.

He then started the wagon to head to Fort Madrid, now only about an hour away. He'd tell Ernie what had happened and arrange for Jim to get buried then he'd turn around and head back.

———

Sergeant Pete Orris entered the command tent and found it empty except for Colonel Beaumont but didn't ask why it was almost deserted as he came to attention, saluted and asked, "You sent for me, Sir?"

The colonel returned his salute and replied, "Have a seat, Sergeant."

Pete sat down across from a large, folding table and waited.

"I just finished talking to General Magruder and he wasn't very happy. You're related to Private John Keeler, is that right?"

"Yes, Sir. He's my brother-in-law."

"Early this morning, Private Keeler and three others deserted."

"Again?" Pete blurted out before realizing he'd interrupted the colonel.

His commanding officer seemed not to notice and continued, saying, "Again. Only this time, he was successful. According to others in his company, he was the leader of the four men who not only deserted by stealing one of our longboats but did so while they were on picket duty. If that wasn't enough, after Colonel Bushnell sent four men to track them down, they ambushed and killed the four men."

Pete was numb with the news. He'd been the one to convince John to enlist and before, he'd just been a source of embarrassment with his shenanigans but now, he'd done much, much worse.

"What can I do, Colonel?"

"They took that longboat up the Red River. Do you have any idea where they'd be going?"

"Well, if I'd guess, I'd say they're going to where my ranch is in Hardeman County."

"Why would they row that far instead of just going to the nearest town?"

"When we enlisted, we rode in with a nearby rancher named Ellis White. He's a good man, one of the best I've ever met. He was a sergeant in Colonel Bushnell's brigade."

"Yes, I know about him. Go on."

"Ellis was always ahead of everyone else in his thinking and almost a year before the war, he cleared off most of the cattle off of his ranch and took some of mine and drove them to Abilene. He paid off almost all of his hands and even after paying me, he still had almost eight thousand dollars.

"He left some with his foreman to run the place when we left. He didn't tell anybody where he put the money, and John must have asked him a couple of dozen times on the ride to Henrietta about it. I don't doubt for a second that with Ellis gone, he'd head to the ranch and hunt for that money."

The colonel nodded, then said, "That makes sense. Now, General Magruder wants those four men hanged or shot, it doesn't matter which, but he was furious about what they did, and ordered me to make sure that they pay for what they did."

"Yes, Sir. I can see that he'd want that."

"What I want, Sergeant, is for you to lead three men to do the job. I'll supply you with horses and food to track them down. I wouldn't get too close to the river, though. You'll have to swing wide around that Yankee camp that's keeping an eye on us from the west. Those four are about twelve hours ahead of you, but you should be able to move faster than they can."

Pete nodded and said, "I'll get started right away, Sir."

The colonel then leaned back and said, "Pete, you've been with me right from the start, and you're one of the best men I have. I'm going to be honest with you. We've been tilting at windmills for quite some time now. The Yankees have finally figured out how to fight and between Sherman down here and Grant up in Virginia, we're getting our butts whipped. Now, tomorrow, we're going to be crossing the Mississippi into Louisiana and chasing General Banks' army. We'll probably push them for a while, but it won't do anything more than make this damned war last a while longer."

He slid some papers across the table and said, "These are discharge papers for you and the other three men. The army won't be here by the time you could get back anyway. Take the horses and weapons in lieu of your mustering out pay. You go back to Hardeman County and that wife of yours and start fixing what the politicians broke."

Pete stared at the liberating papers for fifteen seconds before he slowly picked them up and slid them into his blouse pocket. The persistent whisper of his upcoming death died as he realized that in a few short days, he'd be seeing Mary Jo again. He wanted to jump up and cheer, but he was still sitting before his commanding officer.

"Will that be all, Sir?"

Colonel Beaumont smiled, rose, extended his hand, and as Ellis shook it, he said, "Go to the quartermaster. He's been briefed. Good luck, Mister Orris."

Pete held back his urge to grin then replied, "Thank you, Sir," then just before he turned, the colonel had one more thing to add.

"Oh, and just to let you know Sergeant White didn't get hanged. He was given his parole because he saved a Yankee captain from being hanged by none other than your brother-in-law. They captured him when he was escorting the captain back to his lines."

"*Ellis is alive?*" he exclaimed.

"Unless he did something stupid on the way back to his ranch. He's probably back there already using that hidden money to build it back up."

That news released Pete's grin then he saluted the colonel even though he was technically a civilian now then did an about face and exited the command tent.

Once outside, he read the names on the other three discharge papers wished they were different men then hurried off to find them. Once he'd pulled them all together, they'd head over to the quartermaster's tent and prepare to start their chase. He knew where the Yankee brigade was camped, but once he was past the camp, they should have an easy ride to Hardeman County and to Mary Jo.

———

Mary Jo was sitting with Sara Mae in the kitchen having tea with sugar and fresh cream while Sonny and Mandy were on the front porch drawing on their chalk boards.

"Couldn't you have slipped me a note or something?" Sara Mae asked.

"I couldn't take that risk, Sara Mae. I wanted to tell you so much that it hurt. He just had me terrified."

"I'm sure that Ellis is going to make him pay for what he did to you and Lou Gordon."

Mary Jo sipped her tea then asked, "So, Sara Mae, you finally have your wish and you're living with Ellis. He told me that you own his heart and soul, but wished you owned the rest, too. Does that mean that you're not sleeping together?"

"Yes, and it's torture for both of us."

"When he told me that Pete was still alive, I felt like a fire exploded inside me. My Pete's coming home and I'm so excited, even if it's going to be a year. I was worried that Pete might be ashamed of me or angry, but Ellis said that he wouldn't be. I guess men talk to men differently than they talk to us."

"I know. He told me some of the things John said about me and the children when he did talk about us. He said that John called me a cow. Can you believe it?"

"Oh, I can believe it, Sara Mae. That bastard didn't deserve you. Ellis does, though, doesn't he?"

Sara Mae's eyes smiled as she looked at her sister and replied, "He does, and I feel so very lucky to be here with him. He loves Sonny and Mandy, too. They think the world of him. I know it makes me sound like a heartless witch, but I want to get a telegram telling me that John was killed. Ellis says that it's unlikely because John avoided dangerous places, so it could be a long time before we know what John is going to do."

"Personally, I don't think those marriage vows of yours are worth a pile of beans. Didn't John promise to 'love, honor and protect' you?"

Sara Mae nodded but said, "I know he did none of those things, but just because he broke his promise doesn't mean much to Ellis, I'm afraid."

Mary Jo stared at her older sister, smiled and said, "Then we'll just have to see if we can convince him to have you join him in his bedroom, or have you already asked?"

Sara Mae smiled back then sighed and said, "I offered to do just that. I think he was close to letting me too, but asked to postpone what we both wish to happen. I bumped into him in the barn and he had to catch me and then we had an extended, glorious few minutes of exploring before he stopped. I knew he was in agony when we left the barn and I wasn't much better, but he still slept alone."

"I could tell on the ride over here that he was, um, anxious, shall we say. You really stirred him up, Sara Mae."

"I know. He stirred me up, too. It's more like a bottled tornado than just being stirred up."

"Did you want me to go back to the Big O, so I don't get in the way?"

"No. No. You stay here. We can talk freely now, and I don't think it would make any difference anyway. Ellis is a strong man and he'll do what he thinks is right regardless of the consequences or what he may want to do. When he finally accepts that John is my husband in name only and he's my husband in every other way, then he'll let me into his bed and his life."

"I hope that's soon, Sara Mae. Now, let's talk about things that don't involve sex. I'm already getting excited about seeing Pete again, and if I dwell on it too much, I'll get all frazzled."

Sara Mae laughed and said, "Okay. Did I tell you about the chickens?"

———

Ellis rolled the wagon, two steers and two horses into Fort Madrid and pulled to a stop in front of Smith's Dry Goods and Sundries, hopped down then crossed the porch and walked through the open doors.

Ernie spotted him as he entered and waved him over before Ellis could say a word.

"I got a telegram for ya, Ellis," he said as he reached under the counter and pulled out a sheet of paper.

Ellis accepted the telegram and just slipped it unread into his pocket.

"Ain't you gonna read it, Ellis? It's mighty good news."

"Ernie, I saw Jim Abigail leavin' the Big O this mornin' trailin' two cattle and his saddle horse. I got kinda worried about Mary Jo and rode over there. I found her strapped down to the bed and she told me that Jim was gonna run. I chased him down and caught up with him about three miles north of here. He pulled his pistol and took a shot before I could get mine out of the holster, but he missed, and I didn't. His body is in the back of the wagon and I need to get him buried. Who's doin' the buryin' these days?"

Ernie's mouth dropped open but quickly shut before he said, "Take it down the street to Abner's livery. He handles the buryin'."

"I'll do that in a minute. Do you want the cattle?"

"Sure. I give 'em ten dollars' worth of credit for each critter."

"Is that Yankee dollars or Confederate?"

"Yankee dollars, of course. I ain't gonna cheat 'em."

"Okay, do I leave 'em with the butcher?"

"Nope, take 'em down to Abner's for that, too. He keeps 'em in one of his corrals until we need 'em."

"Okay, I'll do that. And put the credit on Mary Jo's account. They're her steers."

"Okay, I'll do that."

"Ernie, after I empty that wagon, I don't want to go back with it empty, so I'll fill it with hay and say a half a cord of firewood."

"That'll run you three dollars, Ellis."

"I'm gonna drop off the body and the cattle then I'll be back and load up the wagon."

"See ya shortly, then."

Ellis gave him a short wave before leaving the store and climbing back into the driver's seat. His quick dousing hadn't done a very good job and he'd have to use a stone to get the rest of the bloodstains off the seat, but that was for later.

After he'd dropped off the body and the cattle at Abner's, who didn't seem overly shocked at Jim's demise nor the method, he returned the wagon to Ernie's feed and grain where they loaded the firewood and then filled the rest of the space with hay.

Once that was done, Ellis let the draft horses drink and rest for the return trip while he went to the café and had something to eat and a lot of water.

When he returned to settle with Ernie for the hay and wood, he found the proprietor busy with Mrs. Morris, so he walked the aisles to buy some things for the children and maybe something special for Sara Mae. He'd pick up something for Mary Jo too, now that she would be staying with them. It also meant that he'd move into the bunkhouse where he'd left the rattlesnake hide.

He bought a small box of hair ribbons for Mandy then a harmonica for Sonny and a checkerboard set for everyone along with a couple of decks of playing cards to teach Sonny the intricacies of poker.

He then had to figure out what to get Mary Jo and bought her a hairbrush thinking if she had one, it was back at the Big O. He'd have to make a trip back to the ranch house to get her things anyway, but she could always use a new one.

But even after searching for another ten minutes, he hadn't found anything that he thought would be right for Sara Mae. She'd bought all of her clothes already and he simply couldn't find anything that would suit her.

He finally gave up and walked to the front of the store, set them on the counter and Ernie began adding up his total, including the hay and wood.

"Ernie, I want to get somethin' special for Sara Mae, but nothin' seemed right. You got any ideas?"

"Ladies always like jewelry, Ellis."

"I ain't so sure that she would, though. Besides, you ain't got any."

Ernie reached down under his counter, pulled open a drawer, extracted a wooden box and set it on the wide shelf.

"I told ya, Ellis. Folks trade for things a lot."

He opened the box and Ellis saw a mishmash of chains and sparkly things and began to rummage as Ernie watched.

Ellis pulled out one item after another and nothing seemed right for Sara Mae until he found an unusual, silver ring with a pair of hands holding a heart.

"What's this, Ernie?" he asked as he showed him the ring.

"I got that from an Irish feller. He said it's what they call a claddagh ring and it stands for friendship, love and loyalty."

"It looks about the right size, so I'll take this."

Ernie smiled as he closed the box and returned it to the drawer.

"Altogether, your total is $13.50, but I guess you can afford it, ain't that right?"

"Sure," he replied as he took out one of the twenty-dollar bills from his own stash that Jim Abigail was trying to steal.

Ernie gave him his change and Ellis took the bag but put Sara Mae's ring in his pocket.

Ten minutes later, he was driving the wagon out of Fort Madrid when he finally remembered to read the telegram that was stuffed in his right pants pocket.

He pulled it free unfolded it and read the amount. Seven thousand eight hundred dollars and forty-five cents as of May 1, 1864. The interest rate must have been higher than he'd expected, probably because everyone was borrowing because of the war.

That was a lot of cash to have so far away, so he figured his best bet was to open an account in Henrietta and have half of it transferred there. He now had another thousand dollars in bank notes and the thousand dollars in gold under the anvil. He didn't doubt that he was the wealthiest man in West Texas right now.

He was in a good mood as the heavily loaded wagon trundled north to his ranch.

————

By the time Pete and the other three recently discharged men mounted their horses to head west with their Spencer rifles and full saddlebags, it was late in the afternoon and the murdering deserters were already more than sixty miles ahead as they rowed upstream.

John and the others had finally gotten the knack of rowing and had overcome the night's muscle fatigue. They still took breaks but found that two could stop rowing take a break and then the other two could rest. There was only a minimum drop in speed when only two rowed because the current from the earlier spring rains had dropped off considerably.

They expected to reach the Fresh Water Creek tributary in three more days and had no intention of slowing down. They had incentive.

————

Sonny and Mandy spotted the wagon rolling toward the ranch and popped to their feet as Sonny shouted, "Mama! Uncle Ellis is comin'!"

Sara Mae and Mary Jo both rose from the kitchen table and walked quickly down the hallway, crossed the main room and stepped out onto the porch.

As they shaded their eyes against the glaring Texas sun, Sara Mae said, "That wagon is full and he's trailing two horses, so I don't think that Jim Abigail made it to Fort Madrid."

"I hope he emptied his revolver into that bastard!" her sister snapped then looked at the children and said, "Excuse my language."

"It's okay, Aunt Mary Jo, I heard it before," Sonny said.

"Knowing your father, I'm not surprised," she said under her breath as they all continued to watch.

———

Ellis had seen the sudden appearance of the two adults and waved. He was almost home, and it was almost all over now. With Jim Abigail's exit from the mortal plane, there was now just one real obstacle before he could really get on with his life and that bastard was two hundred miles away and probably working his hidden still in the woods.

But as he was close enough to the house and was able to clearly see Sara Mae, he wondered why he was being so damned particular about John Keeler. He'd just killed a man, and nobody had even blinked. He knew it was the right thing to do but still, with no law around to investigate, *how would they know?*

What was the difference with Sara Mae? He loved her and she loved him. The one who was supposed to love and protect her had done neither and may never return. Even if he did come back, it surely wouldn't be to become the father and husband he should have been.

He knew that no one in Fort Madrid would even whisper a hint of disapproval and knew of three other couples that had lived together without marriage and that was before the war. Now he suspected it was a lot more common with all of the widows desperately seeking some form of stability. Ellis remembered Linda Harrison back in Henrietta and didn't doubt for a moment that he wouldn't have even had to propose marriage for her to join him.

With the next rotation of the wagon wheels, Ellis rotated his own decision of what to do about Sara Mae. He was glad he'd bought the ring now and began to suspect that it was almost a nudge from The Man that it was the right thing to do.

Once he'd committed to the notion, he felt a weight lift from his shoulders. As far as he was now concerned, Sara Mae was a widow and he would be her husband from this day forward. When they finally were able to clarify John's fate, they could go to Henrietta and get married officially.

He was practically bubbling inside as he turned the wagon onto his access road. He'd have to delay his talk with Sara Mae until they could be alone, and he gave her the claddagh ring, but he couldn't wait to tell her.

Sonny was the first to bound from the porch when Ellis was still a hundred yards out then Mandy bounced behind him before the sisters stepped down from the porch more sedately, despite Sara Mae's urge to race out ahead of her children.

Ellis slowed the wagon enough to let Sonny clamber up beside him then had to stop to pick up Mandy and set her on the seat before getting it rolling again.

"You bought a lot of hay and wood, Uncle Ellis," Sonny said.

"Yup. I figured it was kinda stupid to bring this wagon back empty."

"Did you shoot Mister Abigail?" he asked.

"Yes, sir. He took a shot at me with his pistol but missed, and I shot him right where you're sittin' now. I gotta clean off those stains, though."

Sonny glanced at the dark red splotches and moved two feet to his right.

"What happened, Uncle Ellis?" Mandy asked.

"I'll tell everybody what happened after we let the tired horses drink and rest. Okay?"

"Okay."

He pulled the wagon to a stop before the sisters and looked at Sara Mae with new eyes.

"I just told Sonny and Mandy that I'd tell you all what happened after I let the critters rest and drink, so I'll roll to the trough in a little bit, but I did have a shootout with Jim Abigail and left his body in Fort Madrid."

"You did some shopping, I see," Mary Jo commented as she looked at the full wagon bed and noticed the bag as well.

"Yes, ma'am. I'll see you shortly."

He smiled and looked at Sara Mae one more time before snapping the reins and getting the wagon rolling again.

Mary Jo turned to go back into the house, but after two steps, she noticed that Sara Mae was still frozen in place then walked back to her sister.

"Sara Mae? Are you all right?"

Sara Mae blinked then looked at Mary Jo, smiled and said, "I'm fine. I just, well, I'm fine."

She began stepping toward the porch still unsure of what she had read in Ellis' eyes. There was something very different yet very enticing about the way he'd looked at her and she simply didn't know how to react.

Ellis stopped the wagon near the windmill set the handbrake then helped Mandy down as Sonny hopped to the ground.

It took him a few minutes to take the two draft horses out of harness and lead them and the two geldings to the trough while the children waited on the back porch.

He then led the four animals to the corral and left them inside without removing the saddles yet but took the saddlebags with the money, hung it over his shoulder then walked back to the wagon and removed the cloth bag.

"Okay, folks, let's go inside and have a nice talk."

He trailed the two excited children into the kitchen where Mary Jo and Sara Mae were already sitting at the table.

"Did you get anything to eat in Fort Madrid?" asked Sara Mae.

"Yes, ma'am. I'm fine."

He picked up Mandy set her on Sara Mae's lap then set the sack and the saddlebags on the floor took the last open chair and then removed his tired gray hat and set it atop the saddlebags.

"Okay. The part you can all figure out is that I caught up with Jim Abigail less than an hour outta Fort Madrid. He was waitin' for me, and after we shared some words, he surprised me when he yanked the wagon to a stop and drew his pistol. He took the first shot and missed from about fifteen feet. I guess the wagon was still rockin' and it threw off his aim.

"I hit him square with my first shot and then I had to take his carcass into Fort Madrid where I had him buried. Mary Jo, I left the two steers with Ernie, and he put twenty Yankee dollars on account for you. I didn't want to bring the wagon back empty, so I bought some hay and firewood."

"Strangely enough, we noticed," Sara Mae said with a smile.

Ellis smiled back and replied, "I keep tellin' you that you're the smartest one around, ma'am, and this proves it. I'll bet nobody else figured that out."

Everyone laughed before Ellis continued.

"While I was there, I figured I might as well do a little more shoppin', so I picked up a few things," he said as he picked up the cloth sack.

He reached inside and pulled out the biggest item, the checkerboard set and put it on the table.

"This'll help pass some of the quiet time," he said then, after taking out the two decks of cards, he added, "So, will these. I'm gonna show Sonny how to play poker."

"What about us?" asked Sara Mae, "I'd like to learn, too."

"I ain't sure that's a good idea, Sara Mae. I'd hate to lose to you and have you demandin' all sorts of payment."

Sara Mae giggled at the idea but didn't say anything.

Ellis pulled out the box of hair ribbons and handed them to Mandy, who said, "Thank you, Uncle Ellis," before she opened the box and pulled a yellow ribbon out and handed it to her mother.

He gave the harmonica to Sonny, and then surprised Mary Jo when he gave her the hairbrush.

"Ellis, this is much nicer than the one I have. Thank you."

"You're welcome, ma'am. I figure I can ride over there tomorrow and pick up your things."

"Where will I be sleeping?" she asked.

"You can take my room and I'll move out to the bunkhouse."

"Are you sure, Ellis? I don't mind moving back to the Big O."

"That ain't what you told me before, Mary Jo. Don't worry about it. I'll be fine."

He then set the empty bag on the floor and Mandy asked, "What did you buy for Mama?"

"Oh. I musta forgot to get her somethin'. I'll remember the next time."

Both Mary Jo and Sara Mae suspected differently, but neither commented as he picked up the saddlebags.

"Sara Mae, remember I told you that I thought Abigail was holdin' back some of the money I gave him when I left so he could buy the ranch after the war? Well, there's over a thousand dollars of it in here, so that means that we're in a real good place about money. I got a reply from the bank in Kansas, too."

He then pulled the telegram and handed it to Sara Mae. She had already noticed that Ellis had said 'we're in a good place for money', and not 'I'. So, when she looked at the mind-boggling number, she was stunned.

"Ellis, why is this so much?"

"I figure they were payin' higher interest 'cause of the war and everybody was borrowin'. I figure it might be a good idea to have some of that money put into the bank in Henrietta. What do you think?"

Sara suddenly understood, or hoped she did, why Ellis was including her in the decision but right now, it was nothing more than hope.

"I think that's a good idea from the smartest person on the ranch," she said as she handed him back the telegram with a smile.

Ellis took the telegram back then said, "Now, tomorrow, after I get Mary Jo's things, I intend to head back to Fort Madrid and get that buckboard and the chickens. But first, I need to get that wagon emptied."

"I'll help, Uncle Ellis," Sonny said.

"You'd better, mister. That's a fine musical instrument I gave ya, and you need to work it off."

Sonny grinned and as Ellis stood, he popped off his chair then the two males in the room left the kitchen to begin unloading the wagon.

Sara Mae watched them leave and wondered what surprise Ellis had in store for her and hoped he expected to give it to her tonight in the bunkhouse.

———

It took Ellis and Sonny almost an hour to unload the wagon while Sara Mae and Mary Jo cooked supper. When they finally finished, they took off their shirts and let the water being pumped but the turning windmill flow over their heads and then let it run over their sweaty torsos before putting their shirts back on.

"Thanks, Sonny. You did a good job."

"Thanks, Uncle Ellis. It felt kinda good to get somethin' done."

"It does, don't it?" he asked with a smile as they walked onto the porch and stepped into the house.

Dinner conversation was spent talking about what was going to happen the next few days, during which Ellis announced his decision to go to the Comanche village and retrieve his herd.

"Why so soon, Ellis?" Sara Mae asked.

"Well, in a little while, I plan on hirin' a couple of ranch hands and I'll need a remuda again. I want to give a yearling

C.J. PETIT

to Mandy, too. Sonny has his horse and you have Tippy, but I think a pretty young lady needs her very own horse, too. Isn't that right, Mandy?"

"*I can have a horse of my own?*" she asked with wide eyes.

"Yes, ma'am, and you'll get to pick her out."

Sara Mae asked, "How will you get them back here?"

"I'm sure Rufus will have a few braves help guide 'em back. The Comanches are real good with horses. I'll let 'em take a couple of steers back with 'em as payment, too."

"How long will you be gone?" she asked.

"Oh, I figure three days at the most. Maybe only two if the Comanche are willin' to do it on their own and I can just ride back."

"I think that would be better, Ellis."

Ellis smiled at her and said, "Then I'll make it that way, Sara Mae."

"Good."

Ellis let Mary Jo help Sara Mae with the cleanup while he moved some of his things out of his room and with Sonny's assistance, they took them to the bunkhouse.

As they walked with their full arms, Sonny asked, "Uncle Ellis, can I come along to the village? I'd like to see Uncle Rufus again."

"You didn't figure I'd let you stay here with all of them women folk, did ya?"

Sonny grinned as they entered the bunkhouse and replied, "Thank you, Uncle Ellis."

After dropping off their loads, Ellis and Sonny returned to the house and once in the main room, Ellis took a sheet of paper from the stack on the corner and picked up a pencil.

Sonny watched as Ellis began writing numbers then doing some adding and subtracting which Sonny hadn't done before.

"What are you doin', Uncle Ellis?" he asked.

"Tryin' to get an idea of how much money to put in different places. I ain't none too happy about havin' so much cash on the ranch. Sooner or later the word gets out and all sorts of bad boys will be payin' us a visit to try and steal it.

"Now this big number here is what we got in the bank in Kansas. These other two numbers are the cash and the gold under the anvil. Now, I don't want to have much more than five hundred dollars in the house, but the nearest real bank is in Henrietta. So, if we take some there, and have the bank in Kansas send some of our money, we can keep most of it close enough where we can get to it. I don't wanna keep it all in the bank in Henrietta 'cause I ain't sure of how safe it's gonna be after the war. I gotta talk to your mama about it, too."

Sonny looked at the numbers and asked, "Can you show me how to do the cypherin', Uncle Ellis?"

"You bet, but don't go askin' me how to be talkin' right. You should be talkin' more like your mama than me. I'm just an ignorant cowboy and that's okay if all you're gonna do with your life is handle dumb critters, but you gotta do better, Sonny. You're as smart as your mama and you gotta use them brains to make somethin' of yourself."

"Can't I just be a cowboy like you and Uncle Rufus?"

"Sure, you can. But that doesn't mean you gotta talk stupid."

"Okay, but if I don't talk too much like my mama, don't get mad."

Ellis smiled at Sonny, ruffled his hair, and said, "I promise that I won't do no such thing."

Sonny grinned back as Ellis folded the sheet of paper and put it in his pocket before returning the pencil to the cup.

———

"How much longer are we gonna go today, John?" Hick asked as they rocked back and forth with the oars in their hands.

"Just another hour or so. We did pretty good today and I figure we'll be there in three days if the current stays low."

"Good, 'cause my arms ain't happy and my back ain't much better."

"It ain't fun back here, either, Hick," Eustice Smothers yelled from the back seat.

———

The four gray riders had cut the deserters' lead to forty miles by the time they had to pull over for the night, but Pete didn't think that the horses could keep up this pace for two more days. They'd covered almost eighty miles since leaving the camp, but had to swing wide around the Yankee camp, so they still had a hundred and sixty miles ahead of them. With luck, they'd reach his ranch in three days.

———

The sun was setting, and Ellis was sitting on the edge of the porch with Sara Mae. The children were inside playing checkers with Mary Jo, who'd used that as an excuse to give her sister time with Ellis.

"I think I'll put up that porch swing when I get a chance, Sara Mae," Ellis said as Sara Mae sat shoulder to shoulder with him.

"That would be nice," she answered.

After a long pause, Ellis said, "Walk with me, Sara Mae."

Sara Mae just nodded then they both hopped to the ground, and Ellis took her hand as they began a slow stroll down the access road.

"I did buy somethin' for you when I was in Fort Madrid, Sara Mae, but I wanted to wait until we were alone to give it to you," he said as he reached into his pocket and pulled out the silver claddagh ring.

After they stopped, he held it out to her and said, "Ernie told me that this is an Irish claddagh ring and see the two hands holdin' the heart? He said that the man who traded it told him it meant friendship, loyalty and love. I know it's not a wedding ring, Sara Mae, but it doesn't matter to me anymore. I'm going to slide this on your finger and ask you to be my wife and when we finally solve the John issue, we'll go to Henrietta and get married proper."

Sara Mae's splayed her trembling fingers before her, and Ellis slowly slipped the band onto her empty ring finger.

"I don't know all the words, Sara Mae, but I want you to know that I love you and will always be here for you. I'll honor you until the day I die."

Sara slowly turned to face him with tears rolling down her cheeks as she whispered, "Aren't you supposed to kiss the bride?"

Ellis pulled he close and after she'd put her hands behind his neck, he kissed her just as he had in the barn and felt the same thrill he'd felt then.

They separated and looked into each other's eyes for a few seconds before they turned and continued walking away from the house with their hands locked together.

"Are you still going to sleep in the bunkhouse?" she asked softly.

"Yes, ma'am. But maybe, if Mary Joe don't mind, we can go to the Big O ranch house now to get her things."

Sara Mae giggled softly then said quickly, "Let's go and tell her while you saddle the horse."

"Only one?"

"When I saw you riding in with Mary Jo on your lap, I'll admit to being jealous of my own sister, but you can satisfy my fantasy now by letting me ride on your lap to her ranch house."

"Jealous? Why would you be jealous?" he asked as they turned around.

"Oh, are you really going to tell me that having Mary Jo pressed against you didn't get you excited?"

"No, ma'am. I ain't about to lie to ya. It was kinda difficult for me, but I kept thinkin' about our time in the barn while she was sittin' there."

Sara laughed and replied, "That, Mister White, was the best answer you could give me."

They reached the house and Ellis kissed her once more before trotting quickly to the barn to saddle Tippy while Sara Mae almost floated into the house.

As soon as she walked through the open doorway, Mary Jo could see a level of joy on her older sister's face that she'd never seen before and suspected it was all about Ellis.

"Mary Jo, Ellis and I are going to go to your house, and we'll bring your things back for you, but we won't be coming back until the morning," she said as calmly as she could manage as she displayed the ring to Mary Jo.

Mary Jo rose, walked to her sister hugged her and whispered, "I don't care if you don't come back for a week. I'm so happy for you, Sara Mae. You deserve some joy in your life. I'll mind the children."

"Thank you, Mary Jo. I need to pack some things."

Sonny and Mandy watched their mother disappear and looked at their aunt.

"I'll be watching you for the night. Okay?"

Sonny then looked at Mandy and both children started giggling and it soon infected their aunt.

———

Ellis saddled Tippy in record time then led the mare out of the barn, mounted and walked her to the front of the house where he remained in the saddle waiting for Sara Mae.

She trotted out of the house less than a minute later carrying the cloth sack that he'd left on the kitchen floor and handed it to him before stretching out her arms.

Ellis could feel that there were mostly clothes in the bag, so he set them on the saddle horn then lifted Sara Mae onto the soft bag and after clutching her waist and feeling her arm tighten around his set the mare at a medium trot to the southwest.

"This is nice," she said as she rested her head on his chest.

"You know, ma'am, that I could take advantage of you as we ride along."

"Any advantage you take would be to my advantage as well," she replied.

Ellis dropped the reins and took advantage of having Sara Mae where she was, and they let Tippy handle the navigation as they both engaged in serious kissing and touching as they bounced over the trail to the Big O.

By the time they reached the ranch house, Ellis was almost unable to lower Sara Mae to the ground but managed to get her there without damage and once she was standing on solid ground, he handed her the bag and said, "I'll be in shortly, wife."

"I'll be waiting, husband," she replied as she danced away and hurried into the house.

Ellis watched her and then turned Tippy to the barn and in less than five minutes was leaving the mare drinking at the trough as he jogged to the house heading for the front of the house where he could see light coming from the windows.

When he entered the main room, he stopped and gaped at Sara Mae. She was wearing the yellow dress, and he could tell instantly it was all she was wearing.

Sara Mae was breathing rapidly as she saw the look on Ellis' face and knew the impact that her wardrobe change was having on him. She felt so liberated with just the thin layer of cotton covering her as she slowly began to walk toward him.

Ellis tossed his hat aside then dropped his gunbelt to the floor with a loud thunk as he took a step toward Sara Mae.

"You are the most woman I've ever met, Sara Mae, and now, I swear, that means even more than just what I meant before. You are beautiful."

"We both know I'm not, Ellis, but it's not important what I think, only that you told me I am. Now make love to me like the husband that you are. I want you so badly and I can't wait another moment."

Ellis was too full of Sara Mae to even talk as he took her in his arms, kissed her passionately and then the dams holding back their lust exploded and the small ranch house at the Big O erupted in sounds that had never echoed from its walls before as the mighty flow of released desires raced through each of them.

The yellow dress was the first piece of clothing to be tossed aside as the couple undressed, kissed and felt each other as they wove their way to the nearest bed.

Ellis had long given up any expectation of prolonging the consummation of their joint declaration of marriage once he'd seen Sara Mae in the yellow dress, and Sara Mae didn't care a lick as she let herself experience love and passion as she'd never come close to enjoying before.

Ellis may not have taken the time he'd hope to, but he still talked to Sara Mae and did things to her that had only dwelt in her fantasies. It was a raucous, chaotic fifteen minutes before they finally both reached the ultimate expression of love and passion then collapsed onto the bed, gasping for air as the sweat dripped from their naked bodies.

"My God, Ellis!" Sara Mae said between gulps of air, "I thought I was going to die!"

"I was in heaven already, Sara, and you took me there," Ellis replied as his chest rose and fell under Sara Mae's head, her long brown hair everywhere.

"Are you all right with this, Ellis?" she asked, "I know you were worried because I'm still married to John."

"No, Sara Mae. I finally figured out that he wasn't really a husband to you or a father to Sonny and Mandy. All he ever cared about was himself. I love you, Sara Mae and I'm never gonna regret what we did. I'm so very happy to be your real husband now."

Sara Mae purred as she slid on top of him then kissed him and said, "Thank you, Ellis. I've never felt more like a woman than I do right now."

"If you'll wait a little while, my woman, I'll make you happy again."

"How long must I wait for you to do that, my man?"

He put his hand behind the back of her head, kissed her passionately and then answered her question without saying another word.

By the time they finally slept, it was well after midnight, and neither had given one thought of retrieving Mary Jo's things.

CHAPTER 8

The first to be moving the next morning was John Keller and his three fellow deserters as they pushed their longboat into the Red River just after sunrise. While there hadn't been any rain where they were that night, the heavy downpour from a strong thunderstorm in the hills west of Hardeman County had added enough water to the river to add to the strength of the current, and after just a few minutes at the oars, they noticed the change but were powerless to do anything but fight the increased flow.

Between the four of them, they had eighty-six dollars and change, but it was all Confederate money and they knew that it wouldn't go far. The driving impetus to reach the Slash W and find Ellis White's hidden cache was their source of power as they pulled on the oars.

————

Pete Orris and his three men were on the road twenty minutes later but kept their horses to a slow trot for the long ride ahead, knowing that they'd still be gaining on the much slower moving boat. They weren't concerned about any highwaymen as each man was armed with a Spencer carbine, courtesy of the Yankee cavalry, enough ammunition for roughly ten shots apiece, and various pistols. Worries about any potential thieves aside, they still kept their eyes open because it was ingrained in them after three years of fighting.

The other three men that were riding with Pete were all married, and two had children. Only Walt Harrison from Henrietta didn't as he'd married his wife, Linda, just before leaving. Pete wasn't happy with the colonel's choices, especially Walt Harrison. While not in John's league for malingering, he was probably only a rung or two up that ladder.

The other two, Bill Hotchkiss and Lenny Mowbray, weren't so bad and had been married much longer, but Pete thought that neither man was too anxious to return to his wife. Neither spoke as disrespectfully about his wife as John had about Sara Mae, but Pete was curious about what they would do when they returned. He already knew that there were a lot of widows that were anxious to find a man to take them in and wasn't sure either man would even go home.

But that was irrelevant as the only thing that mattered to Pete, aside from finding John and his fellow deserters, was to return to the Big O and Mary Jo.

———

It was mid-morning by the time the Big O ranch house was no longer occupied, and Ellis and Sara Mae returned on Tippy leading one of the Big O horses carrying two bags of Mary Jo's things hung over its saddle.

Ellis hadn't bothered asking Sara Mae if she wanted to ride the horse, and she didn't even think of asking in the first place.

They enjoyed their new status every second that they could until they were close to the Slash W ranch house and believed they should show some measure of discretion.

"Are you still going to Fort Madrid?" Sara Mae asked.

"Yes, ma'am. If it's okay with you."

"As long as you get back before dinnertime, mister."

"I'll make sure I do that, Sara Mae."

Sara Mae smiled at Ellis before turning to look at the nearing ranch house and wanted to talk to Mary Jo in the worst way. The night she'd spent with Ellis had been more than just inspirational; it had been epic.

———

"Aunt Mary Jo, they're comin!" shouted Sonny as he looked out the front door.

"So soon?" Mary Jo asked rhetorically as she laughed and walked down the hallway with Mandy.

When she reached the porch, she waved at her sister and Ellis, and as Sara Mae waved back, Mary Jo could already see the glow on her face and had as many questions as Sara Mae had answers.

Ellis pulled Tippy to a stop before the front porch then lowered Sara Mae softly to the ground before dismounting.

After tying off the mare to the hitchrail, he looked at Sonny and asked, "Is your horse all saddled and ready to go?"

"I can't saddle him yet. I'm too small."

"I know, Sonny," he said with a grin, "I was just funnin' with ya. Let's go and get him saddled while your mama and aunt go and talk."

"Are we still goin'?" he asked as he jogged behind Ellis.

"Now that's a silly question. Why would I want you to saddle your horse if we weren't headin' to Fort Madrid?"

Sara Mae watched them leave then turned to Mary Jo and said, "Let's have some tea and we can talk."

"This should be interesting," Mary Jo replied as they entered the house with Sara Mae holding Mandy's hand.

———

Ellis and Sonny were off Slash W land ten minutes later, trailing the brown gelding that Ellis had found after the gunfight near Montague and were making good time as they headed south, but they weren't heading for Fort Madrid. He was going to visit the Chesterfield ranch first then, if that worked out, he'd go to the Andersons and see about those chickens.

When they reached the road to Henrietta, they turned east instead of west and soon spotted the Chesterfield place and turned down the access road. It wasn't that much different than the last time he'd seen it on the way out of Fort Madrid three years ago.

He and Sonny pulled up before the ranch house and just before he shouted his presence, Abe Chesterfield popped out of the doorway and said, "Why, if it ain't Ellis White himself. I heard you was back. Step down and come on in."

"Thanks, Abe," Ellis said before he and Sonny dismounted.

When they entered, Abe asked, "So, what brings you by, Ellis?"

"A couple of things, Abe. I recall before I left that you had a buckboard that you were tryin' to sell and was wonderin' if you ever did sell it."

"Nope. Still got it. That war sure did mess things up quite a bit. There ain't too many folks lookin' for a buckboard these days. If you give me twenty Yankee dollars, you can have it."

"How's the grease and harness?"

"I kept it workin' good, but don't have any horses. All I got is my two mules."

"Sounds like a deal, Abe. You wouldn't happen to have any dogs you can spare; would ya'?"

Abe laughed then replied, "You might say that. It seems that all I got around here is dogs. You want a couple?"

"Sure. I'll take a couple of dogs and that buckboard. How are they with chickens?"

"I don't figure they care much one way or the other. You gettin' some from the Andersons?"

"That's the idea. I'll tell you what, Abe. You may not care about the dogs, but I'll take a couple, pay you for the buckboard and after I get my herd back from the Comanches, I'll run one of the horses down to ya."

Abe scratched behind his neck and said, "You're gettin' the bad end of the stick on this deal, Ellis, but I sure could use a horse."

"Good enough," Ellis said as he pulled two ten-dollar bills from his pocket handed them to Abe then they shook hands and left the house to check on the buckboard.

Ellis let an excited Sonny pick out the two dogs, but they really didn't look like the coon hounds he expected to find.

They had thicker coats and weren't as skinny. Their ears were peaked too, rather than floppy like a hound.

It didn't matter what they were to Sonny as he quickly found two young males that he liked, and Abe put cords around their necks to keep them from running off as Ellis harnessed the brown gelding to the buckboard.

Ellis and Sonny drove the buckboard out of Abe's ranch thirty minutes after arriving with their two saddled mounts trailing behind. The two dogs were on the back of the buckboard and Sonny was leaned over the back of the seat rubbing their heads.

"Can I name 'em, Uncle Ellis?" he asked as Ellis turned west.

"I'll tell you what, Sonny. I'll let you name one of 'em and you let Mandy name the other one. That sounds fair to me."

"Me, too. I'll name the one with the white tip on his tail and Mandy can name the one with the black tip."

Ellis grinned as the two dogs bounced behind him trying to get Sonny's attention.

He almost reached Fort Madrid when he turned left again and picked up the rather poor southern trail that led to the Anderson farm. He was grateful for the spring-supported seat and the large wheels of the buckboard as it bounced over the rough ground.

"They sure are big for coon dogs," Sonny said.

"I reckon they ain't coon dogs at all, or maybe just a little bit. That was a few years back that I heard Abe had coon dogs, but I guess some other kinda dog got in there among his bitches and had himself a good time, maybe even a coyote or a wolf."

"That can happen? I thought it had to be the same kinda dog."

"Nope. Coyotes and wolves are both dogs of a sort and those boys in back sure look like they got something else inside 'em. But they look friendly enough and I'm sure you and Mandy will have a good time with 'em."

"Where will they stay?"

"In the barn, I reckon. I was gonna get 'em to keep the mice and rats outta there, but they can keep the coyotes and foxes away from the chickens, too."

"Maybe we shoulda got a girl dog too, so we could have puppies."

Ellis laughed then said, "We can always go back. I don't figure Abe is gonna be short of dogs for the rest of his days."

Sonny smiled at Ellis before they hit a big bump and the buckboard lurched almost dumping Sonny in back with the dogs.

They turned down the access road to the Anderson farm ten minutes later and could already see chickens just about everywhere. They had two large coops with nesting boxes, but there were dozens of loose chickens pecking at the ground.

"Lookit all those chickens!" exclaimed Sonny as he pointed.

"We gotta be careful we don't squash 'em. It'll be good to see how our new furry friends act around 'em, too."

They rolled the buckboard close to the front door, and Mabel Anderson stepped out of the nearby barn at the sound. Ellis knew her and her husband Ed well enough, but he knew their sons, Jack and Buddy, better because he'd served with them for three years and were both still back east with his regiment.

"Howdy, Mabel," he said as she neared.

"Glory be! I heard you were back, Ellis, but I thought folks was just goin' a bit silly. What happened?"

"I got myself captured by a Yankee picket line and they gave me parole, so I came back here. When I left, Jack and Buddy were both fine and that was only a couple of weeks ago. Like the rest of us, they lost some weight, but that's because they didn't eat any of their mama's good cookin'."

"Thank you for the news, Ellis. Letters only show up when they write 'em, and neither boy was all that good with his writin'. What brings you by?"

"Well, Mabel, I'd like to buy some chickens for my ranch, so I wouldn't have to drive to Fort Madrid all the time just for eggs."

"Step on down, and we'll talk with Ed. He's kinda under the weather right now, so I've been takin' care of the birds."

"Thank you, ma'am," Ellis said before clambering down as Sonny hopped down from the other side.

"How many do you want?" she asked as they climbed the steps to the front porch.

"I reckon you'd know better than me, Mabel. I figure a dozen eggs a day and maybe a chicken a week for the pot would suit me about right."

"Well, I think three dozen hens and a couple of roosters would do that and you could always come back and buy some more if you need 'em."

They walked into the house and Ellis saw Ed sitting in a chair with his leg on the table. He looked pallid and was sweating even more than he should have in the warm room.

"Howdy, Ed," Ellis said as he removed his hat.

"I heard what you told Mabel, Ellis, and I'm glad you got outta there. I kinda cut my leg a few days ago and it's swollen up some."

Ellis nodded, understanding that infection had set in and with no doctors within fifty miles, the chances of Ed living another month were slim.

"Bad luck there, Ed. Mabel says three dozen chickens would do the job along with a couple of roosters. How much would you like for the birds?"

"Well, if you want the cages to move 'em, how about two dollars a dozen?"

"I don't know, Ed, that seems mighty cheap for all those egg-layers, how about I give you twenty Yankee dollars?"

Ellis could tell that it was probably more cash than the Andersons had seen the entire year. They probably bartered their eggs and chickens with Ernie for their supplies.

"That's right kind of you, Ellis. Are you sure you can part with that much cash?"

"I'm in good shape, Ed. I sold most of my herd up in Abilene before the war."

"I heard about that. There's all sorts of talk about the Ellis White treasure. I'm kinda surprised you ain't been visited by all kinds of bad sorts."

"I was kinda. Just yesterday, my old foreman tried to run off with some of the cash I left him to run the place. I caught up with him north of Fort Madrid and had a bit of a gunfight. I'm here and he ain't, so you can figure out how that went."

Ed nodded then Mabel said, "Let's go out there and get those chickens in some cages for you, Ellis."

"Yes, ma'am," he replied, then smiled at Ed and said, "You get better, Ed. I'm probably gonna need some teachin' on how to handle these ornery chickens."

Ed laughed and said, "Nah. They ain't hard at all compared to those four-legged critters you have to herd all over Texas."

Ellis laughed then waved at Ed as he and Sonny left the house with Mabel.

After they'd stepped down, Ellis took the harness of the buckboard and followed Mabel.

When they reached the barn, Mabel said, "We'll pick up three cages inside. They're good-sized, so each one can handle a dozen chickens."

Ellis and Sonny each took a big cage and Mabel grabbed a third then carried them to the buckboard and slid them onto the back behind the two dogs who watched curiously.

"You just get the dogs?" she asked.

"Yes, ma'am. I hope they'll be okay with the chickens."

"You never know with dogs," she said as she began to walk to the first big chicken coop.

Ellis led the buckboard to the coop then stopped near the door and set the handbrake.

"What kinda chickens are those?" he asked.

"They're Rhode Island Reds. They're good egg-layers."

"Lordy, Mabel! Couldn't you find some Texas Tans or even some Georgia Greens?"

Mabel laughed and said, "Sorry, Ellis. This is what we've got."

"I guess I don't have to tell nobody that. Let's load 'em up."

Ellis found that catching chickens wasn't as easy as he expected, and Mabel had two of the cages full of the birds before Sonny and Ellis filled their one and both of Mabel's had the roosters.

"Just put them into a coop with water and feed and nesting boxes. You'll have to clean it, too."

"Thanks, Mabel," he said as he reached into his pocket, then pulled out a twenty-dollar note and handed it to her.

Then he said, "Mabel, if there's anything I can do to help, just come and see me at the Slash W. That ain't no empty words, neither. I figure you're gonna be needin' some help and I'll see that things are okay 'til your boys come home."

Mabel knew what he meant, but neither mentioned Ed's condition as she replied, "Thank you, Ellis. I'll keep that in mind."

Ellis nodded then he and Sonny climbed into the buckboard then he released the handbrake and waved to Mabel before turning it around and heading for the access road then turning north.

Once they were back on the trail, Sonny asked, "What was wrong with Mister Anderson?"

"His leg got infected from whatever cut it. I don't think it's gonna get any better, either. I saw too many men die or lose limbs from even small wounds that got infected and without any doctors to help him, I figure Ed Anderson won't be around long."

"Oh. Does Mrs. Anderson know?"

"Yup. I'm sure she does and so does Ed, but there's nothin' anybody can do now."

The idea that someone could die from a simple cut put a damper on the trip home, but after they reached the northern road, Ellis knew he had to get Sonny back into a normal frame of mind.

"You didn't bring your new harmonica, did you, Sonny?"

"Sure. It's in my pocket."

"Well, give it a try! A couple of those boys in my company were pretty good with 'em."

"I don't know how to play it. It sounds funny."

"Go ahead and try anyway."

Sonny pulled out the harmonica and began to blow, creating the normal boy concerto of mixed notes that had neither rhyme nor rhythm.

"See?" he asked as he stopped playing.

Ellis said, "Give it here and I'll show you how a master harmonica player uses that fine instrument. When I was a boy, I had me a mouth organ and folks thought I was so good that by the time I was grown up, I'd be playin' in an opera house in front of passels of folks, maybe in New Orleans or even New York. Now, you listen and hear how it's done."

Sonny quickly handed him the harmonica and Ellis gave him the reins to the horse. He took a deep breath and rammed all the air he could through the chambers of the harmonica resulting a painfully long, ear-splitting single note that soon had the two dogs howling and the chickens all flapping their wings as they tried to escape from their cages.

Sonny had his hands over his ears as he laughed until Ellis stopped and exchanged harmonica for the buckboard reins.

"Now, yours wasn't so bad, was it?"

"No, sir," Sonny replied with a grin.

With the good mood restored, Ellis drove while Sonny practiced on his harmonica.

———

"What made him change his mind, Sara Mae?" asked Mary Jo, who had totally altered her view of Sara Mae as anything close to Puritanical.

"He said it was after he shot Jim Abigail. It was a fair fight, but he'd just killed a man and there were no consequences. When he saw me and the children again when he was returning, he said that it dawned on him that John didn't care and had forfeited his rights as a husband and father and he actually looked at me as his wife. He even said he felt as if he'd gotten divine approval."

"Wow! That's pretty impressive. Does this mean I have to move out now?"

"He said he'd still stay in the bunkhouse because he wants to make sure it's safe. He doesn't want you to live alone."

"It would have been better than living with that bastard."

"Well, you're here with us now and soon, Pete will be home."

Mary Jo sighed and said, "I hope this damned war is over sooner than Ellis thinks it will be. I'm afraid that Pete won't make it. He was a lot like Ellis and always had to take charge. Men like that are the ones who get shot. Ellis said he'd already been shot in the stomach and somehow survived."

"I know. Ellis was shot twice, but John never even got a splinter."

Mary Jo paused then smiled, "Just make sure you don't get any splinters on your behind when you go sneaking off to that bunkhouse at night."

Sara Mae closed her eyes, smiled and said, "I wouldn't care if it was the size of a pencil if it meant spending the night with Ellis," then she shivered as she wrapped her arms around herself as she relived last night.

———

If the Red River had been a straight waterway, John Keeler, Hick Smith, Eustice Smothers, and Al Hartman would have been a hundred miles ahead of their pursuers by the time Ellis turned his chicken-loaded buckboard onto his access road. But the Red River, like almost all rivers, was a winding, treacherous passage that meant as their second full day of rowing continued, they were only thirty miles ahead and at the rate that Pete and his three men were gaining, they would have passed the deserters and been waiting for them when they arrived at Fresh Water Creek.

But as the four riders were just two miles out of Bonham, Lenny Mowbray's gelding snapped his left foreleg when it dropped into an unexpected and unnoticed six-inch deep hole. Lenny had gone flying, and they had to shoot the animal. Getting another horse was almost impossible, unless they stole it, and Pete wasn't about to let that happen.

Pete decided that they had enough time to double up, which would slow them down considerably so, after transferring the scabbard and saddlebags to Pete's horse, Lenny Mowbray climbed up behind Walt Harrison and they started west again at a reduced speed. Lenny would switch to ride with Bill Hotchkiss when they stopped for breaks, which now would be more frequent.

Pete was familiar with the Red River's snaking path and thought that with the deserters' lack of rowing skill, he'd still be gaining on them. He was right, but the rate of closure had been reduced to just a couple of hundred yards an hour, which meant that he couldn't afford any more delays.

———

John Keeler, Hick Smith, Eustice Smothers, and Al Hartman were working much better as a team now. They didn't even spend too much time talking as they stroked their oars. They'd had their own delay a few hours earlier when they ran aground on a sand bar and had to drag the longboat free from the mud, but their delay didn't have any other consequences and were soon back in the center channel and making good time.

When they did talk, the conversation was about two things: Ellis White's money and women. John had told them about Sara Mae and in fact, had almost been advertising his wife as he had already set his sights on Mary Jo. With each pull of the oars, the idea of finding Mary Jo alone in that house on the Big O took first place over Ellis' secret bank, which wasn't going anywhere. He hadn't even mentioned her to the others. Sara Mae was good enough for them.

———

Ellis pulled the buckboard to stop, smiling at a waiting Sara Mae as he pulled the handbrake.

Sonny hopped down from the other side and trotted around to the front.

"Those don't look like coon dogs, Ellis," she said as she looked at the two bouncing animals.

"No, ma'am. I don't reckon Abe Chesterfield kept their mamas locked up and some other boys of one sort or another snuck in there."

Mary Jo walked to the back and saw all of the squawking chickens in the three large cages and said, "That's a lot of chickens, Ellis."

"Yes, ma'am. We need to get 'em in their coop and then show the dogs their new home in the barn."

Mandy was staring at the dogs when Sonny said, "Uncle Ellis said I get to name the one with the white tip on his tail and you get to name the other one."

"Is he mine?" she asked as she looked up at Ellis.

"If you want him, he is. Now, if you each want one of them dogs, you gotta take care of him but mostly, he'll take care of himself."

"Okay. I'm going to name mine Happy," Mandy said, "because he looks like he's smiling."

"I'm going to name mine Stoney, 'cause I like General Jackson," Sonny announced.

"Okay, you two, you can follow me around to the chicken coop and after we get them cages outta the buckboard, you can have your dogs. Then I gotta see to the horses."

Ellis climbed back onto the buckboard, released the handbrake and drove it slowly toward the barn as everyone else walked behind.

After reaching the chicken-less coop, Ellis hopped back down, trotted to the back then unloaded the three cages. He untied the dogs' restraining cords and let them hop down then gave Happy's cord to Mandy and Stoney's cord to Sonny. After Sara Mae opened the door to the coop, he carried the three cages inside and one by one, introduced the chickens to their new home. He left the cages inside then tossed in handfuls of hay until the bottom of each cage was covered.

Ellis hurried through the gate then after looping the rope around the nail to keep it closed, he looked at the chickens who seemed to be trying to establish a pecking order.

"Well, ladies, we got eggs for as long as we want 'em."

"And that Sunday chicken dinner, too," Sara Mae added as she took Ellis' hand.

Ellis squeezed her hand feeling that his home even without the herd of horses, was now complete. He had a wife and family and he didn't give John Keeler a second thought any longer.

Sara Mae said, "We're going to go and make some lunch, Ellis, but no chicken this time, I'm afraid."

"There's always rattlesnake, ma'am."

Sara laughed then she and Mary Jo began to walk to the house leaving Ellis alone with the chickens as Sonny and Mandy had both taken their new dogs to the barn.

"Rhode Island Reds," Ellis muttered before turning around and then leading the horse and buckboard to the trough still trailing Tippy and Sonny's horse.

———

It was mid-afternoon before they all sat down to lunch and Sonny told his mother about Ellis' harmonica lesson and tried to repeat the horrendous sound that Ellis had created but didn't have the lungpower to do it.

As they were nearing the end of the meal, Sara Mae asked, "Ellis, Mary Jo asked if she would be moving back to the Big O now, and I told her that she'd be staying here. Is that right?"

"Yup. I'd feel a lot better knowin' you were safe, Mary Jo. A pretty young woman like you livin' alone would attract varmints. Even with all of the widows this war is makin', you'd stand out. If you gotta stay here a year until Pete comes back, then you will."

Mary Jo asked softly, "What if he doesn't come back?"

"Mary Jo, I figure Pete's got himself one helluva guardian angel. I heard about that gut shot that he took and didn't even get infected. You gotta believe he's comin' back. In fact, I'll tell you what, Mrs. Orris, now that Sara Mae and me are gonna stay together, why don't you two start plannin' for when Pete comes back. Maybe we'll build a bigger house closer to this one so you and Pete will have room for all of your young'uns. We sure got the money for it. We got enough Yankee cash to do damned near anything we want to do."

"But that's your money, Ellis. Not ours," Mary Jo protested.

"No, ma'am. It's our money, meanin' mine and Sara Mae's. If she wants to help her little sister and brother-in-law, she can do that," then he smiled at Sara Mae and said, "Ain't that right, Sara Mae?"

She smiled back and replied, "Yes, Ellis. I'd be more than willing to help Pete and Mary Jo."

Ellis then looked back at Mary Jo as he said, "So, Mary Jo, no more worryin' about Pete. That guardian angel of his will be guidin' him right back here to you and by then, you and Sara Mae will have everything all figured out."

Mary Jo smiled at Ellis. She'd still worry, of course, but the idea of planning for Pete's return lifted her spirits because it put substance to what had only been hope.

"Thank you, Ellis. Sara Mae is a lucky woman."

"She's the most woman I ever met," Ellis said as he rose, turned to Sonny and said, "Let's go and feed them chickens."

Sonny and Mandy both hopped up and followed Ellis out the door then heading for the barn and the big bag of chicken feed.

After they'd gone, Mary Jo said, "Why did he tell you that you were the most woman he'd ever met? You surely aren't fat and I'm a good three inches taller than you."

Sara Mae smiled and said, "What Ellis meant…"

———

As the sun disappeared below the horizon, Pete's group had already pulled off to the side of the roadway to set up camp. The loss of the horse had slowed them down more than Pete had expected, so they hadn't even made it halfway to Gainesville. He seriously began thinking about leaving one of the men in Gainesville, but that would put him at a serious disadvantage when they found the deserters.

They all had Spencer carbines, which would normally be an advantage, but none of them had ever fired the weapon before and didn't have enough spare ammunition to practice. The other problem was that losing an extra set of eyes to spot the deserters could be critical.

His biggest advantage was that the murderers probably didn't know that they were being pursued and John didn't know that Ellis was not only still alive, but at his ranch. Pete wished they had a telegraph out there so he could wire Ellis and warn him that John and three others were coming, and he could let Mary Jo know that he was going to be back in two more days.

But as he thought about it, he wondered if they hadn't run a telegraph line out to Fort Madrid by now. He didn't think it was likely because all of the resources were being devoted to the army, but when they stopped at Gainesville tomorrow, he'd ask if the telegraph line had been extended to Fort Madrid.

———

John Keeler kept the longboat gliding west for two more hours after Pete had been forced to stop for the night, so when they pulled ashore to set up their camp, they were twenty-five miles ahead. The mosquitoes, while not as bad as they'd been at the confluence of the Red River and the Mississippi were still a plague preventing a restful camp.

"Where do you figure we are, John?" asked Hick Smith.

"No more'n two days out I reckon. I figure if we were to head straight south, we'd almost walk into Gainesville after a three-hour march."

Al Hartman asked, "Why don't we just go down there, grab us some horses and get away from this damned river?"

"We gotta avoid towns, Al. We killed four boys back near the camp, and I figure the colonel's gonna wire ahead and have everybody lookin' for us."

"I suppose," Al replied as he poked at the fire.

"Listen, boys, in just a couple of days, we're gonna be eatin' good, have women, and all that Yankee money will be ours."

"You don't care if we diddle your wife?" asked Hick.

"She ain't nothin' to me. I married her 'cause her pappy gave me her dowry. I still kinda poked at her 'cause she was my wife and was there, but if you boys want her, you go right ahead. I got other plans."

"What other plans?" asked Eustice.

John figured it really didn't matter because he was in charge, so he replied, "I'm gonna corral my sister-in-law. I had my eye on her for a while. We lived in the same house with her, but she didn't like me none. I figure that's all gonna change when we get back."

Hick laughed, then said, "Why? You ain't changed. How come you figure she's gonna like you now?"

"I don't care if she likes me or not, Hick. What's gonna change is that I'll let her know that she's mine now."

"What does she look like?" asked Al.

Once he'd let the news out about Mary Jo, John didn't see any reason to hold back his description of his sister-in-law as he remembered her when he'd spied on her.

When he finished, he spent almost as long describing a naked Sara Mae to let them all fantasize about his wife and not Mary Jo, having already staking claim to her as his woman.

———

Ellis rolled the dried rattlesnake skin and set it under one of the bunks, still unsure of what use he would make of it. He'd tidied up the bunkhouse as much as possible, anticipating a visit from Sara Mae later that night.

He had removed his gunbelt and hung it on a peg and all three of his rifles were leaning in the corner. He'd left the shotgun and shells in the house as both women knew how to use it, but decided that he'd keep his Henry, Sharps and the J.F. Brown with him along with the saddlebags of ammunition.

Satisfied that the bunkhouse was ready for his hoped-for visitor, he was going to blow out the hanging lamp, but left it burning instead. Seeing Sara Mae in her female glory was a thrill in its own, and once she'd realized that it was nothing to be embarrassed about, she'd done more than just accept their unclothed state. Sara Mae had been liberated and despite ten years of marriage, had felt like a schoolgirl, discovering new passions and cravings.

———

Once Mandy had drifted off, Sara Mae slipped out from under the blankets and tiptoed out of the house, knowing that Mary Jo was probably quietly giggling in her bed. But Sara Mae didn't care as she stepped out into the moonlight, feeling the cool breeze tug at her nightdress when she quietly stepped down from the porch and hurried toward the light of the bunkhouse, growing more excited with each step.

When she pulled open the door and saw Ellis waiting for her, she shuddered then closed the door behind her.

That night, their lovemaking was more tender and somewhat subdued as Ellis was able to take his time and express his love for Sara Mae. But the volume increased noticeably in the small bunkhouse as they progressed and finally reached a crescendo before suddenly lowering to a few huffs and expressions of gratitude to the almighty.

Sara Mae stayed for another hour as she and Ellis just held each other on the narrow bunkbed.

"Sara Mae," Ellis said softly, "I'm a completely happy man because of you. I have a wife and two wonderful children that mean more to me than this ranch or anythin' else. I know I keep tellin' ya that you're more woman than any other woman I ever met, and you know why. Every day that we're together, I think you're more woman than you were the day before."

Sara Mae kissed him as she slid her hand across his sweaty chest and simply whispered, "I love you, Ellis."

He knew that she'd have to return to the house soon and was concerned that they might fall asleep, so he asked, "When do you have to go back?"

"Not yet. I want to stay like this for as long as I can."

Ellis just let his hand slide all the way down her slippery back and then kissed the top of her head. He was so utterly content that he didn't think there was anything that could ruin their lives now.

———

Sara Mae had managed to stay awake and slipped out of the bunkhouse around midnight, returning to the bed with Mandy for a few hours of sleep.

The next morning was fairly routine and Mary Jo was thoughtful enough not to say anything, but she did let her older sister know with grins and winks that she was aware of Sara Mae's surreptitious trip to the bunkhouse.

After a filling breakfast of bacon, eggs and biscuits, Ellis assigned chores to Sonny and Mandy that included milking the cow, feeding the chickens and cleaning the chicken coop. The children would be accompanied by their dogs, which made the jobs less annoying.

Happy and Stoney both seemed to attach themselves to their small human partners automatically, which Ellis couldn't figure out. The dogs were friendly enough to the adults but seemed bound to Sonny and Mandy when they weren't sleeping. Ellis was pleased with his decision to get the dogs and seeing they were always near the children.

Before he left to add some hay to the corral and show Sonny how to milk the cow Sara Mae asked, "When are you planning on going to the Comanche village?"

"Tomorrow. I figure me and Sonny can get out there by early afternoon, have Rufus talk to the Comanches about movin' the herd then be back here the next day."

She nodded and asked, "Then you'll hire some ranch hands?"

"Yes, ma'am. I'll do that the day after we get back."

She walked close to Ellis and whispered, "I'm going to miss you tomorrow night."

"That's tomorrow night, ma'am. Not tonight," he whispered back.

Sara Mae smiled as Ellis grinned then turned and left the kitchen trailing both children.

———

Pete and his men reached Gainesville just before ten o'clock, and after stopping at the café for a late breakfast, he wandered over to the Western Union office and asked if it would be possible to send a telegram to Fort Madrid and was surprised to discover that he could.

He quickly wrote:

MARY JO ORRIS BIG O RANCH FORT MADRID TEX

WILL BE ARRIVING IN TWO DAYS
NO LONGER IN ARMY
CHASING JOHN AND THREE OTHERS
THEY ARE USING RED RIVER
WARN ELLIS

PETE ORRIS GAINESVILLE TEX

The operator said, "Two dollars," which surprised Pete, but he still gave him the money.

After he'd heard the operator tap out the message, he left the office and had to hunt down the others who were talking to a group of women near the church.

Ten minutes later, they were riding out of Gainesville heading west for Montague.

———

In Fort Madrid, Ernie Smith was helping Mrs. Monroe load her wagon when the telegraph began to chirp.

He turned to Eddie Baxter, who hung around the store and was an unpaid assistant, but had received and sent messages for him in the past and shouted, "Get that, will you, Eddie?"

Eddie was already near the counter, so he replied, "Yes, sir," then trotted around to the key and tapped out the acknowledgement code before he picked up the pencil and realized there wasn't any paper next to the key as there usually was.

So, as the message began arriving, Eddie just remembered it before he grabbed a piece of used butcher paper and caught the last few words before tapping out the message received code. He should have requested a repeat, but he never had before and didn't want to let the sending operator think he didn't know what he was doing.

When he finished, while Ernie was still helping to load Mrs. Monroe's wagon, he found some clean sheets of paper and copied the message from the butcher paper, but he'd missed some letters and decided he'd just make sense out of what he wrote.

MARY JO ORRIS BIG O RANCH FORT MADRID TEXAS

WILL BE ARRIVING IN TODAY
NO LONGER IN ARMY
CHASING JOHN AND THE OTHERS
THEY ARE USING RED RIVER
WANT ELLIS

PETE ORRIS GAINESVILLE TEXAS

Satisfied that it made some sense, Eddie left the message on the counter for Ernie.

When Ernie finished with the load, he walked into his store, picked up the message and asked, "Eddie, is this right?"

"Yup. It looks like Pete's gonna show up here real soon."

"Well, that'll make Mary Jo right happy. I wonder what took that operator in Gainesville so long to get this sent? That's a good two-day ride from here, but Pete's sayin' he's comin' today."

"Maybe Pete had him hold it until he was almost here."

That made no sense to Ernie, and he was just about to ask for a retransmission, but thought there was nothing urgent in the wording, so he didn't. If Pete was arriving today, there wasn't even any reason to send it to the Big O, either.

He folded the message, wrote 'Mary Jo Orris' on the back and put it in the box marked 'TO BE DELIVERED'.

———

The remainder of the day had settled down to routine at the Slash W now that the chickens and dogs had arrived.

Ellis took advantage of the lack of urgency to climb the windmill and repair the missing blade. That took longer than he'd expected, but while he was up on the top of the spindly structure, he could see his herd and the Big O ranch house and its small herd and thought it might be wise to move the smaller herd to the north with his herd to make it easier to care for both groups.

It would be easy to keep them separate once he had ranch hands and made sure all of his critters were branded then they could search for mavericks, too. He'd seen signs of some of the unbranded cattle when he'd made the trip to the Comanche village and would see if he could spot any tomorrow when he went to get his horses.

By the time he climbed down from his repaired windmill, it was dinner time and he needed to wash up. He needed to take a serious bath one of these days too, as he didn't want to offend Sara Mae. Maybe he'd take a quick ride out to Fresh Water Creek after supper and do that.

———

That night, when Sara Mae made her hurried trot to the bunkhouse, she found a squeaky-clean Ellis waiting for her, but hadn't commented, even if she did have a chance before he scooped her into his arms.

CHAPTER 9

Ellis was the first to awaken the next morning and had saddled both the gray gelding that he'd given to Jim Abigail and Sonny's horse before he walked into the kitchen for breakfast.

Sara Mae set his plate of bacon and eggs next to his cup of coffee before sitting next to him and asking, "Are you ready to go?"

"Yes, ma'am," he replied before shoveling a forkful of eggs into his mouth.

"I made you and Sonny some bacon and egg sandwiches to take with you."

"Thank you, Sara Mae."

"How many horses will you have when the herd is back?" asked Mary Jo.

"I ain't quite sure. It could be anywhere between twenty and fifty, dependin' on what the Comanches will be keepin'. If it wasn't for Rufus, I wouldn't get any of 'em back."

"Is Rufus coming with you?" asked Sara Mae.

"Nope. I asked him, but his wife was pretty big when I saw her, and I don't think he's gonna want to leave her. Besides, I don't know how much longer the village is gonna stay there. Game's gettin' pretty low accordin' to Rufus."

"Well, you get back as soon as you can, Ellis," Sara Mae said as she touched the back of his hand.

"You can count on that, Sara Mae. I know you'll be missin' the sweet sound of my harmonica playin'."

Sara Mae laughed and replied, "That's not the instrument I'll be missing, Mister White."

Mary Jo blasted coffee out of her nose as she began to laugh and cough.

Sonny and Mandy didn't know what had caused their aunt to react that way but didn't ask either.

After taking the bag of sandwiches from Sara Mae, Ellis kissed her softly then smiled at her before turning and walking with Sonny out the back door.

Sara Mae took a deep breath and stood with Mandy and Mary Jo without saying anything.

———

Sonny had asked if Stoney could come along, but Ellis told him that the dog was too young to make the trip as fast as they'd be riding, so after Sonny said goodbye to his dog, they mounted, waved to the ladies on the back porch and rode northwest, casting long shadows across the ground.

Ellis had his Henry in the right scabbard and the Sharps in his left but had put the J.F. Brown in a scabbard on Sonny's horse just to keep it with him. Sonny was still too young to fire any of his weapons but was growing quickly and Ellis suspected that he'd be ready next year.

The thought of 'next year' brought a smile to his face as they trotted across the ranch. Ellis envisioned his life already spread out before him and liked what he saw. He could see Sara Mae by his side watching their son handle cattle while a grown-up Mandy had to fight off the young men. He even saw other, younger children that were his and Sara Mae's but didn't have enough imagination to see their faces. But the thought of an even larger family kept the smile planted on his face.

————

Pete, Walt, Bill and Lenny had passed through Montague by the time Ellis and Sonny were leaving Slash W land, and despite the double-loading, were still gaining on the rowers now ten miles to their north and only six miles ahead.

"I want to get past Henrietta by the time we set up camp," Pete said loudly.

"We ain't gonna stop in Henrietta?" asked Walt.

He was hoping to find Linda and not sure he wanted to get involved in another gunfight, especially now that he wasn't in the army anymore. Pete Orris had no authority over him now and had made the mistake of giving each man his mustering out papers.

"Not if we can keep going. We'll see how it goes. I don't trust John Keeler at all, but he'll want to get to the ranch as fast as he can, and we can't afford to waste time," Pete replied, but was glad he'd sent the telegram. At least Ellis would be ready.

Walt didn't reply but was determined that when they got to Henrietta, he'd let Pete know that he wasn't going a step past the town limits. They only had three horses anyway.

———

Pete was right to be concerned as the deserters had picked up their stroke rate to reach the ranch as soon as they could. All of John's talk about that wife of his had created a bonus incredible incentive to reach their goal, and John already had his own.

They may not have been pulling away from their unrealized pursuers, but they were no longer losing any of their lead, either.

———

Ellis and Sonny had pulled over for a break shortly before noon, and he'd given Sonny a sandwich and when he pulled his from the sack, he found a small note inside.

He held off reading the note until he'd wolfed down his sandwich and washed it down with water from his canteen. Then after stopping the canteen and hanging it back on the gray gelding, he pulled the note from the bag and unfolded it.

My Dearest Husband,

I address you this way because it is who you are. I have never been loved as you love me, and I will be forever grateful.

Return to me as quickly as you can, hold me in your arms and make love to me as only you ever have.

Your loving wife,

Sara Mae White

Ellis smiled, carefully folded the note then slipped it into his empty vest pocket. This note would not be crumpled for the trash bin as the one from Linda Harrison had been.

Sonny had seen his face as Ellis read the note and knew it was from his mother and expected it was a love note because of the way she and Ellis behaved together now. Ellis was his and Mandy's father now and Sonny couldn't be happier.

"Okay, Sonny, let's go and get our horses," Ellis said as he smiled then stepped into the saddle.

"Yes, sir!" Sonny exclaimed as he climbed onto the back of his gelding.

———

It was mid-afternoon when Ellis and Sonny walked their horses into the Comanche camp and were greeted by a smiling Rufus Green.

"Come to get your horses, boss?" asked Rufus as they dismounted.

"That's the idea. Got all sorts of news for you, too," Ellis replied.

"Come on in. Red Deer will take your horses."

Ellis and Sonny handed their reins to Red Deer then followed Rufus across the center of the village to his tipi.

"Silver Dawn is gettin' close, so she's in her mother's lodge. I'm livin' by myself now."

"Well, I hope that ain't too long, Rufus," Ellis said as he ducked to enter the flap.

"So, boss, are you livin' alone, or did you and Sara Mae come to an understandin'?" he asked as they all took a seat.

"It took me a while to figure it out, Rufus, but I finally got to thinkin' that John ain't never been a real husband to Sara Mae and wasn't no father to Sonny here and Mandy. He ain't comin' back, so as far as I'm concerned, Sara Mae is a widow and now she's my wife. As soon as we get word of him either dyin' or runnin' off, we'll get married proper in Henrietta."

"I'm real happy for you and her, boss. She's a good woman, like my Silver Dove."

"She's the most woman I've ever met, Rufus."

"So, what news do you have?"

"Well, Jim Abigail must not have figured on my comin' back, and a couple of days ago, he tied Mary Jo to the bed and made a break for it. I spotted him driving the wagon and trailin' a couple of steers and his saddled horse, rode over to the ranch untied Mary Jo then chased him down. I almost screwed up when he surprised me, but he missed his first pistol shot from twelve feet. I swear I heard that bullet buzzin' past my right ear. I found most of the money that he held back, Rufus, and I brought you three hundred dollars for the lost pay he owed ya."

"I don't need the money, boss," Rufus protested.

"You can do a lot of good for your people with it, Rufus. Yankee money goes pretty far these days."

Rufus realized that Ellis was right then nodded and said, "Okay, boss. You got me."

Ellis grinned as he pulled the bills from his pants pocket and handed them to Rufus.

"What else is goin' on?"

"Well, me and Sonny got a bunch of chickens and a couple of dogs for the ranch and Mary Jo is livin' with us right now, too."

Rufus was about to ask how that was working out now that Ellis and Sara Mae were spending time together, but with Sonny sitting there looking at him, it wasn't the time.

"How long is she gonna stay?"

"As long as it takes before Pete comes back, so it could be a while. That war ain't endin' soon enough to suit the boys who are dyin'."

"I reckon not."

"Rufus, can you have some of the Comanches drive the herd back to my place for me? I kinda want to get back to the ranch by tomorrow afternoon. They can take a couple of steers back with 'em, too."

Rufus grinned and said, "I'm sure that Sara Mae is missin' Sonny right bad and that's why you gotta get back. They already got paid for mindin' the horses, boss, you don't have to give 'em two beef critters for bringin' 'em back."

"No, that's okay. Some of those older steers need to go anyway. How many horses are we talkin' about now?"

"Well, after they take their half of the foals, you'll wind up with forty-two."

"That's better'n I expected."

Sonny then pulled his harmonica from his pocket and said, "Look what Uncle Ellis bought for me, Uncle Rufus."

Rufus smiled at Sonny then said, "Don't you figure you oughta start callin' him pa or papa now?"

Sonny whipped his eyes to Ellis waiting for some form of permission.

Ellis smiled and said, "Well, Sonny, which one will it be?"

Sonny replied, "I used to call my father 'papa', so can I call you 'pa'?"

"Sounds good to me, Sonny. I wouldn't want to get called what I called your father anyway, and it wasn't 'papa'."

With that issue settled, the rest of the afternoon was spent catching up on the events of the days since he'd seen Rufus last.

Before supper, Rufus talked to the chief to arrange the movement of Ellis' herd back to the Slash W and the disappointment about losing the horses was somewhat mollified by the gift of two steers.

———

Pete and his three men rode into Henrietta late in the afternoon and pulled up before Wharton's Dry Goods to pick up some supplies for the last push, and all of them noticed the War Widow's Laundry next door.

"Will ya lookit that," Lenny Mowbray said as they stepped down.

"I'm going to get the supplies," Pete said as he headed for the open doors to the store.

"I'll catch up to ya," Walt said as he and the others grinned and began walking to the laundry.

Pete knew his authority had greatly diminished, so he didn't push it as he walked inside the dry goods store.

When the three men entered the laundry, Walt stopped in his tracks and asked, "Linda? What are you doin' workin' here? I ain't dead."

Linda was staring at Walt with wide eyes as if she'd seen a ghost. She'd never really been notified of Walt's death, but after years of being alone without a single letter from her husband and with her money gone and an overwhelming wish that Walt was really dead, she had gone to work at the laundry to make just enough to get by and maybe find a husband like Ellis White. She wasn't the only woman in the place running under the false flag of widowhood, either

She finally said, "Walt? I thought you were dead! You never wrote me a single letter."

"Well, I ain't dead, so you get yourself out from behind that counter and get over here. We're goin' home."

"But...but the house is gone. I lost it when the bank foreclosed. You didn't send me any money, so I had to work."

Walt really didn't care about the house all that much. It wasn't anything to brag about, but he did want a place to be alone with Linda and he wanted it now. All that talk of naked women had him fired up.

"Where are you livin'?"

"I have a room at Morgan's Boarding House."

When she hadn't taken a step from behind the counter, Walt walked around the shelf grabbed her by the wrist and said to Bill Hotchkiss, "Tell Pete that I ain't in the army no more and not to come lookin'. You only got three horses anyway. Tell him you can go faster now."

Without waiting for an answer, he yanked Linda out of the laundry turned east and fast walked her down the boardwalk to Morgan's Boarding House. She was having to jog to keep up and was horrified when passersby watched her being dragged like a pig to the slaughter which was how she felt.

Bill Hotchkiss looked at Lenny Mowbray, shrugged, then said, "I guess we'd better go and tell Pete."

Lenny replied, "What about the widows, Bill? I ain't goin' back to that harpy I married."

"I ain't either, let her think I was killed or somethin'. But let's go with Pete to that ranch and see what that's like. Who knows what'll happen? Pete said he had a lotta Yankee money."

Bill nodded then the two men left the laundry turned west and after walking a hundred feet entered the dry goods store.

Pete wasn't shocked by the news and wasn't as displeased as he should have been. Walt wasn't a deserter anyway, so there was nothing he could do, and he was right about being able to ride faster now.

He paid for the purchases with almost the last of his Confederate dollars then the three men mounted their horses and left Henrietta.

———

309

Just twenty minutes after being pulled into her small room at the boarding house, Linda Harrison lay on her bed with Walt already snoring beside her. *What had happened to him during the war?* He wasn't overly gentle before he left, but she really didn't know him that well after only three days of marriage. It had been a sudden thing brought on by his upcoming departure but even in his enthusiasm of their wedding night, he hadn't been like this. He'd been brutal and had actually slapped her twice when she hadn't been fast enough to comply. Walt Harrison had become a beast.

She looked at his sallow, thin face and was almost unsure that he was really her husband at all.

———

The four deserting murderers were still six miles ahead of the three pursuers as they continued to row against the slowing current of the Red River.

John decided to push as long as they could today because he knew they had to be close now. If they kept rowing after sunset, then they should reach the mouth of Fresh Water Creek by noon tomorrow.

———

By the time sunset did arrive, Pete's posse had pulled over to camp about forty miles from Fort Madrid while the rowers still managed to put another three miles behind them before they beached the longboat on the shore and set up their camp.

When both groups were asleep, there was only eight miles between them, yet each had no idea how close they were.

———

While Sonny slept, Ellis spent the time talking with Rufus about anything they could think of after Rufus told him that the village would soon be moving and both men knew it was unlikely that they would see each other again.

By the time they did get to sleep, it was almost midnight.

———

Sara Mae was finding it difficult to sleep as she had Mandy tucked in close. She'd only spent such a short time with Ellis, yet she missed him terribly. She shouldn't be sleeping with her daughter; she should be sleeping with her real husband who was up north in the Comanche village.

She didn't know how much longer things would stay this way and began to think that maybe they should spend some of that money and build another house now, or at least make this one larger.

She'd talk to Ellis when he returned tomorrow.

Her last thoughts before she drifted off was her deep wish that the whole issue with John would be solved soon, as she felt uncomfortable with the notion that he could pop up at any time. When Ellis had told her of his two attempts at desertions, the possibility of his making another, successful attempt, had lingered in her mind.

She had no idea just how close her legal husband was when she finally slipped into a deep sleep.

———

The next morning, with the blinding Texas morning sun in their eyes, Ellis and Sonny were already in their saddles, saying their farewells to Rufus and Silver Dove, who was standing by his side. As much as he'd miss Rufus, Ellis knew they had to get back to the ranch, so just an hour after sunrise, they waved and started out from the Comanche village.

Ellis had only been gone a day, yet he already missed being able to just be with Sara Mae and that need spurred him to move the gray gelding at a higher speed than they'd taken on the ride to the camp.

———

John had his fellow deserters in the longboat and rowing about the same time that Ellis and Sonny left the Comanche village. It was a beautiful late spring morning, but none of them cared about the weather as they pulled on the oars. John had told them to keep an eye out for the mouth of Fresh Water Creek as they rowed west.

———

Pete and the remaining two men were the last to be moving, probably because Pete had difficulty in convincing the other two that heading west was where they should be going and not back to Henrietta. The only thing that kept them moving that way was when Pete promised to give them each twenty Yankee dollars when they got there. He didn't have the money but assumed that Ellis wouldn't mind.

So, almost an hour after the rowers began to push the longboat upstream, Pete and his two ex-privates started riding west at a medium trot.

Pete wasn't going to go to Fort Madrid and just as Ellis had done a couple of weeks earlier, he decided to ride straight to the Slash W. He was worried that with the delays he'd encountered, John and the other murdering cowards would already be there, and all he could hope for was that either they hadn't reached the ranch yet, or Ellis was ready for them. Then there was always the chance that they weren't even headed for the Slash W and were already drunk in New Orleans or somewhere else.

————

Back at their common destination, Sara Mae and Mary Jo were taking care of all of the chores that had to be done daily. Sara Mae had milked the cow, while Mandy had fed the chickens and Mary Jo had brought more hay to the horses.

Once all the morning chores were done, Mary Jo asked, "What do we do next?"

"We could start digging up the ground for the vegetable garden. Ellis said he'd do it, but I don't mind."

Mary Jo smiled and said, "I don't mind either, but aren't you worried about being all sweaty and dirty by the time Ellis returns?"

Sara Mae grinned then replied, "Let's go grab our hoes and shovels, sister. My husband will have me any way he finds me. We'll be just sliding around on each other earlier than usual."

Mary Jo laughed, and they walked out to the barn where Mandy was already cleaning up after both dogs had left gifts for the humans.

After they marked off the new large vegetable garden near the potato and onion patch, the taller, stronger Mary Jo began to turn the earth using the spading tool with its four wide blades. Once she'd turned some of the earth, Sara Mae followed with the hoe, breaking up the clumps and preparing the ground for the seeds. The new garden was only about fifty feet from the windmill, and she'd ask Ellis if he could get a hose to run water to the ground for irrigation.

She suddenly giggled when she realized how she'd already become accustomed to thinking of Ellis as the man of the house…her house and her home.

———

In Henrietta, Walt had taken Linda's small amount of savings and sent her back to the laundry while he went looking for work.

It should have been easy to find a job with the scarcity of men around to fill them, but Walt's no longer thought that working in the livery, or stocking in the dry goods store were good enough anymore. They owed him for going to war and fighting for them, and they all seemed ungrateful. No one would give him a well-paying job that didn't require a lot of effort.

After searching for almost two full hours, he headed to Jessop's Saloon for a beer. He hadn't had one in years.

When he entered the place, he expected to find it empty and it may have been close, but there was a table with two boys playing poker and both seemed familiar. He sauntered over to the table, and when he was close, they both looked away from their hands and grinned.

"Well, lookit what the cat dragged in! How come you're back, Walt?" asked Bob Schmidt.

"I just got back from doin' somethin' stupid," Walt replied as he pulled out a chair and sat down.

Jesse Voorhees tossed down his hand and said, "That's what we told ya before you set off. You shoulda stayed here with us. Instead, you go and get married and then try to get yourself killed."

"Well, I just finished havin' my time with Linda, but I need some cash. What have you boys been doin'?"

Bob Schmidt replied, "Not much. We had a good racket goin' stealin' stuff and sellin' 'em on the black market, but Sheriff Eason got word of it and they kinda threw us in prison for a couple of years. We just got out two months ago and we're just gettin' settled, but we're thinkin' of movin' on 'cause the sheriff's been watchin'."

Walt glanced at the bartender, who wasn't looking then said, "I was let outta the army early 'cause me and three other fellers had to chase down some deserters that murdered the boys that were sent to bring 'em back. The sergeant that was in charge told the colonel that they was headed for a ranch in Hardeman County 'cause the rancher that owned it left a lot of Yankee money on the place."

That news piqued the interest of the two men, and Jesse Voorhees asked, "You figure it's still there?"

Walt nodded then replied, "Pete Orris, the sergeant, sure thought so. He even said that the owner, a feller named Ellis White, would give us more money for stoppin' those deserters. Now, I don't figure those four boys we were chasin' went that way anyhow 'cause it don't make any sense. Why would they row upstream when it's a lot easier to just float with the current? Anyway, the only one who was thinkin' that way was the sergeant. But if we wait a few days, the two that went with him, Bill Hotchkiss and Lenny Mowbray, should be comin' back this way and we can ask 'em about it."

315

"How much are we talkin' about, Walt?" Bob asked.

"Well, if he sold all of his cattle up in Abilene before the war even started and even after payin' off the hands, we all figured he had to have more'n six thousand Yankee dollars somewhere on that ranch. There ain't no bank closer than here, and he ain't gonna travel no eighty miles just to store the money. He's got it buried somewhere on that ranch of his."

Jesse nodded then said, "I don't see why we gotta wait for those two fellers to come back, but we ain't got any horses, either. What are we gonna do, walk?"

"Hell, Bob, I bet I done walked a thousand miles in the army. Eighty miles ain't nothing but a short stretch of the legs. You boys got any guns?"

"Just our pistols," answered Jesse.

"Same here. Let's do this. We pack up some food then in a couple of days, we set out. We can get there in four days easy. We show up on that ranch at night and wait 'til he's sleepin'."

"I don't know, Walt. That's mighty risky and there's just too many things we don't know about."

"Well, I'll see what I can find out and meet you boys here again tomorrow."

"Where are you gonna find things out?" asked Bob.

"Just ask around. White went through here just a few days ago, and I figure he stopped by a few places to get supplies and do some other things before he went to that ranch. I bet he even visited the widow's laundry to try out one of the widows, too. Linda tells me that was what some of 'em were doin'. Is that right?"

Jesse snickered then answered, "She's got the right of it, but she sure didn't offer me or Bob anything. I don't think she likes us much."

"Well, she musta put on airs or somethin' while I was gone, 'cause she sure wasn't very cooperatin' when I got back. She knows I'm her husband now, though."

Bob and Jesse both laughed before Walt said, "Why don't you two start askin' around, too. His name is Ellis White and he's got a ranch in Hardeman County somewhere near Pete Orris' place. I can't remember White's ranch, but Pete's place was called the Big O."

"Maybe he's got money, too, Walt," Jesse suggested.

"Maybe. I'm gonna have a beer and start askin' around, beginnin' with the bartender."

Walt then rose and headed for the bar.

———

Ellis and Sonny were still more than an hour's ride from Fresh Water Creek when John and his longboat made the awkward turn and headed about a half a mile upstream before they decided it was too narrow and they weren't making any headway.

They pulled the longboat to the creek's shoreline, clambered out and threw their knapsacks and canteens over their shoulders as they hefted their rifles and climbed onto the flat ground of the northeastern corner of the Slash W ranch.

"How much further do we have to go?" asked Hick Smith.

"We're on his ranch already, but the ranch house is about three miles that way," answered John as he pointed to the southwest.

"Let's get goin'!" exclaimed Eustice as he began striding away.

The other three men quickly caught up with him and with an ever-rising level of excitement, picked up the pace.

———

Pete's group was just entering Hardeman County from the east and were just a mile from the southeastern border of the Slash W, but instead of turning toward Fresh Water Creek, Pete's desire to see Mary Jo again, made him turn toward the west and the ranch house.

But after a couple of minutes, he turned to Bill Hotchkiss and said, "Why don't you and Lenny head north to Fresh Water Creek? It's about four miles from here. If there's nobody there, ride back southwest and you can find the house and barn easily enough."

Bill thought about it for a second, didn't see any problem with the delay because he figured they were on a wild goose chase from the beginning, so he nodded then waved to Lenny and both rode off to the north to check for the deserters that he knew wouldn't be there. They were probably in New Orleans having a good time by now.

———

Pete spotted the ranch house just five minutes later and kicked his tired horse up to a fast trot when he saw specks at the back of the house. It could be Ellis and Sara Mae, or it could be Mary Jo and Sara Mae and that possibility made him focus totally on the ranch house.

The first one to notice Pete was Mandy, who was watching the chickens when Happy and Stoney both suddenly turned to the north and barked.

When she saw the rider, she knew it couldn't be Uncle Ellis because he was alone and coming from the wrong direction, so she and the dogs all ran around the side of the barn and as soon as she spotted her mother, she shouted, "Mama! Mama! Somebody's coming!"

Sara Mae and Mary Jo both turned and faced in the direction that Mandy was pointing and soon saw the lone rider about a mile and a half out.

"Who's that?" asked Sara Mae.

"I don't know, but it's not Ellis and Sonny."

"I'll get the shotgun, Mary Jo," Sara Mae said then she shouted, "Mandy, go into the house! Now!"

Mandy didn't hesitate but began to run to the house as her mother raced inside and by the time Mandy was entering, Sara Mae was exiting with the shotgun where she found Mary Jo still staring at the approaching rider.

Sara Mae slowly walked beside her younger sister and asked, "Do you know who it is?"

Mary Jo's eyes were wide as she replied quietly, "I think it's Pete."

At first, Sara Mae believed that Mary Jo was just being hopeful, but after another minutes, she recognized the uniform and soon picked up the three stripes on his sleeve, just like the ones on Ellis' cut-off sleeve she'd kept in her drawer. When the rider suddenly yanked off his hat and waved it wildly over his head, Sara Mae knew that her sister was right. Somehow, Pete Orris had returned.

Mary Jo was waving back just as frenetically as Pete set the exhausted animal to a gallop to close the last few hundred yards. She took to heart Sara Mae's statement that her husband wouldn't care how dirty or sweaty she was when he returned. *Pete was home!*

Sara Mae still had the shotgun, but once she was sure it was Pete, just walked back to the house and stepped onto the back porch to watch.

Pete's heart was threatening to burst out of his ribcage when he leapt to the ground and flailed forward into the waiting arms of his wife almost knocking her over in the process.

He then wrapped her in his arms, lifted her from the ground and kissed her as tears flowed from both of their eyes.

Sara Mae just smiled and watched the incredible joy on her sister's face before she suddenly realized that either Pete deserted or the war was over, and they didn't know about it. If the war was over, that meant that John would either be returning soon or disappearing.

She set the shotgun against the back wall then walked to where Pete had finally lowered Mary Jo to the ground as they just looked at each other.

Before Sara Mae could speak, Mary Jo quickly asked, "Pete, what are you doing here? Is the war over?"

"No, sweetheart. I've been mustered out. It's okay."

"But why? Were you hurt or something?"

"No. John and three other men deserted and stole a longboat to row upriver. General Magruder sent me and three other men to chase them down because I thought they'd be coming here."

"No, they didn't show up."

"Not yet, but they aren't very good at rowing and the river winds a lot, so they had to go further, too. They're probably a good twenty miles downriver at least, unless I was wrong that they were coming this far. I sent two of the men up to take a look at Fresh Water Creek, so they should be back here soon. I just wanted to see you again."

"I'm so happy you're here, Pete. I have so much to tell you."

Pete then noticed Sara Mae and said, "Sara Mae, I'm sorry, but John should have been hanged more than once for the things he did, but somehow got away with it. I've been given orders to shoot or hang him and I intend to do it, too."

Sara Mae replied, "Good. I don't ever want to see him again. Besides, Ellis is my real husband now."

Pete then looked around and asked, "Where is Ellis? I sent a telegram from Gainesville telling him I'd be arriving shortly and to warn him about John and the others."

321

"We never got a telegram, Pete, and Ellis is up north at the Comanche village getting our herd back. He should be back in a few hours, though," Sara Mae replied.

Pete was still holding onto Mary Jo and said, "It's good to hold you again, Mary Jo. I should have listened to Ellis and stayed here with you. You shouldn't have had to live alone for so long."

Mary Jo bit her lip and said, "Um, Pete, let's go inside and talk."

Pete glanced north but didn't see anyone then replied, "Alright. The other two should be here shortly."

He took Mary Jo's hand, and Sara Mae followed them into the house then passed through the kitchen to find Mandy in order to give her sister and Pete private time to talk and hoped that Ellis had been right about Pete's reaction to the news. He'd been right about everything else so far and wished for Mary Jo's sake that his streak remained intact.

———

Ellis and Sonny were less than an hour out of the ranch and had to stop to rest and water their horses when the quiet day suddenly became a fireworks display.

———

The four deserters were walking at a rapid pace but were still wary of being discovered by a ranch hand or one of those Comanches that John had spoken of, so when they picked up the dust cloud of the two approaching riders, they all quickly dropped to the ground and leveled their rifles.

"Who do you figure it is, John?" asked Hick.

"I don't know, but damned if it don't look like they're wearing gray."

"You think they're deserters?" asked Al.

"Nah. They got horses and why would they be way out here? They're lookin' for us, boys. I'll bet that bastard brother-in-law of mine told the colonel that I was comin' here and he sent 'em after us. Nothin' else makes any sense."

"Do you think they spotted us?" asked Eustice.

"It don't look like it. Let 'em get close and then we open fire."

"Alright," replied Hick.

———

The reason they hadn't been spotted was that neither Bill Hotchkiss nor Lenny Mowbray thought that the deserters were anywhere close to Fresh Water Creek. They were just chatting and laughing about being able to get out of the army legally and figuring on asking Pete for more than just the twenty dollars he'd promised them. If Ellis White had all that money that they heard about, then he could afford at least fifty dollars and maybe more.

So, they rode straight at the four prone riflemen not noticing them in their filthy gray uniforms which blended in with the prairie grass and dirt but still would have seen them if they'd been paying attention.

When they were less than fifty yards out, even inattentive Lenny Mowbray finally spotted them but instead of reaching for the Spencer carbine, pointed and shouted, "What's that?"

His question was answered by the four blasts from the muzzle loaders and the mammoth cloud of gunsmoke that suddenly erupted from the ground before them.

Their horses reared in shock as two Minie balls slammed into Lenny's chest, knocking him over the back of his horse while Bill Hotchkiss only took one hit, but the lead slug ripped apart the left side of his chest splintering ribs destroying his left lung's upper lobe and then leaving his chest after fracturing two more ribs.

He was still alive as he tumbled to the ground but didn't stay that way very long.

The four shooters quickly scrambled to their feet and raced to the two horses that had trotted just a few yards away after the sound had echoed away.

John and Hick chased after the horses while Eustice and Al Hartman examined the two dead bodies, didn't recognize either of them, but searched their pockets for money.

John caught Bill's horse first and quickly mounted, noticed the Spencer then tossed his musket to the ground and pulled the carbine from its scabbard before holding it high above his head.

"Whooeee, boys! Lookit what I got!"

By then, Hick had caught up with Lenny's horse, stepped into the saddle and made the same discovery.

Eustice and Al had come up empty, so they walked over to the horses and Al asked, "Can we double up with ya?"

"I'll take Al and Eustice can ride with Hick," John replied as he helped Al onto the back of the horse.

———

Pete was listening with a barrel of mixed feelings as Mary Jo told him about Jim Abigail. He was horrified, angry, and a bit jealous, but placed no blame on his wife.

She had just told Pete of Jim Abigail's gunfight and death when the combined echoes of the four-rifle volley rolled across the yard and reached his ears.

Mary Jo stopped and asked, "What was that?"

"Gunfire. I don't know if it was my men or John and his that pulled the triggers, but you need to get Sara Mae and Mandy then all of you need to get out of here. Go and hide in the loft in the barn and take that shotgun that Sara Mae had with her," he said as he quickly rose then looked at his wife and exclaimed, "Go!"

Mary Jo nodded then as Pete ran out the back door, she turned to find Sara Mae, who had been listening in Sonny's room with Mandy, walking towards her with the shotgun already in her hand.

They left through the back door and could see two riders coming as Pete raced for his horse that had wandered to the barn to get some hay.

Sara Mae grabbed Mary Jo's arm and said, "We can't go into the barn. They'll look for us there. They can already see us."

"Where else can we go?"

"Follow me," she said as she headed toward the barn, watching the two riders as she did.

Once they were blocked by the barn, she angled toward the bunkhouse, holding Mandy's hand in her left and the shotgun in her right. When they reached the bunkhouse, Sara Mae closed the door and they all took seats on the bunks to catch their breath.

"Why do you think it's safer here?" asked Mary Jo.

"They saw us going into the barn and this door is closed. By the time they look for us, if they get past Pete, then I'll be ready for them with both barrels pointed at the door."

Mary Jo felt sick. Pete had finally returned to her and he may die just a few hundred yards away.

————

Ellis and Sonny heard the same gunfire as it echoed off the northern range of High Hills and after a few minutes of hard riding, spotted the two double-loaded horses heading for the ranch house.

"What's happening, Pa?" asked Sonny loudly as they kept their horses at a fast trot.

"I ain't got no idea, but I'm gonna find out. When we get about a mile out, I want you to pull up and stop near that lone pine tree. Don't argue with me, either. Your mama wouldn't be happy if you got hurt."

"Don't let them hurt her, Pa," Sonny shouted.

"I'm gonna make 'em sorry they ever set foot on our ranch, son."

Ellis pulled the Sharps out of its scabbard as they closed the range. It had the range and firepower he needed, then he'd switch to the Henry for rapid fire.

———

Once Pete realized that he was alone and facing the four deserters, he had to modify his tactics, and left the horse where it was, pulled one of the Spencers from its scabbard and wished he had more ammunition. He was sure that the deserters now had the other two Spencers, but he wasn't sure that they knew he was here.

He left the barn, cocked the Spencer and quickly walked around to the south wall facing the bunkhouse and with the wall on his left shoulder quickly headed east and soon reached the back end of the chicken coop. He stayed hidden as he peeked around the corner and watched the two horses as they approached and soon recognized John Keeler who had a Spencer carbine in his hand.

After stepping around the corner, he leveled the Spencer and aimed at John, sure that he was the reason they were even on the Slash W.

John didn't spot Pete yet, but Al Hartman, who didn't have anything else to do as he clung onto John, did.

He shouted, "Shooter to our left!"

John whipped the horse to his right as did Hick Smith who had heard the shout.

Pete squeezed the trigger just as they turned, and his shot went wide left, missing John by over a foot. He quickly cycled the lever, but the expended cartridge didn't pop free, so he had to spend precious seconds trying to extract the useless brass giving Al and Eustice time to drop from the back of the horses and hit the dirt, so they could reload their muskets.

Pete was concentrating so hard on trying to make the Spencer functional again that he hadn't noticed the two men drop to the ground.

Once their horses were free of the extra weight, John and Hick bent over their horses' necks and raced toward the house to get behind Pete.

In the bunkhouse, Mary Jo had her face pressed against the door, watching through a crack as the fight unfolded. It was already murderously hot in the bunkhouse and both women were sweating profusely. It may as well have been a sauna.

Sonny had pulled his gelding to a stop before they reached the single tall pine in the middle of an otherwise empty expanse of ground while Ellis kept his gray horse moving. He'd heard Pete's shot, but didn't know who had taken it. He knew it wasn't a shotgun, so it couldn't have been Sara Mae or Mary Jo, which meant that someone else was there and was trying to stop the four men in gray who were still too far away to be identified.

But he did see the two men on the ground as he passed within eight hundred yards without being seen by the attackers.

Mary Jo, on the other hand, spotted him and said loudly, "Ellis is back! He's behind them and I don't think they see him!"

Sara May felt a surge of hope with the news and didn't doubt for a moment that Ellis would prevail. She just hoped he would do it before they took Pete away from Mary Jo.

When Ellis was less than four hundred yards out, he cocked the Sharps and slowed the tired gray gelding to a regular trot and kept his eyes focused on the two men reloading their muskets. The fact that they were ramming home powder and ball gave him a real edge. He only glanced once at the two riders who had raced out of sight around the back of the house. He'd deal with these two first.

Pete had finally pulled the trouble-making brass free with the tip of his knife blade and reloaded the chamber with another .56 caliber cartridge but when he looked, he didn't see John and the other rider anywhere, and the two men on the ground reloading were at a bad angle to waste one of precious shots.

In all the excitement, he hadn't noticed where Mary Jo and Sara Mae had gone and assumed that they were in the loft, so he had to keep John and the other man from getting into the barn. He then forgot about the two men on the ground about two hundred yards out and began to walk along the southern wall of the barn, keeping his eye on the house, expecting them to come toward the barn doors where they had to have seen the women enter.

Ellis finally pulled his horse to a stop at around two hundred yards, aimed at the shooter on the left who was finally finished his reload and squeezed the trigger.

The Sharps slammed against his shoulder and the .45 caliber round spun from its muzzle and less than a third of a second later, slammed almost dead center into Al Hartman's back, pulverizing his eleventh and twelfth thoracic vertebrae and slicing through his spinal cord before ripping apart his diaphragm and stopping in his chest. He spasmed but didn't scream before he collapsed to the ground.

The loud report of the Sharps reached Eustice Smothers' ears just as the bullet slammed into Al, and he automatically whipped his rifle around to try and fire at the surprise shooter. But to be able to aim at Ellis, he had to at least get to a seated position.

After firing, Ellis had slammed the Sharps back into his scabbard, grabbed the Henry, and levered in a fresh round as he kicked the horse back into a high rate of speed.

John and Hick had heard the shot and thought one of their own had fired at the shooter near the barn, so they didn't pay much attention as they slowly worked their horses behind the house to try to flank the barn shooter.

Eustice was bringing his musket to bear when Ellis opened fire at over a hundred and fifty yards. It was outside of the effective range of the Henry, but he knew those rounds would distract the shooter enough to either make him hold his fire or take a rushed shot. He might get a hit, too.

Eustice wasn't surprised when the ground just to his right exploded when Ellis' first .44 hit the dirt, but the sound of the rifle that sent the bullet was different. He'd been forced to regain his target when a second bullet blew a hole in the ground just to his left, which did surprise him. *What kind of gun did that man have?*

He hadn't lost that much of his sighting after the second .44 hit the dirt, but he was shaken by the rapid rate of fire and jerked his musket's trigger, sending the heavy slug of lead on its way, but the resulting gunsmoke obscured his ability to see if he'd hit his target.

He hadn't hit his target and by the time the smoke had cleared enough for him to realize it, his target had fired again at less than a hundred yards and the .44 found a home in

Eustice's chest, just to the left of center. He just flopped onto his back with a .44 lodged in his heart.

Mary Jo almost shouted, "I think Ellis got both of the ones on the ground, but I can't see the first two!"

John and Hick both soon realized that they had a problem when they heard the rapid sequence of lighter caliber fire.

"Is that one of them Yankee repeaters?" asked Hick as they pulled their two horses to a stop behind the house.

"That's what I figured. That means that somehow, Ellis is back. I heard he bought one before the war, and I know he didn't take it with him."

"Now you tell me. So, what are we gonna do?"

"First, we get off these horses. You take the back of the house, check out the new shooter and I'll head around the front and see if I can get the shooter out near the barn."

"Okay, John," Hick said before both men dismounted.

Hick then cocked the hammer to his Spencer and began a slow walk to the back of the house while John did the same toward the front.

Mary Jo could see Pete as he walked slowly across the back of the barn watching the house and Ellis as he walked his horse closer, but she couldn't see either of the two men who were behind the house.

Hick still couldn't pick up Ellis yet as he reached the edge of the back porch and took a deep breath. The shooter could be close, so he'd have to aim and fire before the man knew he was there.

He brought his Spencer to his shoulder, leveled the sights and quickly stepped out from behind the house and swept the sights across the vista, until they found Ellis just sixty yards away.

Ellis was expecting the shooter and already had his Henry prepared to fire when another rifle sounded, and Hick Smith staggered to his left before tipping over and dropping to the dirt. Ellis whipped his eyes to his left, then was shocked to see Pete Orris standing by the barn with a smoking Spencer carbine in his hands.

Before he could do anything, Ellis wanted that last shooter who had to be behind the house where the third shooter had been. He waved to Pete then walked his horse slowly toward the back of the house where he expected to find the shooter with his rifle pointed where the dead body lay on the ground near the porch.

Pete then made the mistake of watching Ellis make his approach when he should have been watching the front of the house.

John had seen Hick get hit just as he reached the front porch and as he swung his cocked Spencer around the house, he saw Pete Orris standing there focusing on the back porch.

John grinned and said under his breath, "Idiot. You just made Mary Jo a widow."

He quickly settled his sights, squeezed the trigger and less than a second after the Spencer released its deadly missile, Pete spun to the ground as his carbine flew from his hands.

John quickly recycled the Spencer but didn't wait to see where Ellis was as he raced across toward the barn where he'd seen Mary Jo and Sara Mae enter with Mandy. He needed protection from Ellis' rifle.

But when Mary Jo had seen Pete get hit, she screamed, threw open the door and as she took her first step, she saw John suddenly change his direction then run towards her with his rifle and she quickly backed into the bunkhouse, knowing that Sara Mae had the shotgun ready.

Once inside, a terrified Mary Jo grabbed Mandy, dropped her to a bunk and lay on top of her as she exclaimed, "He's coming! He's coming!" but didn't specify who 'he' was.

Just after spotting the two horses behind the house, Ellis heard the report from the front porch then quickly dismounted and began to jog to the front of the house. Whoever was still alive out there was now a threat to Sara Mae, Mandy and Mary Jo. He didn't know if the last shooter had shot Pete or if Pete's guardian angel had saved him yet again, but he had to stop the bastard now.

John didn't know where Ellis was, but his best chance now was inside that bunkhouse. He'd use Mary Jo as a shield, but suspected that Sara Mae was in there as well, and she'd be even a better shield if she was there for a couple of reasons. He didn't care if she got shot and he knew full well that Ellis White was sweet on her and his wife was smitten with him, too.

What he hadn't counted on was the shotgun Sara Mae was pointing at the half-open door.

Ellis was rounding the front of the house then finally with a shock of recognition, identified John as the last shooter, but had a bad angle to fire as John neared the bunkhouse door. Then he thought it didn't matter as the women should be hunkered down in the house by now and once John entered the bunkhouse, there was no place for him to go. He hadn't been able to place Mary Jo's scream from the back of the house and thought it might have come from the front room.

So, he held fire as John knocked the door open with his foot and saw Sara Mae pointing the shotgun at him.

Sara Mae was stunned when she saw her husband standing just six feet away from her and as much as she wanted to pull the trigger, she couldn't. He may have been a terrible husband and father, but he was still the father off the little girl who was on the bunk just three feet away.

John stepped inside, keeping his rifle pointed at his wife and said, "Drop it, Sara Mae, or I'll shoot you and you know I will, too."

She knew with morbid certainty that John would shoot her without a second thought and slowly lowered the shotgun to the bunk on her right side.

"Now, get step back all the way to that back wall," he said.

Sara Mae was disgusted with herself as she slowly stepped back.

John reached down picked up the shotgun then set his carbine, still cocked, against the wall.

"Sara Mae, you're gonna finally be of some use to me. You're gonna keep me from gettin' shot."

Sara Mae finally asked, "What are you doing here, John? Did you desert again?"

"Yup. And now I'm here to get Ellis' money and anything else I fancy, like your sister here," he replied as he ran his free hand across Mary Jo's backside.

"Ellis is going to kill you for what you did, John, no matter what you think."

"I'll bet he's been diddlin' you since he got back, hasn't he? But you know what, I don't care at all. You ain't never been anythin' to me other than a meal ticket. Those two brats you bore were probably some other bastard's. But I don't care about that, neither. Right now, lady, you're my ticket outta here and Mary Jo and Mandy are comin' too."

Ellis had only realized his mistake when he walked quietly toward the bunkhouse and heard the voices inside.

Now he had a real problem. If John walked out with a cocked gun pointed at Sara Mae, even if he were to shoot John, it was likely that the rifle would go off, killing her.

He knew he didn't have much time to come up with a solution, and it had to be the right one.

Ellis still couldn't come up with an answer when he heard a loud groan looked for the source then spotted Pete Orris rolling onto his back and reaching for his head. Ellis could see some blood, but as soon as Pete had groaned, he found his answer. Now it was just a question of timing.

He quietly walked around the back of the bunkhouse and then stepped about halfway along the east side. He could see Pete on the ground and brought his cocked Henry level. He had to put this bullet exactly where he needed it to go and it had to arrive at exactly the right time.

John heard Pete's groan as well but didn't turn from Sara Mae. His plan remained the same, but he had to alter it to take care of Mary Jo's husband, too. He knew that Pete wasn't an immediate threat and that Ellis was, so he'd have to be careful when he finished off his brother-in-law.

"Stand up, Mary Jo. I want all three of you near the door, and you remember that I got both barrels of this shotgun pointed at your backs."

Mary Jo hadn't heard Pete but slowly rose then helped Mandy to her feet. Sara Mae took her hand and they stepped to the doorway.

John then exchanged the shotgun for the Spencer. He'd need to have a second round ready after he shot Pete, but first, he had to draw out Ellis.

"Alright, ladies, you walk about twelve feet outside and stop," he ordered.

After they left the bunkhouse, John began scanning for any signs of Ellis and didn't see so much as a hint of movement.

When the women stopped, John shouted, "Ellis! I know you're out there and if you don't come out right now, I'm gonna put a bullet through Sara Mae, and then through Mandy and then Mary Jo!"

His shouted threat echoed across the ground, but the only reaction came from Pete when he heard John's voice.

As he struggled to get into a sitting position, Mary Jo saw him move and shouted, "Pete! You're alive!"

John snarled, "Shut up! He ain't gonna be for long and your sister ain't either if Ellis don't show his face soon. Start walkin' real slow toward the barn."

Mary Jo wanted to rush to Pete but the terror of having John just a few feet behind her with that gun kept her feet moving at a slow pace.

Ellis soon had the back of John's head in his Henry's sights and kept them there as he followed Sara Mae with the cocked Spencer. He had to fire high to make sure he didn't hit any of the shorter women or Mandy. He just had to wait for John to take the muzzle of that Spencer away from Sara Mae's back.

John kept scanning to his left at the house but still hadn't seen Ellis never suspecting that he was standing just a few feet behind him.

Pete's vision was blurry, and he could see movement ahead and knew it had to be Mary Jo, Sara Mae and Mandy walking in front of John, but they were just a blob to him.

He shouted, "I'm going to kill you, John. I was told to hang you or shoot you for what you did. It's time to face justice."

John laughed and yelled, "You ain't in any shape to do nothin' but die, Pete, and I'm gonna handle that in a few seconds. Where's your pal, Ellis? Did he run off leavin' you to die?"

Pete couldn't see Ellis, but suspected that he was nearby, so he pointed at the blur and shouted, "There he is! Right behind you!"

Ellis thought Pete had lost his mind and almost squeezed the trigger when John laughed and said, "You think I'm fallin' for that old trick? You must think I was born yesterday."

Ellis exhaled softly as he maintained his target now almost thirty yards away.

Pete's ruse had failed and now he began to suspect that Ellis had been shot. *If he was there, why hadn't he shot John yet?*

John said, "Hold up. I got a job to do first."

After the women halted, he quickly moved his Spencer's muzzle away from Sara Mae then turned it to face a sitting Pete Orris just fifty yards away and brought the sights in line with Pete's chest.

He was grinning as Ellis' .44 slammed into the back of his neck just below the skull and nicked his mastoid tip behind his left ear before drilling into the side of the barn.

John Keeler collapsed like a sack of potatoes onto the Slash W dirt and the Spencer rifle clattered to the hard earth beside him but didn't discharge.

Sara Mae and Mandy both whipped around as Ellis sprinted toward them and Mary Jo raced to Pete without even seeing or caring who'd taken the shot.

Ellis dropped his Henry as he scooped both Sara Mae and Mandy off the ground and kissed his wife.

Sara Mae then pressed her face against Ellis' chest and began to sob as she exclaimed, "I'm so sorry, Ellis! I should have killed him! But I didn't! I could have gotten us all killed!"

Ellis put his hand on the side of her face as he said in a soothing voice, "But you didn't, Sara Mae, so don't say another word about it. You're officially a widow now and officially my wife, and I'm usin' my husbandly rights as head of the household to forbid you from ever blamin' yourself."

Sara exhaled and tried to smile, but burst into another bout of tears as she buried her face deeper onto Ellis' shirt.

He looked down into his daughter's eyes and said, "Sonny calls me 'pa' now, so I figure you should too."

Mandy didn't dare look back at what used to be her father as she just nodded.

He kissed her on the forehead then lowered her to the ground as he wrapped his other arm around his shuddering wife.

———

After reaching Pete, Mary Jo dropped to the ground and was using her skirt to clean the blood from Pete's head while he protested that he'd be okay.

She said, "Ellis said you had the best guardian angel of anyone and now I believe him."

"I think I have two angels," Pete said as he tried to focus on Mary Jo.

"Can you stand if I help you, Pete?" she asked.

"Let's try," he replied as he used his hands to push from the ground as Mary Jo lifted.

He balanced himself against the wall of the barn and then put his arm around her shoulders.

"Let's go to the kitchen and see if we can get you cleaned up," she said before they began a slow walk toward the house.

———

Sara Mae finally pulled her head from Ellis' chest and asked, "Where's Sonny?"

"I told him to stay near the lone pine up north. I'll let him know it's safe to come back down and then I'll clean up this mess."

"Kiss me again, Ellis. Please?" she asked.

Ellis pulled her tightly against him and kissed her softly.

After they separated Ellis asked, "Will you be all right now, Sara Mae?"

With her eyes closed she replied, "Yes, but I don't want to see him, Ellis. Take us to the house."

Ellis didn't reply but took her hand and Mandy's to escort them away from the bloody scene. Mandy had her eyes open but was looking away as they passed John's body without a glance then Sara Mae opened her eyes again when she was sure that she was past the body.

They entered the front door and found Mary Jo tending to Pete's head wound.

"Pete, what the hell happened?" he asked.

"John talked three other troublemakers into deserting with him and they stole a longboat to make their escape up the Red River. You'll probably know them when you find their bodies because they were all in your outfit. They sent four men after them and all four were killed, which really got General Magruder riled up. They asked me to go after him and even gave me my discharge because they said they'd all be gone by the time I returned. We rode as fast as we could, but lost a horse, and after I had to leave Walt Harrison in Henrietta because he found his wife working in the widow's laundry, the three of us got here just about the same time that those four arrived."

Ellis asked, "Was his wife's name Linda?"

"I think so. Did you know her?"

Ellis smiled at Sara Mae and said, "She left me a note askin' me to see her again, but I tossed that one. I got a keeper of a note yesterday, though."

Sara Mae smiled up at Ellis then reached over and took his hand.

"So, there are two dead bodies out there I need to pick up?"

Pete replied, "I'll help, Ellis."

"No, it's okay. I'm gonna go and get Sonny and then I'll harness the wagon and start loadin' them onto the bed. I might be able to make it to Fort Madrid and back before sundown. I just need to know the names of your boys. Like you said, I'll know the others."

He didn't wait for a protest, but quickly strode from the kitchen and stepped out onto the porch then turned left to start collecting horses. The two from behind the house were at the trough with his gray gelding and Pete's was in the barn, so it wouldn't take long.

After he'd gotten the two loose horses into the corral, he mounted the gray gelding and headed for the lone pine.

Sonny had been watching all of the gunfire from the pine tree and had been terrified when he saw so many men being shot and hoped that none of them was his new father. When he spotted Ellis riding toward him, he quickly mounted and rode to meet him.

Ellis held up the gelding as he waited for Sonny, who arrived just thirty seconds later.

"What happened, Pa?"

"Four deserters, including your father, showed up in a boat and I guess they figured on startin' trouble on the Slash W. Anyway, your Uncle Pete and some other soldiers showed up on horses to find 'em and hang 'em for murdering other soldiers, but there was a lot of shootin' that I'm sure you watched. John Keeler and the others are all dead and so are all of the soldiers except for your Uncle Pete who was grazed in the head by a bullet. He's gonna be okay, though."

Sonny took a second to digest all of the information, but finally just asked, "What are you going to do now, Pa?"

"Well, you're gonna go and help your mother and sister. They were kinda upset by what happened. I'm gonna harness a wagon, collect all the bodies and then take 'em to Fort Madrid."

"I can help."

"I appreciate the offer, son, but I think you could help a lot more with your mama and Mandy."

"Okay. Were the dogs hurt?"

Ellis grinned and replied, "No, sir. I don't think so. I bet they were hunkered down in the barn after that first volley. They're just young'uns, so I won't be callin' em cowards, but if they start runnin' from those chickens or mice, I might hang that moniker on 'em."

Sonny laughed then said, "I'll check on them while you harness the horses. Is that okay?"

"That'll be fine."

———

After Ellis had gone, Sara Mae sat at the table while Mary Jo and Pete talked, but didn't listen to their conversation. She was twisting the claddagh ring around on her finger and thinking about the horrendous gunfight and how Ellis had protected her and Mandy. She began to think of the mistake she'd made with the shotgun but didn't try to rationalize the error. She'd almost gotten Mandy and Mary Jo killed because of her inaction. She knew that John was out there and what he was trying to do, but she had still frozen when it was critical that she pull the trigger.

She suddenly vowed that she had to show the same courage that Ellis and Pete had shown, and she'd begin by getting over her fear of seeing John's body. Just seconds after making that decision, Sara Mae stopped twisting her ring and committed to being more than just a wife to Ellis. She would be his full partner.

———

When Ellis and Sonny reached the barn, they dismounted, and Sonny quickly found Stoney and Happy hiding under the wagon. When he called to them, they both trotted out wagging their tails as if nothing had happened.

After Sonny left the barn leading the two canines, Ellis unsaddled the gray and then Sonny's horse, hung his canteen over his shoulder, then harnessed the draft horses to the wagon. He didn't think it would take that long to load up the bodies, and he'd start with John, so Sara Mae wouldn't have to see his carcass anymore.

He kept glancing at the house hoping that no one exited as he began the grisly task. He was so accustomed to handling dead bodies after three years of carnage that now it wasn't any different than picking up that dead rattlesnake, and in John Keeler's case, it was exactly the same thing.

After tossing John's body unceremoniously onto the wagon bed, he just led the team around to the back of the house and after identifying Hick Smith, added his carcass to the back of the wagon.

He then boarded the wagon and headed for the two that he'd shot as they lay on the ground. He had a good idea who they were long before he found them because John always hung out with the same small group of troublemakers.

After dumping Eustice Smothers and Al Hartman's bodies into the wagon, all that remained was to find the two that had ridden in with Pete. He followed the trail left by the double-loaded horses and after forty minutes, he spotted them on the ground.

He loaded them with more care than he had the others, but the wagon was full now. He'd picked up the discarded weapons he'd found and laid them next to the bodies.

Ellis then turned the wagon back toward the house and just needed to get the names of the other two from Pete, then he'd pick up his Henry that he'd left on the ground near the bunkhouse and drive to Fort Madrid.

He may have been physically drained but knowing that the whole question of John Keeler was now behind him calmed his mind and smoothed whatever lingering wrinkle in his soul had remained.

But as he drove the creaking, bouncing wagon, he began to look at motive. John wouldn't have come back for Sara Mae, and even as pretty as Mary Jo was, he couldn't see that being enough motive to come two hundred miles. It had to be the ranch and the only thing that made his ranch that much more valuable was the money that everyone seemed to know was there. Even if he stored the money elsewhere, those damned rumors would persist, and he remembered how even Ed Anderson had commented about the stories.

He was still trying to come up with some solution but was still a bit foggy when he approached the back of the barn, rolled past the chicken coops and parked the wagon near the bunkhouse. After setting the handbrake, he hopped down, took the four muzzle-loaders from the wagon and carried them into the bunkhouse, set them on a bunk before leaving again, snatching his Henry from the ground and walking briskly back to the house.

He'd swung wide of the house on the way back so nobody would see the wagon, but before he reached the back porch, he saw Sara Mae standing on the edge with her arms folded.

Ellis said, "I'm gonna to be leavin' for Fort Madrid in a few minutes, Sara Mae. I just need to get some water and the names of those other two from Pete."

"I'm coming with you, Ellis," she said firmly.

Ellis gawked at her for a moment before replying, "What? Sara Mae, I got a wagonload of bodies and it's gonna be smellin' mighty bad by the time I get to Fort Madrid."

"I don't care. I'm coming. Mary Jo will watch Sonny and Mandy. I want to come with you, Ellis. I told Mary Jo we'd be back before sunset. Is that right?"

"I figure it might be a little later, but not much," he said as he stepped onto the porch.

She hooked her arm through his before they walked into the kitchen where Pete sat with Mary Jo. Sonny and Mandy were already in his room playing checkers, per their aunt's direction.

"Pete, Ellis needs the names of the other two men who came with you," Sara Mae said.

"The taller one was Bill Hotchkiss and the other man was Lenny Mowbray. I wrote them down," Pete replied then gave Ellis the short note so they could have markers placed on their graves.

Ellis took the paper and said, "We'll be back around sundown," and was going to say more, but needed to get that wagon moving, so he held his tongue.

"We'll be waiting, Ellis, and then we need to talk," Pete said.

Sara Mae took Ellis' arm before he replied, "Okay," and they walked out the door.

Ellis filled two canteens before they headed to the wagon where he helped Sara Mae into the driver's seat before climbing up next to her. She took a deep breath, looked at the wagon bed, found her dead husband's bloody face and stared at it for almost a full minute as the team pulled the wagon away from the bunkhouse.

After she turned back to the front, Ellis asked, "Why did you feel like comin' along, Sara Mae?"

"I had to, Ellis. I never want to be a liability again. I know you've seen a lot of death over the last three years, and probably some before that, but this was the first time for me, and I have to get past it. I think I have, and I don't want to be some spineless woman that depends on her husband all the time. I want to be able to help when you need me, and I want to be your partner as well as your wife."

"You're gonna be both, Sara Mae. I'll help you with your shootin' and things, but you never were no spineless woman. You raised Sonny and Mandy to be good young folk on your own and protected 'em from that worthless dead husband of yours. It's not a matter of sand, ma'am. It's just knowin' you have it. You'll be even more of the most woman I've ever met, and even though we got a messy load behind us, I'm real happy to have you along."

"Thank you, Ellis," she said as she locked her arm tightly around his.

"Sara Mae, I was thinkin' about why John came back here and I'm sure it was because of the money he and everybody else seems to figure we got here and that's got me worried some. Pretty soon all of those soldiers are gonna be comin' home and there are probably already deserters like John out there who heard the stories. I imagine a few of 'em might think about comin' here and startin' trouble. I don't wanna give up the ranch 'cause it's our home, but I want to know what you think."

Sara Mae had been wrestling with the same problem before Ellis mentioned it and was no closer to coming up with a solution than he was.

"I know, Ellis. I can't see how we can stop the rumors or what may happen because of them. I agree that we shouldn't leave, especially now that we're finally able to live our lives as we wished."

He looked at Sara Mae, smiled and said, "We'll figure it out, sweetheart. Probably before we get to Fort Madrid."

Then he asked, "How was Pete doin'?"

"Quite well. The bullet must have barely touched the side of his head. He talked to Mary Jo after you left and just like you said he would, he didn't blame her at all for what happened at the Big O with Jim Abigail and he said that he wished he'd been the one to shoot him."

"I kinda figured it was that way just by the way he was lookin' at Mary Jo when I walked into the house. Do you figure they'll just talk while we're gone?"

"I wouldn't bet on it, husband. You sergeants seem to have an awful lot of bottled up lust, but I'm proud to tell you that Mary Jo was stunned about how we spent that first night together. She said that Pete, even when they were first married, was never so, um, prolific."

Ellis laughed, kissed Sara Mae, then replied, "That's because he didn't have the most woman in all of Texas."

Sara Mae smiled as she hung onto Ellis while the wagon rolled on and the stink from behind them was gratefully swept backwards as they drove into the light breeze.

———

Back at the Slash W, rather than shock Sonny and Mandy, Mary Jo and Pete snuck out of the kitchen and hurried to the bunkhouse. It may have still been a sauna inside with a lot of deadly hardware on the neighboring bunk, but sweating was the least of their concerns as they rushed inside and closed the door behind them.

————

It was late afternoon when Ellis pulled the wagon to a stop before Ernie's store, then helped Sara Mae down before entering the doorway.

When Ernie spotted them walk through the entrance, he said, "Glad you folks are here. I got a telegram for you to take to Mrs. Orris, Ellis, and a letter, too."

Ellis said, "That telegram was supposed to warn me about four deserters that were comin' to attack the ranch and that Pete was on his way to stop 'em. When did it get here?"

Ernie blanched and as he handed the telegram to Ellis, said, "It showed up two days ago, but didn't say anything about a warnin'."

Ellis read it quickly and said, "This doesn't make a lick of sense, Ernie, but it doesn't matter now anyway. I got six bodies out in the wagon and before I bring 'em down to Abner, I need you to identify one of 'em for legal reasons."

"Who's that?" he asked as he walked around the counter.

"John Keeler. He and three others deserted, killed the four soldiers who they sent to find 'em, then came here to steal what they could."

"Lordy!" he exclaimed as he headed for the door followed by Ellis and Sara Mae.

After looking at the six corpses, he identified John Keeler easily enough then asked, "Okay, Ellis, that's John. Now what?"

"I don't know if it's legal and all that, but just write me a letter or somethin' that says that you saw his body. That oughta be good enough for what I need it for."

"Okay. I'll do that while you get that load down to Abner's."

Ellis nodded then helped Sara Mae onto the driver's seat, climbed up beside her then started it moving down the street to Abner's livery.

It took almost half an hour to unload them and Ellis gave him thirty dollars to put them in the ground along with Pete's note with the two names and pointed them out to Abner. The others didn't deserve any markers.

They stopped at Ernie's on the way back, picked up his statement, the letter for Mary Jo from Pete then made a stop at the Ernie's Café for a quick supper before beginning the drive back.

Neither had come up with a solution to the money problem that was the exact opposite of almost everyone else's money problems, but the issue would generate more problems soon enough.

As they bounced along on the driver's seat, Sara Mae asked, "I wonder how the telegram got so mixed up?"

"It happens more than you might figure, especially with somebody like Ernie who doesn't send a lot of 'em. It's okay, though. I was probably already gone by the time he coulda sent it out to the Big O and it was empty anyway."

"I wonder what Pete wrote in the letter."

"I wonder if he's even gonna let her read it. I mean, he's here now."

"I was here when you read my note," she said.

"I know that, ma'am, and I'm happy you are, too."

"Are we still going to build a house for Pete and Mary Jo?"

"We'll talk to them when we get back. They've got the ranch house down on the Big O, but I figure you'd be happier havin' 'em closer now that we can."

"I would. But right now, I'm just happy to have you close. We're going to be pretty busy for a while, aren't we?"

"Yes, ma'am, and that means all kinds of busy."

Sara Mae laughed and just exhilarated in the sense of freedom and belonging that filled her; freedom from John and belonging to Ellis.

———

By the time the wagon turned onto the access road, the sun was setting, and Ellis and Sara Mae were glad to be back and weren't surprised to see Sonny and Mandy on the front porch with Pete and Mary Jo sitting beside them.

"I gotta get that porch swing built," Ellis said.

Sara Mae was waving as she replied, "One more thing on our list, Mister White."

Pete and Mary Jo had long since returned to the house, having only spent twenty raucous minutes in the bunkhouse before spending another ten minutes trying to restore their wardrobe and dry off somewhat before leaving their hot honeymoon hut.

Ellis pulled the wagon to a stop near the front of the house and after hopping down, helped Sara Mae to the ground then they joined hands before walking toward the porch.

"I see you have an empty wagon, Ellis," Pete said when they were close.

"Yup. I had Abner make markers for your two boys, but the others are just gonna be put in the ground. How are you doin'?"

"Better than I thought I would. Mary Jo told me what happened. That must have been a tense few seconds waiting to take that shot."

"I was worried about some sweat drippin' into my eyes at a bad time, but once John took that muzzle away from Sara Mae, I had him."

Mary Jo said, "I have coffee ready."

"You all go inside. I've gotta take care of the horses and I'll be right back," Ellis said before kissing Sara Mae then turning back to the wagon grabbing the harness and leading the team to the barn.

Sara Mae stepped onto the porch took Mandy's hand and everyone walked inside already talking about the day's events.

Ellis took care of the team and after setting the wagon outside the almost full barn headed for the house without bothering to stop and wash this time.

When he walked through the open door, he recognized the need for another project when he found all four chairs filled and Sara Mae had Mandy on her lap. He needed a bigger table and more chairs as he doubted that this would be the last time there would be this many in need of seating.

He poured himself a cup of coffee as Sonny rose to offer him his chair.

"That's okay, Sonny," Ellis said, "my behind is kinda sore from sittin' on that wagon seat most of the day."

Sonny grinned then sat back down as Pete asked, "It's getting a bit late to make that ride to the Big O and I'd rather not get there at night after all of today's excitement. Do you mind if we stay here tonight?"

"Nope. That's fine. Me and Sara Mae won't mind sharin' the bunkhouse."

Mary Jo smiled and said, "So, I've heard."

Sara Mae then smiled at Mary Jo and asked, "Did you have to remove any splinters, dear sister?"

Mary Jo blushed lightly as the two sisters remained smiling at each other but didn't answer the question.

Then Ellis pulled out the telegram and letter before saying, "Mary Jo, Ernie had this telegram from Pete that was supposed to go to you, but it's too late now to do any good, but he also gave me a letter to you from that galoot sittin' there. Now, seein' as how it's addressed to you, I gotta give it to ya. If you wanna have an argument with your husband about it, that's between the two of ya."

353

Mary Jo glanced at Pete then accepted the letter and telegram.

"Pete, can I read it?"

"You may as well, but you might want to wait until later when we're alone."

She smiled at Pete then slipped it into her dress pocket.

Once the sleeping arrangements and letter ownership were resolved, they began a long conversation about everything that had happened over the past few weeks that had led to the gunfight on the Slash W.

————

Walt Harrison hadn't gotten much information about Ellis White until Linda returned to the room after a day's work at the laundry. The other women had crowded around her to ask about the sudden appearance of her husband and his abrupt and rude behavior in taking her from the laundry.

Linda hadn't masked her combination of disappointment, confusion and now fear that his return had evoked and dreaded having to return to her room but had nowhere else to go.

When she entered the room, she found Walt already sitting in the one chair waiting for her, so she sat on the bed without saying a word.

Walt finally asked, "I been told that you women at the laundry have been offerin' services to men to make money on the side or to find a man. Did you do that?"

Linda shook her head and replied, "No. I haven't been with a man since you left."

"You been lookin' for a husband?"

Linda found it difficult to lie because of the very nature of the laundry, so she answered, "Yes. I told you. I thought you were dead. You never wrote me a single letter."

Walt then asked quietly, "You try to hook up with a feller named Ellis White a few days ago?"

Linda blurted out, "How did you know?"

"I just figured you might. You found out about all of his money, didn't ya?"

"No. I didn't know he had a lot of money. He was just, well, he was very nice."

Walt snorted then said, "Linda, you tell me the truth, or you'll be sorry. Did he give you any money?"

"Just for his laundry. That's all."

"Was it Yankee money or Confederate?"

"Yankee."

Walt nodded then said, "Now, tell me whatever else you know about this feller."

Linda was afraid of the consequences, so she honestly told Walt all she knew about Ellis and his ranch.

When she finished, he rose and escorted her from the room for supper. Linda wasn't anticipating what would happen when they returned but felt like she'd betrayed Ellis White and worried about what use Walt would make of the information.

———

Ellis and Sara Mae didn't create much noise when they slipped under the blankets on one of the cots in the bunkhouse. Both were just too emotionally and physically spent from the long, terrifying day and had been satisfied to just hold each other before they slipped off to sleep, expecting nothing but routine problems for a while.

CHAPTER 10

Pete and Mary Jo left the Slash W to return to the Big O early in the morning, driving their own wagon trailing his horse and the one Walt had used.

Then after they left, the family's day began with the chores of milking the cow and taking care of the chickens. The dogs had recovered from the scary day and were shadowing Sonny and Mandy again.

Sara Mae moved her things into Ellis' room and Ellis spent an hour cleaning guns then setting all of the long muzzle-loading rifles in the corner of the bunkhouse. He had no idea what use he would have for them, so he'd take them down to Ernie the next time he went to Fort Madrid and give them to him to sell. Ellis imagined that some of the locals wouldn't mind having one of them and Ernie could keep whatever they paid.

The entire day was one of blessed routine and work as Sara Mae cleaned her house while Ellis moved saddles and took care of the horses. He then greased the wagon's wheels and the buckboard's as well before lunchtime.

Pete and Mary Jo visited for a while to fill in the gaps in last night's conversation and returned to the Big O after lunch.

While they were there, Pete accepted Ellis' suggestion that they move the small Big O herd in with his, and they planned on doing that in the next few days.

After lunch, the whole family set to work on the vegetable garden. Sara Mae had asked about getting a hose run from the trough to the garden, and Ellis had thought that it would be better to just make a cut in the corner of the trough, and with the lay of the ground, when the windmill was pumping the water, the excess would flow to the ground and they'd carve an irrigation ditch to the garden.

Sara Mae had grinned as she wiped the sweat from her forehead and said, "Now, who's the smartest one on the ranch?"

They managed to get most of the ground broken up that afternoon, but it still needed more work and then they had to plant the seeds after they created their irrigation system.

———

In Henrietta, Walt Harrison was back in the saloon, explaining what Linda had told him about Ellis White and was convinced that he was living alone and had the money. He figured that if they started out in the morning for Fort Madrid, if they didn't see Bill Hotchkiss and Lenny Mowbray on their way back, then a lot of things could have happened. He suspected that Bill and Lenny might have back shot Pete to make their own withdrawal and were livin' it up on that ranch right now.

Jesse wasn't so sure, but Bob Schmidt figured they didn't have anything else to lose, so he agreed with Walt. Tomorrow, they'd start walking west and to him, the excitement of not knowing what they would find was almost as good as the thought of possible riches.

———

That night, after Mandy and Sonny were in bed, Ellis and Sara Mae decided that the bunkhouse would allow them more privacy and soon trotted out into the night.

———

Friday morning dawned gray with a threat of some serious, and welcome rain.

The threat of moisture didn't mean that chores didn't get done nor did it stop them from finishing preparing the ground for the vegetable garden. The lack of sun did make it less stressful, and just as they were preparing to dig the trench for the irrigation system, they were stopped when Sonny spotted a dust cloud on the horizon.

"Pa, somebody's comin'!" he shouted, pointing toward the northwest.

Ellis and Sara Mae both looked that way, but just watched with hoes in their hands.

"Who is it, Ellis?" she asked in a normal, unconcerned voice.

"Unless I'm wrong, I think it might be Rufus."

"You can see that far? I can only make out a speck."

"I'm just guessing, Sara Mae. From that direction, it's either Rufus or another Comanche comin' to tell me that the herd's back where they belong."

"Does that mean I get my horse, Pa?" asked Mandy.

"Yes, ma'am. But if we find you a yearling, you can't ride her until it's another year older, but you'll have her here to make her your friend and you can introduce her to Happy, too."

Mandy didn't care if she couldn't ride her horse for a year. She was just as happy being able to have a new animal friend.

Sara Mae then said, "I'll go and get the coffee ready. My husband is never wrong."

Ellis looked at her and just laughed as she smiled turned and walked to the house with Mandy following. Ellis watched Sara Mae walk away with appreciating eyes.

Ellis and Sonny both identified Rufus just ten minutes later and waved to let him know that they had.

Rufus waved back and couldn't help to keep himself from smiling. Silver Dove had insisted that he go with the other braves and visit his friends as he was no use to her anyway. So, yesterday, he'd joined the band that had driven the herd to the Slash W. He'd picked out the two steers that they'd be taking back with them and they'd already turned back. He'd catch up before they reached the village.

He was still grinning when he reached them, and Ellis and Sonny's matched his, tooth for tooth.

He dismounted then after shaking both of their hands, he said, "We dropped off your herd near the cattle, boss, and I marked two old steers for 'em. They're already headed back, so I won't be stayin' long. Silver Dove told me I had to go, but I didn't argue much."

"Come on in, Rufus. Sara Mae is puttin' on some coffee and I'll tell you all that happened in the past few days."

"She stayin' with ya now, boss. You know, stayin' with ya?" he asked with raised eyebrows.

"Yup. She's my wife now. I'm the one who made her a widow, too."

They stepped onto the porch as Rufus said, "Now, that story is gonna be worth the trip."

Sara Mae smiled at Rufus when he entered and said, "Ellis tells me that your wife is going to have a baby soon."

"Yes, ma'am. She's with her mother now and I figure it'll be before we move the village, maybe in the next day or two."

They all took seats with Mandy on Ellis' lap for a change and Rufus asked for the story.

After ten minutes, Sara Mae poured the coffee as Ellis continued talking.

When he finished, Rufus said, "I'm glad for you both that that bastard is gone and so is the one that took Mrs. Orris. Havin' her husband home musta been a real surprise."

"It was a helluva homecoming, Rufus," Ellis said before taking a sip of the coffee.

"You hire any hands yet?" he asked.

"Nope. I figure I'll do that in a couple of days. I ain't had enough time to go lookin' yet."

"The reason I'm askin' is that a some of the Comanche bands up north are makin' noise about raidin' 'cause the bluecoats are gone and there ain't a lot of menfolk, either. Chief Long Elk don't cotton to the idea, and we'll be movin' the village another day's ride northwest in a little while, so you probably don't need to worry none. But havin' a couple of extra hands might be a good idea."

"Thanks, Rufus. I've got plenty of firepower, too."

"Good. Well, I'd best be headin' back. I don't want those boys takin' any extra cattle or horses with 'em."

Both men rose, then Rufus smiled at Sara Mae and said, "I wish you every happiness, ma'am."

She smiled back and said, "Thank you, Rufus, and I hope you have a strong son or daughter soon."

Sonny then stood and followed Rufus and Ellis as they left the kitchen.

When they reached Rufus' horse, they shook hands again then Rufus shook Sonny's hand before saying, "Your new papa is the best man I ever met, Sonny. You be like him and I'll be proud of ya."

"Yes, sir," Sonny said before Rufus smiled then mounted his horse, waved then wheeled his mount to the northwest and set off at a medium trot.

Sonny watched him leaving and asked, "Pa, are we ever gonna see Rufus again?"

"I reckon not, Sonny, but you remember that man. He was the best man I ever met."

Sonny nodded then he and Ellis returned to the kitchen.

———

After Linda had gone to the laundry, Walt left the boarding house found Jesse Voorhees and Bob Schmidt and the three started their long walk to Hardeman County before mid-morning.

They had forty-two dollars in Confederate bills and three dollars and thirty cents in Union money. Each man was armed with just a revolver and had enough ammunition for four to six extra shots, depending on the man. Walt wished he'd hung onto that Spencer but didn't feel like lugging it eight miles, either.

Walt had been doing some serious thinking after talking to Linda and had modified his plan accordingly. As they began walking, he explained that because of the unknown situation on the Slash W, that it would be a better idea to head for the Big O first.

"Why would we wanna go to that place when all the money's at White's ranch?" asked Jesse.

"We don't know what's goin' on over there, and I know where Pete's ranch is. I figure if the deserters made it to the Slash W and ran into Pete and his boys, there was a shootout and whoever came out on top is still there and I don't want to run into 'em with just pistols. So, if we swing south of that other ranch and go to Pete's place, we at least get some horses and maybe some rifles. Who knows, maybe we'll even get us some cash there, too."

Bob said, "Okay, but we got a few days to figure out things."

"Yup," replied Walt, "and then you boys will come to see I'm right."

Jesse snorted, but they all kept up the rapid pace.

———

After lunch, Ellis and Sonny mounted their horses to go to the northwest corner and check on both the cattle and horse herds. Ellis wasn't sure what to expect when he did a count of either, but he did want to bring a yearling back to Mandy.

After thirty minutes, they spotted both herds and within minutes, Ellis was pleased with his initial count. He was pretty sure that he'd only lost the two steers that he'd offered and when he finished his horse count, came up with the promised number.

"It looks like they're all there, Pa," Sonny shouted over the hoofbeats.

"Yup. Now, let's go find a nice yearling for Mandy," he yelled back.

There were six yearlings in the herd, and he let Sonny pick his sister's horse, and he did it quickly when he found a handsome young filly with a deep red coat, dark brown mane and tail and two back white stockings with a white slash on her forehead. She was the one that Ellis would have chosen for Mandy as well.

She was a bit skittish when Ellis approached her but let him loop a rope around her neck and lead her away from the herd. Another mare, probably her mother, took a few steps in their direction, but then stopped when her new colt trotted to her side.

"Your girl will be visitin', ma'am. And my girl will be ridin' her when she does," Ellis said as he saluted the mare.

When they returned thirty minutes later, Sara Mae and Mandy were waiting on the back porch with big smiles and when they were fifty yards out, Mandy exploded like a shot from the porch and flew across the yard creating her own dust cloud while her mother laughed.

"Is she mine? Is she mine?" she shouted excitedly when they came to a stop.

Ellis handed the trail rope to Sonny and said, "Yes, ma'am. She's your filly now."

Sonny slid from the saddle then led the red filly to Mandy and handed her the rope.

Ellis dismounted and waved to Sara Mae who then stepped down from the porch and walked to her family.

"She's really pretty, Ellis," she said when she was close.

"Just like our little girl, Sara Mae," he replied as he took her hand.

Sara Mae nodded then whispered, "Yes, just like our little girl."

"Sonny, let the horses get somethin' to drink and then lead 'em into the corral."

"Yes, sir," Sonny replied before he and Mandy turned and walked toward the trough leading their horses with Happy and Stoney trotting behind.

Ellis led the gray to the trough with Sara Mae walking beside him.

"You don't think we'll have a problem with the Comanches, do you, Ellis?" she asked.

"No, ma'am, I reckon not. If they're two days' ride north, I don't figure they'll bother comin' down this far and Rufus will let 'em know that we have a passel of guns, too. I don't know how many they picked up over the years I been gone, but it can't be that many."

"I hope your streak of being right continues, Ellis."

"This one I'm pretty sure about, ma'am. We still gotta figure out somethin' to do about the money, too. We'll leave the gold under the anvil, but I still have too much cash around here. I gave three hundred to Rufus, and I figure we can give a couple of hundred to Pete and Mary Jo to get 'em goin' again, too, but that won't do a damned thing to stop those stories from spreadin' around."

Sara Mae nodded then said, "I'm going to go back and start supper. I don't think I'll be seeing Mandy for a while."

"That's a good guess, Mrs. White," Ellis said before pulling her close, kissing her then before he let her go, he let his wandering left hand let her know that he was still very fond of her.

A smiling Sara Mae waltzed to the porch and skipped inside the house looking back at her husband once more before going inside.

Ellis watched her leave then led the gray to the corral where he unsaddled both horses and removed the yearling's necktie.

"Now, you come out here and talk to that filly a lot and rub her neck to let her know you're her friend, Mandy. Sing to her, too."

"What about Happy? Can he come in, too?"

"Yup. All the critters that live here have to get used to seein' the other ones."

"Okay," she replied before opening the gate a bit to let the two dogs inside.

———

That night as Ellis and Sara Mae lay in their normal bed, deciding that the children had to get used the noise sooner or later, Sara Mae said, "We just had a pretty normal day, Ellis. I hope this is the start of a long trend."

Ellis absent-mindedly slid his hand across her wet skin and replied, "I'd like it to be that way, Sara Mae. I'm all for excitin' things, like what we do when we're alone, but the other kind I'd rather just stayed away."

Sara Mae giggled lightly and said, "I wouldn't mind a little more excitement in that arena right now, Mister White."

Ellis was more than happy to oblige.

———

Walt, Jesse, and Bob had walked further than they'd expected because of the lack of sunshine, having covered more than a third of the distance by the time they'd stopped to make camp.

Walt was in better shape than the other two because he'd spent so much time marching, but Jesse and Bob weren't too bad because neither had owned a horse since being sent to the prison.

But the miles they'd put behind them that day meant that with any kind of luck, they'd reach Fort Madrid in three days, not four.

———

In Henrietta, Linda Harrison was both relieved to find that Walt was no longer there but disturbed as well. That intense questioning about Ellis White led her to believe that he'd gone off to Fort Madrid to cause trouble.

She thought she'd warn Ellis and send him a telegram in the morning.

———

The next morning, Ellis had the cut made in the trough right after breakfast and Sara Mae and the children watched as water escaped from its wooden dam made a short waterfall and splashed into the hole that Ellis had dug. Once the hole was filled, the water then flowed down the channel they'd created and then branched into six more gouges in the ground before winding into the vegetable patch.

"There will be more water on this side, Ellis," Sara Mae said as she pointed to the water's six entry points into the garden.

"Yes, ma'am, but that water will keep flowin' and when the dirt turns into mud, the water should keep goin'. Then we just put that board over the cut in the trough and most of the water flow will stop until we want to let it go again."

Sara Mae smiled and said, "Now, you're just rubbing it in, smart man."

They planted the seeds two hours later and would have peas, carrots, corn, tomatoes and even strawberries if the soil was good enough. None of them knew much about farming, but Ellis did know about fertilizing and had more than one source. He did warn the children not to use dog fertilizer as it would kill the plants not help them, but didn't have an answer as to why it was that way.

———

Walt Harrison, Jesse Voorhees and Bob Schmidt had started their day's walk early because the sun was already making it hot, which shouldn't have been a big surprise in June in West Texas. Walt even reminded them that it was Sunday, but neither of the other two appreciated his attempt at humor as they trudged along the roadway with sweat already dripping down their backs.

———

It hadn't taken long for Linda Harrison to find out that Walt had walked out of Henrietta the day before with two of his old acquaintances, Jesse Voorhees and Bob Schmidt. Those two were bad news and she'd had the mistaken belief that Walt was past that association. The fact that he'd gone off with them only reinforced her suspicion that they were heading for Ellis White's Slash W ranch.

She sent her telegram at eight o'clock, just before going to the laundry, hoping that she really would be a widow in a few days.

———

Later that day, Ellis and the rest of his family loaded onto the buckboard and trailed the horse that Bill Hotchkiss had been riding when they left Henrietta and headed for Abe Chesterfield's ranch so Ellis could fulfill his promise.

They arrived at the ranch two hours later, and Abe Chesterfield was tickled pink with the gelding then offered Ellis a bitch to go with the two curs, but Ellis had demurred, saying if the time came, he'd return to pick one up, but right now, the two boys were more than enough.

They left Abe's place and decided to stop at Fort Madrid because Ellis wanted to pick up some fresh beef at the butcher. He may have had over a hundred critters on his land, but he grew 'em and let the butcher end 'em.

He pulled the buckboard to Ernie's store helped Sara Mae down then Mandy while Sonny scrambled down the other side.

"I'll be back in a few minutes, Sara Mae," he said as he headed for the butcher.

Sara Mae waved then she followed Sonny and Mandy into the store. Ellis had given her ten dollars and she wanted to see if she could find a ring for him. She wanted to stake her claim.

Ernie saw them enter and said, "Howdy, ma'am. I just got a telegram for Ellis. Is he comin' in?"

"Yes. He'll be here shortly. Who is it from?"

"A lady named Linda Harrison in Henrietta."

Sara Mae blanched before she asked, "What did she want?"

Ernie wasn't one to stand on formalities, besides with John Keeler gone, he was sure that Sara Mae and Ellis were going to be married, so he handed her the telegram.

She read:

ELLIS WHITE SLASH W RANCH FORT MADRID TEXAS

BELIEVE HUSBAND WALT AND TWO OTHERS
HEADING YOUR WAY
LEFT YESTERDAY MORNING AFOOT
PISTOLS NO RIFLES
MAKE ME A REAL WIDOW

LINDA HARRISON HENRIETTA TEXAS

Sara Mae was disturbed by the message for two reasons. Three men were coming to start more trouble and Linda Harrison wanted to be a widow and expected Ellis to make her one.

She slid the telegram in her pocket then said, "Thank you, Mister Smith. Ellis told me that he bought this ring from you. Do you have any men's rings?"

Ernie grinned then said, "Yes, ma'am. I think there are a couple in the box," then reached under his counter and soon produced his jewelry box.

Sara Mae quickly began sorting through the items, now feeling a greater sense of urgency to get it on Ellis' finger. She found one gold band and one that was either silver or white gold, but what had been used to create the ring was unimportant. It was the same color as her claddagh ring, so she took the ring from the box and asked, "How much would this one cost?"

"Three dollars would do it, Mrs. White," he replied, gambling that she would appreciate the form of address and could tell by her light blush and smile that she did.

"Can I hold onto this while we do some more shopping?"

"Yes, ma'am. If I can't trust you or your husband, then there's nobody I can trust."

She smiled at him, then walked to the aisles to find her children and buy something else to disguise the cost of the ring.

————

Ellis arrived with his butcher paper-wrapped steaks a few minutes later then set them on the counter while he walked down the aisle to talk to Sara Mae.

Ernie figured he'd let Sara Mae tell Ellis about the telegram after having seen the look on her face as she read it.

Sara Mae had picked up some more peppercorns and some brown sugar by the time Ellis arrived, and looked up at him.

She pulled the telegram from her pocket and said, "Ellis, this arrived this morning from Linda Harrison. It looks important."

Ellis didn't comment about the sender but quickly read the message and said, "This is about what we been expecting, Sara Mae, just a bit sooner than we figured. If they're walkin', then they won't make it here any earlier than tomorrow afternoon, so me and Pete will be ready for 'em. She even said all they had was pistols, so it won't be bad. Maybe we can scare 'em off."

"But she expects you to make her a widow."

"Well, ma'am, first, I gotta make sure that you don't become one. Now let's get your things together and we'll head back so I can talk to Pete and get a read on this."

"Okay," she replied then called to Sonny and Mandy before she and Ellis walked to the front of the store.

Sara Mae knew that her bill would be way too high for what she'd purchased and Ellis would be sure to notice, but when they reached the front of the store, Ernie quickly said, "I don't have any change right now, Ellis. I'll add it all to your next bill if that's okay."

"Not a problem, Ernie. In fact, here's forty dollars to put on account in case me or Sara Mae forgot to bring enough with us," he replied as he handed him two twenty-dollar notes.

"That'll work, Ellis," Ernie said as he accepted the money then smiled at a relieved Sara Mae before Ellis picked up the steaks and they left the store.

As the buckboard rolled easily northward, Sara Mae was still troubled by the telegram as much by the sender as the content. Ellis had said that he'd only talked to her twice and for no more than ten minutes altogether, yet she felt she knew him well enough to send him a telegram, and not only that, but expected to be a widow in a few days.

"You said Linda Harrison was pretty, Ellis. Is she as pretty as Mary Jo?"

"Almost, but she still isn't nearly the woman my wife is. I keep tellin' ya, Sara Mae, that you are the most woman I've ever met and there ain't ever gonna be another woman that even comes close."

Sara Mae felt a bit foolish as she clutched Ellis' arm in hers and let out a deep breath, no longer concerned about Linda Harrison in the least.

———

After they reached the house, Ellis helped Sara Mae and Mandy to the ground then after Sonny bounded down, he handed the bag to Sara Mae climbed back up, waved and turned the buckboard to the southeast toward the Big O.

The thing that had bothered him about the telegram was that three men on foot were actually a bit more of a problem than horse riders. If they showed up late, they could walk right into the house. He only hoped that Happy and Stoney were already old enough to react to the arrival of strangers.

As the Big O ranch house loomed ahead, his new concern was that he hoped he wasn't barging in on any private time between Pete and Mary Jo. It was still an hour before sunset, so it wasn't as likely, but he still recalled that time with Sara Mae in the barn during the daytime and if it hadn't been for his own sense of righteousness, they would have given a whole new meaning to the term 'barn raising'.

But that worry vanished as he spotted Pete out back near the barn splitting logs then when he caught Pete's eye, he waved and watched Pete slam the axe head into the log and wipe the sweat from his forehead with what might have been a white handkerchief at one time, but was gray now.

He pulled the buckboard to a stop beside him pulled the handbrake and stepped down.

"What's up, Ellis?" he asked.

"I got a telegram from a Linda Harrison in Henrietta about her husband and two others walkin' this way and she figures they're out to give me some trouble. What do you think? Is he the kind that'll start shootin' first?"

Pete replied, "I'm not sure. I didn't really care for the man, and of the three the colonel picked, he was probably the least reliable and a bit too unpredictable. I figured the colonel sent those three with me because he didn't care if they came left. But if he's coming with two others, then I can't see any other reason for him heading this way."

"I figure it's the stories about the Yankee money I got here that's drivin' 'em here."

"I wouldn't be surprised. That's my fault if that's the reason, and it probably is. I needed to give him and the other three a reason to come here and told them I'd give them twenty Yankee dollars for following the orders of their commanding officer because they were all civilians once they got their discharge papers. If the colonel had been smart, he would have postdated those orders two or three weeks ahead, so I'd have some measure of authority."

"Well, Pete, if they left yesterday mornin', I figure the earliest they could get here would be late tomorrow and that's what's got me a bit spooked. If they come at night on foot, I might not see 'em quick enough. If I had those dogs longer, I could trust 'em to let us know they were there, but they're young and might not do a damned thing but wag their tails at 'em."

"Well, I'll tell you what, Ellis. Tomorrow, how about if me and Mary Jo come over for supper and then, before the sun goes down, we ride a perimeter search and if nobody's there, we set up a watch."

"The moon's past half full, so we should have enough light to do that, too. I appreciate it, Pete."

"Are you going to have chicken for supper?" he asked with a grin.

"Maybe," he replied then asked, "What did Mary Jo think of your letter?"

"She cried. I was in one of those moods where I thought I was going to die if I crossed the Mississippi and wrote a letter telling her how much I loved her."

"I imagine she's gonna keep that letter for the rest of her days, just like I'll keep the note that Sara Mae wrote me when I was goin' off to see the Comanches about gettin' my horses back."

"Are you going to let me read it?"

"Hell, no. Sara Mae wrote it to me, and my eyes are gonna be the only ones to see it, at least 'til I figure Sara Mae won't mind."

"Just kidding, Ellis."

Ellis grinned and replied, "I know. Well, I'd better get back to my wife and young'uns and let 'em know what's gonna be happenin' tomorrow."

Pete gave him a short wave before Ellis clambered onto the driver's seat, turned the buckboard around and started back to the Slash W.

———

Despite the heat, Walt, Jesse and Bob had managed just as much distance, if not more, the second day, crossing more than half of Wilbarger County before they pulled off for the night. They'd been helped by the frequent creeks and streams that crisscrossed the county, giving them the ability to keep themselves hydrated.

When they started their campfire, they were only twenty-one miles from Fort Madrid and Jesse and Bob had agreed to Walt's plan to go to the Big O first.

———

After the children were in bed, Sara Mae asked Ellis to join her on the porch, rather than turning in themselves.

She took a seat on the edge of the porch and waited for Ellis to sit beside her before she said, "Ellis, you'll never know just how happy you made me when you gave me the claddagh ring and told me that you were my husband now, even if we didn't have the paper announcing it to the world."

"I am your husband, Sara Mae, and always will be."

"I know, but I wanted to let anyone who sees you know that I'm your wife and always will be."

Before Ellis could reply, she slid the silver ring from her pocket and said, "Ellis, I can't remember the words from the last wedding I attended, and they didn't sink very deep anyway, so can I put this ring on your finger and just tell you that I'll love you until the day I die?"

Ellis smiled at her and held out his big hand, letting her slide the ring onto his finger as she said softly, "You are my husband, Ellis Mitchell White, and I promise to love you every moment until I take my last breath."

Ellis then kissed her softly and whispered, "And you, Sara Mae White, are my wife, and I will love you and cherish you long after the sun stops shinin' and the moon loses its glow."

She kissed him again and they slowly lowered onto the porch and began seriously kissing and touching each other before they sat back up then dropped to the ground and scampered to the bunkhouse to consummate their marriage…again.

CHAPTER 11

Ellis had been giving more thought about how to handle the three gunmen heading for his ranch after Sara Mae had fallen asleep under his arm and decided he didn't like the idea of waiting for them to arrive. Men on foot were more unpredictable and might not come directly to the Slash W. They might go to Fort Madrid first to get more information or maybe a rifle or two. He didn't know their financial situation but suspected they didn't have much money on them.

The next morning as he ate his ham and eggs, he said, "Sara Mae, the more I'm thinkin' about those three, the more I figure it might be smarter to head east along the road to Henrietta a ways and see if I can spot 'em. They won't know who I am, and I'd be able to handle it better."

Sara Mae replied, "What about Pete?"

"I figure Pete can stay here with you, Mary Jo, Sonny and Mandy and keep an eye out. If I don't see 'em after an hour or so, I'll come back here in the afternoon."

"When will you leave?" she asked calmly.

Ellis had to smile at her lack of anxiety and answered, "I figure I'll leave here in a couple of hours or so. Now, I don't figure they'll get here before tonight at the earliest, so it ain't likely that I'll run into 'em today. If we still haven't seen 'em by tomorrow mornin', then I'll go out lookin' again only real early."

"Okay. Will you show me how to fire a real gun before you leave? The shotgun only is good for short range, isn't it?"

"If you wanna do serious damage, you can reach out a good eighty yards or so with the buckshot I got loaded, but to make sure, you'll need one of those Spencers. Now, the problem is that there ain't a lot of ammunition for them guns. Each one still has seven cartridges in its stock, but there's only six more left. If I show you how to shoot one, it can't be very often."

"How about your Henry?"

Ellis knew it would be a much better weapon for her to use and he still had plenty of ammunition, but he really wanted to take it with him when he rode east to hunt for those three. It was the rapid-fire advantage the Henry gave him that could be critical.

"I'll tell you what, Mrs. White. I'll show you how to fire the Henry, but I gotta take it with me when I ride out there. I'll show you how to fire the Spencer, but it's gonna have a much bigger kick and it's heavier and harder to get that new cartridge ready to fire."

"Alright. When can you show me how to shoot?"

"Right after we finish breakfast, ma'am," he replied with a slight smile.

Walt, Jesse and Bob had started the last leg of their journey at seven o'clock, and Walt guessed they'd be at the Big O by early afternoon.

Sara Mae had no problem with the Henry and after firing just four rounds, Ellis was pleased with her ability enough to let her dry fire the Spencer.

She had more difficulty with the bigger rifle and its stiffer lever, but after half an hour, Ellis figured that it was good enough to enable her to fire the gun.

"Keep this one in the kitchen, Sara Mae. You'll have seven shots, but you won't need that many. Pete has two of 'em at the Big O and he'll bring 'em over."

"When will he and Mary Jo be arriving?"

"Late afternoon, I reckon. He made some joke about havin' chicken for dinner, or at least I thought he was funnin'."

"Well, while you're gone, I'll go and wring a Rhode Island Red neck and we'll have chicken and gravy for dinner."

Ellis grinned then leaned over kissed Sara Mae slid his hand across her smooth bottom and then said, "I'll be lookin' forward to it, ma'am."

Sara Mae smiled back and replied, 'I'll be looking forward to more of that too, mister."

He took her hand and they returned to the house, each toting a rifle.

––––––

An hour later, Ellis had saddled the gray gelding, slipped the Henry into its scabbard then mounted and walked him to the back of the house.

"I'll be back in a few hours in time for that chicken dinner, Sara Mae. If you hear gunfire then you grab that Spencer and give the shotgun to Sonny, but I think it'll be quiet enough."

Sara Mae just smiled at him and waved before he turned the horse to the south and set him at a slow trot as he headed down the access road.

―――――

He wasn't even three miles from the ranch when he pulled up to a stop after he spotted a dust cloud heading for his ranch. If it had been the three men, there wouldn't be a dust cloud unless they'd stolen some horses along the way which wouldn't be out of the realm of possibility.

He left the repeater in its scabbard as he started south again, watching the dust cloud and soon making out a single rider, not three, but remained wary.

Ellis was less than a mile away from the rider when he recognized that it wasn't a man in the saddle but a woman, and after another two minutes, he identified Mabel Anderson, then immediately understood why she would be riding to the Slash W. Her husband must have succumbed to the infection.

When she finally reached him, he could see the pain and sadness on her face confirming his guess but waited for her to say something.

"Ellis," she finally began when she pulled her horse to a stop, "Ed...Ed passed away last night, but I didn't find out until this morning. I know it's asking a lot, but could you help?"

His own issues were set aside as he replied, "Yes, ma'am. I'll do all I can. What would you want me to do?"

"Could you come back with me and help to get him from the house and take him to Fort Madrid?"

"Yes, ma'am. Let's head back right now and I'll take care of it."

She wheeled her mount around then she and Ellis began walking their horses south again.

"Thank you, Ellis. I know that you figured out that this was going to happen when you stopped by the other day. Ed and I both knew it was inevitable, but that didn't make it any easier. He had me sleep in the other bedroom so I wouldn't be there when he passed."

"Ed was a good man, Mabel. Are you gonna be all right?"

"I think so. I know the boys will be coming home when this God-awful war is over, but I may need help until they do."

"Anything you need, Mabel, you just ask."

"Thank you again, Ellis."

———

As Ellis and Mabel crossed the eastbound road to Henrietta, Ellis glanced that way and didn't see anyone which gave him a measure of relief. The three men hadn't arrived yet and by the time he had Ed's body in the wagon and brought to Fort Madrid, he should still have enough time to do his quick search and head back to the ranch to have a nice chicken supper with everyone.

The reason the road was empty was that Walt had shifted their direction to the northwest when he spotted the distant High Hills and knew that the Big O was on the South Fork of the Pease River. So, when Ellis was riding to the Anderson's farm, the three men he'd missed spotting were actually five miles to his northeast and only eight miles from the Big O or the Slash W.

———

By the time Ellis had hitched Mabel's wagon, carried Ed's body out of the house and begun to drive back to Fort Madrid, the three men had reached the road to the Slash W and stopped.

"You figure that heads up to White's ranch?" asked Jesse.

"I reckon so," replied Walt, "but it don't matter none. We'd be spotted before we got within two miles of that place if anybody was lookin'. Now, Pete's ranch house is either empty, or close to it, so we do a little scoutin' and then I'll come up with a way to sneak in there."

"Alright, Walt," Bob said, "but I'm gettin' tired of walkin' and mighty hungry to boot, so you'd better come up with it fast enough."

"Don't go worryin' about it, Bob," Walt said before they began walking due west toward the Big O, now just three miles away.

———

Mary Jo was baking some biscuits to bring with them for dinner while Ellis was out in the barn, picking up some hay to move to the corral. They only had four horses, two courtesy of the CSA, but he knew they'd have more soon enough now that Ellis has his herd back.

Ellis had only touched on the idea of joining the two ranches, and although Mary Jo was very happy with the idea, Pete was just a bit hesitant because he suspected that Ellis was helping more because of Sara Mae than anything else. He was wrong, but his pride was tweaked by the belief. He hated to admit that he was beholden to any man, even Ellis.

The two Spencer carbines were leaning against the wall in the kitchen, but he was wearing his Colt New Army pistol as he worked.

———

Ellis drove the wagon to Abner's livery then he and Abner slid Ed's body from the bed and accompanied by Mabel, carried it into his less-than-immaculate mortuary in a shed behind his livery, but Mabel wasn't offended at all. It was just the way it was and at least Ed would get a burial and have a marker, which many men didn't.

"Thank you, Ellis," she said after he and Abner lowered Ed's body onto a long table.

Ellis stepped back and said, "You're welcome, Mabel. I've got to head back and take a quick look for those three men I told you about, but if you want to stop by for some company sometime, I'm sure Sara Mae would be glad to see ya."

"I'll do that, Ellis," she said before kissing him on the cheek.

Ellis smiled at her then turned and left Abner's mortuary, untied the gray gelding from behind the wagon mounted and trotted east out of Fort Madrid.

———

From over a thousand yards out, Walt had spotted the smoke drifting out of the cookstove pipe and saw Pete tossing hay into the corral, but no one else. His location meant that if they walked north a little bit, they'd be able to block his view with the barn, so they soon headed that way watching Pete as they did in case that he spotted them before they disappeared.

Less than two minutes later, they were just eight hundred yards away from the back of the barn without being detected. Then they stopped so Walt could tell them what they'd be doing next.

Walt still kept his eyes trained on the barn as he said, "It looks like it's just Pete, and I'm guessin' that wife of his he was always talkin' about is in the kitchen. Let's see how close we can get before he sees us. Pull your pistols, but don't cock 'em yet. We just stroll nice and easy keepin' that barn between us and him. If he sees us, we run like crazy to get to him. If he gets near the house, I'm gonna throw a shot his way to make him run back, but you boys hold your ammunition."

"Okay," Jesse said as they each slid their revolvers from their holsters and began a slow walk toward the barn.

———

Ellis was only three miles out of the Slash W when they began their final approach. He'd ridden a mile or so down the eastern road and after not seeing anything for another five miles due east, he had turned around and headed back to the ranch confident that they hadn't arrived yet.

———

Pete was still unaware of the three men who were now just two hundred yards away but out of his sight as he carried another armload of hay to the corral.

Everything changed just a minute later when Mary Jo popped out of the house to tell Pete that the biscuits were ready and if he was being a good boy, he could have one.

Her right foot never reached the dirt when her eyes grew wide, as she pointed at the three men and screamed, "Pete! They're right there!"

Pete whipped around still couldn't see them but yelled back, "Get inside!" then raced to get to the house and the Spencers.

Walt, Jesse and Bob instantly began their hundred-yard dash to the house, and Walt cocked his hammer and fired a rushed shot to keep Pete from making it to the porch, but Pete had been under fire a lot over the past three years and wasn't fazed. He flew onto the porch and dashed through the open door where he found Mary Jo trying to cock one of the two Spencers.

"Leave them, Mary Jo," he said, "They're too close now. Go to our bedroom and lie on the floor!"

Mary Jo shook her head and shouted back, "No, Pete! I'm not leaving you anymore."

She then crawled to his side and waited for the three men to start shooting.

The men slowed down when they reached the barn and Walt looked at the ranch house.

"Jesse, you stay here and keep an eye on that back door. Me and Bob are gonna make a rush for the front door 'cause they won't be expectin' it and we only need to worry about Pete anyway."

Jesse quickly said, "Okay."

Walt then looked at Bob and said, "Let's go!" and both sprinted away from the barn expecting gunfire to erupt through a window before they reached the front porch but made it without a shot being fired.

When they stopped near the porch, Walt and Bob had to catch their breath for a little while before they could enter the house.

Pete was in deep trouble and didn't know how to get out of it. He knew that they had the barn covered and he wasn't close enough to the window to see the front of the house, so they could be out there right now. If Mary Jo hadn't been with him, he'd just make a mad dash out of the kitchen into open ground where he had a better chance of seeing and hitting them, but she had to be protected.

Mary Jo was well aware that her mere presence was keeping Pete from doing little more than waiting for the assailants to arrive and was seriously thinking of doing exactly what Pete would have done if she wasn't there. If she ran outside the door then Pete would chase after her and get out of the house.

She was just about to make that suggestion when they heard a creak out front as a board shifted under the weight of one of the men, and all she could do was to try and get out of Pete's line of fire.

"Pete, I'm going to go to the back of the kitchen, so you can shoot at them," she whispered.

It may not have been hiding in the bedroom, but it was better than where she was, so he just whispered back, "Be careful, Mary Jo. I'm not sure if my guardian angel is that powerful."

Mary Jo smiled at Pete, kissed him, then stood and took a slow step toward the back of the kitchen.

———

Walt and Bob had their pistols cocked now as they crossed the main room and headed down the hallway toward the kitchen, where they knew Pete Orris was holed up.

Suddenly, there was motion and both men fired.

The house echoed with the loud reports and the two .44 caliber slugs of lead raced the twenty-two feet down the hallway. Bob's shot drilled past Mary Jo's back by three inches, but Walt's bullet slammed into her left side, throwing her to her right as it mangled bone and tissue.

Mary Jo didn't have a chance to even scream before she fell against the sink then dropped to the floor as blood quickly pooled on the dry wood.

Pete did scream and almost tossed away his pistol when he saw his wife take the hit and fall lifelessly to the floor, but he kept it in his hand as he spun back toward Mary Jo and just as he took a step, he heard the shooters coming down the hallway.

Walt and Bob had realized immediately that they had shot Pete's wife, but didn't think twice about it. They were only concerned that Pete was still there with his pistol and now was probably enraged enough to rush at them, but the thick cloud of gunsmoke filled the hallway, blocking their vision.

Smoke or no smoke, Pete's absolute fury drove him to attack but even then, his tactical skills kept him from being foolish. He wanted to kill all three of those sons-of-bitches.

"You bastards!" Pete shouted as he aimed his pistol at the hallway entrance, fired one shot then immediately cocked his hammer and stepped to the edge of the hallway.

After Pete's missed shot, Walt gave a stop sign to keep Bob from getting any closer to the kitchen as he expected Pete to come barging down the hallway in a heartbeat.

But despite his immense wrath, the only part of Pete to enter the hallway was his Colt-bearing right hand and arm, then as soon as it made its appearance and before either of them could react, he fired his second shot. The .44 catching Bob in the right side of his gut and dropping him to the floor. The loud grunt followed by the loud crash and thump of a pistol hitting the wood let Pete know that one of the shooters was down, but two were still active.

Walt immediately turned and ran into the main room then just as he entered the kitchen end of the hallway, Pete unloaded two more quick shots at the gray shadow of the fleeing shooter but the massive amount of gunsmoke in the house gave Walt just enough cover to avoid being hit as he ducked to his right in the main room then dropped to the floor to be able to shoot Pete when he followed.

After throwing the last two shots at Walt as he disappeared and believing he might have left the house Pete's top priority now was to see to Mary Jo. He prayed that she was just wounded but had little hope. His precious, beloved Mary Jo had been hit in the chest at close range and he was almost certain she was dead.

He reached his wife's body in seconds, took a knee and began to weep at the sight of her damaged body and her lifeless, staring eyes.

Pete had seen so much death in the last few years, he thought he'd become immune to the sight, but not this. Not his Mary Jo. But even has the tears continued to slide across his face, he knew he was in a bad situation. If he had any hope of getting revenge on the two remaining shooters, he had to get to the Slash W and get Ellis.

The two Spencers were forgotten as he stood and walked to the open back door, took a deep breath and then shot out of the room across the back porch and without breaking stride, kept his legs churning as fast as possible as he headed north away from the barn.

———

Jesse had heard all the gunfire and had heard Pete's scream, so as far as he was concerned, the gunfight was over and now, he, Walt and Bob had possession of the ranch and began to think about that pretty woman that was inside and probably cowering in a bedroom.

He holstered his pistol, then stepped out in front of the barn just as Pete exploded from the back of the house.

"Son of a bitch!" Jesse swore as he grabbed his pistol again and began to chase after him.

Walt heard Pete's sudden break clambered to his feet and raced through the hallway, glanced at Mary Jo's body in the corner, but kept running as he passed through the open doorway.

By the time he reached the porch, Pete was more than a hundred yards away and still running.

He spotted Jesse as he reached the back of the house and shouted, "What happened? How the hell did he get past ya?"

Jesse pulled up, realizing that Pete was well out of range and they were tired after their earlier sprint, so he just replied, "I thought you got him. I heard him scream."

"That was 'cause we killed his wife. We didn't mean to, but she kinda surprised us."

"Where's Bob?"

"Pete got him. He's inside and still breathin', but he took that bullet in his gut and I don't figure he's got long."

"What do we do now? Do we get horses and chase after him?"

"Nope. I don't wanna take a chance. All this gunfire probably reached the Slash W and I figure his pal Ellis White will be comin' here shortly. I saw two Spencers in the kitchen, and that'll give us the edge. I figure it'll be better if we rest up and get ready for him."

"Okay. Let's go inside and get them Spencers."

They took one more look at the disappearing Pete Orris before they returned to the house.

Once inside, Jesse looked at Mary Jo's body and said, "Now that's a real shame, that is. What do we do with her?"

"Get her outta here before she stinks this place up. Let's get her out to the barn."

"Okay. When we're there, I figure it'll be a good idea to saddle a couple of horses too, in case we need 'em real fast."

"Okay. Let's get her outta here," Walt said as he stepped over to Mary Jo's body and grabbed her ankles.

———

Once he was far enough away and realized that he wasn't being pursued, Pete slowed down to a walk to get his breath, but was driven by his incredible anger, anguish and intense desire for revenge.

With tears still slid down his face as he walked quickly northeast, following the familiar path between the two ranch houses and hoped that Ellis had heard the gunshots and was already on his way.

———

Sara Mae and both of her children had heard the gunfire and she'd kept them close as she gave the shotgun to Sonny and picked up the Sharps. She didn't know where Ellis was but like Pete, she hoped he was close enough to hear the shots.

———

Ellis was already at a medium trot when the first shot fired by Walt to try and keep Pete from the house reached his ears. At first, he thought it might be Pete or even Sara Mae trying the Sharps, but it wasn't the right sound. He slowed the gelding so he could listen better, and soon heard more gunshots and recognized them as the lighter reports of pistol fire then stopped the gelding completely to get a better sense of direction.

He was facing the Slash W, and it was torture to him remain static, but knew it was critical. When he heard the next shot from the west, he knew it was the Big O and the sense of relief he felt gave him a feeling of shame just for acknowledging its location, but now he had to act and not dwell on how he felt.

He pulled the Henry and turned the gelding west and set him at a fast trot toward the Big O.

Ellis was scanning the open landscape as he rode looking for any movement and after five minutes, he spotted a man on foot heading for the Slash W. He was sure it was Pete, so rather than keep going to the Big O, he quickly turned the gelding north to intercept him.

Pete hadn't seen Ellis yet because he was focused on the trail leading to the Slash W which is where he expected to see Ellis, but when he heard hoofbeats to his right, he whipped his head to look in that direction expecting it to be the two shooters who must have saddled his horses to chase him down.

When he recognized Ellis, he stopped quickly wiped the tears from his eyes and waited.

Ellis glanced to his left, saw the Big O ranch house in the distance, but didn't see any movement on the ranch, so he kept riding and soon reached Pete.

"Pete, what happened?" he shouted as he brought the gelding to a stop and dismounted.

Pete was still fighting the tears that threatened to erupt again as he quickly answered, "They snuck up really close to the house, Ellis. All three of them. They trapped me and Mary Jo inside and two came in the front door and shot Mary Jo before I could even get a shot off."

Then he almost screamed, "They killed Mary Jo, Ellis! They killed her!"

Ellis was stunned by the news but there would be time for grieving later. Now he and Pete had to clear the ranch of those bastards.

He grabbed his canteen from the saddle and handed it to Pete without saying anything.

Pete upended the canteen and drank every drop before giving it back to Ellis.

"Where are they now, Pete?" Ellis asked.

"Still in the house. I'm pretty sure I got one of them, and I thought they'd chase after me, but they didn't. I think they're going to hunker down and wait for us to come after them."

"Do they have your Spencers?"

"Yes. They were in the kitchen when I made my break."

Ellis glanced back at the ranch, then said, "Let's get back to the Slash W. We've got another four hours of daylight, and I wanna get those bastards before the sun goes down."

Pete nodded as Ellis mounted, then helped Pete onto the saddle behind him before setting off at a slow trot to the Slash W.

As they rode, once Pete had given him a more detailed report of what had happened, Ellis began planning a strategy for dealing with the two men. If they'd only had their pistols, he could get close enough and use the Henry to pick them off almost with impunity, but those Spencers gave them a good three-hundred-yard range, so he'd have to come up with some other way of finishing them off.

"How much ammunition did you have for those Spencers altogether, Pete?"

"Not much. You actually have more of it than they do. I think it's fourteen rounds."

"Okay. We'll talk for a bit while you're saddling a horse back at the Slash W."

"I want to them, Ellis. I want them bad."

"I know, Pete, and we'll get that done. I'm just sorry that all that damned money is at the root of this. If it wasn't there, they wouldn't have come this way at all."

"Ellis, those kinds of men would have come sooner or later. We both saw them in the war. Men like John Keeler were almost freeloaders on the backs of the fighting men. Don't go blaming yourself. Blame the ones that deserve it."

Ellis nodded, but didn't feel any less guilty.

———

Sara Mae was standing on the front porch facing in the direction of the Big O and the source of the gunfire when she spotted a single rider in the distance and soon recognized Ellis' gray gelding. Then less than a minute later, she felt her stomach drop when she realized that he had a passenger. She had lost either a sister or a brother-in-law then when she noticed that the passenger was riding behind Ellis and not on his lap, she set the Spencer carbine on the porch floor and began to cry.

———

Ellis saw Sara Mae and Sonny on the front porch and knew that Sara Mae had already understood what had happened well enough to start mourning for her sister. His heart went out to her even as he was planning on taking revenge for Mary Jo.

When he was close to the porch, Pete slid down and trotted away toward the barn anxious to prepare for his return to the Big O with his sorrow pushed aside by his anger.

Ellis dismounted then tied the gelding at the front hitchrail before stepping onto the porch and wrapping his arms around his sobbing wife.

"What happened?" she asked with a subdued, shaking voice.

"Those three men who were comin' here musta gone to the Big O first. Pete told me that they snuck up on him and when he saw 'em, he ran to the house and made it to the kitchen with Mary Jo. She wouldn't leave him but when two of 'em came in the front, she figured it was better for Pete if she was out of his line of fire and started to walk to the back of the kitchen.

"That's when they shot her. I don't know if they knew they were shootin' a woman or not, but it don't matter what they were thinkin'. Pete got one of 'em, so we're gonna head down there shortly before the sun goes down and finish off the other two. I need my other two long guns and Pete's gonna take one of the Spencers."

Sara Mae sniffed then said, "I'm not going to ask you to be careful, Ellis. I know you'll do what you have to do but come back to me after you've killed those two sons-of-bitches."

"I will, Sara Mae, but me and Pete gotta get ready to go."

"I know," she answered softly then kissed him quickly before turning and walking back into the house.

Sonny looked up at Ellis and said, "I'll take care of mama."

Ellis was reaching for the Spencer when he suddenly said, "Wait. Sonny, go with Uncle Pete to the barn while I go and talk to your mother."

Sonny was about to ask why but instead, he just hopped down from the porch with the shotgun and trotted toward the barn.

Ellis walked into the house explained his idea to Sara Mae and when she didn't object, he gave her a quick kiss then strode quickly out of the house to join Pete and Sonny carrying both Spencers.

As soon as he left the room, Mandy walked to her mother and asked, "Mama, what happened to Aunt Mary Jo?"

Sara Mae's eyes erupted in a second round of tears as she pulled her daughter to her lap and had to force herself to answer the question.

———

Back at the Big O, Walt and Jesse, after moving Mary Jo's body to the barn, had to do the same for Bob's corpse. They each had a Spencer now then spent another half an hour looking for anything of value and finding little, which irritated them both.

But they did find some food and fresh biscuits, so they made some real coffee and had some eggs and bacon while they kept an eye out to the east for the expected appearance of Ellis White and Pete Orris.

———

Ellis had loaded both the J.F. Brown and the Sharps, so when he, Pete and Sonny rode out of the Slash W, Ellis had the Henry in his right scabbard, the J.F. Brown and its Amadon scope in the left scabbard and the Sharps in his bedroll. Pete had a Spencer and one of the four muzzle loaders that he'd been carrying for years. He'd also reloaded his pistol but hadn't wasted the time to clean it yet. Sonny had one of the muzzle loaders in his scabbard, but it wasn't loaded.

Sonny and Pete stayed sitting in the saddle as they watched Ellis set the gray to a fast trot and ride due south away from the ranch.

"Do you understand what you need to do, Sonny?" Pete asked.

"Yes, sir. It's kinda easy."

"It is, but don't get all excited and do anything stupid. Okay?"

"I won't, Uncle Pete. How much longer do we have to wait?"

"Ten minutes or so. We're going to ride a lot slower than your father, so he'll be ready by the time I get there."

Sonny nodded but wasn't sure that anyone would mistake him for his much taller father, even at a mile and with his father's gray hat perched on his head.

———

Ellis rode past the same trail road where he'd seen Jim Abigail making his attempted escape just ten days earlier and thought it felt like ten months. He wanted at least another mile before he made his turn to the west. His whole idea for using Sonny as a deception was based on his assumption that the two men in the house would be primarily focused northeast toward the Slash W. They might be watching other directions as well, but they'd have a limited field of view from inside the house as Pete had painfully discovered. Once they saw two riders approaching, they wouldn't bother looking anywhere else either.

Today he believed that he'd make better use of the sniper rifle than when he'd fired into the chart table.

He turned the gelding west and kept his eyes to the northwest, making sure that he couldn't see the ranch house. He was familiar enough with the landscape to know where he was even without seeing the structures.

Ellis guessed that Pete and Sonny should be starting out by now as he kept riding.

———

Pete and Sonny started riding along the trail between the two ranches at a slow trot after ten minutes and kept the pace even as the barn and ranch house popped over the horizon just five minutes later. It was important that the two shooters caught sight of them.

As soon as Pete thought they were close enough to be seen by the two men in the house, he told Sonny to make his break north.

Sonny nudged his gelding away from Ellis who kept the same pace heading southwest while he rode away faster, creating a huge dust cloud to mark his passage.

———

Jesse was watching the northeast from the kitchen while Walt was in the main room watching the southeast when he saw the dust cloud on the horizon and soon identified two riders.

"Here they come, Walt!" he shouted.

Walt grabbed his Spencer quickly trotted to the kitchen and immediately spotted the two riders coming from the direction of the Slash W.

He had watched for less than a minute when Sonny made his sudden break.

"There goes one of 'em!" Walt exclaimed as he gripped the Spencer.

Jesse said, "He's gonna come around from the north while the other one comes straight at us. I figure he'll try and stay behind the barn like we did so we can't see him when he gets closer."

"That's what I figure, too. He's probably got one of the Spencers with him, so we need to make sure he's close. I'll tell you what, Jesse. As soon as the one that's comin' this way gets out of sight when he's in line with the barn, I'm gonna run out there and wait for him on the south side of the barn. I think the other one's gonna wait until we're under fire, but you keep an eye in that direction. I'll draw him in real close and once I get him, I'll walk back here, and we can see what the other one does."

"I'll go out there, Walt. I owe it to Bob."

"Okay, Jesse. Just don't rush it. Give him time to get close."

"Don't worry about it. I wanna be sure I put a chunk of lead into his hide."

Walt just nodded as they continued to watch Pete with an occasional glance at the disappearing Sonny.

———

Less than mile south of the ranch house, Ellis had turned north and was riding at a medium trot. He'd expected both men to stay inside the house, and when Pete opened fire with the musket then he'd fire at the smoke from their return fire with the J.F. Brown. Once they were pinned down, Pete would toss a Spencer round in their direction every thirty seconds or so to give Ellis a chance to get closer and use his Henry, but he might use the Sharps, depending on the situation.

He'd spotted Pete about a mile or so to his northeast and didn't see Sonny, so everything was going better than he'd hoped when things abruptly changed.

When he caught sight of Jesse suddenly leave the house to jog to the side of the barn, he thought he'd been spotted but then realized that the man wasn't even looking his way and was still staring in Pete's direction, but he was sure that neither man could see the other.

He immediately pulled the J.F. Brown from the scabbard and slowed the gray to a walk to keep the noise down. He was only eight hundred yards away when he made the change in speed, so he had to keep switching his view from the barn with its uncovered shooter and the house which may be hiding the second shooter who could have him in his sights.

Jesse was concentrating on where Pete should be by now as he slid his left shoulder along the barn's wall. He tossed his hat aside as he neared the corner of the barn stopped, cocked the Spencer then began stepping carefully toward the edge keeping his eyes glued to the east, knowing that Pete would soon be visible and in range.

He was almost to the edge when he finally spotted Pete just four hundred yards out and walking his horse with a rifle in his hands. Jesse grinned because he knew he hadn't been spotted and Pete was riding straight into his trap.

———

Walt had been trying to figure out the strategy that the two were using as he continued watching the distant Sonny who still almost a mile out and was barely moving. *Why was he going so slowly?*

———

Pete could tell that Ellis was about ready to shoot, so he knew that he must have had a target, but he practically had a death wish after the loss of Mary Jo and almost hoped that he missed. He wanted his revenge and if he died, then so be it. He wasn't going to bother a guardian angel if he really had one. As far as he was concerned, nothing else mattered now except the death of those two heartless bastards who had stolen Mary Jo from him.

———

Ellis was less than two hundred yards from the barn hadn't seen any movement from the house yet and figured he'd never get a better opportunity. He could see that Pete was within range of the barn-shooter, so it had to be now.

He pulled the gray to a stop, pulled off the lens caps of the telescopic sight cocked the hammer of the J.F. Brown then aimed the rifle at Jesse, who was just now beginning to bring his Spencer level.

He didn't feel even a bit of anxiety or shame about taking the shot. This wasn't about justice or playing by the rules. This was war.

The scope was really unnecessary as he could have made the shot easily enough using the iron sights as the long optical tube was offset to the left, but Ellis wanted this shot to be perfect.

He let out his breath and his index finger slowly began to contract. The rifle butt suddenly rammed against his shoulder and about a half a second later, the .45 caliber bullet slammed into the right side of Jesse's skull, scrambling his brain before blowing the left parietal bone into fragments as it left before drilling though the barn's wall and almost hitting Walt's horse.

When Jesse's body collapsed to the ground, Pete accelerated toward the barn as Ellis slid the sniper rifle into its scabbard and snatched the Henry free before he started the gray toward the front of the house at a medium trot. He assumed that Pete would realize that the original plan of trying to draw fire from the house was replaced with a modified one now that one of the shooters was already dead and Ellis was a lot closer to the house than he'd hoped to be.

But Pete didn't care about any plan now. He was sure that Ellis had just killed one of them, and that meant that the last one was still alive and in the house. He hoped it was Walt Harrison as he quickly approached the barn.

Ellis lost sight of Pete when he was on the other side of the barn but had to concentrate on the house now just a hundred yards away and already within range. He just didn't know where the last shooter was.

———

Walt had been watching Sonny, still confused by what he was doing when the J.F. Brown's loud report bounced off the house. He thought that Jesse had taken his shot, so he turned and looked out of the other window just as Pete reached the barn.

"Son of a bitch!" he swore as he scrambled to the east-side window to get Pete into his sights.

He cocked the Spencer's hammer then had to assume a kneeling position to get low enough to get a clean shot.

———

Despite Pete's almost insane desire for revenge, it hadn't reached the point where he disregarded all tactical thought, so when he reached the barn, he suddenly yanked the reins to drop to the ground for a more stable shooting platform.

The dust was still rising when the kitchen window shattered as a .56 caliber round blasted through the glass and raced across the ninety-two yards and punched into his horse's neck as its head was being brought up by the sudden yank on its reins.

Pete was already swinging his leg from the right side of the saddle when the gelding took the hit and as the brown horse began its death fall to the left, he tumbled to the ground on the right, losing the Spencer as he hit the dirt.

He quickly scrambled to the fallen carbine, cocked it and fell to his stomach in a prone position taking aim just below the kitchen window.

_____

Walt thought that he must have hit Pete when both horse and rider went down, but still levered in a new round and cocked the hammer as he waited for the dust to clear.

_____

Ellis didn't know what had happened to Pete on the other side of the barn but that shot had served the same purpose as in their original plan and had identified the location of the last shooter.

He was only fifty yards out when he dismounted quickly, let the gray go and cocked the Henry's hammer as he tried to get a good angle on the kitchen.

He'd only taken four steps when another shot rang out, but this came from Pete's location and he saw the wood on the wall beneath the kitchen window splinter as the Spencer's large caliber bullet smashed through and was immediately followed by a loud scream of pain from inside the kitchen.

Ellis shouted, "I'm goin' in, Pete! Hold your fire!" then raced toward the front porch.

Pete knew he'd hit the shooter but despite Ellis' shout, he fired a second round then after levering in another cartridge, cocked the hammer and fired again then again and by the time Ellis entered the house, he had emptied the Spencer of all seven rounds. When the hammer fell on an empty chamber, he jumped to his feet dropped the carbine to the ground and pulled his pistol as he ran toward the back porch.

Ellis had stopped in the main room when he realized that Pete's anger and anguish had made him continue firing at the wounded man in the kitchen and didn't blame him at all. If they'd shot Sara Mae, he would have emptied every weapon he owned into him and then probably stabbed him and then burned the bastard.

When there was the pause, and Ellis assumed Pete's Spencer was empty then began a slow walk down the hallway with his cocked Henry ready to fire at any movement although he doubted it there would be any.

He reached the devastated kitchen and found Walt Harrison lying on the floor surprisingly still alive, but his left shoulder was shattered, and blood was flowing onto the floor. There were big holes in the wall behind him from the repeated rifle fire, but only one bullet had struck him.

Walt glared up at Ellis but said nothing as Pete's loud bootsteps echoed on the back porch before the door flew open and Ellis saw the wild, killing look on his face.

Pete just glanced at Ellis before his eyes focused on the dying Walt Harrison.

He aimed his pistol at Walt's face and snarled, "You greedy, worthless bastard! You killed my wife and there isn't a place in hell that's bad enough for you!"

Walt continued his silence but just continued his glare but shifted it to Pete.

Pete then aimed his pistol and Ellis suddenly shouted, "Wait! Pete! Don't make it easy for him. Don't end his pain!"

Pete nodded then looked around the kitchen spotted Mary Jo's blood and knew that they'd moved her body.

He released his Colt's hammer slid it into its holster and said, "Okay, Ellis. I've got this now. Go and find my Mary Jo and drag that other one's body into the front room."

Ellis had an idea of what he was planning to do but just walked between Pete and Walt, trotted out to the porch and headed for the barn which was the most likely place to leave a body, so it didn't attract vultures. When he entered and found Mary Jo's body, tears began to drip from his eyes, but he still walked inside, made sure she was straight before covering her with a horse blanket. He then grabbed the ankles of the dead man nearby and dragged him out of the barn and toward the front of the house.

After getting him onto the porch, he trotted back and grabbed the second one with half of his head blown off, and pulled him across the dirt, up the two steps onto the porch and kept going when he reached the main room before dragging the first body inside where the powerful stench of kerosene was already filling the house.

"They're both inside, Pete! I'll be out in the barn!" Ellis shouted as he trotted out of the front door across the porch, then kept going toward the barn.

————

Pete stared at Walt Harrison who was still very much alive, and if he'd had proper medical treatment even the crude treatment of the army surgeons on the battlefield, he could have survived the wound.

Pete said, "You're going to die in pain, Walt. I'll live with mine and it will never leave, but yours will be a pain like you haven't imagined until you've reached the eternal pain that waits for you in hell."

Walt finally spoke, snarling, "Go to hell yourself, Orris."

Pete took out a match from the box near the cookstove, struck it on the cast iron side then after the match flared to life, he stepped toward the open door, tossed it four feet to the floor, and only stayed until he saw the flame ignite the pool of kerosene around Walt's boots burst into a roaring fire.

He then turned and jogged out of the house as his victim screamed in pain that would never be enough before smoke began to pour from the door and the broken window.

Ellis stood by the barn door watching the expected fire almost explode to life as Pete walked quickly towards him not even glancing back at his ranch house.

When he reached Ellis, he said, "I never want to see this place again."

Ellis just asked, "Where do you want to bury Mary Jo, Pete?"

"Not here and not in Fort Madrid where John is buried. Can we dig a grave near your house?"

"That's what I was thinkin'. I'll harness the team. Do you want to ride back and tell Sara Mae that I'll be bringin' her back? You can pick out the place and begin diggin'."

Pete was about to ask to switch roles but decided that it was better this way, so he just nodded then said, "Alright. I'll go and get Sonny and we'll head back."

Pete then glanced inside saw Mary Jo's covered body then took a deep breath turned, then took one of the two saddled horses inside and led him out of the barn to get the discarded Spencer.

As Ellis began harnessing the wagon team, Sonny sat on his horse about a thousand yards north watching the ranch house burn as its smoke reaching thousands of feet into the sky already. He didn't know why it had caught fire but had seen his Uncle Pete and Ellis talking, so he knew they were okay.

When his uncle began riding from the barn, he set his horse at a medium trot to meet him and hopefully find out what had happened.

———

After harnessing the team and moving the wagon from the barn, Ellis then returned, slid his hands under Mary Jo's body then lifted her easily and carried her to the wagon. He set her down on the bed and had to slide her slightly forward. He then tied the last remaining saddled horse in the barn to the back in case the enormous fire spread before he retrieved his gray gelding, tied him to the back of the wagon then clambered into the driver's seat and set off for the Slash W.

———

Sonny knew enough not to ask for too many details just because of the look on his uncle's face, but Pete still gave him a quick account of what happened and what he would do when they returned to the Slash W.

"I can help dig, Uncle Pete," he said.

"I appreciate the offer, but I need to do this myself, Sonny," he replied.

Sonny just nodded and then let his uncle ride quietly beside him as they drew closer to the ranch house.

———

Sara Mae and Mandy were on the porch when the smoke from the ranch house fire first appeared on the horizon. The gunfire had still frightened Sara Mae and the smoke had only made it worse, but she had to be strong for Mandy.

Mandy asked, "Is that a fire, Mama?"

"Yes, sweetheart. It's your Uncle Pete's ranch house or barn, I think. They're the only things down there that could make that much smoke."

Mandy began to cry again and asked, "Is...is pa okay?"

She was worried herself, but still managed to smile at her daughter and reply, "Yes, Mandy, I'm sure he and Uncle Pete are fine. We'll see them soon."

Mandy wasn't convinced but stopped crying and just nodded.

They continued to watch and after a few more minutes, spotted two riders on the horizon.

Mandy immediately perked up, pointed and exclaimed, "Here they come, Mama!"

It didn't take long for her to recognize the horses. It was Pete and Sonny and that realization terrified her. *Where was Ellis?* The sight of just Pete and Sonny riding alone suddenly created a heart-ripping belief that Ellis had been killed.

She had to move to the edge of the porch and sit down as she tried to restrain her despair-induced shaking. Pete had been made a widower today by those greedy men and now she was a widow at their hands.

Mandy sat beside her, and Sara Mae wrapped her daughter in her arms as she fought back tears. She had promised Ellis that she would be stronger, but not for this.

Mandy could feel her mother's shivering arms and didn't understand why she was so upset. Her father and her brother were coming home. She hadn't even thought that it might be her uncle and not her father riding with Sonny.

When Pete and Sonny were close enough, Sara Mae dropped from the porch with Mandy then they both stood and waited impatiently for them to arrive. Sara Mae dreading the news that she expected to hear.

Pete pulled his gelding to a halt then dismounted as Sonny dropped from the saddle. He led his horse the twenty feet to Sara Mae and looked at her mournful, terrified eyes, believing she was simply sad because of her sister's death.

"Ellis will be bringing Mary Jo here in a little while, Sara Mae. I'm going to find a place to bury her on the ranch and start digging her grave."

Sara Mae blinked then excitedly asked, *"Ellis is alive? He's coming back?"*

Pete didn't understand her surprise but replied, "Yes. He's fine. I burned the house, Sara Mae. I never want to set foot on that ranch again."

Sara Mae was so relieved that she began crying again before she picked up Mandy and held her close.

Pete just took his horse's reins and headed for the barn.

Sara Mae set Mandy down then looked at Sonny and asked, "What happened, Sonny?"

He told her the abbreviated version of what his Uncle Pete had told him then added what he'd seen.

Sara Mae glanced back toward the smoke, didn't see Ellis, then said, "Let's get some food into you and bring something to your uncle. When your father comes back, we'll need to help."

"Yes, Mama, but I need to get the horse in the barn first."

"Okay, you do that and then you come inside and eat."

"Yes, ma'am," he replied before he led his horse away.

Ellis was driving the wagon as fast as he dared with his precious cargo. He'd glance back at the bed and then the burning house as he drove but soon picked up the Slash W ranch house. He didn't see anyone outside but hadn't expected them to be there after Pete had arrived.

He didn't know how to expect Pete to react to Mary Jo's death. He knew it must have been a shock to watch her get shot and die just feet away from him, but he wasn't sure how long it would take Pete to get past her death. He knew how much he loved his wife and with her gone, he had nothing that mattered to him anymore. His ranch was pretty much a barn and maybe two dozen head of cattle and four or five horses. He didn't even have that much money either.

Pete was a good man and Ellis still considered him more than a friend. He was still family. He'd let Pete sleep in the bunkhouse and see if he'd be willing to stay and help him with the herds. He was sure that what Pete needed more than anything right now was time to heal.

He was just a mile from the house when his mind made the obvious connection to Linda Harrison, who was now a real widow. He'd send her a letter rather than a telegram to let her know that Walt was dead, but he'd include a lot more now. It would be the strangest letter he'd ever written, and he'd want Sara Mae's help.

———

Pete had taken a pickaxe and shovel from the barn then quickly started walking northeast. He aimed for a small hill that was just a hundred yards from the barn. There were no trees nearby, but that didn't matter.

When he reached the top of the hill, he scanned the vistas and could see the High Hills on both north and south horizons, Clear Creek running from west to east to the north, and the tall column of black smoke twisting into the sky in the southwest, which was the only blemish to the view.

He marked out the plot dropped the spade then began to swing the pickaxe with serious intent smashing into the hard Texas soil creating clumps of dirt. He'd broken up the top crust of tough soil and had already begun shoveling when Sara Mae, Sonny and Mandy began climbing the hill.

He was startled when Sara Mae said, "Pete, we brought you a sandwich and a canteen."

Pete lowered the spade to the ground accepted the offered sandwich but before taking a bite, he said, "Thank you, Sara Mae. You're very thoughtful. Have you seen Ellis yet?"

"No. But he had to do some things before he left anyway."

"I know. When you see him, have him drive the wagon over here. Would you please?"

"Of course," she replied as he took his first bite.

She handed him the canteen then smiled turned and walked back down the hill with her children while Pete watched her leave. He found himself not only crushed by the loss of Mary Jo but a bit jealous of what Ellis now had and he never would. It wasn't the kind of jealousy that most attributed to a man as he looked at a woman but a complete juxtaposition of his and Ellis' thoughts from just a month earlier.

He drank half of the canteen finished the sandwich then set the canteen down and picked up the spade to begin digging in earnest.

———

Sara Mae, Sonny and Mandy were all on the front porch waiting when Ellis pulled the wagon to a stop then climbed down after setting the handbrake.

He wordlessly walked to Sara Mae and enveloped her in his arms letting her understand just how priceless she was to him.

After he let go, she said, "Pete asked that you drive the wagon to that small hill where he's digging the grave, but I think he needs to finish on his own. Why don't you come inside and get something to drink and eat while you tell us what happened?"

"Alright," he answered as he took her hand.

Ellis would wait until they were alone to tell her the reason for the fire and his decision about how to help Pete.

———

It was forty minutes later when Ellis drove the wagon, without his gray or the second horse attached, slowly toward the hill with Sara Mae and the children walking behind in an informal funeral procession.

Pete had the hole deep enough and had set aside all of the rocks he'd unearthed during the shoveling. He was sitting on the hill drinking the last of the water as he watched the wagon heading his way.

He was almost numb now having expended so much emotion during the day. The sun was setting, and he felt as if the day had lasted a lot longer than twenty-four hours. It had been a lifetime.

He stood as Ellis brought the wagon to a stop. Ellis had taken the time to wrap Mary Jo's body in one of the wool blankets from the bunkhouse rather than leaving her cocooned in a horse blanket.

Pete then walked slowly down the hill to the wagon then stopped at the tailgate and looked at the blanket-wrapped body of his beloved, young wife.

Despite his almost dazed demeanor the sight of her body made him close his eyes and shudder as tears began to roll down his face again.

Ellis had stepped down and was standing beside Sara Mae, but neither said anything to Pete as his grief overwhelmed him. They both knew that Pete wanted to be the one to set her into her eternal resting place.

After a minute of release Pete opened his eyes wiped his face then turned to Ellis and asked quietly, "Can you help me get Mary Jo off of the wagon, Ellis?"

"Of course," he said as he stepped to the back and after he helped slide her body from the wagon held onto her knees while Pete slid his arms underneath her torso then lifted her from the wagon's bed.

As he carried the body up the hill, Ellis, Sara Mae and the children followed. When he reached the top he turned to Ellis and held Mary Jo out to him, so Ellis took her in his arms as Pete hopped down into the grave.

Ellis then bent at his knees and lowered the body carefully to Pete's outstretched arms. Pete then gently placed her on the floor of the hole and then asked that Ellis start handing him the stones from the pile. One by one, Ellis handed him the rocks and Pete placed them carefully over his wife's body until she was covered. He then held up a hand to Ellis who helped him out of the hole.

Once outside he wordlessly picked up the spade and began to shovel dirt onto the rocks.

It was an eerie scene as the only sounds were the rhythmic slide of the spade's blade into the pile of loose dirt followed by the thump of the dirt hitting the bottom of the hole. The deep red sky added to the almost unearthly effect.

The sun was almost gone when the dirt pile was gone and a mound covered the gravesite.

Pete dropped the spade then stepped back from the gravesite.

Ellis and Sara Mae expected him to say something, but he didn't. He just stared at the dirt in silence.

Finally, Sara Mae said softly, "Goodbye, my beloved sister. I'll come and visit you often and you'll always be alive in my heart."

Ellis didn't feel as if he had any right to say anything, but Mandy said, "Goodbye, Aunt Mary Jo. You made me happy."

Sonny glanced at his mother then looked at the grave and said, "Goodbye, Aunt Mary Jo. Say hello to the angels for us."

Pete then looked at Sonny and then at Sara Mae before turning his gaze back to the grave took a deep breath then said softly, "I'm so sorry, Mary Jo. I know that you've already forgiven me for my mistakes but know that I'll always love you."

When Pete finished Ellis felt obligated by Pete's words to add his own confession, so he said, "Mary Jo, it's not Pete's fault. You know that. It's mine. Those men shoulda never come here and would have stayed where they belonged if it wasn't for me. I'll do all I can to make things right, and hope you'll be forgivin' me."

Pete glanced at Ellis but didn't say anything before he picked up the spade and pickaxe and everyone left the hill. He put the tools in the wagon bed but began to walk back to the house. Sara Mae and the children walked with him while Ellis climbed onto the wagon.

———

An hour later, Pete was lying on his back in the bunkhouse staring at the ceiling asking himself what the point was of going on anymore. He was so empty that he didn't even care if the sun rose tomorrow morning. The only thing that kept him going was when he was able to focus on those few marvelous days that he'd been able to spend with Mary Jo.

In their bedroom, Ellis had Sara Mae still in her nightdress, pulled in close to him.

"Ellis," she asked quietly, "what are we going to do about Pete?"

"I've already been thinkin' about that. He's really bad right now and it's gonna take him time to get better, so I figure the first thing we can do is get him back to just workin'. Let him start thinkin' ahead and not behind. Then I have somethin' else that I kinda thought might help, but I need your help with this one."

"Go ahead."

"Now, hear me out before you get all mad at me, but what I was gonna do was send a letter to Linda Harrison. I need to anyway 'cause she's a real widow now and has to know about it. Then I was gonna tell her about Pete and ask her not to go and get married for a while."

Sara Mae lifted her head up quickly then asked, "What?"

"Now, calm down, ma'am. It may not come to a damned thing, but when I was talkin' to her in Henrietta, I thought she was a fine woman and darned near as pretty as Mary Jo. She was a lot like her, but different, too. I guess she made a bad choice in her husband, just like you did. I figure if we can be this happy, then maybe she can make Pete happy too, but it's gonna take some time."

Sara Mae lowered her head to Ellis' shoulder again then said, "Okay. I'll agree to the premise and we'll see how Pete does. I thought you might have died in that gunfight after I saw just Pete and Sonny returning and I thought my world had ended and I'm sure that's how Pete is feeling right now."

"I know. It's gonna take time, Sara Mae."

Sara Mae nodded. It would most assuredly take time.

CHAPTER 12

Early the next morning, Ellis headed out to the bunkhouse while Sara Mae cooked breakfast.

He opened the door and found Pete still lying in the bunk, but awake and dressed.

"Did you go to sleep like that?" he asked.

"What difference does it make?" Pete replied.

Ellis walked to the opposite bunk sat down and stared at his brother-in-law.

"Are you a woman all of a sudden, Pete?" he asked harshly.

Pete turned his head and glared at Ellis before snapping back, "What's wrong with you? I lost Mary Jo yesterday or have you already forgotten?"

"No, I ain't forgotten, and ain't ever gonna forget, and you won't either. But we got cattle to take care of and a whole lotta more work to get done around here. Now I ain't gonna insult you by makin' you a ranch hand, but I can ask you real polite if you want to be my partner on the Slash W."

"Why? I don't have a damned thing and I'm not accepting your pity or charity, either."

"Boy, Pete, you are turnin' soft on me. I figured if we combine the Big O with the Slash W then we'll have more land and access to Clear Water Creek and the south fork of the Pease River, too. I'm bein' kinda greedy if you ask me. I figure

---

that'll make you a third partner in this deal. Me and Sara Mae each get the other third. What do you think?"

Pete stared at Ellis looking for any signs of pity or sympathy but finding none.

He slowly asked, "What about the house?"

"I figure when the time comes, we rebuild it closer to this one, like I was plannin' on doin' anyway. We can use that cookstove, though. We should move it out of there soon, too, 'cause I figure some fellers woulda seen that fire and are thinkin' about doin' some lootin'.'"

Pete said, "Any looters who want to do the work to steal a damned cookstove can have it."

Ellis grinned scratched his head and replied, "I guess you're right, Pete. That would be kinda stupid. So, what do you say? I figure we can move your herd over to mine this mornin' then get to figurin' out how to get our ranch back to where it was before this damned war started."

Pete slowly said, "Our ranch," then sat up and added, "Alright, Ellis. Let's go and move those cattle."

"We gotta fill our stomachs first, Pete. Let's wander over to the house."

"You go ahead, I'll be right behind you. I need to wash up first."

"Good enough, see you shortly."

Ellis stood then quickly walked from the bunkhouse, relieved and somewhat surprised that Pete hadn't shot him after that 'woman' insult.

When he reached the kitchen, Sara Mae looked at him questioningly and he said, "Pete's gonna be in shortly for breakfast, my beloved wife. He's now a third partner in the ranch and you, ma'am, are also a third owner."

Sara Mae glanced at the open door then asked, "Is he better?"

"Much better'n I expected, and maybe we can get him back to normal faster than we figured."

"I hope so."

By the time Pete entered the kitchen, he was shaved and had a smile on his face which almost shocked Sara Mae.

Pete had accepted the offer of a partnership in the ranch not for the possibility of making any money, but for giving him a new start and a chance to get on with his life. His loss of Mary Jo and the burning of his ranch house had left him empty and directionless but after just one short talk with Ellis, he found a direction and a purpose in life again. He just hoped he could keep this feeling but wasn't convinced that he could.

After they had breakfast, the two men left the house to move the Big O cattle to the Slash W's herd.

After they'd gone, Sonny said, "Uncle Pete isn't so sad today."

Sara Mae replied, "No, he's not. Your father made him a partner in the ranch and he's going to stay here now and help."

Mandy smiled and said, "Good. I like Uncle Pete and didn't like to see him so sad."

"Neither did I, Mandy," Sara Mae replied.

———

As they moved the cattle, Ellis and Pete talked about the other improvements they'd have to make, including hunting for some mavericks that Ellis had assured him were there, breaking the horses that were still had a bit too mustang in them despite the Comanches' care and finding the loose horses that they knew were there as well.

By the time they returned for lunch Pete, while not close to being recovered from his loss, had committed himself into the work, letting the constant flow of sweat help wash away his anguish.

That afternoon, while Sara Mae and the children tended the vegetable garden, Ellis and Pete returned to the Big O barn to make sure it was untouched by the fire, and they both walked through the still smoking remains of the house finding that the only thing that was recognizable was, as expected, the cookstove.

They did find the charred bodies of the three men and used the tools in the barn to dig a hole in the center of the ashes, then dumped what was left of the three killers into the hole with the burned weapons and covered it with a combination of ashes, dirt and debris. Neither man had said a single word during the burial which was more of a trash disposal.

When they returned to the Slash W each man was covered in soot and sweat and their disgusting appearance drove them to the waters of Fresh Water Creek with a bar of soap and orders from Sara Mae that they not return until she could see their skin again.

After supper, Pete left the house to walk to the hill and visit Mary Jo while Ellis talked to Sara Mae about what they had done at the Big O and Pete's surprising progress. He then went into the main room sat at what passed for his desk, and with Sara Mae sitting beside him, he penned a letter to Linda Harrison with her guidance.

Dear Linda,

Thank you for the telegram warning me of those three men. They are all dead, but not before they killed my sister-in-law, Mary Jo Orris, in her own kitchen with her husband, Pete, just a few feet away.

This letter serves two purposes. I'm letting you know that you are now a widow. That's the easy part. The other one is much harder to explain.

First, I need to tell you about my situation. When I first returned, I married Mary Jo's older sister, Sara Mae. She was a widow too, and I've loved her for years, but never thought we could be together.

When I met you, I believed you were a charming, smart young woman and if I hadn't already been in love with Sara Mae, I probably would have returned to Henrietta to get better acquainted. It is my high opinion of you that inspired the second reason for the letter.

Pete was devastated by his loss but is doing better now. Pete Orris is one of the best men I know, and I just made him a partner in the ranch. I know that he really will need a good woman to fill the hole in his heart left by his wife's death, and I can think of no other woman that would be capable of doing it except you.

So, what I am asking, Linda, is that you deflect any offers of marriage for a month or so until we can bring Pete back to his normal good nature. When that happens, I'll let you know and if you're willing, I'd bring you back to the Slash W. We'll have a new house built nearby, too.

I know it must be hard at the laundry, so I'm enclosing thirty dollars to see you through.

If you'd rather not, I'll understand, but keep the money and send me a letter either way.

Respectfully,

Ellis White

P.S. Pete is better looking than me.

He'd added the postscript on his own, so when he handed it to Sara Mae for her approval, she laughed when she saw it.

"I don't think so, husband. But then I'm prejudiced."

"You keep thinkin' that, ma'am, and I won't complain. So, is it okay?"

"It's perfect. When are you going to post it?"

"Tomorrow. Do you need anything from Fort Madrid?"

"No, sir. Just come back in one piece."

"I'll try, ma'am, but I ain't makin' any promises."

Then Sara Mae's smile left her lips as she asked quietly, "Ellis, is Pete really doing that well? I know that I'm putting on a brave face, but I still feel such a sense of loss and she was his entire world. Even when he smiles, I can see the pain and almost vacant look in his eyes."

Ellis stopped folding the letter looked at her and replied, "I ain't that sure, Sara Mae. He's been through a lot in the war, and even though he ain't said anything, that don't mean it ain't sittin' inside him. Most boys don't talk about what they saw or had happen to 'em in those battles or skirmishes, and I always figured that was a bad thing to do. Me, I talk about it and get it out, but Pete doesn't. He keeps it all bottled up in his head. When Mary Jo died, I know how angry and hurt he was, but then I figure he put it all back inside, just like he did in the war. I just don't know what to do about it."

"Do you think he could go mad?"

"I don't know, Sara Mae. I plumb just don't know. We just need to keep an eye on him and maybe I can get him to talk about Mary Jo more. But for now, I'm just gonna keep him busy so time can fix him."

Sara Mae nodded and said, "I hope he gets back to himself, Ellis. He's too good a man to waste."

"That he is, ma'am."

———

The next morning, Ellis rode out alone to Fort Madrid while Pete learned about taking care of the chickens and milking the cow from the little people. He seemed to be fine, maybe even better than yesterday, so Ellis wasn't worried when he left.

Sara Mae was doing laundry, including Pete's, so she had a full day of work just doing that and wished that Mandy was older. As she plunged one of Ellis' shirts into the sudsy water, the loss of Mary Jo suddenly hit her again as they'd usually done laundry together and the jokes that they'd passed had made the tedious job pass more quickly.

She held the dripping cloth in her hands without moving for a few seconds then sighed and continued scrubbing.

———

After arriving at Fort Madrid, it took Ellis almost half an hour to post the letter when he had to explain to Ernie and a veritable crowd of eight men and three women what had happened at the Big O. The fire had created massive rumors and stories, so Ellis didn't really have a choice anyway.

The positive part of the gathering was that Ellis was able to put out the word that he'd be hiring ranch hands in a month or so, and four of the older men said that they'd be interested.

When he was leaving, Ellis thought that he should really check on Mabel Anderson and see how she was coping with the loss of her husband, so he headed for the chicken farm, reaching the access road just twenty minutes later.

He dismounted, tied off the gray then as he stepped onto the porch, he spotted a sheet of paper hanging from a nail on the door.

GONE TO CHESTERFIELD'S. IF YOU WANT EGGS OR CHICKENS LEAVE MONEY IN BOX.

Ellis grinned glanced down at the empty box then turned and trotted down the porch steps, mounted and then wheeled the gelding around and trotted away. Mabel was going to get herself some furry companions. It was a good idea now that she was living alone and wasn't sure when her boys would be back.

———

He was in a good mood as trotted north and began to think that everything would be settling down to a normal routine. With the added land of the Big O, he estimated he could handle a herd of almost a thousand cattle now. He wouldn't be moving any cattle until he had at least three hundred head, and that wouldn't be likely for another couple of years. By then the war should be over and the expected chaotic revenge-fueled aftermath would be in full swing. He didn't think that West Texas would be impacted nearly as much as the more populated and desirable part of the South.

Ellis was turning onto his access road when he saw Sara Mae walk out of the house stop on the porch and wave. He returned her wave then kept his eyes on her as the gray trotted toward the house. She seemed disturbed, and Ellis began to worry.

He pulled the gelding to a stop and was dismounting as Sara Mae stepped down from the porch.

"What's wrong, Sara Mae?" he asked as he tied off the gelding.

"It's Pete. About an hour after you left, he walked out to the hill and he's been sitting out there ever since."

"Have you talked to him?"

"No. Honestly, I was a bit worried about what might happen if I disturbed him."

"Okay. I'll go and talk to him."

Sara Mae gave him a weak smile but still kissed him before climbing onto the porch and returning to the house.

Ellis began walking to the hill wondering what the best approach would be to deal with Pete. He was equally split between shocking him with a 'grow up' spiel and just a direct man-to-man talk about the war and death. He decided he'd shift in either direction depending on Pete's mood.

As he walked up the incline of the small hill Ellis spotted Pete sitting like a statue at the foot of Mary Jo's grave and Ellis wondered if he'd shot himself or something but didn't see any blood.

When he reached the top, he passed on Pete's right then sat on the ground and looked at the blank face of his brother-in-law but didn't say a word.

They both sat that way for almost ten minutes with the broiling Texas sun roasting any bare skin. Ellis didn't even wipe away the sweat that was dripping into his eyes as he kept them focused on Pete.

Finally, in a low monotone Pete asked, "What do you want, Ellis?"

"It ain't what I want, Pete, it's what you want that's got me wonderin'."

"What I want is buried six feet below that dirt. Can you bring Mary Jo back to me?"

"You know I can't. Nobody can do that. You were doin' pretty good there for a while. Why are you so bad now?"

"I thought I could get over it, but I can't. I'll never get over it, so what's the point?"

Ellis paused then said, "Well, then, I guess you're just gonna have to end it, so we don't have to keep feedin' ya."

He pulled out his Colt Dragoon and handed it to Pete.

"You want me to shoot myself?" Pete asked as he looked at the big pistol.

"Well, you might as well do it and not waste another fifty or sixty years. Then when you're all dead, you'll be in heaven with Mary Jo and then she'll tell you how mad she is."

"Why would she be mad? We'd be happy again."

"Nope. She'd be madder'n hell 'cause she'd be hearin' Walt and them others down in the fires below laughin' 'cause they won after all."

Pete stared at the Dragoon then said, "It still hurts, Ellis."

"I know that. But you gotta make Mary Jo proud of you. Don't let those bastards get their victory. Every day that you are livin' and makin' a better life for yourself is another day that Mary Jo will be smilin' and happy for ya."

Pete handed the pistol back to Ellis and said, "I'll try, Ellis, but I'm never going to marry again."

"Now, that's a real waste, Pete. You're one of the best men I ever met and with all of those widows out there needin' a good husband, you're just cheatin' one of 'em out of a chance to have a man to provide for 'em and make 'em happy. I'm sure that Mary Jo would be tellin' you the same thing, too."

Pete exhaled but didn't reply before slowly getting to his feet. He remembered the last letter he'd written to Mary Jo and how he'd told her exactly that.

Ellis rose, slid the pistol into his holster then said, "Sara Mae was kinda worried about you, Pete. I'd appreciate it if you didn't go scarin' her that way. She's sad enough over losin' her sister, you know."

"That was thoughtless of me, Ellis. I'll apologize when we get back."

They began to walk down the hill and Ellis said, "You know what you oughta do, Pete, is for you and Sara Mae to just talk about the good times you both had with Mary Jo. I'll bet Sara Mae has some stories about when Mary Jo was a little girl that you ain't even heard yet and I think just talkin' about 'em will make her feel better."

A slight smile crossed Pete's face as he said, "I imagine so."

———

At the supper table, Pete and Sara Mae did start sharing Mary Jo stories and Sara Mae found it amazingly comforting to tell the stories of a mischievous young Mary Jo as the memories leapt into her mind.

Ellis may not have been able to bring Mary Jo back to Pete, but the stories that filled the ranch house that night brought her back to life in his heart and in Sara Mae's, too.

———

For the next six days after summer officially arrived a nasty heat wave, even for West Texas descended on the area. Each ride out to the herds required four canteens of water and every chore was physically draining even those that were done early in the morning.

But the water kept flowing from the windmill pump, and after having to modify the simple irrigation system the young vegetable plants were still thriving, courtesy of the water and plenty of manure. Even the strawberries were doing well.

On the seventh day the heat wave ended in spectacular fashion with a horrendous thunderstorm that spawned two tornadoes near the ranch along with several gulley-washer torrents of rain. The twisters didn't impact the ranch at all, but one did touch down near Fort Madrid and took out Abner's livery barn and mortuary. The four horses in the livery were killed but no people died in the storm.

The thunderstorm did usher in much cooler weather, and Ellis figured it was time to build that porch swing for Sara Mae.

Pete's recovery was noticeably better, and even though he still visited Mary Jo's grave each day, he was able to talk about her and not feel morose in any way. He'd even admitted to Ellis that he'd been premature in his statement about never marrying again because he knew that Mary Jo wouldn't want him to live the rest of his life as a hermit.

Ellis hadn't received a reply from Linda Harrison which could have been for a number of reasons, so he hadn't mentioned her to Pete but the day after the thunderstorm, he found he didn't need to tell him about her.

They were cutting boards for the porch swing when Pete nonchalantly asked, "Say, Ellis, that telegram you got from Walt Harrison's wife. What was her name again?"

"Linda. She sure is a pretty young woman and real nice to spend time with, too. For a lady who's had to put up with the likes of Walt Harrison, she was still a pleasant person."

Pete just grunted then continued to saw the board and Ellis didn't push the issue.

They had just finished assembling the porch swing and were carrying it out to the porch when they noticed a buggy approaching from the south.

"Do you know anybody with a buggy?" Pete asked as they continued to lug the large swing to the house.

"Nope. Let's get this onto the porch and wait for 'em. I can't see them bein' any trouble, not in no buggy."

Pete laughed before they reached the porch carted it up the steps and set it on the floor of the porch.

The buggy turned down the access road and Ellis soon recognized the passengers and smiled.

"It's Mabel Anderson and Abe Chesterfield. Now that's kinda interestin'," Ellis said.

Abe pulled the buggy to a stop then after climbing out, he walked to the other side and helped Mabel exit.

"Afternoon, Ellis," Abe said as they approached the porch.

"Afternoon, Abe. Mabel. What brings you by?"

"Can we talk inside, Ellis?" he asked.

"Sure thing, let's go inside and I'll have Sara Mae join us."

After everyone was seated with Sara Mae sitting close beside Ellis on the couch after giving him a curious look, Abe explained the reason for the visit.

"Ellis, after Mabel lost Ed, she come by to get a couple of dogs for protection and I figured well, it was kinda a waste for me to be livin' alone with the dogs and her to be livin' alone with her chickens and I'll admit I was always fond of Mabel.

So, we're gonna get hitched and live in one place. That's why we come to see ya."

"Congratulations to you, Abe. You too, Mabel. So, what can I do for ya?" Ellis asked.

"Well, we don't need both places and I figured that it would be easier to sell my place 'cause it was bigger and set up as a ranch. Now, all I got is dogs on there now except I might have some mavericks runnin' lose up on the north end somewhere. I just ain't had the need to go out there much. I was thinkin' that you might want to buy the place. I don't know of anybody else who's got any kind of cash these days and me and Mabel could sure use some."

Ellis really didn't need the ranch because it wasn't bordering the Slash W but it had a nice house and barn was four sections and had good water on the south fork of the Pease. His ability to think ahead is what prompted his decision.

"How much would you want, Abe?"

Abe glanced at Mabel before he replied, "Well, if you can give me five hundred Yankee dollars, then that should do it."

Ellis knew that before the war that ranch would have sold for more than double that price even devoid of cattle but now, he doubted if Abe would get three hundred even if he could even find another buyer.

"What are you gonna do with all of those dogs, Abe? Lettin' 'em go wild would really make a mess."

"I know. I'm gonna leave four males at the place that already act like watchdogs and take some with us."

Ellis didn't ask what was going to happen to the others because Sonny and Mandy were sitting on the floor.

"Okay, Abe. I'll give you five hundred in Yankee gold and we'll get that deed transferred. When do you want to do it?"

Abe couldn't believe that Ellis had agreed to the price so easily and in Yankee gold, too!

"How about tomorrow? I'll meet you in Ernie's store and bring the deed with me. You'd have to go to Henrietta to get it registered, though."

"I know. One of these days, we might even have our own town with real county offices in Hardeman County. So, I'll see you tomorrow mornin', Abe."

Abe and Mabel both rose then shook Ellis' hand before turning and leaving the house through the open door.

Ellis, Sara Mae and the children along with Pete all waved as the buggy rolled away and an ebullient Abe Chesterfield waved back as Mabel just smiled.

After they'd gone Pete asked, "Why'd you buy that place, Ellis? And why did you pay him so much? You could have gotten it for a lot less."

"Stupid reasons, I guess, Pete. That money has been nothin' but trouble but gettin' land now at that price seemed a good idea. It has a nice house and barn and good water, too. I'll bet there's probably twenty or thirty head of cattle in those trees near the Pease too. Just thinkin' ahead."

Pete shook his head and replied, "You should have been thinking ahead for less money."

Ellis laughed then took Sara Mae's hand and they all returned to the house. He'd hang the porch swing tomorrow.

That night after a particularly pleasurable time with his wife, Ellis explained his other reason for buying the ranch.

"I thought that might be the reason," Sara Mae replied as she slid her hand over her husband's damp chest, "but you haven't heard from Linda Harrison, either."

"No, ma'am, but even if that don't work out, I figure Pete might be makin' a ride to Henrietta to drop off some laundry."

Sara Mae giggled then kissed him before saying, "As long as you only drop your laundry off with me."

"Speakin' of Henrietta, when do you want to go to get married official-like?"

Sara Mae closed her eyes and answered, "I don't care if we never go and stand before a judge, justice of the peace or anyone else so they can tell us that in the eyes of the state of Texas we are now husband and wife. We married ourselves before I was even a widow, Ellis, and that meant much, much more to me than just some ceremony or papers. If we do have to go to Henrietta for some other reason, like registering that deed or finding Pete a wife then we can get married officially so the children can be Whites and not Keelers, but not just for the sake of making Texas happy."

Ellis kissed the top of her head but didn't say anything else.

———

The next morning, with Pete's help this time, they moved the anvil out of position and Ellis removed twenty-five of the double eagles before returning the gold to the hole and then put the anvil back in place.

"Nobody would look under there, Ellis," a sweating Pete Orris said after they both stood and rubbed their backs.

"That's the idea, Pete. I'm gonna head down to Fort Madrid and pick up the deed then when I come back, we can hang the swing."

"Alright. I'll see you later then."

―――

Ellis returned with his deed to the Chesterfield ranch four hours later just in time for lunch. He hadn't inspected the place yet so Abe would have time to do whatever he needed to do to complete his move to the Anderson farm.

On the ride back he wondered what Mabel's two boys would think of the arrangement when they returned from the war.

―――

The porch swing was hung that afternoon and the first to give it a try were Sonny and Mandy who then asked if Ellis would build them a real swing. He had no real choice in the matter when Mandy asked, "Pretty please?"

The smaller swing was quickly hung from the barn's lifting support an hour later under the restriction that all chores had to be done before they could use it each day.

―――

After hanging the second swing of the day Ellis saddled his gray for his inspection of the Chesterfield place.

After giving Sara Mae a goodbye kiss he mounted and rode down the access road then turned south to head for the Fort Madrid – Henrietta road.

He'd taken the precaution of rubbing Stoney's belly to add his scent to his hands before he rode onto the ranch in case the four guard dogs that Abe had said he'd leave were less than friendly to strangers.

After reaching the road he turned east and as he did, he pulled the gray to a stop when he spotted an oncoming stagecoach.

"Now when did they start runnin'?" Ellis asked himself as he stared at the oncoming vehicle.

He pulled off the road to give the conveyance free passage, and as it rolled past, Ellis stared at the coach's window then changed his direction and set the gelding to a medium trot to give chase.

He caught up with the stage just as the stagecoach was pulling to a stop in front of Smith's Dry Goods and Sundries.

The driver hopped down walked to the boot pulled out a travel bag then set it on the boardwalk in front of the store before opening the door.

Ellis had dismounted and was leading his gelding toward the coach when the young woman that Ellis had seen in the window stepped down.

She was about to ask the driver a question when Ellis said, "Welcome to Fort Madrid, Linda."

Linda Harrison quickly turned smiled and replied, "This is a very pleasant surprise, Ellis. I thought I'd have to get a ride to your ranch."

"I'm kinda surprised myself, ma'am. I didn't even know you was comin' and you never sent me your answer, either."

"I apologize for that. I was still thinking about your proposal when I had my decision made for me after the Henrietta Women's Society had the sheriff shut down the widow's laundry for immoral purposes. I had no place to go, but I still had your money, so I could buy a ticket on the coach."

"Speakin' of the coach, when did they start runnin'? I didn't even know about it."

"I think it was less than a week ago. They built a small way station about halfway, too. I stayed there last night."

"Well, I'll tell you what, Linda, why don't I take you to Ernie's Café for somethin' to eat while we do some talkin'?"

"I think that's a good idea. You need to tell me how you were married so quickly."

"A lot has happened since I got back," he said as he picked up her travel bag and took the gray's reins.

"I imagine so," she replied as they began walking.

"This travel bag ain't very heavy, Linda."

"It's all I have, Ellis."

"We'll fix that later. How come you didn't send me a telegram lettin' me know you were comin'?"

Linda sighed then replied, "I was afraid that if I sent it, you might reply that you'd changed your mind."

"I can see how that might have worried you some, but things worked out okay."

They reached Ernie's small café and took a seat at one of the four tables. They were the only diners in the place.

"Good afternoon, Ellis," Sue Perkins said as she approached the table.

"Afternoon, Sue. This is Linda Harrison. She just got here from Henrietta and will be stayin' with us for a while. Bring her the special and I'll just have some coffee myself. I just ate a little while ago."

"Coming right up, Ellis," she replied then smiled at Linda but didn't say anything before turning to get their food.

"Ellis, the reason I didn't reply was because it was, well, unsettling. I didn't want to be a mail order bride or anything like that. After my marriage to Walt, I decided that despite the scarcity of men, I wasn't going to settle again. That's why I was so obviously attracted to you. I had never acted that way before much less sent a note. I was just concerned that you might leave. I can't tell you how thrilled I was when I saw your return address on the letter and a bit heartbroken when I read it."

"I'm sorry, Linda, but I didn't figure that Sara Mae, that's my wife would be willin' to be my wife when I met ya. You see, when I got back her husband was still alive but back in the army where I was. I knew him real good and he was one of those men that is more like a rattler than a man. When I walked into my ranch house, Sara Mae and her young'uns were there and, well, we kinda married ourselves. There ain't

441

C.J. PETIT

any papers anywhere, but we don't care. Her husband led some deserters in an attack on my ranch and they were all killed."

"So, you aren't legally married?"

"Maybe not in the eyes of the state of Texas, but me and Sara Mae are better hitched than anybody else I know."

After Sue brought Linda's food and Ellis' coffee, before she took a bite, she said quietly, "Tell me what Walt and those two bastards that came here with him did."

As she ate, Ellis explained their surprising arrival at the Big O and not the Slash W, their wild shooting into the kitchen that killed Mary Jo then his and Pete's retaliatory attack. He didn't gloss over any parts of the story, including Pete's setting fire to the house with her husband still alive inside.

Linda stopped eating as she asked softly, "Did Walt kill Mary Jo?"

"Either he did or the other feller. I shot one out near the barn first. But Pete said that there were two shots from the hall and he never checked to see if one or both had hit Mary Jo. I wrapped her in a blanket before we buried her, and it didn't matter anyway."

"I'm so ashamed in my part of all this, Ellis. Walt forced me to tell him everything about your ranch. If I had known what he was going to do, I would never have said a word."

"Linda, you can forget that. Look. You told him about my ranch, not Pete's. He already knew about the Big O before he got back to Henrietta. Pete told me that. I'm sure he already heard the rumors about how much money I had before he got

442

back here, too. He just wanted to know where the Slash W was. It's okay."

"How bad is Pete now?"

"He's a lot better. He's back at the ranch now with Sara Mae and our kids."

"What do you believe his reaction will be when he sees me?"

"Well, ma'am, he asked about you a few days ago on his own thinkin'."

That surprised Linda and she asked, "How did he know about me in the first place?"

"Well, ma'am, I kinda talked about you when he asked about the telegram you sent warnin' me about them comin' our way, but he mighta got more from Mary Jo or Sara Mae, too."

Linda nodded then asked, "Is there a hotel here?"

"Nope. Tyler Mutter, who owns the saloon, rents out some rooms on the second floor but that's where he runs his whore house too, so I don't figure that's a good idea. You come out to the Slash W and stay in my place. Me and Pete can move out to the bunkhouse until we figure things out."

"Won't Sara Mae be unhappy about that?"

Ellis grinned and replied, "I reckon so, but that's somethin' else I gotta tell ya. You see, Mary Jo was a real pretty lady, just like you. Sara Mae was four years older and not as pretty or as well-figured but she's plenty pretty and well-figured for me. Anyway, she always was kinda thinkin' she was second fiddle to Mary Jo and when she found the note you left in my clothes, she figured I might be leavin' the ranch to go back to Henrietta to see you."

"Were you?"

"No, ma'am. It was always Sara Mae. But she asked if you were pretty like Mary Jo and I was honest about it. Now, she's past all that, but I figure the best thing you can do is be your regular, friendly self. She was real hurt when Mary Jo died, and I figure havin' you around to talk to will help her. She needs a woman friend."

"I understand."

"But I don't wanna stretch my luck, either. I'll go and borrow a buggy from Abner down the street, so you don't arrive sittin' on my lap. She told me she was even a little jealous when I was ridin' from the Big O with Mary Jo on my lap."

Linda laughed and said, "That would be starting off on the wrong foot, wouldn't it?"

Ellis smiled and replied, "That, ma'am, ain't the half of it."

After paying for their order, Ellis and Linda left the diner, then with Linda walking with him he led the gelding down to the mostly rebuilt livery and borrowed Abner's buggy for twenty-five cents. How it had escaped the ravages of the tornado was just one of the vagaries of the unpredictable whirlwinds.

An hour after seeing the stagecoach, Ellis drove the buggy out of Fort Madrid with Linda sitting beside him but with a proper two-foot gap. There was no reason to tempt fate.

On the return trip, Ellis told Linda about Pete and told her that if it didn't work out, she could stay as long as necessary, but inside he couldn't see how Pete could resist a woman like Linda Harrison. He'd been close when he was in Henrietta and not many women had gotten that far. Only Sara Mae had made it all the way to the finish line.

———

"Mama, there's a buggy coming!" shouted Mandy as she trotted into the house.

Sara Mae thought it must be Abe Chesterfield, so she just wiped her flour-covered hands on her apron then followed Mandy down the hallway across the main room and onto the porch.

When she noticed the saddled gray gelding trailing the buggy, she knew that it wasn't Abe.

"That's your father, Mandy," Sara Mae said.

"Why is he in a buggy?"

"I think he had a lady with him."

"A lady?"

"Yes, dear. I think that's Mrs. Harrison," Sara Mae said as the buggy turned onto the access road and she stepped down from the porch and waited on the front yard.

Pete was mucking out the barn as the buggy reached the house and Ellis pulled it to a stop, set the handbrake, hopped out and rather than helping Linda, he hugged Sara Mae then kissed her and took her hand as they walked to the other side of the buggy where Linda was already waiting.

Ellis said, "I was headin' to the Chesterfield place and spotted a stagecoach arrivin' and saw Linda in the window. So, we had a chat and I borrowed the buggy from Abner and brought her here."

Linda smiled held out her hand and said, "Hello, Sara Mae. Ellis has been talking non-stop about you."

Sara Mae was prepared to seriously dislike the pretty widow but found it nearly impossible as she shook Linda's hand.

"It's nice to meet you, Linda. When did they start a stagecoach run to Fort Madrid?"

"Just last week, I think, but it will only make the trip on Mondays, Wednesdays and Fridays."

"Well, come into the house and we can talk," Sara Mae said as she took Linda's travel bag from the buggy then turned to Ellis and said, "Pete is in the barn."

The two women climbed onto the porch and entered the house with Mandy following while Ellis headed for the barn, a bit unsure how Pete would react.

Pete was almost finished with his work as Sonny helped and the two dogs just watched the humans labor.

Pete saw him enter, smiled and asked, "How does the Chesterfield place look? Run afoul of any dogs?"

Ellis grinned and answered, "Nope. Never made it to the ranch. I got about a mile out when I spotted a stagecoach comin' in from Henrietta. Seems they started making runs startin' last week. I woulda thought it was a big notion, but nobody told me."

"So, why didn't you go to the ranch?"

"Well, I was holdin' off to the side of the road and when it passed by, I saw a familiar face in the window and chased it down in Fort Madrid."

"Who was it?"

"Linda Harrison. She said that the old biddies in Henrietta had the sheriff close down the widow's laundry 'cause they complained that some of the widows weren't bein' proper ladies. I figure they were all just jealous 'cause they weren't young anymore."

"Linda is here? Why? Did she think she was going to marry you?"

"Nope. She just had no other place to be goin' and wasn't gonna turn into one of those women that the biddies thought they all were. She's a real widow and kinda lost."

"Where is she going to stay?"

"I figure she can stay in the house and I'll join you in the bunkhouse for a while. That house over on the Chesterfield ranch is all set up, so that's probably a good place once we make sure it's okay and has food and everything."

Pete was suddenly very aware of the job he'd just been doing and said, "Um, Ellis, I'm kind of stinky right now. So, before I go inside, I'm going to head over to the creek and wash up a bit. Can you get me a bar of soap?"

Ellis smiled and replied, "Yup. Why don't you take the gray? He's lashed to the buggy I had to borrow."

"Thanks, Ellis. I'll head out to the buggy and you can get the soap."

Ellis nodded, said, "Let's go, Sonny," then he and Sonny left the barn while Pete nervously paced and worried about the unknown.

————

Pete was already riding past the house when Ellis returned to the main room and found Sara Mae and Linda chatting while Sonny and Mandy were engaged in a heated checkers game. They had already assigned the sleeping locations, and as Ellis had expected, he was relegated to the bunkhouse with Pete. He still considered himself and Sara Mae newlyweds and hoped that it wouldn't be for long.

After he took a seat he said, "Pete rode off to Fresh Water Creek to take a quick bath."

Sara Mae looked at Ellis then a split second later, she began to laugh before asking, "What did you tell him? Did he know about the letter?"

"No, ma'am. I told him the truth about Linda's leavin' Henrietta but didn't say a word about the letter. As far as he knows, Linda is here 'cause she had no place to go, which is kinda true."

Linda was smiling as she said, "I'll play along. I think it's better that way."

"Me, too," said Ellis.

They continued talking about what had happened since Ellis had last seen Linda, and Linda would occasionally glance at the doorway. Ellis could see the combination of curiosity and trepidation on her face. None of them really knew how this was going to work out.

It was almost an hour later with the sunset already underway when Pete made his grand entrance.

Linda stood when she heard footsteps on the porch and waited nervously with her eyes locked on the open doorway.

Pete entered the main room stopped and gaped at Linda whose blue eyes grabbed his own eyes like they were roped and hogtied. Neither spoke for a full, incredibly long minute as Linda slowly stood.

Ellis then said, "Pete, I'd like you to meet Linda Harrison. Linda, this is Pete Orris, my brother-in-law."

Pete smiled and said slowly, "Hello, Linda. It's nice to meet you."

Linda replied even more slowly, "Thank you, Pete. It's a pleasure to meet you, too."

Ellis then glanced at a grinning Sara Mae before saying, "I gotta move my things to the bunkhouse."

"I'll help," Sara Mae replied as she rose from her chair.

Ellis nodded then they both walked to their bedroom and quickly removed some of Ellis' clothes, strolled back out to the main room where they noticed that Pete and Linda were both sitting on the couch talking and not even looking their way as they passed.

They'd barely touched their feet onto the dirt when Sara Mae said quietly, "What just happened, Ellis?"

"Beats me, ma'am. Maybe 'cause I liked both of 'em, that meant they were both just good folks and they'd kinda get along."

"Get along? Is that what you call it? That was an awful lot like when I first set my eyes on you, Mister White."

Ellis looked at Sara Mae as they continued to walk and replied, "I suppose so, Mrs. White. I was kinda smitten right off with you too, but figured it wouldn't do me no good."

She latched onto his arm and said, "It's going to be difficult having you in the bunkhouse again without being able to make those nightly visits."

Ellis freed his hand enough to remind Sara Mae that he'd be more than anxious to return to the house or at least manage some private time somewhere else maybe in the barn loft.

———

Two hours later with the sun long gone to rest Ellis and Pete were alone in the bunkhouse and Pete finally asked the question.

"Ellis, now I'm not complaining or anything, but did you have anything to do with Linda's arrival?"

Ellis was laying on his bunk with his hands behind his neck as he replied, "I did. I knew you were gettin' better, but I kinda figured you'd never get fixed all the way unless you had a woman to share your life. Now I ain't sayin' that Linda is gonna replace Mary Jo, 'cause that ain't the way it works. She's not Mary Jo no more than she's Sara Mae. She's her own self. But that bein' said, I was really kinda impressed with her for the short time that I talked to her in Henrietta and if it wasn't for knowin' that Sara Mae was back here, I woulda probably brought her with me. She's that good a woman, Pete.

"So, when those bastards came here and did what they did, I wrote her a letter to let her know that Walt was dead, and she was a widow. That's when I kinda asked her if she could visit and meet ya. It wasn't like I was tryin' to get you married and all, but if it happens to work that way then I know it'll be good for both of ya."

Pete exhaled sharply then said, "Well, I'm not pleased that you wrote the letter without telling me, but I'm really glad that you did. You're right about her not being Mary Jo, but she's a lot like her in many ways. She's smart, fun to talk to and well, just nice to look at, too."

"I'm glad for you both, Pete. Now tomorrow, I gotta take that buggy back to Fort Madrid then I'm gonna head over to the Chesterfield place and after sayin' howdy to the dogs. I'll check on the house then ride out to the Pease and look for any mavericks."

"Ellis, about the Chesterfield place. I know you paid five hundred dollars for it and that's a lot more than I'd get for the Big O, but if things work out between me and Linda can we make some kind of deal, so maybe we can call the Chesterfield ranch ours?"

Ellis snickered then replied, "I figure we can work somethin' out, Pete."

Pete grinned then matched Ellis as he laid down on the cot and slid his hands under his neck and let his mind wander into a much brighter future.

———

After the surprise arrival of Linda Harrison things seemed to advance at an almost frenetic pace on the Slash W.

Ellis inspected the new ranch found the house and barn in good condition and fully functional with furniture, tools and even another wagon. The four dogs that Abe had left to guard the ranch must have run off to make a pack somewhere because Ellis never saw any of them and wondered if Abe had left them there at all.

He found sixteen mavericks out near the Pease but left them there until he and Pete could round them up after he hired the two ranch hands.

Sara Mae and Linda found that they shared many of the same interests and their personalities quickly meshed. Linda was very fond of her children who soon addressed her as Aunt Linda even before she and Pete announced that would soon be her official title. Ellis had been right in realizing that Sara Mae needed a woman friend.

Ellis and Sara Mae would often 'inspect' the Chesterfield ranch now dubbed the Big O because Pete already had the brand and the old Big O would just be part of the Slash W. It was much better than the barn's loft.

That went on for more than two weeks until Pete and Linda finally moved out of the Slash W and set up housekeeping in the new Big O. Just as Ellis and Sara Mae had done, Pete and Linda had simply considered themselves married and so it was.

Ellis hired two older ranch hands, Joe Honeysuckle and Larry Nielson in July and they helped immensely in managing the ever-growing herds of cattle and horses on both ranches.

The summer passed and the war continued with an almost never-ending series of stories of Confederate defeats but life in West Texas remained unchanged. It was only the telegraph that kept them informed of what was happening east of the Mississippi and in East Texas. There were so many Confederate armies that were operating without much coordination that it was sometimes difficult to understand the whole picture but the basic fact that the Union was winning was undeniable.

The numbers of desertions from the Confederate armies was also increasing at an almost unsustainable rate as soldiers were returning to their homes to care for their families which probably just pushed forward the inevitable defeat.

But there was good news too, but that was on the domestic front when in early October both Sara Mae and Linda announced their pregnancies driving Ellis to start adding three more bedrooms to the Slash W house which announced to Sara Mae that he didn't think her pregnancy would be the last.

In January the house was complete although he and Sonny had to make some of the furniture for the new rooms.

Ellis had still not done anything with the money in Abilene because of the war but once a month would ask for his current balance to ensure that it was safe. Abilene, like West Texas, seemed immune from the war while towns in eastern Kansas were not as border clashes between Missouri and Kansas raiders made life difficult.

His money continued to grow each month with the interest adding to the balance. He still hadn't touched the gold under the anvil after buying the Chesterfield ranch, but he and Pete hadn't gone to Henrietta to register the deeds yet either. They were both simply too busy both with keeping the ranches growing and keeping their wives happy.

C.J. PETIT

Fort Madrid continued to expand mostly through the efforts of Ernie Smith. But one of the additions in February caused a sudden and dramatic change in the community.

The war had sucked up almost all of the clergy in the south to act as chaplains but the Baptists had started a missionary service to visit communities that weren't being served by local pastors. When Fort Madrid completed construction of a church in February, Ernie sent out word that on February 12th, Reverend Daniel Ferguson would be arriving to conduct services.

So, on that bright February day in Fort Madrid, Hardeman County, Texas after conducting his well-attended Sunday service, Reverend Ferguson then conducted nine marriage ceremonies, including Ellis and Sara Mae, Pete and Linda, Abe and Mabel, and six other couples. Seven of the women were noticeably with child.

As Sara Mae and Linda continued to swell, Ellis and Pete helped as much as they could to relieve them of their routine work. Mabel began to show up regularly in preparation for her role as a midwife.

Pete was much more nervous about the pending birth of his first child than Ellis was. It wasn't that he wasn't concerned, it was Sara Mae herself who calmed him. Throughout her pregnancy she was nothing less than ecstatic.

Despite morning sickness and the aches and pains that always accompanied carrying the heavy load, she always smiled and assured Ellis just how happy she was because it was true. She may have been smaller than Linda, but she was even more thrilled to be having their baby.

In April, the news of the surrender of General Lee's Army of Northern Virginia reached Fort Madrid which was followed by subsequent surrenders of other major armies. The news itself wasn't critical to life in West Texas but did signify that the long, bloody war was finally reaching the conclusion that Ellis had foreseen five years earlier. The biggest impact was that Confederate currency which had been sliding down the valuation scale finally reached the bottom. No one would take the bills and the Yankee cash that Ellis still had was worth even more, but barter became the most common method of transaction.

But Ellis didn't care about money, cattle or anything else as he sat on the porch swing with Sara Mae leaned against him as the sun set. He could hear Sonny and Mandy laughing in the main room behind them probably because the dogs had done something goofy.

He provided the rocking motion with his longer legs as he looked out across their landscape and recalled the moment when he'd walked into the house almost a year ago and was greeted by Sara Mae with a shotgun in her hands.

There had been so many deaths on this land since that day but the only one that really had hurt was Mary Jo's. Pete and Sara Mae had let her rest in peace on her hill and had gone on with their lives. Soon a new life would be brought into both houses and he hoped more would fill their homes soon after.

But all of it, the war, the shootings and the sadness had faded into distant memories. No, all that mattered was nestled in against his side.

He turned his head to Sara Mae and she looked at him with a gentle smile.

"We have a wonderful life, Sara Mae."

"Yes, we do, and I think it will only get better."

"Every day I spend with you is better than the last, sweetheart. And I still think you're the most woman I ever met."

She laughed lightly as he rubbed her enormous bulge and said, "And for once, my husband, I won't argue with you."

EPILOGUE

Sara Mae was the first to have her baby when she went into labor on May 4th, giving birth to Josephine Mary White just before midnight.

Eight days later, Linda delivered a baby boy they named John Peter.

While the two babies grew stronger, news from the war kept pouring in at a constant rate as each of the remaining Confederate armies surrendered. It wasn't until the end of the month when General Kirby surrendered his Trans-Mississippi army in Galveston that the serious fighting was over. There was no formal surrender of the Confederate States of America, but in August of '66 President Johnson declared the war over.

Ellis still hadn't sold any cattle by the time of that announcement but later that month, he and Pete went to Henrietta registered all of the deeds dropped off their marriage certificates and opened accounts at the new state bank. Ellis finally transferred all of his money from Abilene and closed that account. He gave Pete five hundred dollars to keep things running but Pete only accepted it as a loan.

With the money issue finally resolved, Ellis then kept an eye on the cattle market which was still depressed throughout the year.

Men began returning in droves that year and many were looking for work and not finding any which created problems, especially in the more populated areas. That was an excuse for the Union army to keep the peace and to provide security for the arrival of the carpetbaggers who arrived with Yankee money and a desire to buy land.

Just like the war didn't have a major impact in West Texas neither did the Reconstruction, but it did give Ellis more manpower to be able to add additional ranch hands. By the end of the year, he had four and had expanded the bunkhouse and hired a cook. He and Pete had moved the Big O's cookstove to the Slash W and built a basic chow house near the barn.

When beef prices made a dramatic upswing in '68, Pete and Ellis hired some drovers to add to their own ranch hands and made a drive to Abilene. Between the two of them, they had over three hundred animals in the herd but because of the demand for beef, Ellis had a bigger payout than he had when he'd driven the bigger herd to Abilene eight years earlier.

With the infusion of even more money, Pete was able to finally make the Big O into a profitable ranch and paid Ellis back his loan.

Ellis never heard from Rufus again and would always wonder about his friend and his family. The Comanches had been decimated by disease and in 1867, they signed a treaty that moved the tribe to a large reservation but the government didn't comply with its terms, so there was fighting between the Comanches and the Union army mainly in the panhandle. Ellis hoped that somehow, Rufus and Silver Dove survived both and were living happily somewhere but that's all it would ever be, just hope.

He did however, send a letter to ex-Captain Mike Dunston in Columbus using the address he'd provided on the inside of the saddlebags and in October of '68, he received a long letter in reply which included a picture of him with his wife and young baby.

That drove Ellis and Pete to make the journey to Henrietta where they had several photographs made of their families, but Ellis had a portrait taken of just him and Sara Mae, too.

Ellis sent a family portrait of him, Sara Mae, Sonny, Mandy, Josephine, and little Faith being held by Sara Mae to Mike Duston before they left Henrietta.

When they returned, Ellis took their portrait then walked into the barn and went to work. It took him several hours of careful cutting because the glass had to fit perfectly.

That night after dinner with the fire warming the room and Sara Mae beside him warming his heart and soul, Ellis showed her what he'd created.

Sara Mae looked at the frame smiled, and said, "I'd forgotten about that."

Ellis looked at it and said, "I ain't never forgot it for a second, my love."

They both then looked back at his work as Sara Mae's fingers caressed her claddagh ring.

Behind the glass was an unusual background canvas made of rattlesnake skin. On the left side was their portrait. On the right was a small sheet of paper whose creases had almost cut it in half.

It read:

My Dearest Husband,

I address you this way because it is who you are. I have never been loved as you love me, and I will be forever grateful.

Return to me as quickly as you can, hold me in your arms and make love to me as only you ever have.

Your loving wife,

Sara Mae White

The unusual display would hang on the wall in their bedroom and would become the treasured family memory that would be passed to succeeding generations along with the stories of Ellis White's return from the war to his ranch in Hardeman County and the woman he loved but thought would never be his.

RETURN TO HARDEMAN COUNTY

1	Rock Creek	12/26/2016
2	North of Denton	01/02/2017
3	Fort Selden	01/07/2017
4	Scotts Bluff	01/14/2017
5	South of Denver	01/22/2017
6	Miles City	01/28/2017
7	Hopewell	02/04/2017
8	Nueva Luz	02/12/2017
9	The Witch of Dakota	02/19/2017
10	Baker City	03/13/2017
11	The Gun Smith	03/21/2017
12	Gus	03/24/2017
13	Wilmore	04/06/2017
14	Mister Thor	04/20/2017
15	Nora	04/26/2017
16	Max	05/09/2017
17	Hunting Pearl	05/14/2017
18	Bessie	05/25/2017
19	The Last Four	05/29/2017
20	Zack	06/12/2017
21	Finding Bucky	06/21/2017
22	The Debt	06/30/2017
23	The Scalawags	07/11/2017
24	The Stampede	07/20/2017
25	The Wake of the Bertrand	07/31/2017
26	Cole	08/09/2017
27	Luke	C9/05/2017
28	The Eclipse	09/21/2017
29	A.J. Smith	10/03/2017
30	Slow John	11/05/2017
31	The Second Star	11/15/2017
32	Tate	12/03/2017
33	Virgil's Herd	12/14/2017
34	Marsh's Valley	01/01/2018
35	Alex Paine	01/18/2018
36	Ben Gray	02/05/2018

RETURN TO HARDEMAN COUNTY

Made in the USA
Columbia, SC
14 July 2020